Dodge City Blues

Dan Guenther

To Munk Mead,
Fellow Marine!
Semper Fi;
Dan Guen

Redburn Press   New York   2007

ISBN 1-933704-02-0

Printed in the United States of America
Cover photo and design by Ingrid Guenther
Photo of Cham sculpture of Devi by Dave Scot

Acknowledgments

I would like to thank Dow Mossman, Ed Gorman, and Colonel Bob Fischer, USMC (Ret.) for their thoughts and perspectives on the manuscript.

I must express profound gratitude to Dave Scott, who rescued this book. *Dodge City Blues* was sold to a large publishing house in 1993. After three years the manuscript was returned to me, unpublished, due to changes in editorial philosophy. Subsequently, that original manuscript was misplaced, and the master files lost when my computer crashed. In early 2006, Dave was able to recover the master files of that lost manuscript from the database of my long dead computer. Without his technical know-how and initiative, *Dodge City Blues* would not exist, and Redburn Press would not have been able to publish the lost Vietnam trilogy.

Finally, I would like to thank the Marines of Third Amphibian Tractor Battalion; and the following Marine infantry companies with whom I served: India, Lima, and Mike Companies, Third Battalion, Seventh Marines, from Hill 10 and the Sherwood Forest; and Lima and Mike Companies, Third Battalion, First Marines, from Hill 55, Dodge City, and Go Noi Island, First Marine Division, Fleet Marine Force, Vietnam.

Table of Contents

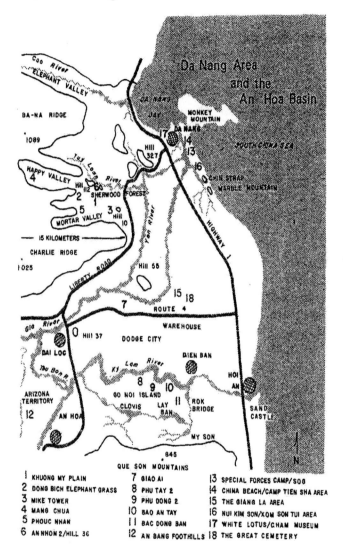

Map of Da Nang Area

1 KHUONG MY PLAIN
2 DONG BICH ELEPHANT GRASS
3 MIKE TOWER
4 MANG CHUA
5 PHOUC NHAN
6 AN NHON 2/HILL 36

7 GIAO AI
8 PHU TAY 2
9 PHU DONG 2
10 BAO AN TAY
11 BAC DONG BAN
12 AN BANG FOOTHILLS

13 SPECIAL FORCES CAMP/SOG
14 CHINA BEACH/CAMP TIEN SHA AREA
15 THE GIANG LA AREA
16 NUI KIM SON/XOM SON TUI AREA
17 WHITE LOTUS/CHAM MUSEUM
18 THE GREAT CEMETERY

Foreword

Dodge City Blues is fiction, a story that takes place in the Dai Loc and Dien Ban Districts of Quang Nam Province, Vietnam. Back in 1969 some of us returned for a second time to Vietnam, and seeing no lasting results from our previous tours, encountered a sense of weariness and dissatisfaction, a kind of ennui a fellow Marine officer once termed the Dodge City Blues. What follows is Sam Gatlin's partial diary, beginning with Laos, and continuing into the bamboo hedgerows of Dodge City and the wasteland we knew as Go Noi Island. No doubt comparisons will be made between this story and Operation Meade River, the largest and most successful cordon and search of the Vietnam War, where seven Marine battalions moved into the thirty-six kilometer square area of Dodge City. But those on Meade River endured the full force of the fall monsoon. This story comes to a close just as the monsoon arrives, a narrative that chronicles how Sam came to reinvent himself in order to respond to the changing demands placed upon him. What he learns from his reinvention will resonate with those, like myself, who have endured the lingering effects of those "Dodge City Blues."

Dan Guenther, December, 2007

"Principles have got to be lost in order to be found."
                    --- Robert Frost

PROLOGUE

Four months into my second tour in Vietnam, I was reassigned to an advisory group in Korat, Thailand. The mission of this advisory group was to train Thai mercenaries for work in the Bolovens Plateau area of southern Laos. Since I had both grunt and track vehicle experience, I fit the profile of the type of person that was needed. Later, I was to discover a well-meaning friend had recommended me for the four-month assignment, thinking I would welcome a change of scenery. During the entire assignment I was never to see a single tracked vehicle, either tank or amphibian tractor, LVTP-5, my military specialty.

My orders took me first to Udon Thani for what was to be an orientation of sorts. A Thai Army sergeant met me as soon as I got off the plane. I noticed the Thai was dressed in tiger-striped fatigues, the kind favored by SOG and Marine Recon back in Vietnam. Without conversation, he drove me to a remote corner of the air base where I was introduced to the Administrative Officer, or AO, of the unit.

Overweight, balding, and wearing those mirror-like, Air Force sunglasses, this AO looked old enough to be my father. In spite of our building's air conditioning, he was sweating like a hog. From our very first meeting this AO struck me as arrogant and condescending.

"You're a Marine," he said, sounding somewhat surprised as he read through my orders.

"Roger that," I replied.

"We don't see many Marines coming into the program. So, Lieutenant Gatlin, what's your claim to fame?"

"I don't have any claim to fame," I replied.

"Right answer, Lieutenant. Okay, let's get down to business. I'll be handling all your pay, and other administrative requirements, including anything you need done while you are out in the field. Do you have a will?"

"A will? That's a big negative."

"Ah, I'll go ahead and draw up a draft for you. I'll also get you a housegirl to take care of your laundry and make your bed. There will be a nominal charge, of course."

"Don't bother. I like to do my own laundry."

"Lieutenant, out here no one does their own laundry; nor do they have time to make beds. And since there is rarely off-base liberty, we found our housegirls support the program in a number of ways."

"Oh, I see."

"I think you will be impressed by the one I send down to you. You will be expected to treat her well. We don't tolerate physical abuse of the housegirls. If, for some reason, she proves unsuitable to you, let me know and I will arrange for a replacement."

That first week turned out to be a fast one, with me getting an orientation to key people and various operations of what appeared to be a clandestine organization. Like my experience with the AO, with the exception of my housegirl, Coco, I found all these introductions quick and impersonal. Folks shared information on a need-to-know basis, so the big picture that I was piecing together was far from complete.

As it turned out, much of my first week's education was left to Coco, a twenty-year old knockout who was of mixed heritage, Cambodian and Laotian. Coco was from Pakse, a relatively big town of 10,000 in southern Laos. Having Coco around more than made up for the lack of information provided by the AO and his associates. Slim as a joss stick, the seductive and sophisticated Coco insisted on giving me a daily massage. Her delicate features bordered on the sublime, and due to her Cambodian blood, she was darker than the Laotian housegirls, with a slight wave to her long hair. But Coco was no lightweight. She was built for speed, and loved to work out on top of me. Fluent in French and several of the Laotian dialects, her English was sufficient for our purposes, and she had other skills that far exceeded my expectations. Her way of communicating transcended both our cultural differences and the chip I happened to be carrying on my shoulder at the time.

"Sam, the AO say you wounded… How so you wounded?" Coco asked one night, out of the blue.

"I had a head injury. An internal thing caused by a mine going off, a traumatic head injury they tell me. But I'm supposed to be okay now," I replied.

"I no understand. Sometime I see your eyes so angry. What for you so… You number one nice young man. How come so pissed off? You no like Coco?"

"No, no… Coco number one! I very much like Coco. Best ever!"

That night I didn't feel like talking. And two weeks later, sadly, I was to learn from the AO that he regularly rotated the housegirls. Keeping Coco around was not an option. So, after a three day orientation patrol just outside of Pakse, I came back to find her gone.

As it was explained to me, Coco decided to cross back over the Mekong to Pakse rather than be a housegirl for another man. I thought about trying to find her, but our pompous AO told me to forget about her. For a long time I wondered if Coco was afraid of me, or if I had in some way offended her. My last girlfriend, an Australian teacher I met on R & R, had dropped me because of what she called my anger issues, my brooding, and my occasional, wild, drinking binges.

Later I was to hear from another housegirl that Coco had tired of spying on me for the AO. It was that simple.

*   *   *

Most of the folks I met in the program were civilian contractors. Led by Special Forces' officers and NCOs on loan to the program, as it was called, these contract folks were combat veterans drawn from a variety of sources - Army, Air Force, Marine Corps - even a few language specialists from the French Foreign Legion.

After an initial three-week orientation in Udon Thani, I was sent north across the border to Vientiane, the capital city of Laos. Vientiane, known as the city of sandalwood, thrived on a bend in the Mekong River amid fertile plains. Along the tree-lined avenues French Colonial architecture crowded the gilded temples, and freshly baked French bread was served next to shops selling noodle soup. The nightlife was outstanding, and my time in Vientiane was all about eating and drinking to wretched excess.

In Vientiane I got to know the Air America people who I would work with further south. Most importantly, I met a number of the Ravens, Air Force Forward Air Controllers, who I would later call upon for close air support. As my orientation came to a close, I began to comprehend the complexity of our mission in Laos; and I was troubled by a number of things, from the use of contractor personnel and Thai mercenaries, to the fact that my own AO used housegirls to spy on those within the program.

From Vientiane I flew down by chopper to Savannakhet for several days, then back again to Pakse for yet another three-day orientation patrol. Situated at the confluence of the Xe Dong River and the Mekong, Pakse was an important traffic junction. From Pakse, routes lead to Vietnam and Cambodia. For the most part, Pakse was a market for agricultural products that came down from the Bolovens Plateau, a fertile area to the north dotted with many French coffee plantations; but close by, in the town of Champassak, was the extraordinary Wat Phou. One of my three-day orientation patrols in Laos used Wat Phou as a rendezvous point.

Older than Angkor Wat, Wat Phou was built by the Khmer in the first decades of the 9th century. Similar to Angkor in architectural style, Wat Phou exuded the same atmosphere of an ancient city lost in the jungles for uncounted centuries. The Wat had stood unused for centuries because it had been built as a Hindu, not a Buddhist, temple. Walking among the ruins I was struck by the beauty of both Wat Phou and the local people, many of whom had Coco's dark complexion and wavy hair. The people I met here always seemed to be smiling, as if they understood something that I didn't.

After Pakse it was back up to Savannakhet and on to Nakhon Phamom, site of a huge electronic intelligence gathering effort. There I met a key player in the Laotian operations. His name shall be Lenny. Lenny was a CIA operative who had extensive experience with the Laotian mountain tribes. Although Lenny's mission was to oversee several bands of tribal guerillas, his influence extended into many areas. He was an ex-Marine who had been decorated in Korea and then gone to work for the Agency, and his operations had taken him all over Asia, even into China.

"So, you're the Jarhead they sent me who knows water operations!" Lenny said upon meeting me.

"Water operations?"

"Yeah, you know those buffaloes or whatever you call them."

"Buffaloes are ancient history. That's World War II vintage. In Nam we use the LVTP-5, the amtrack."

"No shit! I'm thinking of using them in the Mekong, maybe sending one or two up the Xe Dong on a special mission."

"Mekong! The current is way too fast... As for the Xe Dong, I recently flew over a stretch of that river on a chopper flight. I had a good view of the river and all I could see were a lot of sand bars. Shallow water with long stretches of sand bars can be very tricky going for amtracks. Using amtracks also requires a lot of planning and knowledge of currents," I replied.

"I was told that those tracks can carry twenty men," Lenny said.

"That's true, but with so many unknowns I wouldn't recommend using tracks in these rivers. No gray areas with that recommendation. It's a black and white decision, a *no go* as far as I'm concerned. Bad idea. Too uncertain."

Lenny stared at me for a long moment. He was six feet tall, a swarthy, powerful, broad-shouldered man who walked with a slight limp. There were purple circles under his tired, expressionless eyes. The top of his balding head was beaded with perspiration.

"Out here everything is uncertain. And the only thing I know that's black and white is a dead gook."

Thus ended my first meeting with Lenny, and for the remainder of my time in Thailand and Laos the crazy idea of running tracks in the Mekong, and up the Xe Dong, was never mentioned again.

After spending two more days with Air Force types, I was sent to what was to be my official duty station, Ubon Ratchethani. From this duty station it was a hop, skip, and a jump back to Pakse, Laos, where I made my final contact. That contact was a CIA paramilitary officer known by the *nom de guerre* of Fritz Lipske.

Fritz Lipske looked far older than his forty years. A little over six feet, thin and pale, almost scholarly in appearance, he didn't look like the type to command over two hundred Thai mercenaries. But he had a reputation for being very tough, relentless in his pursuit of the enemy, and able to go without sleep for long periods.

I'd been told, in Nakhon Phamom, that Lipske once escaped from the NVA after being held for more than a month in the interior, something unheard of up to that time. The experience had turned Lipske's thick shock of blond hair white. When his troops saw him emerge from the jungle, they were sure that Lipske had returned from the dead, and, forever after that his Thai First Sergeant called him *The Haunted One*. There was an unreal, larger than life quality to Fritz Lipske, who dressed in black jungle utilities and tied back his long white hair with a red bandana.

His radio call sign was Raghead Six. He was high-strung, paranoid, and always on the move. I could never find him when he was needed up at the operations hut; and yes, working with him was like chasing a ghost.

*   *   *

Some weeks later I was sitting alone when a call for help came in over the radio. Fritz Lipske was in trouble. His mistake, he would later claim, was relying too much on the Royal Laotian Army. But for his tough, small group of Thai mercenaries, he would have been overrun.

The enemy'd wanted Paksong, one of the small towns along the southern edge of the Bolovens Plateau. Lipske, with his Thai mercenaries, had hoped to make up for the deficiencies of the Royal Laotian Army… But he miscalculated the strength of the North Vietnamese in the Laotian Panhandle. He'd assumed that with support of a Royal Laotian artillery battery, his road watch teams would be able to control the roads. That assumption had been inaccurate.

The escalation of military activity in the Bolovens Plateau had happened too quickly for the Royal Laotian Army to respond and, as the NVA extended their control westward, Lipske found himself surrounded. The Royal Laotian garrison at Paksong had retreated down the river to Attopeu.

*   *   *

It was an unusually hot, humid night, alive with things blooming in the darkness. My team's mission was to support the emergency extraction of Lipske's team. The tough Thais responded within minutes. When I reached the chopper pad my sergeant had them all formed up, ready to board.

The three black CH-53's that carried my forty-man team were supplied by Air America. Quickly we were over the Mekong, enveloped in the musky scent of the river. Then, we were over Laos, dropping in a wide circle, close enough to the ground so that the fragrance of a million night-blooming flowers rose through the spinning rotor blades of the choppers. I could see the lights of Paksong in the distance. For a brief moment I smelled a burning joss stick and thought of Coco.

At 0130 hours we came over the crest of a hill at five hundred feet. Red and green tracers marked the boundaries of the firefight, and I guessed the distance at three miles. Fifteen hundred feet above our choppers, a heavily armed C-47, Puff the Magic Dragon, was circling, ready to bring on the necessary firepower to suppress the reinforced NVA battalion that had surrounded Lipske's men.

To the west, an Air Force Raven known as Nifty, call sign Crazy Raven, was standing by, linking with additional air support in the form of F-4 Phantoms. By 0145, Lipske was directing Puff to blanket the ground to his immediate north with suppressive fire. Lipske's platoon used that opportunity to pull back into a tight perimeter on top of a small knob... As he consolidated his position, the NVA decided to launch a human wave attack along the northern front of his perimeter. The NVA commanders must've assumed that Lipske's platoon was made up of Laotians rather than the Thai mercenaries. The Thais held their positions, giving Lipske time to use Puff once more.

Huge flares began to pop, illuminating the battlefield. About a hundred NVA who were massing for an assault were caught in the light of the illumination, their position below Lipske's knob revealed, with the cover of darkness gone. All at once Puff opened up, the orange stream of fire sweeping the ground, a deadly, liquid flame playing over the earth.

We were going in as soon as Puff finished the sweeping fire. I gave my men the thumb's-up sign and the order to lock and load. Our chopper banked to the left and my stomach emptied its contents. We began our swift drop into the broad valley below.

*   *   *

It was 0150 when, one by one, the choppers landed to unload my team. We set up a hasty perimeter in the waist-high grass. Moments after landing, the dull thunk of mortar tubes could be heard in the hills to the north. The CH-53's lifted off just as the first mortar rounds began to impact only a hundred meters to our left. We made radio contact with Lipske's team and I gave the order to move out. Within minutes we linked up.

All around us the hills were on fire... The ghostly light of the illumination flares cast grotesque shadows across the grim faces of our Thai mercenaries. Then it grew quiet, with the NVA withdrawing to high ground. At first light the CH-53's returned to extract both our teams. On the way back over the Mekong it occurred to me that my team had accomplished their mission without firing a single round.

*   *   *

Lipske, the self-styled angel of death, was beating a young Laotian scout. The scout was from Pakse, and had been hired by our AO. For reasons known only to him, Lipske had suspected this scout of treachery for some time. The scout's quarters'd been searched, and a large sum of money had been found, too much money for such a humble scout.

This same scout had feigned illness prior to Lipske's departure; yet, when I had formed my reaction team to

XV

rescue Lipske, the scout was discovered enjoying himself with the expensive Thai prostitute he had smuggled into camp.

At first Lipske had two of his Thai sergeants slap the scout around. Then Lipske himself got involved, kicking the scout and jabbing him in the ribs with a hammer. When the young scout failed to respond to his questions as to the origin of the money, Lipske grew increasingly brutal, hammering the fingers of the scout's right hand into a pulp... I had seen enough, but being relatively new, I hesitated to intervene, a mistake on my part. The possession of the money by the scout wasn't in itself an indictment. The money could have come from any number of sources, gambling, dealing drugs, the selling of stolen American goods on the black market. While it was highly likely that the young scout had come by the money through dubious means, there was no real proof that the scout was a spy for the North Vietnamese. All was conjecture on Lipske's part.

The scout lay curled at Lipske's feet, whimpering and holding his crushed fingers to his lips. Lipske stood sweating and bare-chested, breathing heavily, a string of ghostly white wet hair clinging to his face. He dropped the bloody hammer on the ground. Grabbing a sharpened stick from one of his Thai sergeants, he threatened to pull out one of the man's eyes if he didn't reveal the source of the money.

"Lipske, this is senseless. You have no proof!"

"I have all the proof I need!"

"You are acting like a savage."

My words only seemed to anger Lipske all the more, and, in near shock, I watched as Lipske jabbed the stick into one of the scout's eyes before I could stop him. Lipske grunted, holding the scout in a headlock while he pulled out the eye, using the stick as a lever. The scout screamed for his mother. The two Thai sergeants stood by, frozen in fear. Lipske held up the stick with the impaled eyeball for all to see.

This was senseless cruelty. Lipske, wide-eyed and out of control, needed to be contained. The Haunted One had ceased to be a man and become a brute. I rushed forward and butt-stroked Lipske to the head with my rifle.

"That's enough!"

"I'll say when there is enough," Lipske replied, stumbling to his feet.

"Bullshit!" I said, laying it to him again.

A Thai sergeant rushed forward to contain me, but this time Lipske did not get up. Blood was pouring out of his left ear.

"Get control of yourself, asshole. This spectacle is over. Technically, I outrank you, and I am giving you a direct order. If you get up again, I'll put you down for good."

"We should pull out the other eye of this traitor as an example to all," Lipske croaked.

"I'm going to take him to Nakhon Phamom where they are quite capable of extracting the truth," I continued.

I picked up the Laotian and carried him to a jeep. Lipske sat on the ground, making no attempt to get up. Then I was off down the road to Nakhon Phamom.

*   *   *

I made the passage to NKP without further incident. Everyone was shocked by Lipske's behavior; and upon further investigation by our AO, we found that the Laotian scout was a victim of a set-up by an internal agent. It came as a revelation to learn that the suspected internal agent was none other than Coco. While I never understood fully the circumstances of how the AO came by his discovery, other than that the scout and Coco were both from Pakse, it struck me how easily we had been suckered. Who knew what important information had been compromised?

Within hours of the AO's discovery all the housegirls were let go.

When confronted with the truth of the matter, Lipske appeared impervious to the facts, and became totally absorbed in other matters when Headquarters sent two investigators. While the AO took a lot of heat for the circumstances surrounding Coco, Lipske's outrageous behavior caused considerable discontent among the ranks of the Thai. The investigators spent two days gathering information so that Lipske's superiors would be able to respond to the incident. This, of course, did not improve the situation at our base of operations. All of us were on edge, and I kept my back covered at all times, not knowing what to expect from the impulsive Lipske.

The investigators found Lipske lapsing into a kind of daze. When the investigators uncovered more of The Haunted One's past transgressions, Lipske slipped into a state of abject apathy. The shock of the incident had taken a toll on everyone's psyche. Lipske's vicious display had had a particular effect on some of the younger Thai.

One by one, and in small groups, these Thai drifted off, returning to their villages in the north. Only a handful remained of the old company. At week's end, Lipske was seen at twilight walking out into the flood-swollen Mekong River.

He was waist-deep when the swiftness of the current caught him, carrying him quickly to mid- river. Those who watched his passage downstream soon lost sight of him in the fading light.

*   *   *

After Lipske walked into the Mekong the investigators from NKP closed the case. For me, it was just another bad ending. Years later the memory of it would keep coming back to me in bad dreams. But Lipske's death was a beginning as well as an end, and I was told to assume command of what was left of the Thai Company.

A week after the investigators left, headquarters sent down two additional advisors who had been reassigned from the Thai border to support our Laotian efforts. The younger man, Lucas Cain, was a Marine lieutenant who I'd served with in Vietnam. It'd been upon Lucas Cain's recommendation to Lenny that I was assigned as an advisor.

Lucas's role was similar to that of the district advisor in Vietnam. He had oversight of my company as well as the two other companies that worked up on the northern Thai border. While in Laos, Lucas had spent most of his time with embassy, liaison-type duties, evaluating various non-public programs and operations throughout the Laotian Panhandle. He'd worked with the Thai Border Police, and those efforts had taken him north to Chiang Rai on extended training exercises. Those training exercises had crossed into China. Now, with the Lipske incident, as it had become known, Lucas had been sent to oversee our entire program and salvage what was left of our team.

The second man that headquarters sent down was a former member of the French Foreign Legion who had served in both French Indo-China and Algeria. His *nom de guerre* was Renaud. He was a short, squat, and Mediterranean-looking man in his late forties. I wasn't sure of his true nationality, but Renaud spoke a number of languages fluently, including a dialect of one the Laotian mountain tribes, making him of considerable value to the intelligence staff back at Headquarter.

Renaud, unfortunately, had alienated a number of the operations staff with his excessive drinking. However, Renaud was a pal of Lenny's who protected him until one night when a nasty exchange occurred over a Thai woman. That night ended in a drunken fistfight between Renaud and Lenny. Renaud was then banished to the care of Lucas.

In temperament and style Lucas and I were much alike. With his know-how, 'can-do' attitude, and force of character, Lucas inspired my confidence.

"There were almost four hundred men in this unit a month ago," he remembered.

"That's correct. After the incident, they began to drift off," I said.

"We've lost our moral authority… There's no winning their hearts and minds without that. There's no leadership, and there's no cause to believe in without moral authority," Lucas said, taking a drink of his beer.

"You called it. That's the way I see it."

"The truth of our actions speaks louder than words… We sent Lipske down here, and everyone knew he was nuts. They even called him *The Haunted One*. But when he abuses people and resources, the staff up at Headquarters acts surprised."

"Goes with the territory. You got a lot of crazies out here. I hear Lenny keeps the head of one of his old enemies in a big pickle jar."

"Everyone thinks Lenny is crazy too, even Renaud… But Lipske was worse. When we sent him out to lead this company, we really sent a loser. Forget this Haunted One crap, I call this guy Lipske a loser, a loser who screwed things up good. You see, what he did was morally wrong. Not only was it unjust, it was evil. These people know that. And when Lispke the loser walks off into the flooding Mekong and drowns himself, they take that as a sign… That's why so many have drifted off."

"So what's the next step?"

"To find a way to be morally right. Find a way to restore their confidence."

"And they give you Renaud?"

"Yeah. I know. He, too, is like someone from another planet, a real alien. But, hell, figure this, keep him away from liquor and the Thai women and he should be fine."

* * *

The next week found the team on a mission in new terrain. We patrolled for three days, finding nothing. Then heavy rains came in. When the weather broke we called for extraction. All of us were exhausted. Renaud could barely make it to his cot, pulling off his wet clothes and falling into a deep sleep. Lucas and I continued on to the Operations Hut to debrief the staff.

After the debriefing I drank too many beers before I hit the sack. Shortly after midnight I awoke from a bad dream, jumping up from my cot and stumbling across the floor in terror.

"You okay, Sam?" Lucas asked.

"I had a weird dream. I was looking into a mirror and saw Fritz Lipske's face behind me. He appeared to be speaking, but I couldn't hear what he was saying."

"Fatigue. We get too tired and our dreams manifest all our bad thoughts and feelings."

"Bad sign. Maybe I'm losing it."

"No, I think that you were just very tired. And maybe you had too much to drink. When people get too worn out things rise out of their subconscious. Those bad dreams are the result of combat, a kind of appendix to the event. I've heard shrinks call them manifestations."

"Sounds like a mental disorder."

"Or, since we're in Thailand, you could say you saw an apparition in your dream. The Thai believe in apparitions."

"You're talking about ghosts, now?"

"Yeah, that's right. You could say I'm talking about ghosts. "

"Well, I don't believe in ghosts, nor do I believe that people can come back from the dead."

"Even in your dreams?" Lucas Cain asked.

* * *

Outside, the rain was pouring down. The inside of the hut was filled with a haze of cigarette smoke and kerosene fumes. In the light of two kerosene lamps, we'd eaten our modest dinner and were waiting out the rain. To keep off the damp chill, Lucas had crawled into his sleeping bag. After two hours of drinking cognac, Renaud was getting drunk.

That afternoon we'd returned from our third three-day patrol in as many weeks.

The patrol had not gone well. While there had been no casualties, we spent the entire time on the ground evading superior NVA forces. Twice during those evasions Renaud had shown outright cowardice when the NVA had taken us under fire. On the first occasion, he failed to return fire as directed, hiding under the cover of a fallen tree. That first occasion had not escaped the notice of the Thais... The second time we took fire, Renaud simply turned and fled through the forest, much to our disgust.

"Gatlin, I think you are afraid of me! All the Americans are afraid of me. They are afraid of me because I know what they do not know. Americans are so stupid."

Renaud's diatribe on how stupid we Americans were continued, and Lucas and I ignored him. Sober, his self-defeating babble was usually directed at the Air Force types who dominated our organization. But when the irrational Renaud took to drinking cognac, anyone was a potential target. He began to bully me verbally. His contract was up for renewal. I made up my mind I was going to do everything I could to prevent a contract renewal.

"You're drunk. Go to sleep, Renaud," I said.

Lucas got up from his cot and shook his head. He had given up trying to sleep.

"You are both afraid of Renaud! That's why you don't talk to me," Renaud continued.

"You ignorant fuck. You know why no one's talking to you. You can't be depended upon. That's why! In the morning I'm sending you back to NKP with a full report," Lucas said.

"I shit on your report."

"The truth, Renaud. I'm going to tell the truth about how you ran and hid from the NVA while the rest of the team were under fire," Lucas said.

Renaud lunged from his chair, grabbing Lucas's shirt. Lucas fell backwards off his cot but not before punching Renaud in the face. Quickly Lucas was on his feet. Renaud was on his knees, spitting out white fragments of teeth.

With a howl of rage, Renaud rose, drawing an OSS-style stiletto, and in a single, swift motion, stuck the knife in Lucas's right shoulder. Lucas pulled out the stiletto with his left hand and emptied the clip of his .45 automatic into Renaud at a distance of five feet.

*   *   *

After the shooting, I dragged the body out of the hut and called in a chopper to evacuate the wounded Lucas. The next day found me suppressing panic, both as a result of the shooting and at the directive given to me by my superiors. Lenny showed up and told me my team was to return to Laos.

"We are really on to something here. Your team will return to the area of this base camp. Just over this ridgeline you will find a wide valley that has been cleared for agriculture. There you will find a plantation house that an NVA general is using as his headquarters," Lenny said, tapping a wall map of Laos with a long pointer.

"That's just where the NVA chased us back to Thailand on our last patrol," I found myself replying.

"Your mission will be to stand by in case you are needed for support… Without going into great detail, we have a Marine sniper currently on the ground and in position to take out this general. Our man is positioned in this cleared area even as we speak. We have been asked to give him covering fire if he needs it during his extraction."

"That's crazy. How about our extraction? If the shit hits the fan, my team is history."

"You will go back the way you came in. Suck the NVA into an ambush, if necessary."

"That terrain is fucked, thick stands of impenetrable bamboo."

"There are game trails through the bamboo. And there are several speed trails as a matter of fact, where the NVA haul ass with their supplies. You know that."

"No way. Game trails are usually booby-trapped. All kinds of trail watchers monitor those speed-trails. This is a suicide mission."

"We have our orders," Lenny said, using a dirty handkerchief to mop the beads of sweat off his balding head.

*   *   *

It was an absurd mission. My Thai team knew it was absurd. I thought for a moment about what Lucas had said about leadership and moral authority. Was this the way to inspire our Thai team? We didn't win hearts and minds by taking men on suicide missions. My protests were squashed. One of my team told me that Lenny had called me a coward behind my back.

The directive they had given me was clear… There was no running away from their direct order, however absurd it seemed. The absurdity of the plan was heightened by the fact that I was told to take only ten men. A small group could do the job, I was told. A small group should be able to move with stealth, maneuvering close enough so that I could have the Raven Nifty call in air strikes. It was an illusion. With the exception of Lenny, most of the people giving me this order never experienced close combat on the ground, let alone in the tangled bamboo thickets of Laos.

They knew nothing of long-range patrolling in mountainous, jungle terrain; nor did they truly understand how close air support went down.

*   *   *

A chopper set us in at the foot of a long karst outcropping and we got lucky. We found an abandoned speed trail previously unknown to us. We skirted the thick stands of bamboo and made good time, traveling parallel to the base of a limestone karst.

By late afternoon we found the main NVA camp. The NVA bunkers were built into the side of the karst, offering excellent cover from air strikes and clear fields of fire should we attempt a frontal assault of their position. Fortunately, we caught the NVA when they were resting from the heat of the day, dozens napping in their slung hammocks, not suspecting that they were being watched. We spotted only one sentinel, and he was dozing. After all, who would be foolish enough to try to pass unobserved through an NVA battalion-sized unit?

Slipping by the NVA camp without incident, we climbed the ridgeline that separated the cleared plantation lands from the jungle. Carefully, our teams leap-frogged forward, and we reached the summit in less than an hour. As Lenny described, the land fell away into a broad valley that had been cleared for pasture… Small groups of scrawny, multi-colored humped Brahma-like cattle grazed here and there, occasionally lifting their heads to sniff the wind. In the middle of the clearing, surrounded on all sides by short grass pasture, stood the rambling plantation house.

We descended the slope, pressing forward into a thick stand of bamboo, the only cover available. A good three hundred yards of cleared pasture now separated the plantation house from our position. For the life of me, I couldn't fathom where our Marine sniper might be hiding.

If he was in position, as Lenny claimed he was, he was a master of camouflage and stealth…

I wanted to get a better view, and crawled dangerously close to the edge of the thicket. My seasoned Thai sergeant convinced me to halt. For fifteen minutes I sat there, in that steamy thicket of bamboo, dripping with sweat, listening to my inner voice. We could assault the plantation house and blow it to pieces with automatic weapons fire if we had to. But in the process some of us would perish. An air strike was out of the question. It would be folly from our vulnerable position. Then a dog started to bark…

The dog was one of those small, pointy-eared, tan-colored, curly-tailed mutts one sees all over Asia. I've heard them referred to as Pariah dogs. He was pointing in our direction and barking with increased intensity… To remain where we were would be jeopardizing both our hidden Marine shooter, and the team. Lenny had said to remain in position at all costs. But what greater purpose was being served here? Part of me wanted to press forward, assaulting the house and wasting everyone and everything in sight. Another part of me felt the need to withdraw, to spare my men the hardship of this absurd mission. Withdrawing would amount to abandoning our Marine shooter.

I felt totally cut off from all support. The cumulative effect of our days of patrolling was having an impact. My mind was emotionally dead, and I was sure that my Thai sergeant could sense that. By degrees, it seemed that my body was growing numb, losing its energy. When a stinging fly landed on my arm, I watched it impassively…

The Thai sergeant at my side crushed the fly. I smiled. I knew then it was time to withdraw. Forget the repercussions. I felt a greater responsibility for the lives of my team. I made a sign to the sergeant. We would back off and leave while we still could, without a fight. We had done all that we could under the circumstances.

My guess was that back at headquarters they would call me a coward. Those in charge at headquarters would say that I had run away from my responsibilities. But I knew that I was choosing the higher good. With the Thai sergeant in the lead, our patrol began to make its way back up the ridgeline, slipping into the cloak of the dense vegetation. The Pariah dog stopped barking.

*   *   *

The following morning, when we got back to our base camp, Lenny was nowhere to be found. No one said a thing to me about my team's withdrawal. It was as if the whole mission had never happened. Later I called headquarters to request return to my old unit in Vietnam, the 3rd Amphibian Tractor Battalion. The word came back that my transfer was approved, and that our Marine sniper got the NVA general.

Perhaps it was then that my diverse experience in Asia came together, confluent, like the many streams running down those jungle slopes toward the confluence of the Xe Dong and the Mekong Rivers. With that realization I found a kind of closure as I boarded the chopper taking me back to Vietnam, away from the fertile Bolovens Plateau and out of the depths of those Laotian bamboo thickets.

When I made the decision that day to turn away from death I knew, strangely, that I'd also regained the moral authority with our Thai teams that Lucas said we had lost. Call it a decision of conscience. Now I'd made my rendezvous at that place where everything is measured against death, and with the exception of my dreams, I was never to return to Laos. It was all so much ancient history to me.

As our chopper lifted off I remembered the Wat Phou, lost in the jungles for so many centuries, and how struck I was by the beauty of the locals there while walking among those ruins, people who always seemed to be smiling as if they understood something that I didn't, many who had Coco's dark complexion and wavy hair.

DODGE CITY BLUES

CHAPTER ONE: XUAN DIEM CEMETERY

Day One, 0100 hours

Sometime after midnight we got the call from the S-3, Major Hopkins... An army chopper was down just north of Hill 55 near the Xuan Diem Pagoda, pilot and copilot wounded. The new Senior District Advisor from Dien Ban District was with them. Major Hopkins said that the new advisor was an Australian Army Special Air Services hero, an SAS man. I was to get my shit together and what was left of my track platoon so that we could put down a reaction force most ricky-tick.

The moon was full, and this time of year it seemed to rise late in the evening. Now it hung, luminous and bright above the sprawl of rice plains and bamboo hedgerows that surrounded Hill 55, the area known as Dodge City.

"Lieutenant, I mustered nineteen men," Sergeant Chapelle said, glazed-eyed and out of breathe.

"Are you drunk, Chapelle?"

"No, sir. I didn't have more than six beers."

"You look shit-faced."

"I okay, sir. Believe me."

"Hopkins will have our asses if he thinks you're loaded."

"Sir, I'll be fine."

"Stay away from Hopkins. We'll brief the men on the way to the chopper pad."

"You can count on me. But the men ain't happy about going out like this," Chapelle said, spitting.

"I understand. And I know how they feel about this night reaction business. But those Army pilots would come after us no questions asked... And this advisor is supposed to be important. Hopkins says he's come up from the Delta to help us out. He's supposed to be some kind of expert in counter-intelligence. Tell that to the men," I said, grabbing my flak jacket.

The grunts of the First Marine Regiment were all committed to other actions throughout the Dodge City area, and there was no one else to send. My platoon of track rats had been tasked as a night reaction force on two previous occasions. On the first occasion we had used tracks and lost a vehicle to an RPG, or Rocket Propelled Grenade, an antitank weapon similar to the World War II bazooka in the kind of damage it could do to a tracked vehicle. That time we got caught in a cross fire and lost four WIA.

On the second occasion we'd set down in a hot landing-zone and taken five wounded in as many seconds, so it was with great uncertainty that I gathered the reaction force together. I was in my own emotional crossfire, caught between the demands of Major Hopkins for a reaction force and the concerns for my men, men who wondered if I was looking out for them. For all we knew, we could be dropped into the middle of a company of North Vietnamese Army, and this small reaction force was all there was. There was no back up.

"Sir, I'm not complaining. I just wonder whatever happened to the mission we were sent here to perform... And if this advisor is so smart, how did he get himself in this mess?"

"You are drunk. I'm going to tell you the way it is. Then I want you to keep your mouth shut."

"But, sir..."

"Shut-up and listen," I said in a whisper.

"Yes, sir."

"There are a lot of things that we do that are not part of our mission. We're track rats. We're the second team as far as Hopkins is concerned. He's a grunt. And he's going to use us and abuse us. Let's all stay loose and gut it out together. As for that advisor, who knows? Shit happens," I said, feeling conflicting emotions swelling up inside me.

But the Marine Corps depended upon men like Sergeant Val Jean Chapelle. I knew that the most important thing that I could do at that moment was to protect him from Hopkins. At the same time I needed to let him know that I was depending upon him to do the job that only he could do. There are certain things that are best left to sergeants.

"Yes, sir," Chapelle said, spitting on the ground.

"The truth of the matter is that *right now* there isn't anyone else available to pull those people out," I said, my hand trembling as I took out a cigarette.

"Lieutenant, you won't hear anymore bitchin' out of me."

"You all right, Val Jean?"

"Yes, sir."

I was sick to my stomach. My left hand wouldn't stop trembling. I was very tired from the day's efforts. Fatigue was catching up with me.

After checking my shotgun, I grabbed a bag of frag grenades. My shotgun was a standard Marine Corps-issue Stevens which I loaded with double-ought buckshot. Overhead a chopper was circling. The thump-thump of rotor blades shut out all other noise.

Quickly I picked up my bolo and tested the edge. It could split hairs. On my last tour one of my snipers had carried a Kukri. I opted for the bolo, fourteen and three quarter inches of stainless steel alloy.

The great, continuous cutting curve of the bolo was not unlike that of the Kukri used by the British Gurkhas. The advantage of the bolo was that, unlike the Kukri, the bolo could still thrust straight. The design of the bolo was similar to that of the short, fighting sword used by the troops of Alexander the Great. I liked the way it balanced in my hand. I gripped the bolo tightly.

"Lieutenant, they want us down at the chopper pad!" someone yelled.

I snapped out of my daze. My hand had stopped trembling. I could see that my track rats'd stumbled out of their hooches, weapons ready. I could also see an animated Chapelle gesturing in the eerie light of the four-deuce mortar illumination… And to the north, more four-deuce mortar illumination lit the bamboo hedgerows and dry rice paddies. From my vantage point on Hill 55, I had a clear view of the area. The area appeared quiet. I could hear nothing. I could see no tracers.

"Major Hopkins wants us to haul ass, Lieutenant!" a faceless shadow yelled.

I looked at the shadow. It was Slammer, our Navy corpsman.

"Something the matter, Lieutenant?"

"I don't know. I'm just real tired, I guess."

Slammer noticed my left hand. It had started trembling again.

"Hey, we *got to go*! Hopkins wants us right now!"

Major Hopkins was standing at the edge of the chopper pad. Hopkins was the kind of guy you didn't say no to. His broad shoulders made him the biggest shadow at the chopper pad. In the golden glow of the four-deuce illumination, the features of his face exuded a sense of urgency. Word was out that he could be a mean son-of-a bitch.

I had yet to figure out the true extent of Hopkins's role. Officially, he was the S-3 for the First Marine Regiment... The S-3 ran operations. Yet he also had the job of linking up with the people like the new Senior District Advisor from Dien Ban District. Hopkins had great influence over both the commanding officer, and the battalion commanders of the First Marine Regiment. He seemed to be always either implementing some plan, or gathering information upon which to develop some new plan... But I had also seen him bully people. If he found your weaknesses, I had the sense he would exploit you for his own purposes.

"Gatlin! Are your men ready?" Hopkins yelled.

"Most affirmative, sir."

"Lieutenant. We got to get this Australian captain. He's a good man. He's already taken risks for us that he shouldn't have," Hopkins yelled over the noise of the incoming chopper.

Chapelle rushed up to me and gave me a thumbs-up.

"All set, Lieutenant."

"Let's go," I answered.

I watched Chapelle direct the men. He was from Neshoba County, Mississippi, and had just turned twenty. At eighteen he'd already been leading a squad of grunts up on the DMZ. This was his third tour in the Nam. Chapelle had extended to serve with tracked vehicles, thinking that being a track rat would help his career in the Marine Corps. Being with tracked vehicles, either tanks or tracks, was considered to be a plum job.

"Load your men!" Hopkins yelled.

The chopper landed, the rotor wash throwing up shadowy clouds of Hill 55 dust into the night air. The chopper was a Sea Knight, the kind that is boarded from the rear. As soon as the ramp lowered we hustled aboard, all done according to the drill. We could have been going on a mail-run to Da Nang. Within seconds we were in the air, heading into the deep indigo of the night.

*   *   *

The chopper rose in a wide arc above Hill 55, the moon obscured by clouds. To the southwest, deep in the Arizona Territory, I could see tracers from at least three firefights where the Fifth Marine Regiment had trapped a body of NVA. To the immediate south a large firefight raged where Highway One marked the eastern border of Dodge City. This was the big fight that had locked up the resources of the First Marine Regiment. Directly east, where the Korean Marines patrolled, it looked like a whole village was burning. Tonight there was a lot of heavy shit going down.

"Look at all that, Lieutenant," Chapelle yelled above the chopper noise.

"Stay loose, Val Jean," I said.

Chapelle said nothing back. He just nodded and smiled.

"We're going in, Lieutenant!" a shadow yelled.

The chopper banked and we seemed to drop like a stone. My left hand started trembling again. I grabbed the handle of my bolo tightly. The hand stopped trembling.

"Coming in!" the same shadow yelled.

The chopper spun, facing north as it landed. Within seconds the ramp was down and we were on the ground, forming a perimeter at the edge of our landmark. The chopper rose quickly, banked, and disappeared. Everything was quiet. Cold LZ.

"All secure, sir. Cold LZ. We lucked out like a big dog," Chapelle whispered.

I looked about me. Everything was still. Our landmark, the great Xuan Diem Cemetery, lay to our immediate front. On the far side of that cemetery two Army chopper pilots, and the new Senior District Advisor of Dien Ban District, were hiding from a group of the enemy who were probing the area. In the light of the four-deuce illumination I could see the edifice of the Xuan Diem Pagoda rising some hundred yards away.

The cemetery was about two hundred yards square, surrounded by a wall four feet high. Our chopper had set us down on the northeast corner, on a little rise of ground that offered us clear field of fire. The idea was for my group to cross the cemetery to the southwest corner where the Xuan Diem Pagoda's beautiful and historic structure dominated the terrain… Once at the pagoda, my group would be in a position to cover the chopper pilots as they moved towards us over open ground.

The moon chose this moment to poke through the clouds, and a varied geometry of stone stretched out before us. There were the smooth, pastel hemispheres, perfect circles that marked the more prestigious ancestors. Here and there westernized rectangles clustered together, marking family plots and lines of descent. An ancient mausoleum dominated it all, a many-chambered crypt reserved for those of noble blood. In the strange light of the four-deuce illumination the crooked shadows of the stone monoliths swayed to and fro like dancers from hell.

"Waiting on your word, Lieutenant," Chapelle said, looking at me for guidance.

"Let's go, Val Jean. Pass the word that if the shit hits the fan, we will all stand back to back against the northeast corner of the cemetery wall. That's the rally point if people get split up."

"Most affirmative, sir. I'm heading over the wall."

"Go for it."

Chapelle and the first fire team made their move. Although climbing over the wall only took a few seconds it seemed forever, the team moving in slow motion.

I gave the word and my next fire team slipped over... The wall was cool and damp, covered with a slick film of tiny, moss-like plants. The surface was crumbly and seemed to break away from the pressure of my weight. A musty smell permeated the surrounding air. The smell of the dead, I thought to myself.

In the moonlight I gave Chapelle the thumb's-up sign. The plan was to move down along the wall and then move forward. Two fire teams would move abreast in a skirmish line. A third would follow in trace of the skirmish line, and a fourth would secure our position at the wall, covering the rear.

Chapelle moved down along the wall, his fire team following in single file. Mine moved down along the wall in the opposite direction, leaving me in the center of the skirmish line. Off in the distance, on the far side of the pagoda where the downed chopper pilots lay hidden, someone fired an AK-47 on full automatic, emptying a whole magazine.

"Gooks trying to spook those chopper pilots, Lieutenant," my radioman whispered.

"Yeah. Click your handset twice."

During our descent we'd instructed the chopper pilots trapped on the ground to maintain radio silence. A double click on the handset was our signal that we were moving across the cemetery.

An AK-47 fired a second time, spraying the cemetery, rounds impacting and ricocheting off the gravestones. The Marines remained in a low crouch, moving forward slowly and maintaining fire discipline. I signaled them to stop.

Illumination rounds continued to pop overhead, making the night into day, the curious amber light of the illumination about to fade just as another burst forth with a spectacular brilliance. The mortar battery on Hill 55 was shooting these rounds out with perfect timing, the little suns drifting above us on parachutes, fizzling out as they hit the ground.

To my immediate right, a movement caught my eye. A huge toad the size of a hand grenade hopped to the base of a gravestone. The toad squatted, ducking its head as if it were trying to hide. I poked the toad with the barrel of my shotgun and he hopped off onto a pile of dirt where a freshly dug grave lay waiting.

I looked into the grave to see what looked like a body. The body was wrapped in an American poncho. A stench hung in the humid air. It was that rotten, fetid smell of the dead. Two NVA entrenching tools were stuck in the dirt beside the grave. It appeared that our arrival had interrupted a burial.

At that moment an AK-47 round cracked over my head. Another round glanced off a nearby gravestone. I signaled the men forward. The fire teams moved quickly, using the gravestones for cover and maintaining fire discipline. More AK-47 fire swept the area and the men low-crawled the last ten yards to the far wall.

A burst of M-16 fire told me one of my Marines had a target. The return fire was deafening. The ground seemed to erupt before my eyes as various shapes rose out of the shadows to come at us. Green tracers from AK-47's mixed with the golden-red tracers of M-16's. The night air was filled with smoke from weapons firing on full automatic and the screams of men closing hand-to-hand. It flashed on me that we must've cornered a group of the enemy with their backs to the wall.

Rushing forward I slipped on a gravestone and fell into a kind of trench. I scrambled to my feet to find myself eyeball to eyeball with a trench full of Marines and NVA regulars fighting hand to hand. I yelled to the backup fire teams for assistance just as an NVA soldier thrust his bayonet into my flak jacket.

Instinctively, I rammed the rifle barrel upward... The bayonet penetrated through my flak jacket and hung up in my leather shoulder holster. I charged my enemy, kicking his legs out from under him. He let go of his rifle and tried to run. I slipped again in the mud and fell on top of him, my weight driving him down. Screaming, he clawed at my face, digging a finger deep into my eye socket. My body went rigid with sheer panic.

What happened next I can't remember. I only know that the razor sharp bolo found my hand.

The backup fire teams reached the trench and overwhelmed the NVA that remained. One NVA tried to climb over the wall. His head exploded before my eyes. Several fled into the cemetery to be blown away at point blank range by the backup fire teams who fired their weapons on full automatic. In the heat of the firefight all the NVA were killed. With all the confusion and noise, no one heard any of my orders. Everyone was too busy trying to survive. It all happened in less than half a minute.

Mentally, I was calm. I was calm but my left hand had started to tremble again. I couldn't help the trembling. There was nothing I could do to stop it.

In the amber light of the illumination rounds, I counted ten dead NVA. What I thought were VC had turned out to be NVA. We had outnumbered them two to one. Luck had been with us. Each of the NVA had been down to less than five rounds of ammunition. My guess was that we had caught them in the process of burying one of their comrades.

Both Sergeant Chapelle and my radioman had stab wounds. Four more Marines had been shot at close range. Fortunately, those who had been shot had flesh wounds, nothing vital had been hit and no one seemed in shock. I had two Navy corpsmen tending to the wounded.

Slammer, my weird corpsman, approached me, shaking his head.

"Holy shit, Lieutenant. That don't look pretty."

Slammer, unlike anyone else in the platoon, appeared calm and collected. Maybe he was loaded up with some kind of sedative.

My face had deep scratch marks, some of which were bleeding. My right eye was blurry. The spot where the NVA had gouged me ached, but the eye was intact and I could still see out of it.

"Hold still, Lieutenant. Let me check you out."

"Sure," I replied, still trembling.

"Leave it to me, sir. This is what I've been trained to do."

Slammer put some kind of drops in my eye. Soon it was feeling better.

I called Hill 55 to give a situation report. A captain back on Hill 55 suggested that I send a fire team over the wall to try to link up with the chopper pilots. Then he added that we should gather up all the dead gooks for identification, including the dead body in the grave. He was sending out body bags with the pick-up chopper.

I sent my most experienced corporal over the wall with a fire team. The corporal encountered no more resistance, and within five minutes he had linked up with the chopper pilots and the district advisor. The pilots had been within fifty feet of the cemetery wall, hiding under a bush. I radioed Hill 55 to report that we'd picked them up. The captain in the operations center on Hill 55 radioed back that a chopper was on the way. My men who were able then set about the grim process of policing up the dead.

*   *   *

CHAPTER TWO: YIN AND YANG

Day One, 0800 hours

The advisor, Captain Graham of the Australian Special Air Service, opened a lukewarm can of Falstaff beer. I hated Falstaff, but it was all I had to offer him. It appeared that the Senior District Advisor was thirsty.

"Thanks, Lieutenant. That hits the spot."

He wiped his brow and took another long pull on the beer.

"Sorry I don't have anything better, like a Foster's or Victoria Bitter. Or maybe even a tall cold bottle of Toohey's Flag Ale," I said, lighting a cigarette and handing it to the man who wore no visible rank.

"Ah, I can see that you know your aussie beers."

"That's a big affirmative. I had an R&R in Sydney in spring of 1968. Later I went back for a longer stay between my tours in Vietnam."

"I bet you hung out at King's Cross, chasing all those hot aussie women ."

"Only briefly, on my first R&R. I spent a lot of my time down at Cronulla, surfing that nice curl near the Junior Rugby League Club."

"My word! You're a regular *fair dinkum* Aussie."

"I wouldn't go as far as to say that, but I fell for a tall leggy blonde who taught at Woolooware High School."

"Woolooware High School! They were our big rivals in rugby league. I grew up in Sutherlandshire and went to Caringbah High School! Small world. Did you ever get to the Outback?"

"Yeah, but that's a long story. One with a sad ending."

"Well, sorry to hear that. But maybe that calls for another rusty can of warm Falstaff."

We finished our second beer, and went down to the chow hall for breakfast. During the walk to the chow hall I didn't hear a word the aussie captain said. My mind was elsewhere. Maggie, my aussie sweetheart, and I, were at a topless beach north of Cronulla. She was taking off her bikini top and I was opening the first cold beer of the day. We were both hung-over from a wild night of drinking and dancing the night before. My jaw still hurt from where her old boyfriend, jealous of the new Yank in town, had sucker-punched me. A chopper passed overhead and I snapped out of my daze.

Major Hopkins met us in the chow line. For once Hopkins was smiling.

"Captain, the radio call sign Hill 55 uses for your district is X-Ray Delta, so you will be the X-Ray Delta Six," Major Hopkins was saying, woofing down his food.

"That makes me Captain X. And X often stands for an unknown," the Aussie said, smiling.

At that remark Major Hopkins paused in his eating and looked, blinking:

"We're expecting great things from you, Captain. You come highly recommended," he said.

"Thank you, Major, but the truth is that I'm actually only a temporary fix for this job. I was heading up to assist with the Mobile Strike Forces at Command and Control North in Da Nang when I was diverted to this job."

"Yep, that's right. We wanted someone with previous experience as an advisor who could speak Vietnamese. We also wanted someone who had counter-intelligence experience. You fit the profile."

"I was briefed on what happened to my predecessor."

"Yep, Viet Cong assassination squad took him out. They got the guy that ran your PRU team at the same time. Makes me wonder if there's someone on the inside, a spy. How did this squad know when to strike? Anyway, the advisor's job is a tough one. This same VC squad has taken out two other advisors in I Corps over the last three months. Your predecessor was a good friend of mine," Hopkins said.

"Getting on top of that assassination team should be a priority," the Aussie said, pushing away a tray of uneaten food.

"Not hungry, Captain?" I asked.

"Captain Graham, I am going to take that one on," Major Hopkins said. "It's become personal with me."

"Get some!" I said.

"That's right, Sam, *get some*! Its all about taking it to the enemy, but watch who you say that to," Hopkins said, giving me a cold look.

"I'll be doing what I can to help you, Major. It's critical that we all link together. We've got to integrate our efforts as they say."

"That goes without saying, Captain. You probably know that we've had all kinds of problems coordinating with the different districts as well as with the South Vietnamese army."

"I was briefed on that issue. Rest assured that I'm here to change all that as far as Dien Ban District is concerned."

"That's good to hear, Captain. Sam and I look forward to working with you."

"Is last night's action typical of this area?" the Aussie asked.

"As far as the ARVN support we got, that's typical. You can't depend on them," the major replied, shaking his head.

"I see… Sam, how long have you been on Hill 55?"

"Too long, Captain. I've been on Hill 55 way too long."

Both Major Hopkins and Captain X laughed.

*　　*　　*

Day One, 0930 hours

After chow I called for two of my tracks to run the captain to his District Headquarters. The lack of sleep was catching up to me. The newly appointed Senior District Advisor of Dien Ban District hadn't planned to spend the night the way that he had. His plan had been to introduce himself to the Marine Regimental staff of the First Marine Regiment on Hill 55, and be back to District Headquarters in time for dinner. But on the way to District Headquarters his chopper had flown too close to the old Xuan Diem pagoda. The captain wanted to evaluate the terrain around the pagoda close up, the pagoda being a known VC staging area. Several bursts of AK-47 fire had wounded both the chopper pilot and the copilot. The wounded pilot'd set the chopper down, and they had spent the night running and hiding until our reaction force arrived.

"Captain," I said, as we waited for my tracks. "You asked me about how long I've been on Hill 55. Well, this is my second tour with the First Marine Division. I was on this hill on my previous tour for a time. During 1968 I worked tracked vehicle platoons all over the Dai Loc map sheet. I worked for the Seventh Marines on Hill 10, and the Fifth Marines down in An Hoa and the Arizona Territory."

"Sounds like a lot of experience. All that time in the field?"

"Yes, sir."

"You must be a career Marine. All that field time. Then to come back for a second tour."

"No sir. When my time is up I'm getting out of the USMC, Uncle Sam's Misguided Children."

Captain X laughed.

"If you're not planning on a career, why did you come back?"

"It's a personal thing, sir."

"I see. Your reasons have to do with personal conviction. You believe in what we are doing here, supporting the South Vietnamese Army. Is that it?"

"No sir. That's not it. The South Vietnamese people are okay but you can't depend on the ARVN. They're assholes. As far as I'm concerned, Marines are here to kill the VC and their North Vietnamese Army buddies. For me, it's like Major Hopkins said to us. It's all about taking it to the enemy. You see, sir, like Major Hopkins, I've lost some close friends. And I'm real pissed off about it."

Captain X looked at me for a long moment and lit a cigarette. He smoked Lucky Strikes.

"I've also lost friends. And I understand your anger."

"Yes, sir."

"Anger can eat up your insides," the captain said, shaking his head. "But let me ask you something."

"Sir?"

"If a foreign power, under the guise of providing assistance, came into your country and facilitated a coup that resulted in the death of your president, how would you feel?"

"You mean Ngo Dinh Diem. He was a corrupt dictator who oppressed the Buddhists. Anyway, he was losing the war," I replied.

"I don't believe that Diem was losing the war. I know your own Marine Corps Major General Victor Krulak visited all four Corps areas of Vietnam and found Diem to be an effective leader. Krulak's observations were based on interviews with both American and Australian advisers to the South Vietnamese army. I know this because I was one of those he interviewed. At that time the war was going well."

"I've never heard this before."

"Diem put down the organized crime in his rise to power. The people viewed him as someone who could wield power effectively. Like many who were here serving at that time, in 1960, I think he had broken the back of the Communist insurgency."

"Interesting viewpoint."

"Yes. Call it my SAS advisor's perspective. By the way, I also have it on good authority that much of the criticism of the Diem regime was traced back to a journalist named Pham Xuan An, a Reuters stringer. It is now common knowledge that Pham was a Communist agent whose very mission was to influence the American press.

"You're saying taking out Diem was a mistake."

"Absolutely, and to many South Vietnamese the real villain was the American ambassador at that time. I have heard more than one person say that the ouster of Diem was part of a personal vendetta. That same ambassador told your president that he was unable to stop the coup, when, in reality, he instigated it in the first place. These facts are well known in Saigon; and you, Lieutenant Gatlin, wonder why the ARVN leadership won't risk their neck to save Americans."

"You make it sound like we lost our moral authority in their eyes," I said.

"Well, yes. Lieutenant Gatlin, you surprise me. That's one way of putting it."

"I get it. But I've got to tell you, Captain Graham, I returned for my second tour to the same places in Vietnam where I served previously, and I see no lasting results from my previous tour. Nothing's changed. The district advisors, like you, make excuses for the ARVN, and I get real weary of this war. All the Marines on Hill 55 are tired. A Marine officer I know calls it the Dodge City Blues, kind of a combination of weariness and anger."

"It's no good, Lieutenant. Let it go. Let that part go, even if you have to reinvent yourself. If you don't let it go, you'll get to a point where it will drive you crazy."

I didn't reply to the captain. I just nodded. The tracks arrived to pick us up. I called Major Hopkins on the radio to let him know we were heading out. We still had to wait for the engineers to sweep the road.

"That eye going to be all right?"

"The doctor told me to keep it covered for a while. No permanent damage."

The Aussie nodded. Outside, the tracks were revving their 810 horsepower V-12 Continental engines. As we mounted Track One-Three, my lead track, I pondered the captain's observations on Diem as well as my own reasons for being back in the Nam. My being here was all about taking it to the enemy. It was all very personal to me. The amphibian tractors stopped revving their engines. The rumbling ceased as the track engines idled. We headed out the gate toward Route 4.

*　　　*　　　*

Day One, 1000 hours

The amphibian tractor, LVTP-5, was designed as a ship-to-shore vehicle. Upon landing in Vietnam the Marine Corps adapted the track's mission to include transport of men and material on land. It wasn't long before grunt commanders were using and abusing tracks for a variety of purposes, ranging from assault vehicles to living quarters.

"Your wounded track rats, are they all going to be okay?"

"Yes, as far as I know. When they were evacuated off the hill they were in good spirits. They're seasoned. By the way, how should they address you?" I asked, stretching my shoulder.

"Have them call me Captain X. That's my radio call sign, and that's what Major Hopkins seems to enjoy. He's does have a flair for the dramatic."

My right shoulder was bruised from the bayonet of the NVA soldier. The doctor said that there was no damage, but I didn't tell the doctor the whole story. My right arm kept trembling. From time to time the arm tingled and fell asleep. I tried not to think about it. I kept wondering if the trembling was a lingering effect of the head trauma I'd suffered several months ago.

"Hopkins gets real intense," I said.

"I can see that in him."

"Sometimes he gets crazy. Last night there was just too much going on. The Fifth Marines were in a lot of shit, and still are. They had heavy contact all night in the Arizona Territory, and took a lot of casualties… At the same time this big operation with the First Marines has been winding down, and choppers were pulling elements of that effort out to support the Fifth Marines. There just weren't enough choppers available for all that was going down," I explained, chambering a round in track One-Three's M-60 machine gun.

Last night was strange. We'd seen this sudden flurry of activity on the part of the enemy. Firefights were going down all around the greater Da Nang area. It appeared that the lull we'd been experiencing, generally, for the last few weeks, was over. Perhaps there would be more opportunity for what the grunts called payback.

The captain made himself as comfortable as he could in the cramped confines of the bunker on top of Track One-Three. Built of bridge lumber surrounded by sand bags, Track One-Three's bunker was about ten feet long by four feet wide. I preferred the M-60 machine gun to the .30 cal that tracks usually carried. The gun was mounted on the front of the bunker on a tripod that was spot-welded to the track's hull. On my previous tour I had mounted fifty-caliber machine guns on my tracks, but so far this tour I'd been unable to secure fifty-caliber machine guns.

"I'm told Major Hopkins sees himself as a mover and a shaker," The aussie captain said.

"He doesn't back off from anything. Last night was a bitch. But Hopkins found a way… As usual we couldn't get support from the South Vietnamese Army. Our problems linking with the South Vietnamese seem to be getting worse instead of better."

"I understand. We had the same problems coordinating with the South Vietnamese down in IV Corps… I suppose Hill 55 is no different. But one good thing did come from last night's adventure. The body being buried by those NVA turned out to be that of an important VC leader. Hopkins was of the opinion this VC directed the many cadre in the districts surrounding Hill 55."

"Find anything on the bodies?"

"Yes, as a matter of fact… But I'd rather not comment on that. You understand, Lieutenant."

"Sure," I found myself saying, clearly disappointed.

*   *   *

I looked down Route 4. Marines were moving off Hill 55 in the early morning light. Hill 55 was a hub for all the action. It sat in the middle of the Dai Loc map sheet, staging point for Marine operations to all parts of the area. Da Nang lay some twelve kilometers to the northeast. Charlie Ridge rose five kilometers to the west, a great jungle and scrub-covered ridgeline. Ten kilometers to the southwest lay the Arizona Territory where the Fifth Marines had a company of the 308th NVA cornered at this very moment. To the east and southeast lay the South China Sea and our allies, the Korean Marines. Directly to the south lay Dodge City, and beyond the tangled bamboo hedgerows and scrub of Dodge City lay the flat, Go Noi Island plain.

During the last two months the First Marines had conducted a long and highly complex operation throughout that Go Noi Island plain. I had arrived back in the Nam just in time to find myself being choppered to Hill 119 with the tactical command group. That group had representatives from the First Marines, the Fifth Marines, First ARVN Ranger Group, First Battalion of the Twenty-Sixth Marines, Fifty-First ARVN, and the Korean Marines. Hill 119, just south of Go Noi at the northern edge of the Que Son Mountains, offered a clear view of all the action. I remember looking down as we circled over the area to see these ancient ruins far below us. The ruins stretched across a kind of valley, a series of towers and crumbling walls, reminding me somewhat of Wat Phou, only much older.

"Look at those ruins, Lieutenant. They're almost a thousand years old, a religious site belonging to the Chams, rulers of Champa, long before the Vietnamese," someone said as our chopper began a wide, circling descent.

That morning observation had been excellent. The tactical command group and I watched as elements of the Fifth Marines advanced east from Liberty Bridge and elements of the Korean Marines took up blocking positions along the eastern edge of Go Noi. ARVN were positioned to the north of Go Noi.

Crossing over the to Go Noi Island was like entering another reality. The enemy had total control of the place. For many years the island had been a staging area for enemy groups preparing to attack the soft underbelly of Da Nang. I knew this reality first hand. For on my previous tour I had taken my tracks across the flat expanse of the Go Noi Island plain and survived, and so it was with great excitement and a sense of satisfaction that I'd watched the big operation kick off. For too long, I knew, we'd allowed the enemy the sanctuary of Go Noi Island.

As the wing attack and fighter aircraft strafed selected landing zones, I could feel myself getting high on the action. Then, when the attack aircraft flew by at two hundred feet off the ground to lay down a thick stream of smoke, dividing the island for air assault purposes, my left hand and arm began to tremble. Out of the sky the CH-46's descended like great flying grasshoppers. Within minutes a combined force of U.S. Marines and Korean Marines unloaded from the choppers, formed up, and began to sweep north in a coordinated attack...

Three months had passed since that first day. Much had occurred during that three months. Squeezed between blocking forces and advancing Marines, the enemy had been forced to scatter. Some escaped to find their way back to the Que Son Mountains. Most were captured or destroyed, along with numerous bunker complexes and food and rice caches...

Then ten Marine Eimco M64 tractors and nine Army D7E Caterpillers equipped with special tree-cutting blades called "Rome Plows" crossed onto the edge of Go Noi and changed the face of the land, plowing up bunkers and leveling scrub and bamboo hedgerows.

Now, in the distance, with my good eye, I could see smoke rising from Go Noi Island. There, where the First Marines were closing out that big operation, five amphibian tractors from my platoon led by staff sergeant Paul Pabinouis were heading back toward Hill 55. By the end of the day I would be joining those five tracks and Mike Company, Third Battalion, First Marines. Soon, I'd have to think about catching a chopper south... As I watched the smoke I couldn't help but wonder if, in changing the face and character of the land, we hadn't somehow changed history as we had plowed up ancient cemeteries and leveled exquisite pagodas, altering forever the map of Go Noi, and thus the language and experience of the Vietnamese who'd made the island their home.

* * *

"You're quiet, Lieutenant. Something the matter?" Captain X was asking.

"No, sir. Just lost in my thoughts," I replied.

I gave the signal, and we moved down Route 4, kicking up a cloud of red dust. By now the sweep team should have most of the road clear, I thought to myself. Track One-Four followed in trace of One-Three. We stopped to pick up four grunts hitch-hiking out to India Company.

For the moment the captain said nothing. He kept staring at the smoke that was rising in the distance. I stopped the tracks to pick up two more hitchhiking grunts. The sun was now well above the horizon.

"Lieutenant, you talk and I'll listen," he said, at last. "Brief me on the important issues around the Hill 55 area. Things have changed quite a bit since I was in I Corps some years ago. I want your perspective. I need as many perspectives as I can get, especially from those whose opinions I respect."

"Thanks for the compliment. Captain... I'll take a shot at it. Around Hill 55 you have the Marines, three different district advisors including yourself, the ARVN, a limp-dick CIA case officer from Da Nang with his mercenaries, the Provisional Recon Units, that's the PRU's. Then you have the Korean Marines to the south, and east, of us... We have all those resources and a lot of firepower, yet we can't seem to get our shit together. We don't communicate effectively. Everyone fights over turf; and then too, the spooks snoop into everyone else's business. But to me the South Vietnamese are really the biggest disappointment. They don't seem to want to carry the fight to the enemy, either VC or NVA."

"I see. Down in the Mekong they transitioned the old counterterror teams into the PRUs. They were very effective," the captain said, loading his Swedish K.

"We had the same transition here with mixed results. I know two Marine officers who run PRU teams. When they first transitioned from the old counterterror teams to be PRU, Americans commanded the teams, which was good. Now, the word has come down that Americans will no long command the PRU, they will advise. That's fucked. Our local PRU are reluctant to do the things that the original counterterror teams did when they were under the command of Americans. Most PRU can't call in supporting arms, and they're afraid that if they go out without an American in charge, they won't be able to get chopper support, if needed."

"The PRU program is classified. You seem to know a lot about it."

"I worked with the old counter terror teams on my previous tour, and I've hauled these PRU teams out to the bush on my tracks. When you work so closely with a group like that you can't help but pick up on what's going down. I heard via the grapevine that a full Marine colonel runs all the PRUs in Nam. At one point they recruited me. Flew me down to Saigon on an Air America flight, one of those Pilatus Porter planes. But they said I didn't have enough grunt experience to be a PRU advisor, so they sent me somewhere else."

"Sounds like an interesting story."

"Sir, you don't want to hear it."

"Up in the I Corps, I've found the ARVN reluctant to work with the PRU," the Captain said, changing the subject.

"The PRU don't trust the ARVN, and the ARVN downright hate the PRU. It's one of those no win situations. You know, sir, there was an ARVN company just one kilometer away from you last night, but they wouldn't leave their compound. It makes me wonder whose side those ARVN are on. The ARVN's excuse was that they were General Lum's special reserves."

"Not surprising. General Lum supported Diem. He's also a Catholic. Get the picture, Lieutenant Gatlin."

"I do. What a crock!"

"Tell me more about this Da Nang Special Sector. That is something new since I was in I Corps."

The captain looked me directly in the eye, and took another long pull on his Lucky Strike. Major Hopkins had given me the skinny on this SAS advisor. He had served two previous tours in Vietnam. One with the Australian Forces down in IV Corps in 1966; and one even before that, in the early sixties, at the Thoung Duc Special Forces Camp. That early tour had been among the Montagnard tribes in the mountains west of Da Nang. Major Hopkins mentioned a place that I had never heard of called An Diem. An Diem was abandoned by the Special Forces and the various Montagnard tribes came under the influence of the NVA, pressed into service as scouts and couriers.

Captain X looked the part. His build, his lean face and muscular arms reminded me of an all-pro running back, and he had a kind presence about him, as if he had been to the very edge and made it back.

I could see the sweep team up ahead of us. I signaled my driver to slow down. A tank and three trucks were following the sweep team, and were, I thought, further along than I thought they would be. I hoped that they weren't moving too fast.

"Oh yes, the Da Nang Special Sector," I said. "I guess it's now going to be called the Provincial Interrogation Center, the PIC."

"That's a mouthful."

"As I understand it, all district advisors, with the help of the PIC, are supposed to provide leads to the PRU units. Of course, a VC death squad killed your district PRU guy. So, who's on first? Like the old Abbott and Costello routine..."

"It's a big mess according to Major Hopkins. He says lines of authority are unclear."

"Well, as you know the Province Chief has two lines of authority, one political, another military. On paper the Special Sector belongs to the Province Chief, gathering intelligence and reporting on military matters, especially what they term counter terrorism opportunities... In realty, of course, they are paid by the CIA. Right now what the

Special Sector coughs up as intelligence, feeds to the Province Chief's PRUs."

"Down south we called all this the Phoenix Program."

"Yep, its the same program up here. Off Hill 55, Hopkins has had me insert PRU teams on two occasions, using my tracks to mask the drop-off. Both times they got lost. Hell, we had to go back and pick the teams up from the drop-off point, most ricky-tick."

"Lack of American leadership."

"True. And I know of another time, Christ, when a PRU team brought back a couple of heads... The Combined Action Platoon, who worked in that village, said this particular PRU mission was nothing but a vendetta. The PRUs killed some of our good guys because a well-known Vietnamese official didn't get some kind of payoff. What kind of moral authority can we have when shit like that goes down?"

The captain closed his eyes, and took a deep breath, rubbing a thumb and forefinger over his eyelids. He looked tired.

"You okay, sir?" I asked, concerned that the night's events might be taking their effect

"Yeah, I'm fine. I just need a little sleep."

One of the combat engineers on the sweep team yelled *fire in the hole*. We all ducked as a quarter pound block of C-4 blew a box mine in place. Little particles of red dirt rained down on the tracks.

"I don't know, sir. When you figure these ARVN out, let me in on the skinny."

Captain X looked me directly in the eye again. It was as if he were looking right through me.

"It begins by having the ARVN take more responsibility. It's no different than having a new corporal who doesn't act upon his authority as an NCO. You tell that corporal to start acting like he has the rank or you'll take it away from him. ARVN are no different. We need to weed out ARVN officers who won't take the fight to the enemy. Those ARVN who didn't support us last night will be held accountable in the long term. Believe me. It's all Yin and Yang."

"Yin and Yang?"

"Oh, that's another way of saying what goes around, comes around. Yin and Yang is Taoist thought, one aspect of which is that things are cyclical. There is a lot to the viewpoint of the Yin and the Yang. For one thing, there are opposite, conflicting forces and opportunities found in every action and every event. I believe that. But one needs to get down close, into the real flow of things, to understand what those forces and opportunities may be. What that means here in Vietnam is that we have to go live in the village to change things, to get next to the people, to the real flow of events. To do what I am describing requires that we reinvent ourselves and change our approach."

"What you're describing makes sense when one looks at our Combined Action Platoons. They live in the ville and fight with the locals. The CAP teams really work. We just can't put enough of them in the field."

"When the CAP teams live with the Vietnamese they are close to the events going down in the village. They make the most of the opportunities that arise day to day. Get close to the enemy, into *his flow*. That's the answer."

"You'll get along real fine with Major Hopkins. All he does with his free time is read about the Far East, Taoism and Buddhism, that sort of thing; and he likes to play that Chinese chess game called Go."

"That's interesting. He plays a game that is all about containment and control. I'll have to see how good a player he is."

*   *   *

I realized that the captain was probably right. What goes around comes around. But I was burned out. When I got burned out, my head hurt. I started to get headaches. So I needed to keep things simple, and drown my blues in a few beers, try to forget what I knew in my heart that I could never forget, from the shit that went down on my first tour to the Laos debacle. I was looking forward to my next trip to Da Nang. Have to check out the White Lotus for a massage, I thought to myself. After a trip to Da Nang, I'd be okay.

This captain was a complex guy. He had a lot of energy and went about his business with a directness that I liked. What would he think if I told him about my Laotian experience? I began to wonder.

The sweep team stopped once more, finding yet another mine. They blew the mine in place, resuming the sweep at a slower pace. So far the sweep team'd found three mines, not a good sign. The VC had been busy last night. This type of saturation mining had never happened before along this section of road. Route 4 was a major east-west connection, and traffic was backing up behind us. The denial of Route 4 was an embarrassment to General Lum and as well to the district advisors in the area. It was not a good sign and raised all kinds of questions.

A tall hedgerow of bamboo flanked the right side of the road, and ran for about a hundred yards, shading us from the morning sun. It occurred to me that we were in a bad spot if the VC wanted to spring an ambush.

I picked up my field glasses. The whole eastern half of Go Noi Island now appeared to be covered with dense black smoke. I was certain that one of the tracked vehicles supporting the operation, a tank, a track, or a Rome Plow, was burning. No doubt about it. The action was picking up all through the Da Nang area.

Several Marine Corps Phantoms passed high overhead. These fighters were on the way to join other craft supporting the air assault that had developed down on Go Noi. I watched one of the Phantoms making a pass, dropping snakeeyes at five hundred plus knots, maybe three hundred feet off the deck. A second Phantom followed, this time dropping napalm. A plume of flame marked the target; then more black, oily smoke rose above the island.

*   *   *

Day One, 1100 hours

The sweep team was moving at a crawl. All we could do was be patient and let the combat engineers do their job. We had no choice but to wait the situation out. No way was I going to press the sweep team. Let them take all the sweet time they needed.

I offered the captain one of my Marsh Wheeling cigars.

"Try one of these, Captain. Marsh Wheeling is a mild smoke."

The tall bamboo hung overhead, shading us from the bright morning sun. Some of this bamboo, which also marked the southern boundary of the area we called Dodge City, had been harvested. Given all the traffic on Route 4, it bothered me why this stretch of bamboo had not been cleared away entirely. The reasons had to do with General Lum. Lum actually owned much of the land to our north. Thus he called all the shots with how that land was used or abused. In this case he chose not to remove bamboo that would provide the VC with a perfect ambush site. Major Hopkins had complained on several occasions, only to be ignored by General Lum's staff. I just didn't understand this lack of cooperation.

The sweep team paused to rest for a moment in the shade. The driver in the truck just ahead of One-Three began to bitch that the sweep team was taking too much time, and one of the combat engineers on the team made an obscene gesture at the driver.

Captain X stood up and stretched. He lit up the cigar and began to blow smoke rings. I was impressed.

We moved forward onto a slight rise and to our north, in contrast to the action taking place down on Go Noi Island, stretched a serene checkerboard of bamboo hedgerows and rice paddies, vivid green in the morning light. But the serenity was a deception, for this was Dodge City. Those tall, dark bamboo hedgerows hid the VC assassination team that had taken out Captain X's predecessor.

"Maybe you should've taken a chopper back to district headquarters," I found myself saying.

"The hold-up doesn't bother me, Lieutenant Gatlin."

"Captain, I think the lull in the fighting that we have been experiencing during the last few weeks is over," I said, attempting to blow a smoke ring with little success.

"Hey, look at that," my driver yelled.

A bus carrying a load of Vietnamese was coming from the other direction. The bus swung wide around the sweep team, who attempted to stop it… But the Vietnamese bus driver would have none of it. He gunned his engine and sped on towards us. Then the air was split by the crack of an explosion.

"*Holy shit*!" my driver yelled.

The bus rose some ten feet into the air, somersaulted forward onto its roof, and burst into flames.

The engineers fell to the ground. Captain X and I dropped flat on the hull of the track. An AK-47 round cracked by my ear, and I scrambled into One-Three's bunker. More AK-47 fire sprayed the area and the grunts on top of One-Three and One-Four returned fire on full automatic, spraying the bamboo hedgerow and the road indiscriminately.

"Cease fire! Hold your fire! Damn it!" Captain X yelled.

The grunts ceased firing. Captain X jumped down to the ground and ran for the burning, twisted mess that'd once been the bus. Baggage and bodies were strewn across the road, smoldering from the initial fireball of the explosion. The bus had been carrying civilians, mostly women and children. None survived.

"What do you think, Lieutenant?" my driver yelled.

"Command-detonated mine. We better head back up to Hill 55. I don't like the idea of going any further down this road until the engineers do a better job of clearing it."

Captain X returned, shaking his head.

"We'd like to head back up to Hill 55, sir. That okay with you?"

"Yes. Under these circumstances, I think it's best that we return up to Hill 55... I'll get a chopper back to Dien Ban."

The heat of the flames forced the sweep team to fall back. Captain X slumped to one knee, watching the bus burn... I wondered if the new Senior District Advisor was thinking about the Yin and the Yang.

*   *   *

CHAPTER THREE: STICKY-TOED LITTLE LIZARDS

Day One, 1400 hours

I was heading down to the Hill 55 Chopper pad when I ran into Major Hopkins. He had a sour look on his face.

"Lieutenant Gatlin!"

"Yes, sir."

"The colonel was impressed with your actions last night. Because I didn't want to disappoint him I decided not to tell him that half your men were drunk. As their leader, what do you have to say for yourself?" Hopkins asked.

"With all due respect, they were on stand down, sir."

"Get your shit together, Lieutenant. Stand down does not mean that everyone gets loaded. Keep your men ready at all times. That means you keep them sober. That's your job. On Hill 55 we've got to be ready to do the right thing at the right time. That's real simple, is it not? In fact, that's common fucking sense. Are we clear?"

"With all due respect, sir, your request came at us out of nowhere. And actually, being part of a Hill 55 reaction force is not our mission on this hill," I found myself saying. "Rather, I advise your boss, the colonel, on track deployment. I do the same thing for the Fifth Marines down in An Hoa. The only person who gives me direct operational orders is Lieutenant Quick, my company commander. I complied with your request for support last night because it was the right thing to do. As far as I'm concerned, if you are not happy with my men, I'll take all my tracks and drive down Liberty Road to the Fifth Marines. They already have requested my support."

"That's bullshit, Lieutenant. I find your manner both salty and insubordinate."

"Insubordinate! I have never refused to follow a direct order. Major, I think that you're trying to bully me. Now, if you don't want my resources on Hill 55, say the word, and I'm on my way down to the Fifth Marines."

Major Hopkins stood there speechless. Never before had his authority on Hill 55 been challenged. But he could see that I was angry, and he knew that I was right on all accounts... Technically, I could have refused last night's request for support, and my role as a technical advisor for tracked vehicles ran across regimental lines of authority. Hopkins also knew that he had no hold on me. In fact, I knew my threatened departure could only strain the tense relationship he already had with *his* commanding officer. So he took a deep breath. But the more I thought about the major accusing me of insubordination, the angrier I got. Maybe my anger was another effect of my severe head injury. I wondered. The old Sam Gatlin would have approached things much differently with the major. He would have kept his cool, and been more acquiescent. Lately I seemed to have a hair trigger. It didn't take much to set me off.

"Okay, Lieutenant. You made your point. But let me put this another way."

"Sir?"

"You come across to me as someone who is too soft on your men."

"Yes, sir. I'll take that under advisement."

"Advisement! How fucking impertinent!"

"Major, if there is nothing else, I need to attend to my tracks."

"Yes, there is something else. We have a change of plans. Due to the increased level of mining along Route 4, the colonel and I have asked Captain Graham to stay on Hill 55 for a few days. Are those E-1 mine clearing tracks still at Phu Loc 6?"

"Yes, sir, I believe they are."

"Call them up... That is, I'm formally requesting that you have them report to our engineers. Let's start using them to clear mines along Route 4. That's what we're supposed to use them for, to clear mines."

"That's a good idea sir. I'll get right on it."

There *were* people on Hill 55, I reflected, that wanted to kill Major Hopkins... Remarkably, none of them were in my platoon. Also, having been chewed out by full colonels, his tirade didn't bother me. By the end of the day his mind would be caught up with other, more important events, anyway...

*   *   *

Day One, 1500 hours

I found Captain X walking back from the chopper pad carrying a case of Australian Foster's Lager beer. The beer, just flown in from Da Nang, was still ice cold. I directed the captain to the guest hooch. He was grateful for my help.

"Don't rush off, Lieutenant Gatlin. Have a cold beer. I want to talk some more. Tell me about the other districts surrounding Hill 55."

I briefed the captain on how I had worked off Hill 55, during my previous tour in Vietnam, working all three districts surrounding Hill 55. Although Hill 55 was in the Dien Ban District, two other districts were close enough to warrant Major Hopkins's special attention. Ergo, having Captain X on Hill 55 was a great advantage to Major Hopkins in terms of coordination. And, since the First Marines operated across all three districts, it was necessary for Hopkins to coordinate closely with the Army Senior District Advisors in each district so that all parties could link together effectively.

Also, Captain X had a special interest in matters of counter-intelligence, and even Major Hopkins was of the opinion that there wasn't enough expertise in the area of counter-intelligence on Hill 55. Having worked with counter-intelligence matters on a number of occasions, I agreed with that assessment, and would go out of my way to help gather information, probably much to the consternation of some of my men.

The cold Foster's was good. I knew I was heading down to Go Noi Island. I would enjoy the beer while I could, and there was no telling when I'd get back.

"I understand that the regimental commanding officer views you as a hero," the captain said, keeping a straight face.

"Major Hopkins doesn't share that high opinion... He just chewed me out. As for being a hero, *that will never happen*," I replied, blinking, and my sore eye came into focus.

"Oh? Anyway, you're a hero to me, Lieutenant, and it's an excuse to drink some beer. I want you to tell me more about Major Hopkins. We just finished a meeting. I warn you, I continue to be most impressed with him."

"Major Hopkins was just recently promoted... Back on his first tour in 1966 he had a grunt company with the First Marines. He seems to have contacts at all levels. He *works those contacts*. In fact, I would say that Major Hopkins even believes in the adage: 'rules exist to be broken.' Actually, if it were up to Hopkins, I believe he would bring in B-52 strikes on a few of the local villages, just to set an example."

We were sitting on the steps of the hooch when my good friend Lieutenant Wily, a Mike Company platoon leader, walked up. I introduced Captain X as the new district advisor:

"So Wily," I asked, happy to see him. "Did you miss me?"

"Like I would miss a chapped ass!"

Captain X laughed. I smiled and handed Wily a cold Foster's. A swirl of red dust blew up around us and we covered our eyes from the dust. We headed inside the hooch.

As soon as we were in this relative sanctuary, I opened two more of the ice-cold beers and set them on the table. One of those little, sticky-toed lizards called geckos ran across the table, and leaped onto the window screen, followed by another.

"Tell me, sir," Wily asked. "What does the new Senior District Advisor of Dien Ban District think about Hill 55?"

The first little gecko on the window screen ran in crazy circles, the second gecko chasing him.

"No different than down in the Delta. Here the VC seems to be making some sort of move with saturation mines, and booby traps... Then there's this VC assassination team, of course."

"This assassination team runs crazy circles around Hill 55," Wily said. "Like these sticky-toed little lizards here. *They go where they want, when they want.* Everyone in the district is held hostage to this bullshit. They kidnap any locals who protest. Most of those they kidnap are never seen again... We sit on our hill and don't do anything to stop them. Oh, we run our search and destroy missions, but we can't catch them. I must say we're good at tripping booby-traps. My Company's suffered seventeen casualties to booby traps in the past month. In the meantime, everyone is running scared out in the villes. And we don't have a plan, " Wily said negatively.

The littlest gecko ran across the window screen and disappeared. Outside the wind was gusting, blowing swirls of red, Hill 55 dust into the air. It must have been ninety-five degrees, and the grit seemed to drift even through the window screen to settle on the table. The second gecko ran over to the table, and began leaving little tracks in the dust. There was an uneasy silence following Wily's bitter diatribe.

"The captain advised me to reinvent myself, Wily. But I figured you were a better candidate. You need some major attitude overhaul," I said, trying to change the direction of the conversation.

T.T. Wily was from Salina, Kansas. He was over six-feet four-inches, but couldn't have weighed more than a hundred-seventy pounds. Back in Iowa, where I was from, Wily was what we would've called a tall drink of water. T.T. and I had gone through the Marine Corps Basic School together, and thus, whenever we got together, we drank as much beer as we could in what free time we had.

"I'm frustrated. And what's there to reinvent? Your sorry ass?" Wily joked.

"Captain X was telling me about Malaysia. It took twelve years to get things under control there," I said, draining my beer.

"Lieutenant Wily, by reinvent, I mean adapting to each village situation, getting down next to the people, closer to the day-to-day events, and then adjusting our tactics accordingly to deny the enemy his refuge. You Yanks use a kind of search and destroy that doesn't deny the enemy anything. Once you are gone, he creeps right back into the ville. They flow in and out at will," Captain X said.

"I copy that!" Wily said, opening another cold Foster's.

"But your CAP teams, on the other hand, are effective because they stay in the ville. They deny the VC their sanctuary," Captain X added.

"So you're not an advocate of conventional search and destroy?" Wily asked.

"In this kind of guerilla war, search and destroy only works with a proper cordon where no one gets out. It takes surprise and the right level of resources. To work it must be done on a multi-battalion scale and across these artificial district boundaries we create. I see the VC and the NVA exploiting our inability to manage our boundaries. We need the ROK Marines and the ARVN to help us solve that problem," Captain X said, his face flushed.

"Never happen. With all due respect, Captain, never happen" Wily said.

A third gecko appeared and tried to run across the table... Wily grabbed a fly swatter and took a swat at the newcomer. He missed, and the newcomer disappeared under the edge of the table.

Then he appeared again, making an attempt to cross the table to be with his two friends on the window screen. With a quick snap of his wrist Wily brought the swatter to within an inch of the little lizard...

"Is your sorry ass slow, or what..." I said, opening another Foster's.

The gecko leaped onto Wily's Foster's, trying to hide. For a second the confused little lizard clung to wet glass, trying to figure out his next move. Wily struck again, this time tipping over the bottle. But once more the gecko disappeared under the table.

But after a moment, the intrepid lizard reappeared, peeking from under the table, ready to take on the unknown. Wily spotted him and grinned, giving me a wink. I had made up my mind to be on the lizard's side in this conflict, and, watching Wily's eyes, I shoved a table leg at the crucial moment, just as Wily brought the swatter down. Wily missed again.

"Shit! I'm getting slow," Wily said.

The little gecko poked his face over the edge of the table. For a moment he hesitated, on the verge. Wily eyeballed him, deep in concentration, the swatter already raised.

"Some don't know when they've slipped over the edge, Lieutenant Wily," I said, giving Wily a hard time.

"Slipped over what?" Wily asked.

"The edge. You can't get that lizard because you've lost it. Once a person slips over the edge, that's it. They're all done. You just hope that one day they wake up and find themselves. That's all you can do. Isn't that right, Captain?" I said.

"That's right," the captain said, playing along.

"More of your sorry ass bullshit. The only person around here that's slipped over the edge goes by the name of Sam Gatlin. Of course, you're going to reinvent yourself or something like that," Wily said, raising the fly swatter.

The swatter came down on the table with a crash, knocking an ashtray to the floor and raising a plume of red dust.

"Got the little son of a bitch!" Wily yelled.

*   *   *

Day One, 1600 hours

I was into my fourth Foster's when Captain X got the call to report to the Regimental Combat Operations Center. Major Hopkins wanted to see him right away, and since the chopper-pad was next to the COC, Wily and I headed out with the captain. Both Wily and I were to catch a chopper down to Go Noi Island around 1800. It made sense to check into the COC, and see what the situation was throughout the area before we headed down to Go Noi.

The Combat Operations Center, or COC, was buried deep into the red earth of Hill 55. Designed to withstand a direct hit from the enemy's 122 mm rockets, the COC was built with bridge lumber and reinforced with railroad ties. Huge maps of the area surrounding Hill 55 covered the whole forty-foot length of the north wall. Different colored pins and markers denoted the military units and their activities. A corporal scurried back and forth along the maps, pinning three by five cards to various points on the map. A sergeant moved behind the corporal, writing vital information on the cards.

The west wall was further covered with charts and graphs. A sergeant was busy writing the status figures on a chart with a grease pencil. There was a column for those wounded in action. I assumed that Sergeant Chapelle, and the others who were wounded on the reaction force, were counted in the total.

By the south wall, taken up by radios and communications equipment, five men monitored the radios, periodically rising to check with the NCO in charge. Major Hopkins, as S-3, liked to sit at a desk in the center of the COC. Several rows of chairs ran from the center of the COC to the east wall.

"Greetings Captain Graham. We need to talk. Things keep picking up all around Hill 55. Frankly, this increase in activity has caught us by surprise," Hopkins was saying, brushing a cigarette ash off his shirt as we came in.

"I understand your concerns, sir," Captain X said.

"Let me give you a quick appraisal of the situation. The Go Noi operation had been going so well. We'd plowed most of the island flat, and got the better of the enemy in every contact. Things'd been quiet with the Fifth Marines out in the Arizona Territory. All intelligence indications were for a continued lull in activity," Hopkins said, picking up a pointer and slapping it against the map.

"Any word on Sergeant Chapelle?" Wily asked, leaning forward.

Hopkins glanced at us, clearly irritated by Wily's interruption of his situation appraisal.

"Word is that he'll be back tomorrow," Hopkins replied.

"That's good news, Sam. He'll be needed when we get down on Go Noi," Wily whispered.

"Affirmative," I said.

Then Major Hopkins lost no time in bringing all of us up to date on what was happening around the Da Nang. He was all business, a Marine's Marine. As Hopkins was finishing up, Colonel Fry, the Commanding Officer of the First Marine Regiment, entered the COC, and we all snapped to attention.

"At ease, men. *Lieutenant Gatlin*! Good job last night! I just got off the radio with the Division G-2 and G-3. Our Division expressed their gratitude for the efforts of you and your reaction force. I will pass that on to your company commander, next time he's on the hill," the Colonel said.

I looked over at Hopkins, but he didn't appear to blink. Colonel Fry, the commanding officer of the First Marine Regiment, was tall and thin. He looked more like a high school principal than a Marine colonel, and there was an aspect to the Colonel that was almost frail. I'd been told that he had contracted malaria, years ago, during a stint as advisor to the Vietnamese Marine Corps. His skin was blotchy and his teeth looked rotted out. But his eyes were alive with a strange kind of light.

"Thank you, sir. The men in the reaction force deserve the credit. They hung tough," I said, somewhat embarrassed by the compliments, and not knowing what else to say.

"I see... Well, I hope Major Hopkins, here, has had time to brief you on all that's happening. He will be working with you on a recent intelligence development. Division, incidentally, is excited to hear what Major Hopkins has discovered… As a result of what he has found, you will be linking closely with him for the next few days," the colonel said with conviction.

"Yes, sir," I replied, curious as to this development.

Major Hopkins motioned for everyone to be seated for his briefing. He seemed unusually intense, even for Hopkins.

"As everyone here knows, including our guest, Captain Graham, this assassination team has become more active over the last few months. At the end of my briefing I will introduce you to a new resource that will help us track this team down."

The room continued to fill with people. Many stood along the walls and the back of the room. Something big was up. I had never before seen such a large crowd attend. Major Hopkins started the briefing, using a long pointer to review the statistics on the various charts. Then he put down his pointer and motioned to the back of the room.

"Come up here, Hoss," he said. "Let's have everyone get a look at you so that they will know who you are… Everyone, I want to introduce you to a new advisor who will be working with us. His radio call sign will be Seeker Six. He works out of the Da Nang Special Sector. Let me introduce Fritz Lipske. I call him Hoss, that was his nickname when I knew him back on my first tour."

It was as close as I have ever come to fainting while I was in the Marine Corps. I looked up to see none other than Fritz Lipske working his way through the crowd, his long white hair cut off in favor of a butch haircut. He was now sporting a white handlebar mustache, but still wearing those same black utilities. He wore a single brass Montagnard bracelet on his left wrist.

"What's the matter, Sam? You look like you've seen a ghost," Wily was saying.

"Yeah. You could say that."

*   *   *

CHAPTER FOUR: DODGE CITY BLUES

Day One, 1800 hours

Wily, Slammer, and I were about to board a chopper heading for Go Noi Island when Major Hopkins stopped me. He was holding a Polaroid photo in one hand. The scout dog handler we called Mojo Man stood just behind Hopkins with his Scout Dog, Blitz.

"Go ahead and board, Lieutenant Wily. I need to have a word in private with Lieutenant Gatlin," Hopkins was saying curtly, handing me the photo.

In the photo three Vietnamese stood, smiling, in what appeared to be an ancient cemetery. An older man stood in the middle of the group with a young woman, maybe fifteen or sixteen years old, on his left, and a younger boy who hadn't yet reached puberty on the man's right. All three were wearing the black pajamas of the Viet Cong.

"Tell me what you see Lieutenant Gatlin," Major Hopkins said.

"I don't know, sir. Looks like a gook family portrait in a cemetery."

"Correct. The man was Dac Bui, the dead gook the NVA were dumping in Xuan Diem Cemetery the night you broke up their funeral party. The girl is Ani Bui, his daughter. She is a known Viet Cong errand girl. We want her. We think she can tell us a lot of things. We believe the little boy is his youngest son. I'm calling him Half-Pint because no one can tell me his real name... Now use that college education your parents paid for, and tell me what else you see."

"Not sure what else you want, sir."

"Think out-of-the-box, Lieutenant. Look in the background of the photo."

"Looks like the outline of Hill 55 in the background."

"Brilliant, Lieutenant. And what direction does the photographer appear to be facing?"

"Well sir, from the angle that we are seeing the outline of Hill 55, I would guess north. No, wait, it would be north-by-northwest."

"*Correct-a-mundo*! That means that they were standing way down on Go Noi Island, most likely in the big cemetery west of Phu Dong 2. From Hill 55 that's south-by-southeast, and we've got an azimuth within two or three degrees."

"That's pretty good, Major Hopkins."

"It's fucking excellent is what it is. Check out the lower left-hand corner of the photo. See the lid to the burial crypt slid sideways?"

"Tunnel entrance?"

"You amaze me, Lieutenant… Your power to make a great inductive leap passed my test. And here I thought you were just another dumb track rat… Here's a map with the approximate location. Note the coordinates. Now, *I have a request of you.* I want you to get on your tracks and plow through the cemetery until you find that crypt. Mojo Man and his wonder dog, Blitz, here, will assist you in finding this Ani Bui. Blitz will sniff her out if she's there… Right Mojo Man?"

"Greetings, Water Dog Six," Mojo Man said.

Mojo Man greeted me with my radio call sign. While we were operating on Go Noi Island my tracks were designated *water dogs*, and I was the Water Dog Six.

"Nice to see you again, Mojo Man."

"Yes, sir. If this Ani Bui is around, Blitz will sniff her out, wherever she's hiding."

Mojo Man was a ruggedly built black man from Chicago. As a scout dog handler, his job was assisting the grunts within the First Marine Regiment when and where scout dogs were needed. Mojo Man worked with Major Hopkins on a number of his special task teams. Mojo Man was a cool number, and there was something about him that inspired my confidence.

"Take what security you think you need from Mike Company," Hopkins was saying. "Captain Sikes knows that you have a special mission. What he doesn't know is what it is, and I don't *want* him to know. Do this for me and I'll get you another medal."

"Another medal?"

"That's right, or haven't you heard. Our favorite Aussie, Captain Graham, put you in for a Vietnamese Cross of Gallantry for saving his bacon… But that's a gook medal. Find Ani Bui and I'll put you in for a Navy Commendation."

"With all due respect sir, I'd rather have an in-country R&R to Saigon… maybe even Da Nang."

Once again, technically speaking, strangely maybe, Major Hopkins was breaking the rules. Protocol required that he first go through my company commander before giving me this mission. He knew that I knew that, and I knew he knew that; but what we all knew, now, was that Major Hopkins didn't always follow the rules.

"No problemo," he said. "Find Ani Bui *and Da Nang it is*."

*　　*　　*

Day One, 2000 hours

I flew down to Mike Company with Mojo Man, Wily, and Slammer, my corpsman. Mojo man had come prepared, lugging a sea bag full of gas masks and CS grenades. He was an old hand at this tunnel business. Better him than me. The thought of squirming down into those narrow tunnels after the VC made my skin crawl. It took a special kind of person to be a tunnel rat. Captain Sikes, Mike Company CO and Staff Sergeant Pabinouis met us as soon as we landed.

"I understand from Mojo Man that Major Hopkins has given you a special task order. What gives, Sam?"

I immediately began briefing Captain Sikes, the Mike Company CO, giving him as much information as I could without compromising my mission.

"Sounds like another one of Hopkins' wild ass ideas," he said. "I'm reluctant to let you go off on your own with only a squad of Marines as security. Since you are taking only two tracks, I'm concerned for the safety of the men and the vehicles."

I sensed that the captain's ego was bruised because Hopkins had kept him out of the loop, for whatever reason. Much later the reasons for that slight would become apparent, yet, even now, it was clear that Bob Sikes was a real pro.

Sikes was a Naval Academy graduate, and, unlike Hopkins, the Mike Company Commander took the conventional Marine approach to all things military. I had served with many fine officers but Sikes stood head and shoulders above them all. There was something inspiring about his manner. Nothing shook him. He always stayed cool. And there were things that he wouldn't compromise. I once watched him during a very hot fire fight, Sikes maintaining his poise throughout the whole engagement even though his battalion commander, a tyrant known as the Kingfish to all the grunts, was going rabid-ass crazy over the radio.

"What's Mojo Man dragging around in that big sea bag?" Captain Sikes asked, probing.

"Gas masks and CS grenades."

"No CS crystals, I hope. That's a big no no. We've had a written directive come down from division headquarters against their further use."

"Captain, with all due respect, I don't know about such directives. I do what I'm ordered to do," I replied.

"Don't get yourself between a rock and a hard place, Sam… Now I understand why Hopkins doesn't want me involved. As usual, our illustrious major is walking a fine line. Well, whatever it is that you and he are up to, I don't want to know anything about it. And this isn't the first time this kind of thing has happened, Lieutenant. Shit-like-this does not inspire my confidence. So be advised, I've seen others hung out to dry because one of the major's crazy ideas went south. And don't expect him to back you if things don't work out like they should. That's all I have to say on the subject," Sikes said, shaking his head as he walked away.

I looked up to see the moon rising. In the distance, some six kilometers away, I could also see the lights on Hill 55. We were setting in for the night, Sikes having sent out his night patrols. The spot we occuppied had once been a village called Bao An Tay. There was nothing left of Bao An Tay now and the moonlight reflected off the sandy shallows along the Ky Lam River. I rose to make a check of my men's positions, and a bamboo cat let out a cry on the far side of the river.

It was cooling off, and a haze began to hang in the low places over a wide expanse of irregularly plowed ground, cloaking the scattered clumps of elephant grass. Somewhere within that elephant grass someone or something was moving toward us. For the last hour our sensors had monitored this movement, along the southern edge of Go Noi Island.

"What are you looking at, Lieutenant?" Sergeant Pabinouis asked, squatting down next to me.

"Oh, I was checking out our perimeter, and thinking about those gooks we caught in the cemetery last night. Those poor mothers were almost out of ammunition… When they opened up on us they must have known they were history."

"Lieutenant Wily told me the whole story, how Major Hopkins sent our men out when they were on stand down… Lieutenant, there's some in the platoon that's wondering why it had to be tracks rats that went out on that react."

"Because they asked us to. That's why… All the grunts were caught up doing other things. That's the way it was because that's the way it is. After it was all over, he chewed me out because some of our men had been drinking. He told me that I needed to get my shit together," I said. "And that I was giving our Marines too much slack."

"I don't think that's true, sir. Major Hopkins is just messing with your head. Actually, some of the men think that you think more like a grunt than a track rat… They say that you're too eager to please the grunts. It's not all of the men, sir, just some of them. Some of them, they wonder if you're really looking out after their best interest..."

"Pabinouis? You count yourself as one of the some?"

"No, sir. I don't. I just want you to know what's goin' down. That's part of my job as a staff sergeant."

"I see."

"Yes, sir. You know what they think. As for Major Hopkins, some on Hill 55 wonder how long it will be before someone rolls a frag grenade under his hooch."

"Between you and me, I didn't hear that," I said. "But off the record, I understand what you're saying. That's too bad. Hopkins is trying real hard. Speaking of Hill 55, it must be almost due north, for what that's worth," I said.

"Yes, sir, I would say due north."

Pabinouis picked up a handful of sand and let it run through his fingers. He picked up a second handful, and held it in his fist, letting the sand flow out from the bottom of this hourglass in a slow stream.

"How about you, Pabinouis, how are you doing?"

"I'm okay, Lieutenant," Pabinouis said, his smile clearly visible in the moonlight.

Pabinouis, my platoon sergeant, was from New York. He was black and twenty-nine years old, a street-smart Marine who had many talents. The most interesting thing about Pabinouis was that he was an Obeah, follower of a religion that had its roots in the Caribbean. Christianity and voodoo are mixed together in Obeah. Many think of Obeah as more of a cult than a religion. Who is to say? Religion is, well religion, I thought, and it comes in many forms.

For a moment I reflected over the events that had transpired in the Xuan Diem Cemetery. We had been very lucky, and there was more than a grain of truth to what Pabinouis had said about Hopkins. Unchecked, he would run over my track rats for his own purposes. I was grateful to Pabinouis for his feedback, but I already knew that some of the men felt that I was too eager to please Hopkins and the other grunt officers. Yet my eagerness was complicated by my own fears and reservations. I didn't want to be known as someone who backed off from contact with the enemy. In Laos I had chosen to withdraw in order to save lives. That decision still troubled me, for whatever complex reason. It was hard to explain…

*   *   *

Day One, 2100 hours

Half of my tracks had joined Mike Company, Third Battalion, First Marines, earlier in the month as the operation was kicking off. For several weeks we had transported men and supplies, back and forth, from Hill 55 to Go Noi Island while the huge Rome Plows leveled the place. Now that the operation was winding down, Mike Company was to stay on Go Noi to patrol, and with five of my amphibian tractors in support.

Go Noi Island was, always, a nasty place. I'd driven tracks across the length of Go Noi once before, on my previous tour. I'd been lucky that time. Since then Go Noi had grown into a battle ground with the NVA using the island as a staging area for movement into the Dodge City area south of Hill 55. Historically, Go Noi had been a haven for three Viet Cong units, R-20 Battalion, V-25 Battalion, and T-3 Sapper Battalion. Those VC main force units were supported by elements of the North Vietnamese Army 2nd Division. With the recent lull in enemy activity ending, I was sure that both VC and NVA movement across Go Noi would increase.

The primary purpose of our latest operation had been to deny that staging area to the enemy. That denial had not been without a cost. The burned out tank and track hulks scattered across Go Noi Island attested to that fact. These were vehicles lost to mines.

"Lieutenant, the sensors are reporting all kinds of movement. You better get over here," Hog Wright, my communications jock, yelled.

Hog and Sergeant Pabinouis frantically motioned to me as I walked back from the riverbank. Hog called again. He was getting nervous.

"Lieutenant, we informed Captain Sikes about all this movement. He's calling for harassing fire, " Hog said, not looking up from his map.

As soon as those words were out of Hog's mouth we heard the whistle of incoming artillery overhead. There was a muffled explosion in the distance. Where the artillery round impacted, a thick, white cloud erupted from the still haze.

"Willie Peter!" Pabinouis said, climbing to the top of the track to get a better view.

Willie Peter, or white phosphorus, was a terrifying weapon. Particles of white phosphorus burst forth like hot lava, sticking to the skin. I had seen the effects on both prisoners and ambush victims, burn scars that took forever to heal in the muggy heat of the Go Noi Island plain, infected running sores that sapped the will of the strongest of our adversaries.

"Got all kinds of movement now, Lieutenant. That Willie Peter round got them all shook up!" Hog yelled from inside the amphibian tractor.

Hog was an excellent communications jock. He monitored the data being fed back to us from the special sensors that Mike Company's patrols had planted during the previous week. The use of sensors in the area was an innovative approach, the kind of technology Captain X firmly believed in. The technique of using sensors to monitor enemy movement had been around for several years, but many grunt battalions had been slow to adopt the technology. Also unique was the fact that the monitoring equipment'd been installed in our amphibian tractors, and this innovation allowed greater flexibility, employing sensors to gather much needed intelligence.

"I told Captain Sikes that we got *major league* movement toward Checkpoint Clovis... Watch'm drop some VT, fuse-quick all along that stream bed," Hog said, clearly excited by the prospect of catching a large body of the enemy moving under the cover of the haze and elephant grass.

Hog was an intense, wiry little dude. And he had a weird outlook on things. He liked to say that his one stated purpose in life was to close with and kill the enemy. I wondered if he truly believed that. I wondered if Hog had ever been to the edge and back.

"*Get some*, Lieutenant!" Hog shouted, rubbing both hands on his thighs in anticipation of what was to come.

"Patience is the hunter," Pabinouis said, as we monitored Captain Sikes' call for fire over the radio.

"*Shot out!*" someone yelled.

The round burst just above Checkpoint Clovis. VT rounds could be adjusted to explode at various heights in order to shower the area with shrapnel through the use of the quick-quick mechanism. At that point I heard Sikes request that a full battery of 105s be brought to bear on Checkpoint Clovis. A cheer went up from the men as the artillery began to whistle over our heads toward the unseen movement within the haze-covered elephant grass.

"*Get some!*" Hog yelled a second time.

The artillery rounds fell for several minutes. The men hung around the radio, saying nothing, curious as to the outcome… It was clear that the NVA to our south had taken us for granted, and, like a bamboo cat waiting for a small bird in the dense thickets, we had taken them by surprise.

*   *   *

Day Two, 0700 hours

Two supply choppers came in a little after daybreak. Sergeant Chapelle and Lieutenant Kim, our liaison to the Korean Marines, were on board. Sergeant Chapelle crossed the open area between our tracks and dry rice paddy where the chopper landed. He walked slowly from the chopper, bent over at the waist. His middle was wrapped in a broad bandage,

"Sergeant Chapelle! No rest for the wicked!" someone yelled.

Chapelle smiled weakly, raising his hand. I got up and walked over to greet him.

"How are you doing, Val Jean?"

"I'll make it, Lieutenant. Had to get back to the field," Chapelle said, almost out of breath.

"What do you mean? You are all right, aren't you?"

"Had to get off Hill 55... After I came back from the naval hospital, Major Hopkins got on my case," Chapelle said.

"I understand," I replied.

"That hospital is somethin else, sir. You don't ever want to go there. I came in from that dust-off and it was like a nightmare," Chapelle said, a distant look in his eye.

"Stay loose, Val Jean. I know exactly what you are talking about. Just stay loose," I replied.

Slammer came over with a bottle of pills. He offered the pills to Sergeant Chapelle. The pills were downers. Slammer said the pills would help him. Slammer was right, and the pills worked... Within a half hour the Chapelle had calmed down.

*   *   *

Day Two, 0900 hours

Lieutenant Wily, Hog, and I lay in the dark coolness of One-Eight's interior, listening to Janis Joplin. Wily had this thing for Janis Joplin. The morning chopper from Hill 55'd brought the mail, including a package from Wily's brother that had some old issues of LIFE magazine. One issue featured a story about a big rock concert in upstate New York, and showed nubile young girls skinny-dipping in a pond. Of course, several of the girls were tall and slim, with shoulder-length, blond hair.

"Look at those blonds, Sam!" Wily said.

"Holy shit! That's what we're fighting for Wily. That's what makes America great. But we're too late this time. We missed that party," I replied.

"Makes you wonder," Wily said, studying up the photos of the girls more closely.

"Come on, Lieutenant! They're *love children*. Hippies," Hog said, opening his package from home.

"You mean *flower children*. Lieutenant Gatlin met one in Australia," Wily said smiling.

"Roger that, Wily… But my R and R turned into a bummer. On my last night in Sydney, Maggie told me that she still wanted to date other guys. She sure was a beauty. The tallest blond in that photo could be her twin," I said, studying the photo.

"The tall blonde doesn't have any tits," Hog said, peering over my shoulder.

"Hog, don't be an asshole. Lieutenant Gatlin's honey dumped him, even though she had small tits," Wily said with a smirk.

"Please, let's not make mention of Maggie's tits," I said, somewhat irritated.

"Sam, it's better that Maggie told you like it was. Better than getting a *Jody letter*," Wily said, now with a somber tone.

"Hey, Lieutenant Gatlin, first rule of combat is not to bullshit yourself. That's what you always say. There it is." Hog said.

"Someone should tell that to Major Hopkins," Wily said.

"You really don't like him," I put in.

"Major Hopkins is spooky, and he has a reputation as a cowboy. There are a lot of officers on the hill who think Major Hopkins is a half a bubble off center. Some of your men wonder why you didn't push back more over this reaction force business," Wily replied.

"Maybe some of them should talk to me about it," I said. "I'm caught in a crossfire between Hopkins and my role on Hill 55 as the tracked vehicle officer… I know that if I'm not careful, Hopkins will have me running all over the Dai Loc map sheet."

"Call your company commander."

"Lieutenant Quick? That's easy to say. Lieutenant Quick wouldn't take on Hopkins. All my company commander cares about is the money he's making."

"The money?"

"Yeah. He's got part interest in one of the clubs up in Da Nang... That's why he stays in *the Nam*. We're here to kill gooks. Not him, he's probably making a fortune from all his slot machines."

"Slot machines! How did he get into that business?"

"Quick is a former enlisted man with a lot of contacts. He ran a couple of clubs back stateside. He knows that once Nam is over, he's going to lose his temporary commission, so he's trying to make the best of every opportunity."

"That's unethical, big time."

"I copy that. Anyway, that's the kind of guy that he is. He's not going to put his ass on the line for anybody."

"That's too bad."

"Before you make that judgment, we need to make a run to Da Nang and check out his club. It's called the White Lotus."

"The white what?"

"The club that Quick owns a part of," I said, with a smirk.

"Maybe you're right, Sam. Maybe I need to take a trip to this White Lotus. Shake off these Dodge City Blues," Wily replied.

Hog continued to empty out his care package, handing out a number of delights, smoked oysters and cheeses. After eating the cheese and oysters, he took out the tape. It was a tape of Woodstock. He loaded the tape in his boom box.

"*Sounds from the world*, Lieutenant Wily," Hog said.

For the first time all of us heard Crosby, Stills, Nash and Young. Then came Country Joe and the Fish. Finally we got to Jimi Hendricks. Hendricks did a job on the national anthem. A group of grunts and track rats gathered around.

All of us were amazed, listening to the tape, but none of us knew what to make of Jimi Hendrix.

The gunnery sergeant from Mike Company heard the tape wailing… He walked over to Hog and wanted to know what the hell was going on. Awkward situation. I could tell the Gunny wanted us to shut the damn thing off. I produced my special bottle of Jack Daniel's from the dark recesses of One-Six and offered the Gunny a drink, which he took, but in the field the Gunny never took more than one drink, so my ploy only worked some. Back on Hill 55 the Gunny would've drunk half the bottle. Hog shut the tape off.

"Just what the hell *was that*, Lieutenant?" the Gunny asked.

"That's the Dodge City Blues, Gunny," Wily replied.

"Well, Lieutenant Gatlin, I'm glad you had Hog *turn that trash off.* We got men here keepin their heads together for patrol," the Gunny said.

"Lighten up, Gunny. It's only music," Wily said.

"Only music? When you get down to the short stroke we're talkin more than music, we're talking attitudes. I don't like that music. I think that it gives Marines bad attitudes, and my job is to keep my Marines from getting bad attitudes. Lieutenant Wily, that music messes up their brainhousing group, and from the git-go. Personally, music *like that* gives me serious gas, and as long as this old gunny is wired for lights, we ain't going to have that music out here in the field," the gunny said, jutting out his chin.

"Sounds like *censorship* to me, Gunny," Wily said with a smirk.

"Brainhousing group, Lieutenant! It gets in their heads and messes up their brainhousing group! " Gunny replied, loud enough for all my men to hear.

The Gunny then turned and walked away. I got up and followed. I knew the Gunny well. It was clear to everyone that something was bothering him. I also sensed that I should talk to him.

"That Gunny is nuts. He's out of control. I wish that Captain Sikes would do something about him," Wily said behind me.

"Wily, it's men like the Gunny that hold this Marine Corps together," I said half over my shoulder.

"Yeah, well, if you believe that, you and the Gunny are on a manure ride out from the barn," Wily said.

"Wily, the Gunny is just trying to do his job," I replied.

"Well, you watch the Gunny. He may turn and bite you," Wily said.

"Hey Gunny, wait a minute. I want to talk to you," I yelled.

The Gunny stopped and turned to face me. He was just over six feet tall and thin, maybe one hundred and eighty pounds. His thick crew cut was getting gray, and from the lines in his face I would have guessed that he was in his forties. The Gunny's arms were covered with tattoos, and the word was that he had gone ashore on Iwo Jima where he earned the first of his four Purple Hearts. He'd been a platoon sergeant in Korea who had walked out of the Frozen Chosin with Chesty Puller, one of the true heroes of the Marine Corps. It was also known that the Gunny had once been a master sergeant but had been busted for drinking… His eyes seemed to look right through you, and when the Gunny moved through the company area he exuded raw power.

"What can I do for you, Lieutenant?"

"You pissed off, Gunny?" I asked.

"Lieutenant, I am pissed off. I'm pissed off and ashamed. You would think that Lieutenant Wily, and some of these other boot lieutenants, would know how to behave. You would think that they would have enough sense to keep that hippy music *out of the field*."

"Gunny, things are changing. It's that simple," I replied.

"Lieutenant, you are a good young officer. I am proud to serve with you. You are a cut above these other lieutenants. These other lieutenants couldn't have been corporals under Chesty Puller."

"Thank you, Gunny. Let's just give some of the others time," I said.

"*Time*! They're going to be dead, Lieutenant. I just hope they don't kill some of my Marines... I'm just grateful that we have a man like Captain Sikes leading Mike Company. I don't know what I would do if we didn't have his leadership."

"Gunny, what exactly is it that bothers you about Lieutenant Wily?"

"It's his attitude, Lieutenant. He don't treat the old Gunny here with any kind of respect. I don't think that he knows what discipline is. The way he hobnobs with the men makes me want to vomit. He *don't know* that he's an officer, and I am ashamed for him. Major Hopkins and I have talked about him."

"Well, Gunny, Wily seems to get along with the men."

"He ain't an officer. He ain't like you, Lieutenant. I just don't know what's happenin to my Marine Corps. Please don't ever change, Lieutenant. Promise this old Gunny that you'll never change."

"Have you ever talked to Major Hopkins about me?"

"Yes, sir, I have. The major asks about all the lieutenants on Hill 55, you included. Don't worry. I know what to tell him. I covered your backside, sir," the Gunny said, looking me directly in the eye.

The Gunny slapped me on the shoulder and walked away. The Gunny was in his own reality. That reality was governed by the demands of keeping his Marines healthy and combat-ready. The Gunny was the consummate professional. But he had to be watched. For the Gunny could be brutal.

While most of the men respected the Gunny, they also feared him. For the Gunny played a rigid role within the company. He had high standards and was constantly walking through the company area, imploring various corporals and sergeants to inspect weapons and other vital combat gear. He hated sloppiness and ragged everyone on matters of personal hygiene. Occasionally he would explode when a given sergeant or corporal wouldn't take him seriously, raging on and on, that none of us would have survived in the Old Corps.

To the Gunny we were only instruments of the Marine Corps will. The Marine Corps was our mother and our father. As mere individuals we were all flawed. Those of us who didn't meet the high standards of the Corps were worthless and shameful. The Gunny didn't cut anyone any slack, any time, any place. The Gunny was particularly sensitive to some of the comments that my men had made about how the grunts had abused the mission of tracks. He had confronted several of my men about criticizing his grunts, his Marine Corps. Yet, he'd also made a point of complimenting me for my willingness to *use tracks* to support these grunts. This was unusual, for the Gunny had contempt for anyone who wasn't a grunt.

To the Gunny, all Marines obeyed the orders that they were given. Refusal to obey orders in a combat situation was the equivalent of a death sentence. The word was that the Gunny had once shot a man for refusing to obey an order under fire...

The Gunny never seemed to sleep. He often spent his night pacing back and forth like some caged predator in a zoo. He ate little. Back on Hill 55 he would keep company with a select few, usually senior staff NCOs, although he appeared to be on good terms with Major Hopkins. He kept most officers at a respectful distance. For fun he sat by himself and drank Tennessee sour mash whiskey. He drank the whiskey straight, and limited himself to half a fifth a day when the company was standing down. Perhaps the person the Gunny was hardest on was himself.

*   *   *

Day Two, 0930 hours

I was sitting on the top of Track One-Eight looking at the distant mountains to the west. My mind kept drifting back to Maggie and my time in Australia. I thought of that blonde, also, skinny-dipping in Woodstock Pond. My daydream was interrupted by the news from Hog. The VC assassination team working the area had taken out a local French priest. Outside the track I could hear some more commotion. The Gunny was dressing down Sergeant Chapelle. Several of the men were standing next to Chapelle listening to the shouting. I jumped up to check out what was happening. Wily also got up and followed me.

"What's going on, Gunny?" I asked as I approached.

"Beggin' your pardon, Lieutenant. But it appears we got a cherry sergeant here who don't know what his job is!"

"What's going on, Val Jean?"

"The Gunny referred to us as track rats. I explained to him that the men preferred to be called LVT specialists. The Gunny then said we were all Marines. I then said that the grunts shouldn't treat us like second class citizens, sir."

"I'll tell you what's going on Lieutenant!" The Gunny yelled, loud enough for the whole platoon to hear. "Sergeant Chapelle here doesn't want to do his job anymore. That's the problem,"

"Okay, Gunny. You made your point. Val Jean, what's the deal?"

"Sir, all I said was that I think that the grunts aren't using us like they should. The Gunny overheard me and jumped in my shit for not being a good Marine."

"You'd never have been a sergeant in the *Old Corps*!"

"Ease off, Gunny. Everybody just ease off. I want to talk to Sergeant Chapelle," I said, "Alone."

The group began to break up. For a moment the Gunny stood with his hands on his hips as if he wanted some accounting. I said nothing to him, waiting for him to get the message. Lieutenant Wily stood off in the distance, observing the whole situation.

"Lieutenant, I have something to say," the Gunny began.

"Gunny, right now I don't want to hear it. I just want everyone to ease off so that I can talk to my sergeant," I said.

"Yes, sir. I understand. And I know that you will say the right thing, sir. Sir, you are a good officer. Both Major

Hopkins and I got faith that you will square this cherry away. The Gunny knows that Lieutenant Gatlin will do the right thing," he said, walking away.

For a moment, I said nothing. The Gunny'd just given me a veiled threat. I was still trying to figure out the situation. Lieutenant Wily looked at me shaking his head. Clearly Wily was disgusted by the Gunny.

"What's on your mind, Val Jean?"

"Sir, we were talkin' about the mission of tracks. I just said that I thought the grunts misused this track platoon... I was just giving my opinion," Chapelle replied.

At the word *misused* something in me snapped. Maybe it was the suppressed tension of the last two days suddenly rocketing skyward. I blew up.

"Your opinion! Your opinion is something that you are entitled to, Sergeant Chapelle. You are entitled to your opinion and I suggest that you keep it to yourself as long as it's not constructive! I don't want any negativity! Your job is to help me lead these men and make sure that the men got their shit wired together! We need to act in a way that inspires their confidence!"

I turned and walked away, not giving Chapelle a chance to reply. I knew then that I wasn't myself. The pressures of the last few days had got to me. I'd exploded, and I wasn't sure where that emotional explosion had come from. As I walked back to One-Eight the Gunny followed. Maybe I was slipping over the edge.

"That was *real good*, Lieutenant. That's what the old Gunny and Major Hopkins wanted to hear," he said.

But I was in no mood to listen. I turned away from him. Lieutenant Wily followed me.

"What's going on with you, Sam? I couldn't help but overhear you shouting. That's no way to treat a man like Sergeant Chapelle. I don't give a shit what the Gunny says. I heard his reference to Hopkins. Everyone knows where that zealot is coming from!"

"Lay off, Wily. Let me be."

"Who the hell do you think you are, Gatlin? Common sense ought to tell you that you always back your men.

That was a mistake back there, chewing Chapelle out in front of everyone. I'm your friend and I'm telling you that was wrong," Wily said.

"I know. I was wrong. I lost my cool. Now lay off, Wily. Don't tell me about right or wrong. I don't need that. I'll talk to Val Jean when I'm ready."

*   *   *

Day Two, 1000 hours

Lieutenant Kim was the liaison officer to the First Marine Regiment for the Korean Marines. He had flown into Mike Company's position to observe. Major Hopkins had requested his support from the ROK Second Marine Brigade, or the *Blue Dragons*, as the Korean Marines were called.

The Koreans had their headquarters in Hoi An, and their area of responsibility bordered Go Noi Island. Accordingly, some of their number had served as blocking forces on the operation. Lieutenant Kim had been an effective link between Hill 55 and the Korean Marine headquarters. He and I'd become friendly during the last month, and I decided to clue him in on Ani Bui, the girl in the photograph.

"Have you located this cemetery?" Lieutenant Kim asked.

"Roger that. The place is called Phu Dong 2. It's to the north of us about four hundred meters, and runs parallel to an old watercourse. I can show you on the map," I replied.

We cranked up two tracks, One-Six and One-Seven, picked up Blitz and Mojo Man, and headed some four hundred meters to the north. The ground all around us had been plowed flat by the huge bulldozers known as Rome Plows. Once we reached the old watercourse, the terrain changed and we slowed down. Waist high elephant grass stretched in front of us for quite a distance. Just before the watercourse the ground rose slightly, and on the far side, the area was covered with tall reeds where the Rome

Plows'd been denied access due to the wet and mushy ground.

I looked at my map. In the distant past the meandering Ky Lam River had cut across the northern tip of Go Noi Island to form a small pond at the village of An Quyen 2. An Quyen 2 was long gone, deserted and rome-plowed into the earth. The pond remained, connected on its eastern edge to the Ky Lam River by a narrow channel that was more of a muddy mire than a waterway. Covered with green slime, it stretched northwest for several hundred meters, with occasional thick clumps of reeds hiding the opposite bank. To get to Phu Dong 2 we ran parallel to the mire, exposing our tracks, always alert to a possible ambush.

What was once Phu Dong 2 on our map sheet was now only rubble. Here and there the foundation of a house remained but it was clear to us that one big air strike, or maybe a series, had taken the village out. But the cemetery was one of the largest I had seen in Vietnam. Moving slowly forward, we looked for that tall, pastel pink tombstone marking the tunnel entrance. The area was higher than the surrounding terrain. Blitz acted excited. The eighty-pound dog, big even for a German Shepard, was panting heavily. Heat was hard on scout dogs. Then he started to whine.

"What's the matter with Blitz?" I asked, motioning my driver to stop the track.

"He smells something," Mojo Man said, matter-of-factly.

At that point, I directed the tracks to pull along side of each other so that the machine guns of One-Six were pointing toward the south and the machine guns of One-Seven were pointing toward the north. The tall pink tombstone was maybe thirty meters to our front. I ordered Mojo Man to take Blitz and four men to check it out. I would cover him with our track's M-60 machine guns.

*　　　*　　　*

Day Two, 1100 hours

We used the photo as a guide, lining up the tombstone with Hill 55 in the background. To the right of the tombstone was a flat crypt with a concrete lid. Blitz sniffed the lid and began to whine. Mojo Man quieted his dog and had little difficulty sliding the lid aside. The empty crypt appeared to have a tunnel entrance in the side of the wall.

"There's something in that tunnel for sure," Mojo Man said, taking off his flak jacket.

"You sending the dog in?" Kim asked.

"No sir, I'm going in."

"Let's tie a rope to your leg," I said.

"Roger that. Hold my mojo for me, sir. And Buddha be with me," Mojo Man said, handing me the necklace that he wore around his neck.

I looked at the necklace. It had a little jade Buddha tied on it. Mojo Man called it his luck. I wondered if Mojo Man was a practicing Buddhist.

"Sure," I said.

Mojo Man peered inside the tunnel entrance, pointing his forty-five into the tunnel. Blitz continued to whine. Lieutenant Kim held the dog.

"Hush up, dog!" Mojo Man said.

Mojo Man squatted at the edge of the tunnel and listened. The only sound was that of a light wind blowing through the tombstones.

"This is weird," Mojo Man said.

"What's weird?" I asked, my arm starting to tremble slightly.

"The smell," Mojo Man replied.

"What about the smell?" I asked, nervously.

"It ain't normal gook, Lieutenant. It's somethin else. I don't know what. But it ain't normal gook. Smells more like perfume," Mojo Man said, shaking his head.

"Don't feel the need to go in. I'd just as soon gas the tunnel," I said.

"Never happen, Lieutenant," Mojo Man said with a broad grin on his face.

Mojo Man slipped into the tunnel like a snake with a flashlight in one hand and a pistol in the other. He put his gas mask in the side pocket of his pants along with two CS grenades. His tall, thin body disappeared without a sound.

About five minutes passed. The dry, hot wind continued to blow. Sweat ran down my cheeks, cutting through the Go Noi Island dust.

"Mojo Man! What the hell's going on down there?" I yelled.

At that point a shot echoed from the tunnel. I grabbed my pistol and started in. The tunnel was about three feet by three feet, reinforced by plywood and occasional two by four's. I was about five feet into the tunnel when it became apparent that it was going to be tight in spots. There was no way that I could turn around if I had to. I pulled myself forward using my elbows, holding my flashlight in one hand and my pistol in the other. Ten feet ahead of me the tunnel split in a T. From the left side of the T, I heard movement.

"I'm coming out," Mojo Man whispered from down the tunnel shaft.

"You okay?"

"Yeah."

"What was the shot we heard?"

"Gook going through a trap door. Missed him. But I got a little boy with me. There some others back in there. I can hear them."

"Little boy?"

The skinny Mojo Man could navigate the tunnel with no problem, dragging his prisoner behind him. Then, back in the tunnel, I could hear what sounded like whimpering.

"Yeah, caught him in a side tunnel that serves as their pisser. Must have caught him taking a piss."

"Okay, give me a minute. I got to back out. It's hard to back up," I said.

"Stay loose, Lieutenant," Mojo Man said.

The sides of the tunnel were slick; my hands kept slipping on the walls as I pushed myself backward. I was reluctant to grab the two by four supports for fear of causing the tunnel roof to collapse.

Finally I managed to back out the entrance. Mojo Man crawled out right behind me. His prisoner looked to be five or six years old. The boy shielded his eyes from the bright daylight and began to cry.

*   *   *

Day Two, 1115 hours

"I'm going back in to gas the tunnel, and I'm taking some CS crystals with me. There's at least two rooms carved out down there. One had two cots and all kinds of medical stuff, like it was a hospital or something," Mojo Man said.

"The CS crystals will take care of that," I said.

"For sure," he replied, putting on his gas mask.

The little boy looked like the same one in the Major's photo. Major Hopkins'd called him Half-Pint. Kim stood quizzing him, and he seemed forthcoming with all kinds of information. Mojo Man was probably right. This little guy'd been caught apart from the others in the tunnel complex. No doubt the boy's sister, Ani Bui, was still hidden down in the tunnels.

*   *   *

Day Two, 1200 hours

With Blitz roving and two fire teams of four men apiece patrolling the cemetery, I felt confident that we had the area covered.

The rules of engagement governing CS gas were vague at best, but CS gas was the perfect weapon for tunnels. Once inside a damp tunnel complex, the gas tended to gather in the lowest areas first, slowly rising back again to permeate the air. Those caught underground couldn't last more than a few minutes at most once the gas hit them.

They would have to move away from the gas, or escape the tunnel via a hidden entrance.

Even with a gas mask, I could see that the gas affected Mojo Man... He exited the tunnel coughing and wheezing. Blitz grew increasingly agitated. When Mojo Man turned him loose he began to circle the area, nose to the ground. If those underground tried to escape via a secret tunnel entrance, we were sure to catch them.

My understanding was that it was permitted to use CS gas but not the CS crystals. Some argued that CS crystals could do permanent harm to the land. However, even though a directive had come down prohibiting their use, many grunts still used CS crystals to deny the enemy further use of a tunnel complex. Major Hopkins personally directed Mojo Man to use CS crystals. Accordingly, from my viewpoint I was clear of any breaking of the rules.

Then Blitz started digging in the earth at the far end of the cemetery. He'd found a hidden trap door, and when Mojo Man flipped open the door Ani Bui popped up, gasping for air... Three men followed, crawling out while the Marines checked them out for frag grenades.

Our little mission had been a success... I got up on the radio and informed both Major Hopkins and Captain Sikes. Hopkins said, also, that he had Captain X with him back on Hill 55. He added that, within the hour, he and Captain X would fly down to pick up the prisoners. I gave the order to start the tracks and head back to the Mike Company position. As we pulled away from the cemetery I had the feeling that there were eyes watching our departure.

*   *   *

Day Two, 1500 hours

"Great job, Sam," Major Hopkins exclaimed. "I'll call your commanding officer, without fail, today, and tell him that he owes *you* an in-country R & R... What was his name again?"

"Lieutenant Quick. I'm sure that he would be happy to hear that from you," I replied, somewhat cynically.

Major Hopkins was ecstatic that his photo had turned up this intelligence goldmine, and for the past hour Captain X and Lieutenant Kim'd been mining that gold. Both men spoke fluent Vietnamese but they'd had little success interrogating the male prisoners... The three men, hard-core Viet Cong, were all badly wounded. The tunnel was a way station to evacuate wounded VC, and NVA, out of the Dodge City and Go Noi Island area. It was clear that Ani Bui was their temporary nurse, until such time as the men could be carried back to the Que Son Mountains to the south.

Ani Bui's response to interrogation was another matter... Not only did she understand and speak English, her responses came without hesitation. Her manner was open and respectful of the questioning. She claimed she was forced to care for the hard core VC and that, for all practical purposes, her little brother was being held as a hostage against her leaving. The story, I felt, was credible. VC often kidnapped young people, forcing them to support their cause under threat of bodily harm.

In fact, all the time Captain X and Lieutenant Kim questioned her, she clung to her little brother. Technically speaking, both Ani and her brother were classified as non-combatants. Captain X broke off from his questioning to confer with Major Hopkins.

"So, what happens next?" I asked the two men.

"I'm sending these three VC up to the Da Nang Special Sector. Maybe *this new guy Lipske* can get something out of them," Major Hopkins said.

"These men are wounded. They should be treated as prisoners-of-war," I replied flat out.

"If they were NVA I would agree with you, Lieutenant. But these are VC scum. I'm sure Lipske will know what to do. Maybe we should send the girl along with them," Major Hopkins said.

"Ani Bui is a non-combatant. She doesn't belong with the Special Sector. As for Lipske, I have had experience with this man and his methods. If you send these men to Lipske you will be signing their death warrant," I said.

"Something has set you off, Sam," Captain X said.

"Sam, leave these matters to me, and the captain. We will take care of this business… You did good today but what happens now is not your concern."

"Wait, Major, I'm curious. Sam, you said you had experience with Lipske."

"I served in Laos with him. I saw him gouge out the eye of one of his own men. I thought Lipske was dead."

"Laos! You were in Laos, doing what?" Major Hopkins asked.

"I was an advisor to a special mission. The mission never came to pass. But I did have more than enough contact with Lipske. By the way, all this is classified."

"You were with the *Agency*," Major Hopkins said.

"No Comment."

"Major, let me take the two non-combatants back to District Headquarters. We have the means to hold them until we all decide what's the most appropriate course of action."

"That's your call, Captain. Ani Bui is from your district. As for these VC, I'd just as soon put them on a direct flight to hell."

"Major, those wounded VC are another matter. I don't have the facilities to take care of their needs, including the extra security required."

"Then maybe the Da Nang Special Sector is just the ticket. I'll take personal responsibility to see that all their needs are addressed. And, Lieutenant Gatlin, as far as I'm concerned, you are now dismissed. We've wasted enough valuable time jawing over this."

*　　*　　*

CHAPTER FIVE: NIGHT ASSAULT

Day Two, 2100 hours

Back when this operation first got underway, moving my tracks down onto Go Noi Island had been Captain Sikes' idea. Both my men and I would have been happy to stay on the north side of the Ky Lam where things were a little more secure. I made that recommendation but at the last minute Hopkins changed the plan. I'd been disappointed.

"Lieutenant Gatlin, Captain Sikes needs to see you, ASAP!" Hog yelled.

I snapped out of my daze and ran over to Captain Sikes. Three of his four platoon leaders were hanging over him. Sikes was looking to the south where earlier we had dropped the artillery. He was talking on the radio to his fourth platoon leader who was set in a night ambush, just to the north of where we had called in the artillery strike.

"Sam, we may have to take a little ride," Captain Sikes said, not taking his eye from the area we called *Checkpoint Clovis.* "Your buddy Wily seems to be in a tight."

On the map Checkpoint Clovis looked like an elongated bulge that ended in a sharp point along the southern edge of Go Noi Island. Lieutenant Wily had moved his patrol close to Checkpoint Clovis hoping to search the area for bodies or blood trails. Wily was to wait out the night in an ambush site to the immediate north of Checkpoint Clovis. In the meantime a number of NVA had decided to move through the area. In hindsight, it looked like we'd reacted too quickly to last night's successful artillery mission.

None of us expected the enemy to return so fast. Of course, now our dilemma was that our own men were too close to the enemy to use artillery. The situation required a choice between two unpleasant alternatives. According to Hog, the sensors that were still working were reporting very large numbers crossing over to Go Noi... If we pulled our small group back, we were taking a risk having them come under fire from a much larger force. On the other hand, we could attack, a night assault of amphibian tracks into the thick elephant grass around Checkpoint Clovis. I had the sneaking suspicion that the little ride Captain Sikes was talking about was just that, a night assault by moonlight.

*   *   *

Day Two, 2130 hours

I mounted One-Eight and loaded the M-60 machine gun. A squad of grunts packed in behind me, their weapons facing outward. Tracks One-Nine and One-Zero pulled up behind me. The rest of the grunt platoon crowded aboard them, and the driver of One-Zero gave me a thumbs-up and we churned off into the moonlit night...

The marshy watercourse that marks the southern edge of Go Noi Island is called the *Ba Ren*. The Ba Ren is also the southern boundary of Dien Ban District. Historically, the District Chief had done little to insure that the no-man's land along the Ba Ren was patrolled. Such things were left to the coming and going of Marine grunts operating in the area. So it came as a surprise when Captain X, a.k.a. Captain Graham, our new Senior District Advisor to the District Chief of Dien Ban District, came on the radio to confer with Captain Sikes.

The *X-Ray Six*, known to us now as Captain X, wanted a situation report. This was very unusual. In the past former senior district advisors had always observed the formality of going through our chain of command on Hill 55 anytime they wanted a situation report... Clearly Captain X was not one to stand on formality when things were happening within the Dien Ban District. I was surprised. Back at Mike Company's position, Sikes was in the process of complying, as best as he could, with Captain X's request when the elephant grass to my immediate front exploded and hundreds of green tracers began to zip over our heads.

The grunts aboard the tracks dove to the ground for cover. I opened up at point-blank range with the M-60 machine gun from One-Nine. Tracks One-Eight and One-Zero pulled abreast of One-Nine and opened up with their guns. There was a scramble as the grunts on the ground formed into fire teams at the direction of their platoon leader. At his signal I directed the three tracks forward, sweeping the ground to our front with steady bursts of M-60 fire.

Between the Ba Ren and our position stood a tall stand of elephant grass. At that point on the Dai Loc map sheet the Ba Ren is only about hundred feet wide, and more of a sluggish backwater than a flowing watercourse. During the rainy season the same sluggish backwater becomes a torrent. This time of year, however, we had more of a mud wallow with soft banks, than moving river water with still hard bottom in which an amphibian tractor could maneuver, and how these facts escaped me as my tracks moved forward in the heat of the fire fight, I'll never understand. I should have been savvy to what track rats call soft terrain. My guess is I was more concerned about supporting Wily and his men.

Wily and his men were huddled behind a mud dike at the edge of the Ba Ren some two hundred meters to my immediate right... Over the radio I directed the tracks' fire away from Wily's position. It seemed that the NVA were in a long skirmish line, trying to move down a slope and cross the Ba Ren. Illumination rounds from artillery firing from Hill 55 began to pop overhead, making the night into day. I could now see the NVA quite clearly and I ordered my tracks to advance further toward the Ba Ren River.

My tracks' advance closer to the river forced the NVA line of fire to move to my right, toward Wily and his men. It was more luck, maybe, than design. But I could see it start to happen. When part of the NVA skirmish line literally ran into Wily's position, trying to avoid the firepower of my advancing tracks, Wily caught the NVA by surprise. His platoon delivered a deadly, flanking fire killing maybe ten NVA in what seemed as many seconds.

The noise was deafening as Wily's men opened up. Within seconds the air was filled with a smoky haze from the volume of firing, cutting my visibility, and it was then that Hog, who was my feed man for the M-60 machine gun I was firing, pointed to several NVA who were caught in the middle of the Ba Ren. In the light from the illumination rounds I could see their pith helmets clearly. The NVA were chest deep in the water, holding their AK-47's over their heads. That spot in the river appeared clogged with a thick growth of lily pads that were hindering the NVA's attempt to escape. Here and there the placid, white blossoms of water lilies appeared luminous. *We got them where we want them* I remember thinking to myself.

Sergeant Pabinouis was driving my track due to the nature of the mission, and I yelled to him to make a hard left in order to take advantage of what I thought was a target of opportunity. Pabinouis complied with the order, unquestioningly taking One-Nine to the very edge of the Ba Ren River. The soft bank fell away from the weight of the twenty-five ton vehicle, pitching Hog off into the Ba Ren, and me into the driver's hatch where I came to rest upside down on top of Pabinouis.

"Holy shit! Someone help me," Hog yelled.

Pabinouis reacted quickly, turning on the bilge pumps as One-Nine slid like a great steel otter into the Ba Ren. Slime and dirty river immediately began spewing out of the track's bilges as One-Nine bobbed in the water. I clawed my way out of the driver's hatch and back on top of the track. Everything was slippery. The front of One-Nine'd dipped briefly into the Ba Ren, and the track had been submerged enough to pick up a millennium of decaying river moss and stinking algae. I pulled myself over this mess and swung the M-60 around, firing a series of short bursts into the far riverbank.

The gun jammed. Without thinking I grabbed the barrel, burning my hand. At the same time Pabinouis revved the track's engines, and tried to water-steer us so that One-Nine could climb back up the bank and get out of our vulnerable position in the river. The water-steer didn't work, though, because the water was too shallow and One-Nine had become high-centered on a submerged mud bar.

Almost immediately the water came alive with a dozen NVA rice-carriers who must've been hiding under the cover of the bank, on our side of the Ba Ren. While the NVA rice-carriers were unarmed, they were in no mood to surrender. Hog screamed for help. He was in the water to my immediate left, struggling in hand-to-hand combat with an NVA soldier. Then Hog overpowered the NVA, pushing his head under the water. Two more NVA began to board the track. I reached for my .45 and emptied the pistol at point blank range.

Hog popped to the surface, gasping for breath. I grabbed his arm and pulled him aboard just as three more NVA were attempting to climb up the back end of the track. I reached for another magazine for my empty .45. In the confusion my spare magazines had fallen out of the breast pocket of my flak jacket. I felt stupid. Now those spare magazines were lost. Hog lay on the deck of the track, out of breath, his eyes wild with fear as the NVA came toward us.

I, too, was afraid. But it was a fear combined with rage. Another illumination round popped above us, the light casting weird, swaying shadows. I felt that shadow inside me taking over. In the intensity of the moment I was trembling all over. My outer limbs were numb. My mind was clear but upon reflection what I felt was a strange, terrible high. I was lucid, but something atavistic, something ancient and of the blood had taken me over. A darkness cast itself over my soul. I knew later that I had slipped over the edge.

For a brief instant the three NVA paused. One backed off. But one came forward, moving to my left. The other then moved to my right. I knew that they were positioning themselves to rush me. From his uniform I could see the enemy on my left was clearly an NVA officer. He was holding a stiletto and carefully picking his steps on the slippery surface of the track's hull.

The other enemy, shorter than the first, wore only a kind
of sarong wrapped around his waist. He was very
muscular, with powerful arms and shoulders. His eyes
blazed in the light of the illumination, and I saw that he was
covered all over with strange tattoos.

Just reacting, I yanked my bolo from its sheath,
swinging the razor-sharp blade at the tattooed-one with all
the power I could muster. The tattooed-one held up his
hand, trying to block my swing as his hand parted from his
arm at the wrist. He screamed and dove into the Ba Ren.
My backswing caught the NVA officer with the stiletto
along the side of the head. It was a glancing blow, but it
was enough to knock him off balance and into the river.

Track One-Eight appeared above on the river bank to
our left, and began to fire short bursts from its M-60
machine gun into the remaining NVA rice carriers. Hog
regained his breath and quickly cleared and loaded our gun.
Then he began firing steady bursts into the side of the
riverbank should any of the NVA still be hiding in the
bank's overhang. One-Zero approached from our right,
sweeping the river with machine gun fire. The firing
continued for almost a full minute.

I screamed a ceasefire order over the radio. The
machine guns ceased firing. The heavy volume of gunfire
had denuded the water vegetation. Nothing remained of
the water lilies. The last illumination round fizzled out. It
took a moment for my eyes to adjust. In the moonlight
there were little waves on the black surface of the Ba Ren.
A pith helmet floated on the water, just beyond my grasp.
The severed hand of the tattooed-one lay on the deck of the
track. The only sounds were that of the powerful throbbing
of the tracks' 810 horsepower, V-12 engines, and the
occasional belching emission of One-Nine's bilge pumps.

*   *   *

Day Three, 0530 hours

At daybreak Captain Sikes had his men pull the NVA bodies from the Ba Ren River. Most of the NVA appeared to be in their late teens. Hog paid special attention to those unarmed rice carriers that had tried to overwhelm One-Nine. What they had attempted may have been mostly desperation's act, but it still took great courage. Nothing is more terrifying than an M-60 machine gun firing at point blank range. It took more than an hour to get all the bodies lined up along the shore.

At one point in the cleaning up, Hog brought me the tattooed-one's severed hand. He'd picked it up from the deck of track One-Nine. The hand caught me by surprise. The hand was covered with small tattoos, tiny dancing figures and spirals. Hog asked me if I wanted it. I was dizzy, perhaps a bit feverish. There was a gleam in Hog's eye as he held out the severed hand, as if he were holding up a trophy. That part of myself that was the thrill-junkie seemed to take over. Something about the hand, and something about the way Hog approached me, had a strange appeal. It was indeed a trophy of the most terrible kind, talisman to the darkness through which I'd passed physically unharmed the night before. With its tattooed spirals, and mysterious dancers, it seemed almost a charm, part of a dark initiation, and souvenir of combat. I told him to save the hand, but to keep it hidden. A strange feeling of power came over me, but the decision was an error of judgment, I came to know.

At the moment, probably mercifully, I'd also no real time to examine the severed hand or to look at the NVA bodies. I was occupied with getting One-Nine out of the Ba Ren... Hooking One-Eight and One-Zero together, we strung a thick cable out behind them to the back end of One-Nine. I had the men pull apart the thick bridge lumber that we used to build the bunkers on top of the tracks. I then directed them to lay the bridge lumber across the path of One-Eight and One-Zero so that I had a kind of plank road. I hoped this tactic would keep them from becoming mired when we tried to pull One-Nine off the mud bar.

I was feeling dizzy. It was something more than fatigue, maybe the effect of my old head injury. Slammer offered a couple of pills.

"Go ahead and take them, Lieutenant. You will feel a lot better," he said.

I took the pills and washed them down with a half canteen of water, and it didn't take long for the pills to take effect. They must have been some form of speed. Suddenly, I was full of energy.

Even though it was still early morning, the men were sweating profusely. The sweat now poured out of me too; and I felt as if I were on the verge of going out of control, shouting, jumping in and out of the river, my shirt off, mud up to my waist. Yet, I knew that I had to get One-Nine out before nightfall, or the track would be a sitting duck for RPGs. There was one thing that I *didn't want to do* and that was abandon One-Nine.

On my previous tour I *had abandoned* some tracks when defending them had proven to be too risky, and I'd caught a lot of heat over that incident - many of the higher-ups in Division ready to court-martial my ass. Since that time, however, thinking had changed. Now the prevailing notion on the part of the grunts was that it was better to abandon a stuck or isolated track than to risk Marine lives trying to defend an already antiquated vehicle...

And it was with this understanding of the situation that I ran back and forth like a crazy man. At one point, Lieutenant Wily came over to me and told me to slow down, saying that I was pushing the men too hard. I nodded, saying nothing, for Wily and I knew that his comments were made in the spirit of helping me help myself. After Wily walked away, the Gunny came over and told me to keep the pressure on. The Gunny said again that I was his kind of officer, and that Lieutenant Wily should take a lesson from me.

By 0800 hours heat waves shimmered above the hot tracks. I was still feeling dizzy. Slammer was concerned. I told him to forget it, and took out a couple more of the pills. He warned me that they might do strange things to my head. I popped the little white pills anyway, and went back to work. Just as before, the pills had an immediate effect. I was again full of energy, although over time I still would have brief spells of dizziness. I kept working however, and soon my men and I had laid the planking so that we could position Tracks One-Eight and One-Zero. The Gunny slapped me on the back, saying that when we got back to Hill 55 he wanted to buy me a drink of good whiskey. It was the ultimate compliment the Gunny could give.

At 0830 hours we were ready. One-Eight and One-Zero were in line, hooked together, ready to drive over the plank road. Pabinouis was trying to maneuver One-Nine into the right position for hook up, but he was having problems. At that point, I blew up and ordered him out of the vehicle. When some of the other men who were helping didn't move fast enough, the Gunny, who was standing along the bank, also flew into a rage, yelling at the men to get the lead out of their collective ass.

I would drive track One-Nine. Sergeant Chapelle would direct the pull from the riverbank, making sure all efforts were coordinated. It must've been over one hundred degrees easy, by now, and I was seeing spots in front of my eyes… My men moved about like zombies, silent, mud-covered, and miserable. The Gunny smiled and gave me a thumb's-up. It may've been the first time I ever saw him smile. Perhaps misery was the necessary ingredient to make the Gunny smile.

Then, at Sergeant Chapelle's signal, tracks One-Eight and One-Zero moved forward, pulling the cable taut. Ever so slowly One-Nine eased off the mud bar until the back end of the track drew up against the riverbank of the Ba Ren. I gunned the engine and the steel hulk began to emerge from the Ba Ren at a forty-five degree angle.

Suddenly the progress slowed as mud began to build up under the hull. Both tracks began to pull harder, climbing up and onto the plank road. I yelled over the radio for the drivers to ease off, but neither driver had their radio on. I'd made a crucial mistake. Then I yelled to Sergeant

Chapelle, but he couldn't hear me over the engine noise. His attention was on One-Eight and One-Zero, concerned that they might slide off our plank road and become mired in the muck.

There was a kind of pinging sound as several wires on the huge cable snapped and began to unwind. With a great pop, the cable snapped. Instinctively, several of the grunts that had been watching dropped to the ground, the cable passing over their heads. Sergeant Chapelle was caught unaware and the whipping cable caught him at the waist, folding him in half.

Those last seconds of pull, before the cable snapped, had been enough to ease One-Nine over the mud build-up under her hull. With a great surge the old track pulled itself to the top of the riverbank. Once out of the Ba Ren, I shut the engines down and ran to where Chapelle lay face down in the mud.

*   *   *

Day Three, 0900 hours

Major Hopkins and Lieutenant Kim choppered in to check out the dead NVA... They'd come down to Go Noi Island to see the results of last night's action for themselves. During the last two days we had experienced an unusually high level of overall activity. That level of activity had not lessened in the last eight hours. The fact that Hopkins himself had come down to talk to Captain Sikes told me that something big was up.

We evacuated Chapelle on the same chopper that brought Hopkins and Kim in. Chapelle was conscious. He joked that I owed him, big time. I admired Val Jean's humor, but I was stunned by the accident. My company commander would want a full and detailed report. The danger should have been foreseen. It was clearly my responsibility, and I was sure that the attitudes my men had toward me would be affected. I could see that they were shaken, and I couldn't help but feel guilty about the way I had treated Chapelle… I made up my mind that I would make it up to him. If he came back, I would get him a trip to the White Lotus.

No sooner had the evacuation chopper departed than a second chopper landed, an Army chopper; and I was surprised to see Captain X step off. He said that he wanted to check out the bodies himself. His interest was unexpected, like his request for a situation report from Captain Sikes during last night's firefight, as the former Dien Ban District Advisor had left such matters to the Marines. But Captain X had other ideas. Dien Ban was his district and he wanted to keep his finger on the pulse.

"What do you make of all this new activity, Major Hopkins? I thought that we'd kicked all the gooks off Go Noi Island," Captain X was saying.

"I don't know what to make of it, Captain. Large group. Carrying rice. Probably heading up to Dodge City."

"Not a good sign," Captain X replied.

"I agree. We got too much activity all over the Dai Loc map sheet. The Fifth Marines are in heavy contact in the Arizona Territory as are the Seventh Marines in the Que Son Mountains. It's bad news. Everyone and everything is committed. With the level of activity increasing all around Da Nang, the gooks got us locked in for the next few days."

Major Hopkins was cool and calm as he assessed the situation. He had a reputation as a practical man who prided himself on being very detailed and systematic as he went about his planning. Hopkins knew that he had to also keep in tune with what Division called the order of battle. Now he was facing a situation where the resources of the First Marines had been stretched to their capacity. With the level of enemy activity increasing, the next few days would certainly be a test of the major's expertise.

"Got a game plan, Major Hopkins?" Captain X asked.

"Not yet. But it is clear to me that we may have made a mistake. We may have pulled our battalions off Go Noi too soon… But it's a mistake that can be handled, given a few days," Major Hopkins replied.

"But handled how? And handled when? Major, you just said that resources are locked up on the Dai Loc map sheet. It is clear that the NVA are taking advantage of the situation by moving men and material north across the Go Noi into Dodge City... Not only is Mike Company hanging out, but Dien Ban District is in jeopardy," Captain X said.

"We need to buy some time," Hopkins replied.

"And Mike Company will just have to buy that time," Captain Sikes said, approaching the group.

"What about using the Korean Marines? Somehow we have to expand our capacity," Captain X said.

"That suggestion will have to go through to Division. We don't have the authority at this level," Hopkins said.

"That's nonsense. Let's think out of the box," Captain X said.

"That's the way it is," Hopkins replied.

"What about Lieutenant Kim? What is he on Hill 55 for, if not to act as liaison for such matters as this?" Captain X asked.

"It's not that simple. Even if we got the approval, I'm not sure at this point when we could get them in place. We are on an island. You just can't march the Koreans in here. You need choppers, and right now we just don't have enough choppers," Hopkins said.

"What about these tracks? Aren't these called amphibian tractors? Can't they swim across rivers?" Captain X asked.

For a moment Major Hopkins said nothing; then he nodded, and, standing there, I saw a side of Captain X that I hadn't yet seen, an intense aggressive streak.

"Captain Graham, that may be a solution," Hopkins said. "We need to look into that! How about that, Lieutenant Gatlin, could your tracks swim down the Ky Lam to pick up a company of Korean Marines?"

I had an uneasy sick feeling in the bottom of my stomach.

"I don't know about that idea. The Ky Lam is a big unknown, lots of sandbars," I said quickly.

"Time to reinvent yourself, Lieutenant Gatlin. Here's an opportunity," Captain X said, giving me a wink.

"Okay. We will do what we have to, sir. We will do the right thing," I said, wondering what I was meaning.

"Well, let's see what we can do with the Koreans when we get back to Hill 55," Hopkins said, walking up to the line of bodies.

Then Hopkins and Captain X got in an Army chopper, and headed back to Hill 55. By the end of the day, both men were to chopper back down to Go Noi with the word. Lieutenant Kim was to remain behind, on Go Noi, to advise Captain Sikes. The truth was that Captain Sikes would probably give Kim direction. For Sikes was viewed as one of the First Marine Division's rising stars. Sikes was an emerging leader who was known to take the initiative. I had absolute faith that Captain Sikes would ensure that all our efforts were integrated in some fashion so that we weren't left hanging out.

The nineteen bodies were lined up in a row. The Gunny, with his compulsion to find some standard upon which to order everything, had lined them up according to their age. The first body was that of an old man, and the papers on his body indicated that he'd been a VC paymaster. I noticed that this old man had a thin and wispy beard. I looked up at the sky to see a few cirrus clouds at great height. The clouds' trailing and feathery forms were not unlike the long, white strands that the old man had hanging from his chin. This old guy looked like Ho Chi Minh. For all I knew he might've once known Ho. After all, Vietnam wasn't that big of a place. I once put a scale map of South Vietnam on an overlay of the map of the United States to find that South Vietnam was about the size of Florida.

I walked to the end of the line of bodies, most of which were NVA. But at the end was the body of a mere boy. The boy was covered with the same kind of tattoos that I had seen on the tattooed-one. In the middle of the boy's forehead was the same tattoo of the dancer balancing on one leg. When someone checked his pockets, he found a few small bulbs of garlic and a small plastic bag containing what appeared to be charms, charms made of silver rings, bright bird feathers and bits of a strange animal skin. The Gunny said that he thought that the skin was human skin, and he surmised that the boy was not Vietnamese, but a Katu. Katu were a tribe who lived in the mountains along the border with Laos.

I was wired. I wasn't talking much. I was still feverish. It was as if I were floating in my own world, floating in a violent silence.

I sat down in the heat, still floating. I wasn't sure where my head was. Now that I had the time I examined the severed hand. It was a beautiful hand, cafe au lait in color, with intricately tattooed spirals. When examining the tiny tattooed figures, I felt like I was looking at a pantheon of gods. The long fingernails were strong and clear. The fingers were scarred, encircled with interesting patterns of scars.

Hog had been saving a gallon jar of dill pickles behind the radios in One-Nine. I pulled the pickles out of the jar and stuffed the hand into the green dill pickle juice. One by one, in silence, I ate the pickles, gazing abstractly at the bodies. The pickles were still crisp.

The bodies would soon begin to bloat. When those bodies would bloat, one only had to poke a given body with a bayonet to hear it hiss, the gas escaping slowly, making a high, whining sound.

At that point, the Gunny walked among the bodies, cutting the clothing from each body with a razor, and, when he was done with this, the Gunny would pause, turning the corpse over with his boot. It began to remind me of a kind of ritual.

"Making it easier for when the intelligence weenies come down, Lieutenant. Trust me. By the time all the intelligence weenies get down to check out these bodies, they will be ripe. Intelligence weenies like to check out the clothing. That's most affirmative! By God, then it will be up to us to bury them, stink and all!"

I said nothing. I finished the dill pickles and placed the dill pickle jar back behind the radio. I seemed to be living in a daze. I was distracted, all the action and the events of the past two days had caught up with me.

"You okay, Lieutenant?" the Gunny was asking, turning a body with his foot.

I wondered what kind of ritual this was. I wondered *if there was some dark imperative* that governed us all. A number of young Marines watched the Gunny complete his task. This was nothing new. I had seen this all before, and I knew in my heart and my mind that there is this darkness in human experience where things fall apart. All that makes sense is to drift and to try to keep your balance.

"I don't know, Gunny, I feel a little feverish. I think I'm fighting some kind of bug," I was saying.

"You look worn out. You've seen a lot of action in the last two days, maybe too much action," the Gunny said.

"Yeah. Gunny, tell me the truth, what do you make of the situation?"

"It's a bad situation, Lieutenant," Captain Sikes said, walking up.

"Sam, this is the first chance that I have had to thank you," he continued. "An assault using tracked vehicles is a tough thing under any conditions. I just told the Regimental Commander that you led a night assault of your tracks in moonlight. He was impressed, to say the least. Thank you, Sam. You did good!"

I didn't know how to respond. This kind of praise from someone like Captain Sikes left me speechless.

"Thank you, sir," I managed.

"What do you say, Gunny?" Captain Sikes asked.

"Tough situation, Captain," the Gunny replied.

"Yes. Yes, it is a tough situation. But I think that we can pull something together. We just need to rethink a few things. I like this Captain Graham. He's the kind of district advisor that we need.

"I hope your confidence is not misplaced, sir," the Gunny replied.

"Gunny, I admire Graham's way of thinking. He'll influence Major Hopkins for the good. My sense is that this advisor is the kind of guy that won't just sit back and wait for the word to come down," Sikes said.

"He will get hung up in the web, or some bull-necked colonel will squash him like a bug. I admire Graham's enthusiasm. I respect your belief in his energy. But he got his chopper shot out from under him in spite of the fact that the chopper pilot warned him that the area was hot. What was he doing out there in the middle of the night? He scares me," the Gunny said.

"That's odd, Gunny. I didn't think that there was anything that could scare you," Sikes replied, smiling.

"He scares me, Captain, maybe because he reminds me of myself as a younger man. Graham reminds me of another time and another place. He takes me back to another war," the Gunny said.

*   *   *

CHAPTER SIX: THE AWARDS CEREMONY

Day Three, 1100 hours

A chopper brought in a pallet of quart cans of orange juice. I grabbed a couple of cans and sat down inside of track One-Eight. Hog sat monitoring the radio. I opened a can and poured us each a canteen cup full. We sat in silence monitoring the radio.

"Lieutenant, you don't look so good."

"The events of the last few days have caught up with me. Got a low-grade fever. Hog, incidentally, I put that hand in the big pickle jar behind the radios. When no one is around get rid of it for me. If Captain Sikes gets wind of that hand we will be in a world of hurt."

"That's gross. And I was going to have a pickle. By the way, Lieutenant, speaking of gross, have you seen that spider over in the corner," Hog said.

In a corner, under the radio-mount, a large black and yellow spider had spun a web. The spider's body was the size of a twenty-five cent piece. Its legs were two, maybe three inches long.

"How long has that been there?" I asked.

"Don't know, sir. But I like having it around. Call it a pet, my pet spider. The Vietnamese say that its bite will make you sick. Won't kill you, just make you weird out."

"I don't want the fucking hand, Hog. I just told you to get rid of it at the first opportunity."

Hog nodded. Thinking about the severed hand and the spider, I understood how in a combat situation one becomes attached to strange and exotic things. This whole grunt company was a walking testimony to how Marines coveted trophies and *souvenirs* of combat, from NVA belt buckles plundered from the dead to shriveled human ears taken secretly and kept hidden only to be revealed to the chosen.

The disgusting practice of taking human ears had been a no-no since the day Captain Sikes first arrived. Captain Sikes had walked up to one of his platoon sergeants only to find that the man was wearing a human ear on a string around his neck. On the spot Captain Sikes had the sergeant dig a deep grave to bury the ear. I wondered what Sikes would think of the severed hand kept in a gallon jar of dill pickle juice. It was very strange.

I watched the spider moving across its web. It was a beautiful thing. Perhaps this spider was Hog's talisman. We all needed something to bring us luck and good fortune, and we all needed some distraction to take our minds off death's day-to-day presence.

The severed hand would bring good fortune to no one. It was something that represented both pain and death. Keeping the severed hand was asking for trouble. Keeping the severed hand as a trophy was a kind of evil in that it was a memorial to a terrible and violent act committed on another.

Lieutenant Kim stopped by and sat down on the track's ramp. Captain Sikes walked up and sat down next to him.

"Hog's got a pet," I said, pointing to the spider.

"Ah, a spider. Very good," Kim said.

"I just got off the radio with Hopkins," Sikes said. "There is too much going on all around Da Nang, and Mike Company is not one of the priorities. Out here we could find ourselves in a tough situation."

"Say again," Hog replied.

"Hopkins wants to know how many NVA are out there. But we really don't know. The sensors indicate all kinds of movement but we can't translate that into hard numbers," Sikes said.

"And we sit here in this skuzzy track," Hog said, smiling.

"Hog, there are three rules of military intelligence," Sikes said. "And you won't find them written down in any book. One has to learn them from the pros. And one has to learn them from experience… Certain things are just a function of experience. The first rule is that one has to go out and get the information, the intelligence. That's part of what we are doing in this skuzzy track."

"What are the other two rules, Captain?" I asked.

"The second rule is that intelligence has to be interpreted. No one person has all the answers. Different points of view are important in coming up with the interpretation of what is going on. The third rule is that intelligence is perishable. One must act. And that is what we have colonels for," Sikes said, seriously

"So we bring in your Korean Marines?" I asked.

"Roger that," Kim said. "And I believe it will happen. Things have changed with the Korean Brigade. The new Korean colonel is eager. For some reason he has a special interest in Go Noi Island. Colonel Chai will give this Captain Graham what he wants."

"And the plan?" I asked.

"I am sure that our new Colonel Chai will help Major Hopkins with a plan. Colonel Chai will have a plan in five minutes," Kim said, smiling and shaking his head at the same time.

"Between Captain X and your new Colonel Chai, it sounds like Major Hopkins is going to have a plan whether he likes it or not," I said.

We all laughed. It was ironic that Major Hopkins, a man so strong and so intent on keeping things controlled, would find himself driven by the agenda of an eager Korean colonel. Major Hopkins and the First Marines were in a poker game for high stakes, but it was one of those games where people didn't have a lot of time, and there were a lot of wild cards in the deck. And if this new Korean colonel wanted to send in his Korean Marines to make a show, he was probably the dealer in this game. Captain X was a wild card. Lieutenant Kim was a joker. The Gunny and Captain Sikes were two aces holding, waiting for the draw.

*   *   *

Day Three, 1200 hours

At noon Captain X and Major Hopkins returned. I watched the intense and animated Captain X as he talked to Captain Sikes. The Gunny and Kim joined the group and I couldn't help but admire how the enthusiasm and excitement of the aussie captain affected the others. Sikes was right. Captain X was a mover and a shaker. I could feel the sense of a team that he and Captain Sikes were creating.

It was clear to me that part of the plan being developed, with the help of Major Hopkins, would eventually have us swimming our tracks downriver to pick up Korean Marines. Initially, we all would have to move overland to the north as part of the first phase of this proposal. Captain Sikes told me that he was going to gather his lieutenants together to give everyone the word at once. After Sikes left to gather his lieutenants I listened to the Gunny explain the situation to Hog.

The eastern portion of Quang Nam Province was again seeing the highest level of enemy action in I Corps. Both NVA and VC force subordinate to the 4th Front Headquarters were thought to be preparing for ground, rocket, and mortar attacks, in and around the Da Nang area. In addition, we could expect more assassination squad attempts against both local government officials and district advisors.

As I listened to the Gunny, it occurred to me that not much'd changed since the start of my first tour. The names of the NVA and VC units that we were fighting were still the same. The enemy's approach was also still the same, a posture of engaging our forces only when it was to his clear advantage. Now, with our forces spread all over I Corps, the enemy seemed to be taking that advantage just south of Go Noi Island, massing forces in the mountainous hinterland of the Que Son salient for what appeared to be a major thrust at Da Nang.

Captain Sikes returned with his lieutenants and began to outline the game plan. Mike Company was to move overland, to Bao An Tay, in order to interdict the main

crossing sites along the Ky Lam River. Mike Company
was to keep west of the railroad berm. East of the railroad
berm would be the responsibility of the Korean Marines.
Lieutenant Kim would remain with Mike Company for the
duration of this exercise so that Mike Company would have
someone who could communicate over the radio to our
Korean allies. At some point in time, depending upon the
action, my tracks were to swim downriver. We were to
turn into true amphibians in order to pick up the Korean
Marines and carry them to a position yet to be identified
east of the railroad berm.

During the move overland, which was to commence
within the hour, Mike Company was to destroy any enemy
forces, bunkers or caches that were encountered. A
situation appraisal related by Sikes suggested any enemy
units encountered would not defend in strength, but would
withdraw and try to work around us. At this time, our
recon units conducting surveillance operations in the Que
Son Mountains to the immediate south were reporting
movement of large groups of the enemy toward the Go Noi
Island plain. Our continous recon screen to the south and
west would be vital, maintaining up to the minute
information as the groups of the enemy worked their way
north toward our position along the Ky Lam.

I sat listening. Mojo Man and Blitz came up, the dog
wagging his tail. Sikes had finished his briefing and his
lieutenants had left to prepare their men to move out.

"Mojo Man. How's Blitz doing?"

"Blitz is doing good, Lieutenant. But things are
gettin'real interesting, Lieutenant," Mojo Man said.

"That's the way we like it, " Hog said, sitting down next
to me.

"Hog, I think that they's fishin'," Mojo Man said with a
smile.

"Fishing?"

"Yeah. They's fishin'all right, Hog. And they is using
us for bait," Mojo Man said.

*　　　*　　　*

Day Three, 1300 hours

At 1300 hours Captain Sikes asked his lieutenants to gather together around my track. Even though we were on Go Noi Island, Captain Sikes called a formation of those men who were in the immediate area. I was surprised when Major Hopkins told me to fall into the formation with my men. He had a funny look on his face, and I couldn't help but wonder what this stupid formation was about.

Before I knew what was happening, I was called to the front of the formation and presented with the Vietnamese Staff Honor Medal, First Class. The medal was being presented to me for my support of the pacification effort, and cited my actions the night we rescued Captain X. Since Captain X, as District Advisor, was the Army liaison to the South Vietnamese, he had gone to them and requested that I be awarded the medal. Unlike the Marine Corps, if the ARVN are inclined to award a medal, they just do it. Not a lot of documentation is required.

I was overwhelmed. Captain Sikes and his men thought my getting the medal from the South Vietnamese by way of an Army advisor was outstanding.

*   *   *

Day Three, 1400 hours

The grunts were moving out according to the plan. There was one problem, however, and that problem was the bodies of the NVA that lay bloating in the heat. At the last minute, Captain Sikes came over and asked if some of my men would stay behind and bury the dead. Reluctantly, I agreed.

"Oh no," I heard Hog say under his breath.

I grabbed an entrenching tool and jumped down from One-Eight. I wasn't going to ask my men to do anything that I wouldn't do. Burying these bloated bodies was sickening business, and no way was I going to stand by watching while the men gagged at the task.

"Well, Lieutenant. We got shit on again," Hog said.

"Knock it off, Hog. This won't take long if we get everybody digging. Count on this being a real shallow grave."

"Lieutenant, why don't we just dump them in the river?" Hog asked.

"Because the captain told us to bury them."

"Come on, Lieutenant. No one will ever know."

"*The Gunny would know!*" The Gunny bellowed.

Captain Sikes had left the Gunny and a squad of grunts behind for security. Now he stood on a little rise by the river, looming over us as if all of us had been caught in the act of some petty crime.

"Ease up, Gunny. Everything's cool. Your grunts can help us dig and we will get this done most ricky-tick."

"Captain Sikes says they be buried, so buried they will be, most ricky-tick!" The Gunny shouted, jumping down from the little rise of ground on which he stood.

Striding over to the bodies he grabbed the dead Katu boy by the head, and dragged him over to where Pabinouis had begun to scrape a shallow ditch. With a great sweeping motion he threw the dead boy in the fresh trench, grabbed the entrenching tool from Pabinouis, and began covering the boy up with black, Go Noi Island mud. When he was finished he stood up, breathing heavily, sweat dripping off his nose.

"Okay, girls! That's one down! We got eighteen more and the Gunny *can't do it all by himself!*

*   *   *

Day Three, 1500 hours

After taking care of the dead, I walked back to my track. Captain X and Major Hopkins were waiting for me.

"Lieutenant, you're going to have to fly back up to the district headquarters with me," Captain X said.

"Yes, sir. May I inquire the reason?" I asked, perplexed by this sudden development.

"It appears that the Vietnamese want to award you the medal so that some photographers can take a bunch of bullshit pictures," Major Hopkins said with disgust.

"So do I get my R & R along with a press release?" I asked with a smile.

"I don't know about the R & R, Sam," Captain X said. "This event is to demonstrate the mutual cooperation of Americans and Vietnamese within the district. After I got approval for the medal, someone up in Da Nang had a second thought. That thought was to get a little publicity out of your rescue mission."

"But there were no Vietnamese involved with your rescue," I said.

"Roger that," Hopkins said. "We'll have you back down here in a few hours. Right now we're in a tight time frame. We need to meet our colonel. Let's board this chopper that's coming in."

Captain X'd been able to reward me with a medal. Captain X'd been able to free up a company of Korean Marines to help us on Go Noi Island. It seemed now we had the beginnings of a plan, with Major Hopkins of the First Marine Regiment developing some details of that plan. Captain Sikes and Captain X had somehow partnered in this. I sensed that. When we boarded the chopper and headed back toward Da Nang, I knew that Lieutenant Kim's instincts had been right on.

*   *   *

Day Three, 1630 hours

Quite a crowd waited at the district headquarters. A number of senior Marine and ARVN officers I'd never seen before had come down from Da Nang. I counted at least four full Marine colonels, and, at least six ARVN colonels in the group. They all appeared to be enjoying each other's company. According to Captain X, last night our Colonel

Fry had entertained the whole group at The White Lotus. It had been quite a party.

Suddenly I got nervous. My hand started trembling. Major Hopkins was in an intense conversation with Colonel Fry. When he saw me Colonel Fry broke off the conversation with Hopkins.

"Once again, good show, Lieutenant Gatlin. Major Hopkins tells me that you were able to capture several VC down on Go Noi."

"Yes, sir, three hard core VC, all wounded, and two non-combatant," I replied.

"Oh, no mention was made of the non-combatants, nor did I realize these VC were wounded."

"Yes, sir. Wounded seriously."

Colonel Fry gave Major Hopkins a funny look. Hopkins shifted from one foot to the other, as if he were eager to get on with the award ceremony.

"And did you blow up the tunnel complex?"

"No sir. We seeded the tunnel with CS crystals."

Colonel Fry's jaw dropped. Major Hopkins rolled his eyes as if I had brought up an unmentionable subject.

"There has been a directive out for quite some time prohibiting the use of CS crystals. Major Hopkins, you must be aware of this prohibition," Colonel Fry said, obviously concerned.

"Yes, sir. I'll look into the matter," Major Hopkins said, curtly.

At that point Captain X and a Vietnamese Colonel walked up. Colonel Fry turned to greet him and Major Hopkins used that opportunity to pull me aside.

"Watch what you say to the old man. I'll try to cover your ass this time but there are no guarantees. I can't believe you brought up the subject of CS crystals. Someone, namely you, could get his ass in a tight over the use of CS crystals."

"Excuse me, sir. Whose ass? Is this my ass or your ass?" I said, turning away.

*   *   *

Day Three, 1630 hours

Although the district headquarters was surrounded by a barbed-wire enclosure, the crowd had gathered outside the wire due to the limited space and the absence of shade inside the wire. Under a thick stand of overhanging bamboo there appeared to be enough shade for everyone to mix in comfort. What was designed to be a small recognition ceremony for me had suddenly grown to greater proportions. For at the last minute a number of the ARVN officers had decided to award themselves medals for their part in support of Marine operations. What was happening was very political. When Major Hopkins heard about the ARVN awarding themselves medals I thought he was going to have a heart attack.

What I should have realized at the time, but didn't, was that this show wasn't to recognize me. This was a staged event designed to draw attention to what a great job all these senior officers must be doing. Major Hopkins couldn't hide his disgust.

"Let's see if we can get this show on the road, Lieutenant," Hopkins snapped. "If we don't expedite this circus, we could waste a day here while all these people perform."

"With all due respect, Major Hopkins," Captain X said in a low voice. "Let's be sensitive to the Vietnamese. The ARVN have their ways of doing these things. We need to be politically sensitive. That's why we have brought these senior Marine staff down to the district,"

"Captain, with all due respect to you, this spectacle is bullshit and you know it. I worked with some good ARVN. ARVN I respect. But these ARVN didn't do squat to save your bacon. They didn't want any part of the reaction force. And they were asked to help. I know. I'm the guy that asked them. These guys make me want to puke. Without taking anything away from you, Lieutenant Gatlin, this thing here is a joke. This event is an insult to both those ARVN and Marines who have taken real combat risks and shed their blood in the process. We need to get this thing over with so that I can go back to the real war."

"I'm waiting for Colonel Chai of the Korean Marines," Captain X replied, again in almost a whisper. "Lieutenant Kim invited him. Since he's on his way, it would be inappropriate to begin without him,"

"What a crock of shit," Hopkins said.

At that point some of the press began taking pictures of the senior Marine and ARVN officers. Captain X walked over to join them. The picture taking had just been completed when suddenly the scene was interrupted by a burst of AK-47 fire.

The first burst of fire took out two ARVN colonels. A second burst came from what appeared to be a well-concealed spider hole on the other side of the clearing. That burst knocked down four Marines. One of them was Colonel Fry.

A blinding flash followed, knocking both Major Hopkins and me into a stand of bamboo. The concussion of what must have been a satchel charge rattled my brain. My ears were ringing. Blood was dripping from a large cut on my forehead. Dazed, with spots whirling in front of my eyes, I was conscious and still could move. Smoke hung in the air, obscuring much of what was going on. I could hear moans and single pistol shots ringing out. Major Hopkins was lying on top of me with a great sliver of bamboo through his right forearm. He was unconscious and blood was streaming from a wound in his neck.

The clearing was littered with bodies. I could see what appeared to be a VC assassin calmly walking over to the moaning forms and putting a single bullet in the head of each of the wounded. With my ears still ringing, I rose quickly, pulling my .45. I slipped behind the VC who had his back to me, and, as he turned, I fired from within two feet, blowing off the back of his head.

Another burst of AK-47 fire swept the clearing. Masked by the smoke, I backed off to find Captain X semi-conscious at my feet. I pulled him into the cover of the bamboo.

The AK-47 fire continued. Here and there our side began to return fire. Overhead I could hear incoming choppers. I looked up to see Korean Marines firing down from the choppers at ground targets.

Major Hopkins was crawling now, one hand clutching his neck. There was a trail of blood on the ground behind him. If I didn't act, he was certain to go into shock. I yanked him under the cover of the bamboo.

Pulling off one of his socks, I made a compress and was able to stem the flow of blood from the wound on his neck. I then eased out the bamboo sliver from his forearm. Hopkins screamed at the pain.

All around us the choppers were setting down and the Korean Marines were securing the area. Off in the distance I could hear sporadic AK-47 fire as the assassination team retreated. Captain X lay beside Major Hopkins, glazed-eyed and conscious, but unable to speak.

To the right of the clearing, one of our Army choppers set down. It was full of Korean Marines. As the ROK Marines deployed, I carried Major Hopkins to the chopper, yelling at the Army door gunner for help.

When I loaded the Major, I came face to face with Colonel Chai and Lieutenant Kim. Kim grabbed Hopkins and with Colonel Chai's help I loaded three more wounded, including Captain X. I noticed then that blood was streaming from my head wound. Lieutenant Kim pulled me aboard the chopper as it began to rise.

We were a hundred feet from the ground before I let go of my .45. Kim belted me in and placed a bandage on my head. I couldn't help but notice the beautiful Asian woman sitting across from me behind Colonel Chai. She was so calm in the smoky haze that surrounded us. The blood, noise, and chaos in the aftermath of the assassination squad's attack seemed to underscore her beauty.

*   *   *

CHAPTER SEVEN: THE WHITE LOTUS

Day Four, 0930 hours

"Well Lieutenant Gatlin, don't you think that it's time to get out of bed?"

I opened my eyes to see my commanding officer, Lieutenant Quick, sitting on the edge of the bed. He was drinking a cup of coffee. Lieutenant Quick's nickname was Quicksilver. Sergeant Chapelle'd given him the nickname and he loved it. He had the nickname carved on a nameplate made for his desk. It was just one of his many indulgences.

Quicksilver was appropriate. Much about Lieutenant Quick was mercurial. His unpredictable nature often gave way to impulsive behavior and he was governed by changing moods. Yet there was a formal side to Lieutenant Quick. On occasions I had observed the formal Lieutenant Quick first hand, a slick facilitator, one with eloquence and style who was known for his ingenuity in keeping our track company running with zero vehicles deadlined. Then there was his Quicksilver side, a clever rogue whose manipulative nature belied the dark, boyish good looks, and who took pride in ripping off both the Army and the Navy every chance that he could. Lieutenant Quick, also, loved to gamble, at cards, with slot machines, at roulette. It all excited him. His favorite game was hold'em window-poker, with the one-eyed jacks wild.

"Oh shit! My head is in a world of hurt," I was saying, still dizzy.

"You have a concussion and a bad cut on the head... Other than that, they pronounced you to be okay," Quick said. "After they brought you in to NSA they called me. I drove up the beach from Hoi An at daybreak. Doctors say that you are 'good to go' anytime. I thought I'd take you into Da Nang for a little R & R, if you're up to it."

NSA, the Naval Support Activity Hospital, was already on the south edge of Da Nang. Lieutenant Quick had taken a platoon of tracks down to Hoi An with a load of lumber. At low tide tracks could run the hard-packed sand from Marble Mountain without fear of hitting mines. As a favor for Colonel Chai, he was building a big deck onto the Korean Marine Officers' Club, an edifice overlooking the South China Sea known as the Sand Castle.

"Sure," I said. "I'm up for it. I'm always up for a little R & R. How are Hopkins and Captain X doing?"

"They're holding Hopkins for another day. Who is this Captain X?"

"I should have said Captain Graham. He's the Aussie who they made the new District Advisor for Dien Ban."

"The guy you rescued."

"That's the one."

"I saw a guy with an aussie accent talking to some doctors as I walked in. He wasn't wearing any rank."

"I bet that was him. Tall guy?"

"Yeah. Blond hair. He looked fine."

"Good. Sounds like he's all right."

"So… Right now everyone is excited about these prisoners you captured down in Go Noi."

"Credit goes to Hopkins. Shit. He figured it all out from a single photo. As for me, I was lucky just to get off Go Noi Island alive."

I held out my hand. My fingers were trembling.

"You're doing a good job, Sam."

"I just hope my luck doesn't run out."

"Aren't you the one who once said that you make your own luck?"

"Did I say that?"

"That's a big affirmative. Something about being prepared," Quicksilver said, draining his cup of coffee.

"Luck is what happens when preparation meets opportunity."

"That's it."

"Well, I'll be getting both my luck and my shit wired back together. There've been a few times during the last few days that I didn't know where my head was at."

"That's what I hear. You are especially lucky that I am your commanding officer. What's all this I hear about some hand that you got in a pickle jar? You going off the deep end on me?"

"You've been talking to Hog."

"That's right. Hog flew into Marble Mountain this morning from Go Noi to pick up these new sensors from Command and Control North, that SOG outfit. There's some Major Boden there who asked about you."

"Yes, Major Boden, I know him from my previous tour. He's a good guy. I'll have to look him up."

SOG was the Studies and Observation Group staffed by the Special Forces and their montagnard mercenaries. SOG's mission took them into Laos and North Vietnam to gather information. Major Boden was a trusted friend who I had worked with during my period supporting the original counterterror teams. The SOG camp was located in one of the most beautiful spots in Vietnam, just north of Marble Mountain along the shore of the South China Sea, an area we called China Beach.

"Maybe you can go see him when we head back to battalion headquarters. I have some business to get done in Nui Kim Son. While I'm doing that, you can have your reunion with this Boden. Anyway, Hog is a mess. What happened down on Go Noi shook him up. He's waiting outside with my jeep. We'll take him with us to the White Lotus for lunch. I'll tell him to keep his mouth shut about that hand."

Bingo. All things considered, I was a big fan, especially for the moment, of Quicksilver's style and outlook. If you got the job done for Quicksilver, he would cover your ass.

"Go Noi Island shook all of us up," I found myself saying. "That hand is hard to explain. I don't understand it myself. I told Hog to get rid of it."

"Roger that. Whenever you're ready, Lieutenant Gatlin, I'm buying. By the way, I've got a little *mission* for you."

"*Mission*?"

"Yeah. Colonel Chai is going to need our help... Just before I drove up the beach early this morning, I got the word. A group of us are buying some excess gear from the White Lotus. Hauling an ice machine, and some slot machines, down to the Sand Castle is going to be the mission. We're going to expand that club. I'm leasing the slots to Colonel Chai."

"So. What exactly is it that you want me to do?"

"*Haul the gear*. That's all. Call it kind of a supply run."

"That's no sweat. I've made supply runs before. Sounds like a nice break. Of course, with all the shit hitting the fan around Da Nang, it will be hard to break loose the tracks."

"That's for sure, and this supply run is going to be a little more complicated. We'll be haulin' more than a few pallets of beer. We'll be haulin' off a big load of gear for the club. For one thing, you will need an R-1 retriever to lift the ice machine from the truck into the track," Quicksilver said with a smile.

"How many tracks will we need?"

"I've got it all figured out. We will need only five or six. Come on. Get dressed and I'll give you more details on the way in to the White Lotus. Hey! Maybe we'll run into that Queen of Saigon Massage. I'll introduce you."

"No thanks. I'm still walking wounded from getting shit-on in Australia."

"Oh, I'd wait till you see her. Chinese half-caste. She's the one who brought all those hot massage girls up from Saigon. Colonel Chai's hired her to run his club down in Hoi An. I'll try to get you a *freebie*."

*　　*　　*

Day Four, 1230 hours

The White Lotus, located at the intersection of Trung Ne Vuong and Bach Dang avenues in Da Nang, across the street from the famous Museum of Cham Sculpture, Musee'de Cham, rose out of the surrounding grove of tall bamboo, a great stone edifice, grand and serene, a monument to the not-so-distant time when Da Nang was called Tourane, and a bright colonial rest stop along the

humid coast of Indo-Chine Francais. Both the White Lotus
and the Musee'de Cham, built just after the turn of the
century, were made of the same gray-white stone, now
mottled in spots with a kind of dark moss after exposure to
so many years of monsoon rains. The White Lotus was
originally a hotel to house Frenchmen from the Ecole
francaise d'Extreme-Orient, literally the French School of
the Far East, an institute supported by the industrialist
Emile Etienne Guimet. Guimet was obsessed with the
ancient art and culture of Southeast Asia, and spent
considerable time collecting the ancient Cham sculpture,
including many classic pieces from My Son, a group of
ancient temple-towers located in a narrow foothills valley
southwest of Da Nang in southern Quang Nam Province. I
had a brief glimpse of My Son from the air, the day we
kicked off our assault of Go Noi Island.

During World War II Japanese officers turned the hotel
into a brothel, and when the Americans arrived in 1965, the
building had seen better days. However, two enterprising
senior NCOs from the Army had a vision, and they restored
the old hotel to its former grandeur. That vision evolved
into a private club known as the White Lotus, the name
taken from the beautiful white blooms floating on the pond
in the garden behind the hotel.

When Hog, Quick, and I drove over to the White Lotus
for lunch, it had just opened up. The lunch crowd was
waiting at the door, a mixed group of Chinese and
Vietnamese businessmen, several members of the Da Nang
Press Club, military types of all descriptions, American,
Vietnamese, and Korean, with a few of Da Nang's small
Francophone community smoking their Gaulois cigarettes
under the ancient mimosa trees that shaded the hotel's
broad front porch. Late at night the make-up of this crowd
changed. Since all U. S. military were subject to the
curfew, they usually drifted off before dark. But
businessmen and civilian construction workers from all
over the world lingered late, long after midnight, some
going upstairs to see the massage girls one more time,

others disappearing to card games in the back rooms, gambling until daybreak.

"Well, Lieutenant Gatlin, once again you survived. Here's to you, let's get drunk," Quick said, raising his cold Sapporo in a toast.

"What I want to know is how this VC death squad knew about the Awards Ceremony. Something's wrong somewhere," Hog added.

"A lot is wrong everywhere, Hog. This is Vietnam. Clear out your brain housing group," Quick replied.

"Roger that, Lieutenant Quick," Hog said.

"Let's change the subject," I said.

At that point the waiter brought our lunch, prime U.S. military ribeye steaks bought on the Black Market and grilled to perfection, chased down with tall, ice-cold bottles of Sapporo. The discussion took a turn to the subject of beer, and how Vietnamese beer compared to San Miguel from the Philippines or Japanese Sapporo. Hog and Quick concluded that they had yet to find a Vietnamese beer worth drinking. When I told them that I had actually acquired a taste for *33,* brewed down in Saigon, and often referred to as tiger piss, Quick shook his head in disbelief.

"You like that Tiger Piss. Is that fucked or what?" Quick said.

"I copy that, Lieutenant Quick," Hog said, almost choking on his steak with laughter.

Overhead, jet fighters headed out from Da Nang on various missions. I could imagine pilots looking down at the White Lotus as they charted a course for a bombing run along the Laotian Border. Complex thoughts from the past year came back to me. I wondered if the fighter-jocks and other flyboys were the only ones who truly understood the different parts of the war's design. For the pilots were flying high enough above it all where their war fit a pattern.

In the pilots' world there were things that were fixed and permanent, like standard missions and a logistical framework that worked. The pilots' war fit into a big picture game plan where most of them saw their results. The criteria used for measuring a pilot's performance in this war were clear to me. They dropped so many canisters of napalm on designated targets. They took out a Mig in a dogfight over North Vietnam or blew away a convoy of trucks on the Ho Chi Minh Trail.

Down at my level, among the grunts and track rats, it was different. A lot of things didn't always work, like logistics and simply understanding what was going down. Much of the time we didn't understand the big picture or know what to believe. Objectives were always changing, making measurement of our progress unclear. People like Major Hopkins screwed around with the data, especially body counts. Separating fact from rumor was difficult. And at our level it was not uncommon for the plan to change each day. Grunts and track rats lived out on an edge where their reality was profoundly different from those serving in the Division rear. In our war nothing was fixed or permanent. One could move every day for a month, patrolling constantly changing terrain.

Survival for a grunt or a track rat depended on teamwork at the most basic level, where the interactions of the team were often intuitive. Yet, there was a technical part to our reality. It was an intimate thing where each man knew his weapon and the know-how of others with their weapons. In a sense our war was neither derivative nor dependent upon what many called the big picture plan. A grunt and track rat's war was all about on the spot, intuitive judgments, and the firepower we could summon in a given situation. Like the Gunny said, it was a reality that was day to day, and where one had to be careful not to lose his soul.

"What a great place," Hog said, draining his third beer.

"Better pace yourself Hog. We got all day and all night," Quick said.

"Never thought I'd get here," Hog replied.

"Well, Hog, we'll make sure that your first visit is a memorable one," Quick said.

The first time I visited the White Lotus I recalled Homer's *Odyssey* and the story of the lotus-eaters. In the *Odyssey,* eating the lotus led to indolence and dreamy contentment. I thought of how appropriate the name White

Lotus was for this old run down French hotel, filled with
modern day lotus-eaters, each on a journey of their own in
pursuit of the various decadent pleasures the city of Da
Nang had to offer. In the White Lotus one could buy just
about any short-term gratification known to modern man.
It was all there. One could take a short sex trip or a long
opium pipe journey. There was a twenty-four hour poker
game in one of the back rooms. But one had to be careful.
In this Homeric Lotus-land, where the ideal state was
contentment achieved through self-indulgence, the lotus-
eaters carried stilettos and nickel-plated .38 specials; and I
wondered what cyclops might be lurking, hidden within the
deep shade of the tall bamboo and ancient mimosas that
surrounded the White Lotus, waiting until dark to make an
appearance.

After my third beer I began to think about Maggie back
in Australia. I knew what was fixed and permanent in her
life, and I wasn't part of her vision for the future. That
hurt. When I looked at the photos of us back in Cronulla, I
had that same glazed-eyed look as these lotus-eaters who
wandered aimlessly through the crowd at the White Lotus.

All the while I was remembering Maggie and pondering
why she dumped me, Hog and Lieutenant Quick were into
a heavy conversation. Both were getting loaded, and it was
clear that Lieutenant Quick was pontificating.

"The White Lotus has always been owned by a group of
Americans who each had a certain piece of the action, most
of them senior staff NCOs. Oh, there's an occasional
mustang officer like myself. We've run it like a privately
held club with one catch. When one of us has to return to
the States, he must sell off his piece of the action. That
way there's no tax issues back in the world, and we're not
getting crossed up with all the military rules," Quick said.

"Sounds like an incentive to stay in-country, as long as
you're working in Da Nang," Hog replied.

"There it is. I first got involved through an old Marine
buddy. But now I'm getting ready to head back to the
States, and I don't want to give up my share. In the last
year there has been a lot of growth. I'm the guy who

brought in more slot machines. Since I expanded the gambling, things have boomed. So I had a talk with the shareholders and we redesigned the whole deal. We're all going to cash out and get rich. That's what I've been fighting for and that's what makes America great. Call it the pursuit of happiness," Quick said, draining his fourth beer.

"Lieutenant Quick, I want to work more with you. Please keep me in mind if you need any special help."

"Hog, I will keep that in mind. Lieutenant Gatlin, how come you're so fucking quiet? You're not going ape shit on me, are you?"

"I was thinking about a tall blonde back in Australia," I said.

"A tall blonde. Get real, Lieutenant. Ancient history. Like that gook museum across the street," Quick said.

"Maybe I can learn from that history. It will help me in the pursuit of my happiness," I replied.

"Our Mike Company gunny says that in this war happiness is about killing gooks," Hog said, chuckling.

"Now there is one fucked-up person, the Mike Company gunny," Quick said, laughing loud enough to attract attention from several tables.

"The Gunny sees himself as a professional at killing gooks. On the other hand, our new district advisor down at Dien Ban says that this war is about winning the hearts and minds. I think that Captain X is right, and my role is to help those people survive in spite of all the shit that is going down."

"You think too much, Sam Gatlin. Chill. And stay loose. As the grunt Marines like to say, go with the flow," Lieutenant Quick said abruptly.

I chuckled to myself. Go with the flow. Captain X would have called that a form of Yin and Yang.

We were just outside the central bar on the veranda, and had a great view of all the hot women wandering among the tables. I noticed a number of Korean Marine officers come in. Several of them I recognized from my past supply runs down to Hoi An. Leading them was a captain whose nickname was Scar, a bad dude who liked to pick bar fights for fun. Next to Scar was Mr. Toad, an adjutant of some sort. Behind them was Colonel Chai. On Chai's arm was the same beautiful woman whom I had seen on the chopper when the Colonel evacuated me to NSA.

"Now there's a good-looking woman, Lieutenant Quick. How do you like that one, Lieutenant Gatlin?" Hog said, slurring his speech.

"That's the one I was telling Lieutenant Gatlin about! That's Miss Swan! She now works for Colonel Chai and is going to run his club down in Hoi An. I bet the old Colonel gets more than a hand job, what'da ya think, Hog?" Lieutenant Quick said, standing and trying to get Colonel Chai's attention.

I said nothing. I just stared, wondering how well Miss Swan and I would fit together. I couldn't help but feel a pang of envy watching the gracious Miss Swan walk arm in arm with the distinguished, white-haired Colonel Chai.

The head bartender was a prancing fairy everyone called Cowboy. Scar shouted at Cowboy for drinks. Cowboy scurried around behind the bar making the drinks, obviously trying to please the tough Koreans. At one point Scar started throwing ice cubes at Cowboy. Mr. Toad followed suit. Cowboy protested, ducking the flying ice cubes. But the two rough Koreans had tasted blood and the flying ice cubes increased amid wild yelling and laughter.

Cowboy hid behind the bar in order to protect himself. The patrons sitting at the bar pulled back out of the line of fire. The rest of the drunken bar crowd cheered encouragement.

Colonel Chai barked an order and the bar fell silent. He walked behind the bar over to Cowboy, picked him up and gave him some money. Cowboy smiled, bowed gratefully and disappeared out the door. Chai barked a second order and a small Korean Marine security team came through the open French doors and up from the street.

Lieutenant Quick rose and walked over to greet Colonel Chai and Miss Swan. On an impulse I followed. The

Colonel smiled and turned to me, shaking my hand. I bowed to Miss Swan, who took my hand.

"Hello Lieutenant Gatlin. It is good to see you under better circumstances," Miss Swan said, giving me a wink.

Colonel Chai said something in Korean to Miss Swan. She nodded and turned to me, "Lieutenant Gatlin, Colonel Chai has business to discuss with Lieutenant Quick. Would you be willing to accompany me across the street to the Musee' de Cham? Dr. Jean de Fillio, my former mentor, is sponsoring an exhibition. For the first time he has brought together the masterpieces from the two most important Vietnamese collections of Cham art."

*　　*　　*

Day Four, 1500 hours

Walking from the White Lotus to the Musee' de Cham, I soon learned that the cosmopolitan Miss Swan was actually from Paris and not Saigon, daughter of a French army officer and a Chinese mother from Cholon. Her bearing spoke to a wider, international sophistication. Yet she wasn't at all arrogant. Quick was a fool to call her the *Queen of Saigon Massage.* Educated at the Sorbonne, widely traveled, and speaking excellent English, she had accepted Colonel Chai's job offer to run the Sand Castle simply to get out of Da Nang, a city that was growing way too fast for her tastes. She found the traffic jams and the increasing pollution oppressive, preferring instead the cooler, breezy weather along the coast near Hoi An.

*　　*　　*

Day Four, 1515 hours

Climbing the stairs to the Musee' de Cham, Miss Swan's hair, pulled back in a French roll, appeared a lustrous black in the afternoon sunlight. The high-collared, cobalt blue sheath she was wearing had a split up one side, revealing, from time to time, a shapely thigh. Her slim, ivory arms were bare but for a single jade bracelet. I noticed she had a spiral, red and black Yin and Yang tattoo on her right shoulder. In spite of the heat, she seemed cool and relaxed.

Several caramel colored pieces of Cham statuary, each the size of a volkwagen car engine, were lined up at the top of the stairs. Mounted on temporary wooden platforms, they were carved from sandstone and, according to Miss Swan, represented various gods and goddesses worshipped by the Chams. Workers bustled about, unpacking a multitude of crates and small boxes.

"Lieutenant Gatlin, I think you will be pleasantly surprised. These two collections represent the major expressions of ancient art in Southeast Asia, providing a window into history at a time when Champa flourished, a great confederacy of mixed peoples, all speaking classical Sanskrit, and allowing the worship of both Buddhism and the many gods of the Hindu pantheon."

"Miss Swan, I didn't expect this. I once saw those ruins they call My Son from the air. You're helping me understand that culture. Thank you."

"My interest in Cham culture borders on the obsessive. Here, let's walk down this aisle. I'll show you the three major divinities of the Chams."

I followed behind, watching her beautiful ass sway as she took me on a tour, first showing me Brahma, the Creator. Brahma had four faces, representing East, West, North, and South. Next to Brahma was Vishnu with one face and four arms. Behind Vishnu was dark Shiva, the Destroyer, god of violence, with a third eye in his forehead. Then there were the lesser deities set about on stone pedestals, Ganesa, the elephant-headed god of intelligence and Indra, the god of rain. When Miss Swan pointed out Kama, the god of love, in the act of mounting Apsara, a celestial dancer, doggy-style, I told her that she had made me a life-long fan of Cham sculpture. She laughed and gave me a wink. Her laugh got the attention of a small old man shuffling among the musty boxes.

"Dr. de Fillio!" Miss Swan said, waving.

Dr. Jean de Fillio waved back, clearly excited to see Miss Swan. He was old enough to be my grandfather, balding with a white mustache and goatee, his eyes magnified by the thick, Coke-bottle-like lenses of his glasses. The tiny man barely came to my shoulder. A relic from French colonial days, he stood on the stairs of the Musee' de Cham poking a long thin stick of bamboo at his workers and issuing an occasional directive in crisp Vietnamese.

"Ah, Miss Swan! Mon ami. We are still unpacking the collection from Saigon. So good you could make time to visit a sick old man," Dr. de Fillio said, greeting us with a bow and a slight dip of his long bamboo stick.

"Dr. de Fillio, let me introduce you to Lieutenant Gatlin, my escort this afternoon."

The old man nodded, saying nothing, almost as if he disapproved of me. Then he smiled, raising his hand and pointing to the sky.

"*The Devi*! Let me introduce you to the Devi."

The sandstone statue that Dr. de Fillio pulled out of the musty box was the armless bust and head of a beautiful young woman, maybe eighteen inches in height. Mounted on a pedestal, with its tall, ornate hairstyle and ear ornaments, it reminded me of similar work that I'd seen in Laos at Wat Phou. The features were delicate, carved in balanced proportions, and they had a strong resemblance to the inscrutable Coco.

"This is the finest 10th Century Cham piece I have ever seen. It was found here in Quang Nam Province, and is priceless," Dr. de Fillio said, with a reverent tone.

"May I hold it?" Miss Swan asked.

"Of course," Dr. de Fillio replied, passing the bust to Miss Swan.

"Lieutenant Gatlin, meet the consort of the Hindu god, Shiva the destroyer," Miss Swan said. "She is celebrated in songs and poems, and known by a number of different names. I know her as the good Jaganmata, or Mother of the universe, and destroyer of evil. Today she is worshipped by millions as their primary deity."

"Careful, Miss Swan, we don't want to mislead Lieutenant Gatlin. There are many aspects to Devi's divinity, some benign and gentle, and others not so sweet, quite ferocious actually. Devi is a most comprehensive and, shall I say, potent goddess. He-he-he," Dr. de Fillio said, his weak little laugh leaving him breathless.

"That is true, Dr. de Fillio, and I must stand corrected. Let's say I view Devi as the primary feminine cosmic force. She may destroy forces that threaten world equilibrium; but in her more gentle, radiant form, she recreates the universe, bringing wealth and fortune to all those who worship her complexity. Devi is an inspiring model for all earthly women," Miss Swan said, with an enigmatic smile.

"Holy shit," I whispered to myself, feeling the effects of all those tall, cold Sapporos.

*   *   *

Day Four, 1800 hours

Returning to the White Lotus, I found that Lieutenant Quick had finally finished his business with Colonel Chai. He was now carrying on an intense conversation with Hog, but I wasn't listening. After my tour of the Musee' de Cham, Miss Swan was still on my mind. She'd left me to dine with Dr. de Fillio. The Devi, the finest 10th Century Cham piece ever found in Quang Nam Province, now rested in a musty box back at the Musee' de Cham, hopefully under a 24 hour armed guard.

So I settled back to watch all the interesting people passing by in the central bar. I had a great view. Cigarette smoke filled the central bar, drifting out through open French doors into the musty air of the early evening. The slowly turning ceiling fans began to hypnotize me. Moths fluttered about, and little sticky-toed lizards scurried along the walls.

I got up and stumbled toward the restroom, taking a moment to admire the crowded place. The bar was a beautiful thing made of various exotic dark hardwoods. The top was white marble with a full length, wrap-around brass rail. Mirrors ran behind the bar giving the room an illusion of space.

When I walked into the restroom Fritz Lipske and Lenny were standing at the urinals side by side, facing away from me and taking a piss. Lenny had his arm in a sling, and was leaning on a cane. He looked a little worse for wear. Before they could spot me I slipped into a stall, and closed the door, leaving the door open a crack to observe them.

"Yeah Lenny, I wired a hand-cranked field phone to this one guy's balls. You should have heard him sing. So much for the hard core VC, I said to myself. But then he up and died on me. The field phone was too much for the guy. He had a heart attack from all the juice," Lipske was saying.

"That's what happens if you're not careful. You said he was wounded pretty badly. He would have died anyway," Lenny said. "You're lucky you got the information when you did."

"Well, I got two more. Let's see what they tell us."

"Use the old water-torture on them. It doesn't leave any marks on the body, and it won't kill the guy, just fuck him up."

"Hey Lenny, that's not always the case. We had a kid in there the other day and were using that method. I left the room to get a cup of coffee. When I got back, Jesus, one of my stupid PRU, a guy who shouldn't have even been in the room, let the kid choke to death."

"He choked to death on the water torture? I didn't think that was possible," Lenny said, washing his hands.

"Too much water backed up in the kid's lungs, and he choked. Or maybe he ruptured a lung or something. I don't know. *Shit happens*," Lipske said.

"You didn't wash your hands. You should always wash your hands after taking a piss," Lenny said.

*   *   *

Day Four, 2300 hours

Lieutenant Quick and Hog stumbled up the stairs with two massage girls. I'd declined the invitation, and drifted back out to the veranda, then down to another courtyard that was shielded from the noise of the main bar. Cowboy came by and asked if I wanted anything. I told him I wanted to try something new and exotic. At a far table, two men speaking French were drinking something in a tall, green bottle. Both appeared to be quite looped. Bring me some of that, I said.

The two men speaking French got up and shook hands. The smaller one made his exit directly from the veranda to the street. The other man hobbled by my table, supporting himself with a cane. It was Lenny.

"Hi Lenny. Do you remember me?"

Lenny paused, then shuffled toward me, swaying slightly. His eyes were glazed and saliva dribbled out of the right corner of his mouth.

"No. Can't say that I do."

"We worked together out of Thailand for a time. I was one of the Jarhead Lieutenants"

"Yeah, well, you will have to forgive me. I worked with a lot of Jarhead Lieutenants, too many to remember, I guess. And we lost a lot of them, of course. You weren't wounded, were you?"

"No. I was lucky. Looks like you had an accident."

"Accident shit. Got caught in an ambush on the Plaine de Jars. Had to come to Da Nang for decent medical treatment."

"Sorry to hear that."

"You know, I was a Jarhead too. Got decorated in Korea. Always like to work with Jarheads. You can count on a Jarhead to do the job."

"Say," I found myself saying all of a sudden, "Did I see you earlier with that guy Lipske?"

"You know Lipske? He wasn't a Jarhead. No way."

"Worked with him some. I heard he was dead."

"Na. He's okay. He fucked up with some locals and we had to get him out of town. That was all a ploy."

"I see."

"Yeah, and then..."

Lenny was about to say something else when he stopped midsentence. He looked at me closely, shifting his cane, one hand to the other. My mention of Lipske had given him pause.

"Got to go now. *Semper Fi.*"

"*Semper Fi*, Lenny," I said.

Lenny made his way up the stairs with some difficulty. A massage girl met him midway, and took his arm to help him. At one point he turned and stared at me. There was a glimmer of recognition in his eyes. My guess was that he suddenly remembered how we came to know one another.

Cowboy next brought an unopened green bottle, a tall wine glass, and some sugar. He poured the green liquid into the glass. Then he lit a match and heated a spoonful of sugar until it bubbled. This he mixed with the green liquid until it took on a more milky-jade color. "Enjoy", Cowboy said.

I had one drink. Then prepared myself another...

The green stuff was definitely giving me a buzz. Sitting by myself, in the inner courtyard, under the single yard light, the heavy scent of the blooming gardenias was almost overpowering. Insects snapped and buzzed in the vegetation. A cloud of gnats spun under the yard light. The moon was rising. I poured myself a third glass of the green liquid and took a sip. I took out a pen and jotted down some lines. I decided to write a poem.

Blue is the full moon's violent eye.

*This is where nothing
but the blade of clear night
is to be trusted.*

Only the moon hangs firm and eager.

The poem seemed to capture things weighing on my mind. Sure, there were aspects in the natural order of things, like the moon and like the insects that were fixed and permanent, things that would always be there. But there was also ruthlessness and lack of humanity all about me, a brutality that was making me numb. That same brutality and inhumanity expressed itself in the severed hand I kept in that pickle jar.

I tried to pour another glass but spilled most of the liquid on the table. Then I wrote another poem. My eyes kept going in and out of focus. I could hear my heart beat.

We are looking for phantoms,
and phantoms that we are,
again we step outside this village
to wander the landscape in other forms.

Stand absolutely still
and you may catch yourself.

The cloud of gnats spinning under the yard light seemed to move in slow motion. The pale white gardenia blossoms were glowing. All that was fixed and permanent within the inner courtyard was becoming a blur. A passing cloud now hid the moon, but it was as if I could still see the blue outline of the moon through the cloud.

I felt as if I were in sync with the natural things around me. Images that had been with me since childhood, the spinning cloud of gnats, the yard lights on summer nights, ran through my head to give me a feeling of well-being. I thought of what Captain X had said about the Yin and the Yang. Yeah, for sure, the permanent and the temporary flowed together in a constant interaction. Wow. His ideas didn't seem so stupid now. Things were coming together and I could sense that there was a greater unity, apart from the chaos of the last few days.

One of those large green and yellow Vietnamese walking sticks dropped out of the tree above me. The walking stick must have been nine inches long. The strange insect made its way slowly across the tabletop, pausing to sway back and forth, as if it were still on a tree branch.

For some reason Pabinouis and his mojo bag flashed into my mind. Pabinouis truly believed that his luck and well being were linked to some power in that little mojo bag. That mojo bag was real, part of the fixed and permanent inside Pabinouis's brain-housing group. Perhaps the most important part of me, being his lieutenant, had to do with maintaining beliefs that sustained his spirit. And maybe the only true reality of this war had to do with our heads being on straight when it came to knowing how to help men survive both physically and mentally. That was what I needed to remember. That was the truth that came to me in the garden. Tomorrow would bring me back to Hill 55 and my job would be to inspire the trust and confidence of those with whom I served.

"Lieutenant Gatlin, what, in the fuck, are you drinking?"

"Don't know for sure. Wild stuff. I ordered it from Cowboy. I think Frenchmen like to drink it."

"Well, if Frenchmen like to drink it, it's probably fucked."

Lieutenant Quick picked up the bottle and gave it a sniff. He then tasted a bit of the green liquid.

"You fool. This shit is absinth."

"What's absinth?"

"A drink made from wormwood that will fuck you up. It's outlawed in most countries, not in the Nam, of course. It's a kind of liquid dope. I wouldn't drink any more of that shit if I were you."

"No sweat. I'm staying loose remember. I'm *chillin'*. You told me I think too much."

"I'm fucking serious, Sam. Don't fool yourself. The Green Fairy is dangerous."

"Ha! The only dangerous fairy I've seen around here is Cowboy," I said.

"What does the stuff do?" Hog asked.

"People lose fucking control. Hallucinate. Get crazy and run through the streets naked. Shit like that. Real fucking good, Lieutenant Gatlin."

"Lieutenant Quick, I find it amusing that you, with your White Lotus connections and your bizarre wheeling and dealing, should counsel me on what's crazy. But don't worry, I got the message," I said, raising my hands in the air.

Absinth. So that is what the strange green liquid was. I decided that absinth was not the best thing to drink for someone who had suffered serious head trauma.

*　　　*　　　*

CHAPTER EIGHT: THE SWARM

Day Five, 0500 hours

At daybreak we drove down to Third Track Battalion Headquarters. Our headquarters was situated in the Marble Mountain area near five great monoliths rising out of the sand dunes along the South China Sea. Six miles or so south of Da Nang, local legend told of a sea dragon that came ashore and laid a sky-blue egg. When the egg hatched a beautiful woman emerged. Through her magic she transformed the broken shell fragments into the five different land forms, each named for the basic elements that made up the universe: water, wood, earth, metal, and fire.

The tallest of these mountains, one that the locals called the Water Mountain, rose over 300 meters from the surrounding terrain, and was the site of the Tam Thai Pagoda built in 1825. A set of stairs, carved out of solid rock, led to the pagoda, which was the entrance to the famous Huyen Thong Cave. Many believed the cave was a refuge for the Viet Cong. Who knew what was really hidden in the depths of the Huyen Thong?

To the Marines, the Water Mountain was simply Chin Strap, a honeycomb of tunnels and sharp rock outcroppings covered by an abundant growth of vivid green casuarinas. Marines patrolled Nui Kim Son village at the mountain's base, while a SOG Team from the Special Forces camp north of Chin Strap ran an observation post on the top. Lieutenant Quick dropped me off at that Special Forces camp while he finished his business in Nui Kim Son.

"Hey Major Boden, how's the SOG business?"

"Lieutenant Sam Gatlin, late of the old counter terror teams. When I heard that you were back in Nam I figured we would link up at some point. How about a cold Kirin?" Major Boden asked, rising from his desk.

"No thanks, Major. I think I'll pass on that offer. We had a wild night at the White Lotus."

"What do they have you doing these days?"

"I'm back being a full time track rat. No more of that crazy counter terror stuff. How about you, sir?"

"Oh, unfortunately I had to give up my company of Nungs for a desk job. Now, I'm the Command and Control North SOG Liaison to a new part of CORDS. Hush-hush stuff."

"This Phoenix thing."

"Actually, Phoenix is only a piece of it. There's been a total reorganization. All those old counter terror teams have either been eliminated or integrated into the PRU effort, not just at the province level where we worked, but right down to the district level."

"I heard a VC death squad took out both the PRU advisor as well as the District Advisor down in Dien Ban."

"That's right. The PRU advisor had been on the job for less than a week. But we have a lead on that one."

"Anything you can share with me? I work closely with the new Dien Ban District Advisor."

"I know who you're talking about, the Australian SAS guy. He's good, and will shape up his PRU team in short order. Sharing information? Oh boy, that's a tough one. My official answer to you is no. But, given our former work together, I can tell you something that you need to know. Have you heard of the new PIC, the Province Interrogation Center that's been built?"

"That's the old Da Nang Special Sector."

"Well, not really. It's a different animal. Imagine four one-story concrete block buildings, each containing thirty or so solitary confinement cells the size of closets, all of them filled up with suspected Viet Cong or Viet Cong supporters, VC infrastructure guys. And imagine if you can, a central room where interrogation is done round the clock, nonstop. Recently the chief interrogator got a hold of three VC from down on Go Noi Island. They sang like canaries. Enough said?"

"Sounds like an information factory."

"Yep, and it's a productive factory, with all the necessary equipment, a real chamber of horrors. My last trip there really shook me up. This chief interrogator is a contract guy brought in from outside the country. He's a real scary dude. Calls himself the Seeker Six."

*   *   *

Day Five, 1000 hours

A chopper from my battalion headquarters flew me back down to Go Noi Island. When I arrived Sikes said that I looked like shit warmed over. He asked me if I was okay. I said that I was. I didn't want to appear as if I didn't have my shit together. But the fact was that my shit was totally loose. Now that I was on Go Noi I couldn't stop trembling. And my head had started to hurt again.

I found Slammer. He gave me a couple pills to calm me. After about twenty minutes the trembling stopped.

Sikes wanted to get things moving as soon as possible. He said that Major Hopkins and Captain X were back on the job. But one of the Marine colonels from Da Nang who had attended the awards ceremony was dead. Colonel Fry was evacuated out-of-country. Fry's replacement was an Old Corps colonel named Humpski, known only, of course, as "The Hump." Captain Sikes didn't know how many ARVN had been taken out, but of the journalists, two from the Da Nang press center had been killed and and three wounded. The VC death squad had scored big time.

*   *   *

Day Five, 1300 hours

Mojo Man and Blitz the Wonder Dog were working some sixty meters to our front when the enemy sniper popped off his first round. I was with three of my tracks at the western edge of Mike Company's line of advance. Mike Company was spread out, three platoons on-line with headquarters and a fourth platoon bringing up the rear. We were at a spot on the map called Thanh My, which was halfway to our objective of Bao An Tay. The sniper was firing from the ruins of a pagoda to our immediate northwest.

It was close to one hundred degrees, and the dust kicked up from the movement of the tracks just hung in the still air. When the sniper popped a second round every grunt was on his belly, breathing that suffocating dust.

I ordered the tracks to turn broadside to the sniper so that the grunts would have some cover. Captain Sikes told me to open up with the M-60 machine gun on top of track One-Eight. For the moment the M-60 fire kept the sniper's head down. On my signal, tracks One-Nine and One-Zero turned to the west, beginning a flanking move on the ruins of the pagoda that hid the sniper.

The two behemoths then picked up speed and turned directly at the ruins. Traveling at twenty miles an hour the two tracks covered the distance between our position and the pagoda in a matter of seconds. Track One-Eight crashed into the remaining thin wall of the ruined pagoda, climbing up and over the rubble. There One-Eight paused for a moment before executing a spin turn, churning the rubble and leveling the sniper's hideout to a cloud of dust and crumbling clay bricks.

*   *   *

Day Five, 1500 hours

We got the word from Hill 55 to hold up our advance. Everyone needed a break. It must have been a hundred and five degrees now. To our west, in the Arizona Territory, the Fifth Marines had their hands full. I only had to look toward the mountains to see the haze rising, the smoke of the firefights collecting above the windless landscape after more than twenty-four hours of constant fighting.

Helicopters and other aircraft flew back and forth overhead, evidence of the escalating level of conflict. When the aircraft'd passed, and the stillness of the afternoon heat again took hold, in the distances I thought I could hear the whistle of incoming artillery.

"Lieutenant, all I want to know is what happened to my big dill pickles?" Hog asked.

"I ate them."

"All of them?"

"Most affirmative. All of them."

"And you didn't get sick, sir?"

"No. Why would I get sick?"

"I don't know, sir. Sergeant Pabinous and I, well, are worried about you. We see your trembling episodes."

"No sweat," I said, ignoring Hog.

"Well, that's a lot of pickles... There ain't many people, sir, who could eat that many big dill pickles and not get sick," Hog replied, reaching behind the radio to pick up the pickle jar.

"Like I said, I like dill pickles."

Hog sat down and studied the hand floating in the green dill pickle juice.

"Hog, I thought I told you to get rid of that hand," I found myself saying.

I got up, and walked over to Hog. I took the jar, and placed it back behind the radio in its hiding place. Hog's spider moved nervously on its web.

I took off my rain-hat, and with a quick sweep gathered in the spider and its web. A horrified Hog looked up at me as I held the rain-hat, with the captured spider, in front of his face, my fist tightly clenched.

"No, Lieutenant. You wouldn't mess with my spider? You wouldn't?"

"Make you a deal, Hog. You get rid of that pickled hand, and I won't mess with your spider," I said.

Hog looked at me for a moment, saying nothing. Then he smiled.

"*Done*, Lieutenant. But I think that you're beginning to weird out on me," Hog said, shaking his head.

On an impulse I reached over and cupped the spider in the palm in my hand.

"Holy shit! Lieutenant! *What are you doing*?"

"Stay loose, Hog. I'm checking out your spider," I said.

"But he'll bite you. And someone said..."

"Maybe," I said, cutting him off.

I looked at the spider walking across my palm and I knew that he wouldn't bite me. How I knew I couldn't say. The dark, hairy limbs of the spider tickled my palm. Cupping the spider in my palm defied reason. It was a wild impulse beyond my understanding; and as the spider walked off my hand and back onto his web, I was reminded of the walking stick back at the White Lotus.

Hog rushed over to watch as his spider crawled slowly into the confines of the web. Within a minute or so the spider began to spin a new tunnel in the heart of its web. Soon it set about the business of repairing the outer web. Hog and I watched the spider as it spun the delicate threads, threads that seemed to glisten.

*   *   *

Day Five, 2100 hours

Even though it had cooled off, sweat still poured out of me. Getting rid of all the poison from the White Lotus, I thought. Then the word came down to move north. We were to make a night move.

Our rest period had helped everyone. During that time questions concerning how Mike Company was going to operate, and how my track platoon was going to help them operate, kept turning over in my mind. I made up my mind that when Captain Sikes came by, I would take the opportunity to ask him for a private talk.

Captain Sikes believed in what he called private talks. These talks were a form of open door policy that Sikes had with the enlisted men. The Gunny hated the fact that Sikes would allow enlisted men to talk to him without going through the chain of command. But I respected the fact that Sikes was flexible. The fact that Sikes held his private talks inspired my confidence to the point where I felt that I could talk to Sikes one-on-one about my concerns, and my concerns were many. Foremost among them, had to do with my own men's perceptions of how the grunts were intending to use our tracks. My men felt that the grunts didn't really understand how to use tracks. Our recent history as a track platoon was full of what my men would call the misuse of tracks, that misuse expressing itself both in lost tracks and casualties.

To an extent my men were right. Grunts tended to look at tracks as either armor or transport. The fact of the matter was that tracks had been designed as a ship-to-shore vehicle to be used during amphibious assaults. In Vietnam, that design had been forgotten. The practical demands of the situation for hauling men and material over the wet terrain brought tracks inland from the beach. Emergency reaction teams often used tracks as assault vehicles. In those emergencies the grunts used any resource that was available. As a result, tracks had been lost and there had been casualties. That was the nature of war.

Tracks One-Eight and One-Nine started up and headed out. Each track was carrying a squad of grunts on top. For some reason I decided to ride One-Zero. I had the driver start the track. A squad of grunts began to climb on top of the track. The company began to move out. Then we stopped. It was the classic hurry-up and wait. While we were waiting, two gun ships swept by at ground level, the suddenness of their passing jerking me erect.

"How are we doin, Sam?" Sikes said, walking up to my track.

Captain Sikes seemed to have found me before I found him. I jumped down from the top of the track. Sweat was pouring off me.

"Okay, sir. How you doing?"

"Just right! Sam, you don't look so good. You look real tired."

"Yes, sir. Feeling a little feverish. Just fatigue," I replied.

"You sure? I understand you had a concussion. That cut on your head looks infected."

"I'm okay, sir."

"Anyway, thought I'd have a word with you. I wanted to ask you about your sergeant, the one that got hurt pulling out the track. We haven't had time to talk about how it happened."

"I'm afraid that I was moving too fast," I said.

"How's the man doing?"

"I hear that he is recovering," I replied, looking down at the ground.

I was starting to feel a little dizzy. I leaned against One-Zero. Captain Sikes looked at me closely.

"Sam, you really don't look well. Maybe you ought to get on a chopper and head on up to Hill 55. Have Medical check you out."

"Sir, my leaving would leave you short-handed for officers. I couldn't do that to you," I said.

"I understand, Sam. You don't want me using up your tracks or getting them stuck in the mud. I know how you track rats feel," Sikes said with a smile.

"Yes, sir. Frankly, that's part of it," I said.

"What's the rest of it?"

"The rest of it is that I've got too much pride to leave the field over fatigue and a little fever. That's another part of it. Another part of it is that I've got to be here for my men. What would my men say if I abandoned them after what happened to Chapelle. No thank you, sir. I'll stay right here on Go Noi Island and gut it out, fever or no fever," I replied.

"That's your choice and I respect it. Now, is there anything else on your mind?"

"Yes, sir. Are you getting any clear direction from Hill 55 as to how this movement is going to sort out?"

"Yes and no. Yes, in the sense that our reconnaissance teams exploring the trails up in the Que Son Mountains are reporting all kinds of movement. But I think that you already heard that. Also, yes in the sense that our planners up at the division level think that the enemy is massing to make things difficult for us, especially in areas like the Arizona, Dodge City, and the Go Noi. And that means that for the next day or so we will have to sit back in a defensive position up in the northern part of Go Noi to block and perhaps interdict these forces near Bao An Tay. No, in the sense that I don't know what we're going to do beyond, say, a two-day window."

"How about this new Korean Colonel Chai?"

"The only thing I know is what you already were told, and that was that you would probably be picking up some Korean Marines. As for colonels, and that's any kind of colonels, a lot of what drives them is political. If the politics of the situation change for this Korean colonel, he'll back off. He'll be just like his predecessor. Hey, the Koreans are tough, but everyone knows that when the Korean Marines start to get a lot of casualties, they stop patrolling. At any rate, for now it's my understanding that you will be picking up at least a couple of platoons of Koreans. Those platoons will be placed along the northern edge of Go Noi. Lieutenant Kim will be going with you. He'll have all the details."

"That means swimming my tracks down river and back."

"Affirmative."

"No further direction. You were given no further direction on how to proceed?"

"Lieutenant, I don't need any further direction than that. The rest of the direction comes from within."

"Sir?"

"Sam, let me tell you a story. Back in August of 1966, when I was a lieutenant leading a platoon up near the DMZ on Operation Prairie, I had thirty-one men and myself. Over three hundred NVA hit us. We fought for two days and lost only five Marines. We killed over forty NVA. It was nasty. Sometimes hand-to-hand. The men took to calling it the Groucho Marx battle. All that time, all things were confused. I learned right then and there that when the shit goes down the only real direction comes from within. Don't look anywhere else for it, because you ain't going to find it. There it is," Sikes said, looking off to the west, at the mountains.

"You are telling me to do my own thing."

"What I am saying is that out here you are in charge, Lieutenant. Lieutenant Sam Gatlin is the track platoon commander. Don't depend on Hill 55 or some staff weenie up at division to provide direction for you. Down here in Dodge City and the Go Noi you provide your own direction, you're the leader the men look to."

*   *   *

Day Five, 2300 hours

It was Hog who first spotted the swarm sometime close to midnight. We'd been making good time for a night move, and had reached Bao An Tay on the Ky Lam River. Captain Sikes'd called a halt to wait for first light. I sat on the bank of the river and watched. From where I sat, the swarm looked like thousands of small black dolphins, their glistening backs barely breaking the surface of the river. Up close, we'd found it to be a great school of giant catfish, shimmering and undulating, circling in a great spiral. Yin and Yang I thought to myself.

The call of a bamboo cat broke the quiet. Out on the Ky Lam River the huge school of catfish still turned in a great spiral. Mojo Man stood knee-deep in the water, some twenty feet from me, the large swarm of fish churning around his legs.

I sat on the bank of the Ky Lam and looked up in the night sky, watching the stars. The constellation of Orion lay to the north, his giant's belt clearly marked by three stars. The Pleiades, that loose cluster of stars named for the Seven Daughters of Atlas, was visible to the west. The Milky Way spread, directly overhead, millions of stars and glowing clouds of gas light-years across. My fever'd gone. Above me, matter was turning into starlight. Stars were condensing out of interstellar dust. A curious calm came over me.

*   *   *

Day Six, 0530 hours

At first light I waded out in the river. At that point the Ky Lam was shallow, with a sandy bottom, a well-known crossing-point for the NVA. I stood knee-deep among the thousands of catfish, fascinated by the spectacle. I thought to myself how Vietnam continued to surprise and amaze me in so many different ways. It wasn't just the spectacle of war; rather, it was that it was all so foreign.

The swarm kept circling in a clockwise direction. Occasionally smaller groups of fish would break off and spin in a counter-clockwise direction so that there were small counter-spirals within the great spiral. These catfish were similar in appearance to those that I'd caught in the rivers back in Iowa, but this strange group behavior, this swarming together, was unique in my experience.

Then Mojo Man made up his mind to go fishing. When Captain Sikes and I gave him the go-ahead, he tossed a frag grenade into the middle of the swarm. There was a dull thump under the water. Soon hundreds of large catfish were floating belly-up in the Ky Lam, and my track rats and the men of Mike Company ran into the river to gather them up.

We formed an assembly line for the cleaning. Three or four grunts would gut the fish. Sergeant Pabinouis and another track rat would peel off the slick catfish skin with wire snips from the track's toolbox. Then the Gunny rolled the chunks of catfish in corn meal left on board from our civil action efforts. The corn meal had been intended for the use of some Vietnamese villagers. This particular track driver had kept out his share so that he could make corn bread.

Track One-Eight had a propane burner that we used to cook steaks and hamburgers. Hog took over and fashioned a cooker out of a steel ammo box, and it wasn't long before we had a boiling pot into which we were dropping fist-size chunks of juicy catfish. The cooked catfish came out rich and succulent.

*   *   *

Day Six, 0900 hours

Captain Sikes suddenly got word from Hill 55 to set up a position along the river. Accordingly, he set in a perimeter with the Ky Lam River to our back. To our east lay the ruins of the village of Bao An Dong, leveled by Rome Plows. To our west were the ruins of Phu Dong, once the site of a large NVA bunker complex. Facing south a dry rice paddy spread before us, offering clear fields of fire for our automatic weapons.

We would rest until dark. At twilight, we would continue our movement. No reason was ever given for our sudden change in plans. The reasons behind our delay were never explained. From my point of view we were wasting time. Worse than that, we were allowing our enemy an opportunity while we remained in a fixed position. The situation did not inspire my confidence but I kept my thoughts to myself. I didn't want to be viewed as negative by Captain Sikes.

*   *   *

Day Six, 1700 hours

The day passed quickly. I slept through the hot afternoon and woke at about 1700 hours. At dusk we got the word from Captain Sikes. Once again we'd had a change of plans. Instead of another night movement, we were to maintain our position, sending out selected patrols to set up night ambushes.

First Platoon, with Lieutenant Wily as platoon leader, sent out the first of several squad-sized patrols to cover the Bao An Dong area. Since the ruins to our immediate west offered the greatest potential threat, two platoons were to patrol Phu Dong. Third and Fourth Platoons got that assignment. Second Platoon was to stay within the perimeter to provide my tracks, Mike Company Command Group, and the mortar section, with security.

The perimeter was a semicircle about one hundred meters across. M-60 machine guns in both our fighting holes and on top of the five tracks offered interlocking bands of fire should the perimeter be assaulted. Four of the tracks were spread evenly around the edge of the perimeter semicircle. Track One-Eight was pulled back to the edge of the Ky Lam River. There One-Eight provided the Mike Company command group with a headquarters.

"Lieutenant, we should be on the other side of the river," Hog said, sitting down beside me.

"Why do you say that?"

"Come on, Lieutenant. If we were on the other side of the river, we would have more grunt support. Isn't that right, Mojo Man?"

"That's a big affirmative. *The Sky Pilot favors those who have the most firepower*," Mojo Man said.

"We have to stay on Go Noi… We have to stay on Go Noi so that we can control the key points like this river crossing. That's what interdiction is, covering the trail junctions and river crossings with men and supporting arms," I replied, defending the current plan.

"Lieutenant, we got to cross the river and get back to Dodge City. A shit load of gooks could come up from the south and overrun us," Hog said.

"Stay loose, Hog," I replied.

That afternoon's sleep had helped me. My head was clear. On an impulse, I got up and walked down into the river.

"Where are you going, Lieutenant?" Hog asked.

"Just going to cool off."

I walked out in the river until I was about knee-deep in the water. The sun'd set and darkness was upon us. The first stars reflected in the water, and still, all around me, I could feel the catfish brushing against my legs. I lay down in the water, with just my head and shoulders above the surface. The river bottom was sandy and I let myself drift, my body hovering in the slow current of the river, a strange sensation.

While the fish turned in their great spiral, swimming all around me, I looked upriver to see a waning moon begin to rise. Along the shore the looming shadows of the tracks overlooked the river. For a moment, I thought about the complaints of my men, and of their concerns about how the grunts were using and abusing our tracks. The doubts of my men were a cancer that kept growing, and at that instant, under the first stars, I knew that the only cure to that growth was for us to heal ourselves. That healing had to do with reminding ourselves of our common purpose, which somehow had been forgotten. When Mojo Man went fishing everyone pulled together to cook up a great catfish feed. We all hung together to get it done.

There was a lesson for me in Mojo Man's fishing expedition and the catfish feed. Like Captain Sikes said, it was up to me to provide direction for these track rats. I was the leader the men looked to.

I looked downriver and tried to make out the Pleiades. It seemed the surface of the wide Ky Lam River merged into the cosmic dark.

"Lieutenant, you okay?" Hog was calling out from the riverbank.

"I'm fine."

"Are you sure?"

"I'm right, just right. I think I'm reinventing myself."

"Lieutenant, with all due respect, that's some weird shit you're talking."

*   *   *

Day Six, 2300 hours

Close to midnight the listening post directly in front of One-Nine called in movement. Captain Sikes told the listening post to toss out a frag grenade. The frag grenade set off a secondary explosion that shook the ground. It was almost certain that a sapper carrying a satchel charge had been blown away, the frag grenade causing a sympathetic detonation of the satchel charge.

Sikes called in all his listening posts. Wily called in from the Bao An area that one of his squad-sized patrols had heavy movement, and the direction of that movement was toward our position. As soon as Wily completed the radio transmission to Sikes all hell broke loose to the south. The squad monitoring the movement had made contact.

I listened as Sikes called in illumination from Hill 55. I felt a level of comfort with Captain Sikes. Earlier in the evening I'd watched him as he checked out the location of his supporting artillery fire. Now Sikes prepared to call in some of that artillery support, instructing Wily to pull in his two other squads to a prearranged checkpoint.

Wily had his hands full. The firefight in the Bao An area had produced two Marine casualties. From the volume of fire it was clear that the Marine squad was up against a larger force. Through Wily, Sikes directed the squad to break off contact. As Wily relayed information concerning the status and location of the squad, Sikes called in artillery fire from Hill 55.

The first rounds impacted to our southeast. Wily called the adjustment to Sikes who then requested a full fire for effect. Within seconds the batteries on Hill 55 responded. The artillery fire cut a swath five hundred meters long by two hundred meters wide, effectively neutralizing the enemy force.

By 2330 hours Wily'd consolidated his platoon, moving north to the Ky Lam River. Upon reaching the Ky Lam, Wily requested a chopper to evacuate his wounded. Wily was lucky that he was on a bend in the river. The chopper pilot spotted that river bend from the air and dropped down right into Wily's position, coming in low off the wide Ky Lam.

After Sikes brought in a chopper to evacuate the two wounded Marines, he ordered Wily to work his way north along the Ky Lam until he reached our perimeter. At the same time, Sikes directed the two platoons in the Phu Dong area to pull back to the Ky Lam and move south until they linked up with our position.

For a time it seemed that Captain Sikes had things under control. Then, at midnight, the first mortars hit us. Sikes was standing outside One-Eight smoking a cigarette when a mortar round burst within ten feet of him and took out the lieutenant from second platoon standing next to Sikes. For the next five minutes the NVA walked mortars through our position. Mojo Man and I pulled Sikes under the cover of One-Eight. Sikes was hit in the legs and going shocky. The lieutenant from second platoon was dead.

Slammer and another corpsman went to work on Sikes. The Gunny came rushing in, his eyes blazing. The Gunny talked briefly to Sikes. I overheard Sikes say to the Gunny that I was now in command of Mike Company and that I should get Puff on station as soon as possible.

"Lieutenant, you know that they be hitting us as soon as the mortars let up! You know that it won't be shits and grins," the Gunny said, all out of breath.

I picked up the map on which Captain Sikes had written the coordinates. Captain Sikes had one of the best radiomen around. We called him Hair Trigger because he was so quick and on the ball. By the time I'd turned to Hair Trigger he already had Hill 55 on the radio.

"Gunny, make a round of the perimeter. Tell them... You know what to tell them. Hog, I want all the track rats on their radio frequency, listening to me for instructions. Sergeant Pabinouis, I want you topside on this track, covering my ass," I said, the orders just flowing.

The mortars stopped. A Marine fired his weapon once. A frag grenade exploded outside our perimeter, thrown by one of the grunts. Another frag grenade exploded. Mojo Man came rushing in, his dog Blitz panting heavily.

"Lieutenant, we got all kinds of gooks outside our perimeter! Yes, sir, I can tell from the way Blitz is acting," he said.

Hog returned from making the rounds of the tracks.

"All set, Lieutenant. All along the line we got a shitload of movement," Hog said, also out of breath.

"Test to see that everyone is on," I said.

"What?"

"Test to see that everyone is on. Do it now!"

I pointed out to Hair Trigger the coordinates where I needed fire. He was in the process of calling in those coordinates when the second mortar attack began. For another five minutes the mortars fell. During those five minutes, batteries on Hill 55 responded and artillery fire fell all around us. When the mortars finally let up six more Marines were wounded, including Pabinouis.

In the lull after the mortar attack I talked to the Battalion Commander of 3/1, giving him the status on Captain Sikes. We had one KIA and seven WIA, two of those WIA shocky. Over the radio the Kingfish, the Battalion Commander of 3/1, instructed Wily to move north to take command of Mike Company. Wily was about a minute into that move when his platoon came under heavy fire from the north. There was a sizeable NVA force between Wily's platoon and us.

The Battalion Commander of 3/1 then ordered Third Platoon to move south. Two minutes later Third Platoon made contact, sustaining two casualties. The Kingfish told Third Platoon to hold their position. He then asked for my assessment. With artillery falling all around me, I explained our situation as best I could to the Battalion Commander of 3/1.

When our artillery let up, I tried to figure out which coordinates to use in order to give Wily some artillery support. At that point Hair Trigger took it upon himself to go up on the medevac frequency, calling for help from any available gunship. As luck would have it one of the Army Black Cats was over Go Noi, coming back from the south. The Army warrant officer driving that Huey gunship just seemed to drop out of the sky, again coming in low off the Ky Lam River.

I could see now the wisdom of Captain Sikes in choosing this position. With our backs to the broad Ky Lam the gunship had a protected avenue of approach over the water. Quickly we loaded Captain Sikes, Pabinouis and two of the more seriously wounded. When the Huey took off, several bursts of AK-47 fire sent streams of green tracers up into the night sky.

Track One-Six was facing the area from where the fire had originated. One-Six had a fifty-caliber machine gun mounted on top. I gave One-Six the order to open up. The ammunition that the fifty cal was using was linked together in a formidable way, two armor-piercing rounds followed by two antipersonnel rounds, then a tracer. The antipersonnel rounds exploded upon impact like small bombs. One-Six began firing small bursts directly to the south.

All this time I knew Wily's platoon was in deep shit. His people were engaged on three sides, their backs to the Ky Lam River. Third Platoon, still engaged to their front, had managed to pull back to a position that offered cover for the time being. Two squads from second platoon were following in trace of Third. All were effectively blocked from linking up with us.

I gave Hair Trigger coordinates to support Wily. It seemed like forever before Hill 55 responded. Then we had to adjust fire. The NVA broke off contact before I could complete the fire mission. It was 0100 hours.

At 0105 the first rocket-propelled grenade whizzed over One-Six. One-Six immediately responded with the fifty cal. Within seconds more RPGs were whizzing overhead. One struck Track One-Nine on the port side, penetrating the hull and slinging hot slag throughout the interior of the track.

The volley of RPGs must have been the signal for the main body to attack because a series of satchel charges exploded around the perimeter, aimed at knocking out our machine gun positions. I was sitting in the interior of One-Eight, preparing to call in more artillery when the Gunny ran by.

"Gooks in the perimeter, Lieutenant! Gooks in the Perimeter!" the Gunny shouted.

The Gunny had his pistol in one hand and an entrenching tool in the other. Outside, the perimeter seemed to explode. All my tracks were firing their weapons. The noise was deafening and it was hard to see through the smoke-haze that hung in the air. To my right I heard men screaming and shouting through all the confusion.

"Gunny, you better take care of my ass so I can call in some shit to get us out of this mess," I found myself saying, calmly.

The Gunny nodded, saying nothing. Hog got on top of One-Eight to provide our track with security. Mojo Man stood beside me with his M-16 leveled at the track door. RPGs continued to whiz overhead. Rifle rounds cracked the air. Hair Trigger spoke quietly and intently on the radio. I dropped the map I'd been holding for the last hour on the floor. I didn't need it anymore. It occurred to me then that we were in the process of being overrun.

I shut off the track's red interior lights and chambered a round in my forty-five. I pulled my Bolo from its sheath and laid it by my side.

"Lieutenant, we going to have Puff overhead most ricky-tick," Hair Trigger said.

"Roger that. I got the strobe light in my lap. Tell them I'm turning it on to mark our position."

Puff the Magic Dragon, also called Spooky by some Marines, was an AC-47 transport that had been adapted for nighttime warfare. The AC-47 was equipped with fixed, side-firing machine guns that could fire 6000 rounds a minute. In addition Puff carried its own supply of powerful parachute flares that could light up the night to almost daytime conditions. The basic tactic was for Puff to fly in a controlled turn at a carefully set bank angle. Puff then fired a steady stream of rounds directed at a single area. It was awesome. It was also what we now needed to alleviate the pressure.

Overhead, in the far distance, we heard the drone of the AC-47's engines. Figures ran through the smoke. I sat just outside the track door holding the strobe light, watching the interlocking bands of M-60 fire all around the perimeter. Our key fighting holes had maintained their integrity. The

NVA assaulting our perimeter were paying a big price. Then the first parachute flare popped and night turned into day.

The light from the parachute flare revealed scattered groups of NVA falling back from our perimeter. Inside the perimeter I could make out the Gunny swinging his entrenching tool in the ghostly light. At that moment what looked like a stream of liquid fire descended from the sky. When the liquid fire hit the ground it was as if a small tornado had touched down, the 6000 round per minute effect of Puff's side-firing machine guns. The dust and earth kicked up by the liquid fire flew in all directions. The grinding sound that followed was like that heard in a sawmill where giant saws cut through hardwood logs.

For the next twenty minutes Puff circled our perimeter. A glowing stream of liquid fire continued to rain down, and the heavy volume of fire created a surreal, gruesome haze.

*   *   *

Day Seven, 0800 hours

"Well, Lieutenant, we survived that one," the Gunny was saying.

"Roger that, Gunny," I replied.

There was nothing more to say. The two of us were outside of One-Eight sipping C ration coffee. A dusty haze still hung in the air from last night's action.

"You did good, Lieutenant. That's most affirmative."

The Gunny was not one to give compliments freely. I was gratified. Captain X walked up. He had been examining the bodies of dead NVA. He'd counted twelve. There were numerous blood trails indicating the other dead and wounded had been dragged off. Somehow it seemed that there should have been more.

"Thanks for coming down, Captain Graham. You seem to be doing okay," I said.

"I'm not at 100% yet, but I can function. Hopkins is going to be fine. The VC assassination team really shook him up, but he'll bounce back."

"Captain, last night was crazy. We were *beaucoup* lucky. I can't help but wonder where are all these gooks coming from. Our intelligence tells us that the VC and the NVA don't have any manpower left. After what happened to us last night, and what seems to be going on all around Da Nang, I can't believe our intelligence folks anymore. Their estimates don't hold water. I'm afraid that we are going to have Tet all over again," I said.

"Don't blame your military intelligence folks. The blame lies elsewhere, much higher up, at the very top of the chain of command. We Aussies have also thought for some time that a certain U.S. agency has been underestimating the true number of VC and VCI. Their own analysts questioned the low estimates," Captain X said.

"And in the field guys like Hopkins inflate the numbers of VC and NVA killed," I found myself adding.

"Don't be so hard on Major Hopkins, Lieutenant Gatlin. I know for a fact that he questions the same discrepancies that we do. Hopkins has nothing but contempt for the phony numbers. He feels the agency in question decides what their position *should be*, then selects or manipulates intelligence to support that position. Hopkins calls it trying to square the circle."

"When I hear you say these things it turns my stomach," I said.

"Well, as they say, continue to march, Lieutenant Gatlin. Things are in a transition. This agency of yours is backing off. We're going into a mode where the American military is going to assume more direct control over the people who produce these phony numbers. Those changes will affect how we operate. The PRU, for example, will now be under American military oversight. That's a big change."

"Captain, you certainly know more than I do about these things. I find it incredible that this VC death squad seems to operate with impunity."

"I'm going to make finding that VC death squad a priority. My other duties as District Advisor will have to wait. I still have to find an advisor to guide the district's PRU Team. To make matters even more complicated, my PRU Team won't go out without an American to lead them. They're afraid they won't get critical support, either artillery or choppers, if they get into trouble."

"Captain, I can understand their position. Look at the difficulty we have had getting critical support at the right time. It's happening all around Da Nang," I said.

"Yes, it is indeed crazy all around Da Nang. By the way, we know that the code name for this VC death squad is the Warehouse Crew. Lipske got that information from the prisoners Hopkins sent him. This death squad operates out of a place called the Warehouse, a staging area believed to be somewhere in Dodge City. It seems that prior to their assassination mission, this team's purpose was to store rice and bullets to support VC main force units. Ani Bui's father was their cadre leader. Now that those VC main force units no longer exist in any numbers, the Warehouse Crew has targeted certain individuals for elimination."

"If those folks up in Da Nang have all this information, why haven't they smoked these gooks out?" I asked.

"This is all new intelligence. But after this last fiasco, I'm going to be real careful how I deal with both the Army and the Marine Division staff back in Da Nang. Obviously there are some leaks back there. How could this VC team have known ahead of time about the awards ceremony? My plan is to develop my own strategy with the help of you Marines on Hill 55. You seem to be the only resource that I can trust at this point."

"I heard that, sir," the Gunny said, walking up. "Count me in, Captain, if you need someone who knows Dodge City. I'll lead that pencil-necked PRU Team. See if you can find a way for the old Gunny to help you. I'm due to rotate out of the field. If you talk to Major Hopkins, maybe he can pull some strings. You and I could hunt this team down. We would make a good pair, and we could get Mojo Man and Blitz to help us. Yes, sir! Get me that dog Blitz and the Mojo Man and we'll get'em. You see, sir, I know this terrain like I know the back of my ex-wife's behind. Mojo Man knows the terrain as well as I do."

"I can't take you up on that offer, Gunny. We need people with your leadership experience and know-how in the field," the Captain said

The Gunny's manipulation of the situation did not surprise me. Such wheeling and dealing was the way things were done. The truth of the matter was the Gunny's idea had merit. For the Gunny would stay focused. He would be relentless in tracking the death squad. Too often it seemed that our efforts south of Da Nang lost focus, or that the objectives changed before we had time to really gather the right information and execute according to plan.

"Captain, the Lieutenant here did good last night. You would have been proud," the Gunny said again.

"Captain, you mentioned Lipske. What became of Ani Bui and her brother?"

"Unfortunately, Lipske pulled rank on me. Once he pried that Warehouse information from those prisoners, he went to the Province Chief, requesting that I turn over Ani and her brother for interrogation to this new PIC. The Province Chief is sending a PRU team down to pick them up sometime today."

"Captain, we have to stop that from happening. Ani and her brother are non-combatants. We need to do the right thing here. We should try to handle Ani as a kind of Chieu Hoi, someone who is willing to rally over to our side. From what I understand she has been more than willing to talk to us," I said.

The Kingfish, Battalion Commander from 3/1, was landing in a chopper. For a moment, the chopper seemed to distract the Captain. Lieutenant Wily had assumed command of Mike Company and was in the process of preparing for the battalion commander's arrival. He was waving to us to get our attention.

"The right thing, I see your point. Give me some time to think about that," the Captain said.

*   *   *

Day Seven, 0830 hours

The Kingfish always wore his flak jacket and helmet. He was the epitome of what Wily called the nonrisk-taking, straight arrow. Major Hopkins would have called Kingfish risk averse. To me, Kingfish was a big zero. He never smiled, nor did he mix well with the other officers on Hill 55. The strongest thing he drank was Dr. Pepper. In all my experience in the field with Kingfish, I can never remember him taking the time to inquire as to the well being of either my track rats or me.

Kingfish immediately called a meeting, gathering together Lieutenant Wily and the lieutenants from Mike Company. The group also included Captain X, the Gunny, and myself. Kingfish always carried a clipboard.

Kingfish read from his clipboard. He was sweating. After giving us a quick rundown of all the action in the area he said that we had done a hell of a job last night. He added that, for the time being, we were to stay on Go Noi Island, so that we could continue to interdict the enemy. Our efforts were keeping the enemy out of Dodge City. Kingfish then informed us that Dodge City was the soft underbelly of Da Nang, and that a new operation was in the works to protect and deny that area to the enemy. He said that the new initiative was based on recent intelligence provided by the hard core VC we had captured. Almost as an afterthought he mentioned that Seeker Six would be working with us on this proposed operation. Of course, Seeker Six was none other than Fritz Lipske.

We had all heard this soft underbelly stuff before and were wondering if we were to get more support in terms of men. It didn't take long to figure out that more Marines weren't in the cards. Kingfish then asked if there were any questions. When no one asked any questions, Kingfish then began to give us what amounted to a five-paragraph order that we were to follow for the next two days.

As soon as Kingfish mentioned that my tracks were to swim down the Ky Lam to pick up a couple of platoons of Korean Marines, I didn't hear another word he'd said. I was lost in my thoughts, trying to figure out how I was going to do what I had to do.

When Kingfish finished reading his order, he again asked for questions. Once again there were no questions. It was as if everyone were afraid to ask questions. I stepped forward.

"Sir, you mentioned that this new approach was based on recent intelligence gathered by Seeker Six from the VC we captured. Any more details that you can share?"

"No, Lieutenant Gatlin. Nothing I can share. Oh, maybe one thing. In the briefing I attended, Seeker Six said that the three prisoners succumbed to their wounds. Unfortunately they won't be providing us with any more information."

I looked over at Captain X to see his response to that information. He seemed surprised to hear the news about the VC prisoners. When he looked over at me, I could see concern in his eyes. Three wounded VC prisoners from his district turn up dead. Someone should be asking the right questions, especially a senior district advisor who was trying to win the hearts and minds of the people. Maybe no one cared to ask a question at this point, certainly not a big zero like the Kingfish, or Major Hopkins.

This was serious shit. No vague Yin and Yang here. Three wounded prisoners of war were history, probably tortured to death. If that was what happened in the torture chambers of this PIC, an investigation was warranted. Charges could be filled. If Major Hopkins had knowledge of what went down, he was hanging out. I would think that even Captain X was hanging out on this one. Lipske, of course, was a civilian contractor for that *certain agency*, to use an Australian term, and he would probably skate free. No military court for the Seeker Six.

There were no more questions and Kingfish loaded himself back in the chopper. After we all watched Kingfish leave, Captain X called the same group together. This time we got down to real business.

"I think if we work along established lines of communication," Captain X said, "I don't think that we will have any problems. That means we channel all communications back through Major Hopkins on Hill 55."

"That means that no one does anything with the Korean Marines without going through Major Hopkins?" I asked.

"Major Hopkins will be the clearing-house," Captain X said.

"I need direct communication with the Koreans, and I need to operate with some independence from Major Hopkins to ensure that we protect the interests of my men and my tracks. I have an obligation to see that vehicles are not abused," I countered.

"I understand, Lieutenant Gatlin. But we also need to ensure that no one will call artillery on a friendly, nor will we blow each other away in a firefight against each other. As you know, these things have happened before. Now, Lieutenant Wily, this approach will slow us down some, but it is the path of least risk for all concerned. Lieutenant Gatlin, I will make sure that you will have Lieutenant Kim with you to handle any direct communications to the Korean Marines. Again, if we all coordinate through Hill 55, I don't anticipate any big problems. I have great confidence in Lieutenant Kim."

"Yes, sir. We'll have to see how it goes," I replied.

"Captain, I'm glad to have you more closely involved," Wily said.

"By the way, since chopper support for Go Noi Island has been a problem, I would like to offer more support in the form of the gunship that I have at my disposal, should that be necessary."

"Captain X, I agree with everything you have said so far. But I've got an issue to work through. It's called my battalion commander. You bet we need to follow established lines of communication, and they begin with the Kingfish. As the Gunny likes to say, he rides close herd on us. I've got to work through my battalion C.O.," Wily said.

"Of course you do. But view me as a resource. As long as I'm the District Advisor, I've got a role to play in this. My predecessor had a different way of working with Hill 55. I say, let's link closer together to get things done. Let's organize ourselves for results. Let's reinvent ourselves to meet the demands of the situation."

I looked at Wily, and Wily looked at me. What Captain X proposed sounded like it violated the old Marine principle of unity of command. It was one thing to be part of a combat team, yet quite another thing to take direction from someone other than your commanding officer. Wily would be in deep shit if he didn't follow the Kingfish's directive to the letter. Problem was that no one trusted Kingfish. We liked Captain X, but it appeared that he was poking his nose into Mike Company's business. As the company commander, Wily was taking a risk just having this kind of conversation. The Kingfish would have Wily's ass in a Hong Kong minute if he heard about this exchange.

I thought of what Captain X once said to me about when the system became a barrier to getting things done, and how it then becomes necessary to get things done in spite of the system. After the meeting broke up, I pulled the captain aside.

"Bad shit about those prisoners dying," I said.

"I'm caught in a very difficult situation."

"That you are, Captain. Hopkins is really hanging out. If this gets out, who knows what can happen. Hopkins has made a lot of enemies. Charges could be filed. And the situation will get worse if you allow Lipske to get his hands on Ani Bui."

"I don't know what to do."

"Give Ani Bui to me. We'll say that I am using her as a guide down here on Go Noi. I'm willing to give her the benefit of the doubt because she's been so willing to talk to us. I believe her story about being kidnapped by the VC is true. Let's give her the opportunity to come over to our side. If Lipske protests and goes to the Province Chief, we tell them Ani has chosen to work within her district with the senior district advisor. Since Ani will be with me, they won't be able to do shit."

"You've got me thinking. This may be a good plan. No doubt we will encounter resistance from Major Hopkins."

"Fuck him. He would fuck over both of us, given the chance. If he starts to make a big deal over Ani, tell him I will blow the whistle on both Seeker Six and the dead VC. Tell him I will watch him fry in hell over what he has allowed Lipske to do. My company commander, Lieutenant Quick, will back me all the way."

"He'll view that as a threat."

"Damn right it's a threat. Tell him it's a promise. That's something he will understand."

"I'll fly up to the district right away. Expect to have Ani Bui and her brother here within the hour."

"Roger that."

*   *   *

Day Seven, 1000 hours

True to his word, Captain X returned with Ani Bui and her brother within the hour. With Ani under our wing, we lined up our tracks and began to prepare them for the water driving, ensuring that hull plugs were tight and that all bilge pumps were operating.

The cut on my head stopped hurting and my fever was gone. Since we were going to be swimming our tracks downriver, Hog and I made a special spot out of wood from ammo boxes to secure Ani Bui's brother. Having him secure was a good idea all around. I asked Slammer for some more downers so we could give the little guy a sedative. Slammer had what we needed.

Wily then came by for one last rundown. I was to swim my tracks downriver to pick up the Korean Marines. Both Lieutenant Kim and the Gunny were to go with me. I asked for Hair Trigger as my radioman and Wily arranged for that support.

The pick-up point for the ROK Marines was eight kilometers downriver at a river crossing east of a landmark we called the berm. While eight kilometers didn't sound like a long way to go, my tracks had to maneuver over several sandbars and a mudflat in order to get to the pick-up point. The Ky Lam also snaked and meandered in such a way that the northern banks along the Dodge City side of the river provided the NVA with potential ambush sites. The Kingfish'd emphasized that the main reason for moving the ROK Marines via water using tracks was to avoid the many new booby traps and mines that'd been planted across the Lay Ban area of Go Noi Island.

When I thought about those mines and booby traps, a feeling of frustration came over me. In the last weeks we had just completed a big, multi-battalion operation to literally level Go Noi Island. Now, within a matter of weeks, main force VC and NVA had managed to appear out of nowhere, undoing so much of what we'd accomplished. How had these VC been able to slip down into Go Noi to mine the Lay Ban area? Captain X was right. Someone had far underestimated VC strength. The numbers we'd been getting were bogus.

Wily gave me the okay to proceed and we splashed the tracks with One-Eight in the lead. Everything seemed to be working fine.

Then a CH-46 chopper landed. It was the chopper that was to take a sick Marine back up to Hill 55. Sergeant Chapelle was also on the chopper, coming back to the field after recovering from his injury. With Chapelle were two more track rats. These men were experienced water drivers.

Early that morning my company commander, Lieutenant Quick, had got word that we would be splashing our tracks and swimming down the Ky Lam River. He immediately grabbed two experienced water drivers who were hanging about the company area, Weiner Dog and Cornflake, and told them to get on the next chopper south. Luck was with me.

Weiner Dog was a tall, skinny kid about nineteen years old who had only fifteen days left to do in country. He had a narrow face with acne-scarred cheeks and a long skinny nose that made him look like a dachshund. His claim to fame was that he could fix anything mechanical. Back in the states he had been a hot rodder and had worked on dragsters. He never seemed to want to take a bath after fixing whatever he was fixing. There was always dirt under his fingernails and brown clumps of earwax in his ears. Weiner Dog was one of these guys who even when he had been scrubbed down seemed to have a dark cast over his body as if the grease seeped into his very pores.

In contrast, Cornflake was a rugged, clean-featured, blond athlete from Fairfield, Iowa. Cornflake had played linebacker at the University of Iowa for two years before flunking out. At six foot, maybe two hundred pounds, Cornflake didn't look big enough to be a starting Big Ten linebacker. But Cornflake was blessed with excellent hand and eye coordination. He could pitch a frag grenade farther than any one I had ever met, and he could run like a deer.

Needless to say, I was pleased. I was down to one driver per track. Both Cornflake and Weiner Dog inspired my confidence. They could be depended upon in a tight. Having Sergeant Chapelle back was another big plus.

Sergeant Chapelle had a great black and blue mark across his back where the cable had hit him. The doctors had said that there were no internal injuries. With that diagnosis, Chapelle returned to the field. I sensed that something'd changed. There was a new spark in Chapelle's eyes. His posture had changed. He was very alert. I wondered what these changes indicated.

"Lieutenant Gatlin! The Neshoba County Water Dog has returned!

I smiled and gave Chapelle a hug.

"Val Jean, I owe you an apology," I said.

"No sweat, Lieutenant. When we get off this island just help me make the run to the White Lotus."

I put Sergeant Chapelle on Track One-Zero. One-Zero was to bring up the rear. One-Eight would lead. Hog would drive One-Eight, which he was not happy about. Track One-Six was second, with Cornflake as the driver. Weiner Dog was third in line, driving One-Seven. A big and robust Samoan we called Pineapple drove One-Nine fourth in line. On an impulse I switched the fifty cal to One-Nine and asked the Gunny to man the fifty, due to his know-how and experience.

Shortly before we were about to splash our tracks, I felt that curious calm again come over me, that same feeling that I had experienced the night before while watching the stars and floating in the Ky Lam River. That part of me that had been so wired the day before now was floating.

*   *   *

Day Seven, 1100 hours

Ani Bui sat on top of Track One-Eight gazing down at me. When Captain X told her about the Lipske situation, she went right along with the Chou Hoi idea, much to his surprise. Ani understood the danger she and her brother were in; and she was more than cooperative, offering to act as a guide, pointing out potential ambush sites and heavily booby-trapped areas along the river. What an opportunity, I thought to myself, a kind of Yin and Yang. She explained to Captain X how the VC had been able to slip down into Go Noi to mine the Lay Ban area. According to Ani Bui, it was a network that worked under the direction of this Warehouse group. I told Ani Bui that when the time was right, we needed to talk further.

"Lieutenant, got a minute?" Sergeant Chapelle asked.

"Sure, Sergeant. What's up?" I said, snapping out of my daze.

"Oh, it's the men, Lieutenant. They think that we should have crossed back over to the Dodge City side of the river," Chapelle said. "They think this is suicide, staying on Go Noi with the few grunts we have."

"I can imagine how they must feel," I replied. "Especially after all the action we've seen in the last few days. I'll be honest with you, Sergeant. I'd feel a lot better if we crossed over to Dodge City, but we got a job to do hauling Korean Marines. That's our mission. There it is."

Chapelle seemed satisfied with my response. He was doing what he thought a responsible sergeant should do, which was to make me aware of my men's concerns. I was pleased with myself that I didn't overreact to his questioning. I was a reinvention in process, I thought to myself.

For some strange reason I flashed back to one of my college classes. It was spring of my junior year, and an old professor was going on about Odysseus, King of Ithaca, who after the Trojan War wandered for ten years before returning home, a journey marked by many changes of fortune. At one point, when his men are about to mutiny, Odysseus gives a speech that pulls everyone together. But I couldn't remember the content of that speech. I remember being more interested in the dark beauty sitting next to me than I was in the quest of Odysseus. I should have paid closer attention to the lecture.

We then splashed our tracks in the Ky Lam. As Track One-Eight entered the river its many tons created a huge bow wave. Surging forward into the shallows, One-Eight's momentum divided the swarm of catfish. Before the catfish could come back together in their great spiral movement, One-Six entered the river, further breaking up the circling swarm. Then One-Seven splashed and the catfish broke up into even smaller groups. Each track was nine feet high, eleven feet wide, and thirty-nine feet long, and as each churned forward it left in its wake a cloud of muddy sand and river detritus. By the time One-Nine and One-Zero entered the river, the swarm had lost its integrity. I was reminded of what our big operation had done to Go Noi Island, our many battalions and Rome Plows clearing the island of trees and bamboo and leveling all structures, impacting the land and the village culture that had once existed on Go Noi.

It appeared that the quick succession of tracks had messed up the circling behavior of the fish. Then something strange happened. As we headed down the river the swarm began to follow us. I looked back to see that the great swarm had again come together and was beginning to turn in that slow, spiral movement. The river was almost two hundred meters wide at that point. The plan was to keep to mid-river as much as possible in order to lessen the effect of any ambush. It didn't take long for the swarm to catch up to Track One-Zero. There the swarm stayed, turning in that slow, spiraling movement, a dark shadow just beneath the surface of the water.

I looked at the swarm as a mystery. It was, like so much in Vietnam, incomprehensible, a thing transcending the limits of all my previous experience. Certainly every event has a cause, an adequate reason why. I had often thought that nature was not a mere collection of events, a jumble of accidents. Nature was an orderly affair. Planets moved regularly in their orbits. Planted seeds grew uniformly into complex structures. The seasons succeeded each other in order. Everything conformed to a pattern governed by some law or principle.

So I looked at the swarm as part of the order of nature. I wondered if such patterns in nature assumed a designer or architect whose purpose it was to create all this; or if all coordinated activity of nature reflected a single, universal mind. Then it occurred to me that, strictly speaking, it was contradictory to speak of nature as possibly lacking order. Any situation, any arrangement among existing natural things constituted some kind of order.

Sure, I said to myself, there are laws that govern the planets and stellar events. There is a celestial order. On the other hand, from my perspective, down on the ground, there seemed to be no rhyme or reason to the distribution of the stars in the heavens. Each was unique, clear, and bright in its own truth, but unrevealing with respect to the grand scheme of the universe.

That was the Nam. What we had down at our level was disorder, and it was always difficult for me to justify how each death fit into some grand, meaningful scheme. In my state of mind, it was hard to see any rhyme or reason to the uncontrollable events that consumed our day-to-day existence.

Sergeant Chapelle stood on top of his track and stared at the swarm, his glazed eyes wide open. I thought of the Viet Cong who had appeared out of nowhere to plant those mines in the Lay Ban. I wondered how many of those Viet Cong were still hiding out there, waiting for us in Dodge City's tall bamboo hedgerows, much like this huge swarm of giant fish turning slow spirals in the murky waters of the Ky Lam River, their dark shadows hovering just beneath the surface.

*   *   *

CHAPTER NINE: ANI BUI

Day Seven, 1300 hours

On the broad Ky Lam River whole trees, washed down from the mountains during the monsoons, lay just below the surface. One-Eight climbed right up on such a snag and the weight of the track caused the entire tree to rise from the depths of the river. Tangled in the branches of the tree was the body of a Caucasian. As the track eased off of the trunk, the tree fell back into the water.

"Lieutenant, did you see that?"

"Most affirmative, Hog." I replied.

The Gunny directed One-Zero up on a nearby sand bar. I directed the other tracks to turn in a wide circle and headed back upriver to the sand bar. Once all the tracks'd parked on the sand bar, I jumped down and walked over to the Gunny.

"How are you going to get him, Lieutenant?" Hog called behind me.

"I don't know."

"Come on, Marines. Gimme me a hand with this rope," the Gunny said.

"Lieutenant, let me borrow your bolo. I'll need it."

"Sure, Gunny."

I handed the Gunny my prized knife. I didn't want to give it to him but I figured I had no choice. I was glad it was the Gunny and not myself swimming out to gather the body.

"Not much of a current here. I'll go in and get him," the Gunny said.

The Gunny stripped down to his waist and took off his boots. Tying a rope around his waist he waded out into the Ky Lam and swam out to where a few branches of the tree stuck above the surface of the water. Treading water for a few seconds, he then dove under...

The Gunny stayed under the water for almost a minute. He then surfaced, saying nothing. Once he got his breath, he dove again.

"I'm going out to help him," Hog said.

Hog stripped down and swam out to the tree. He made it to the branches just as the Gunny surfaced. Both men paddled about for a minute, talking out a plan. Then they dove together. They seemed to stay down over a minute.

Hog broke the surface with a gasp. The Gunny surfaced seconds later, waving to us.

"Pull the rope in!"

Six of us pulled the line in, dragging the body onto the sandbar. The body was relatively intact. My guess was that it hadn't been in the water that long. I noticed that Sergeant Chapelle's fingers were trembling.

"You okay, Sergeant," I asked.

"I don't know, sir," Chapelle said, lighting a cigarette.

"Here, time to break out some of Slammer's little pills. Take one of these. It will calm you down," I said.

"What is it, sir?"

"Some pills Slammer gave me for doping the kid. It's a sedative. They relax you."

"Beggin' your pardon, sir. I'd rather not. Everyone knows that Slammer goes up and down on pills. He may not smoke marijuana, but he's always popping some weird shit."

"Don't worry about it. If I didn't think it'd help, I wouldn't offer it up. It's something to carry you until we get back to Hill 55," I said.

"Lieutenant, what will the Gunny say if he sees me with these pills. You know how he is," Chapelle said.

"Yeah, I know. He goes crazy over any kind of dope. But I think we've all been getting a little crazy the last few days. I don't think that there is anything to worry about with these pills as long as a person doesn't go overboard and abuse this stuff. That's all."

"Okay, lieutenant," Chapelle said, swallowing the pill.

The little pill seemed to take effect quickly. In a matter of minutes, Chapelle's fingers stopped trembling.

I walked over to where the body lay. It was partially clothed. When we fished it out of the water the hands were still tied behind the back, and I wondered if this person had been alive when he had been thrown into the Ky Lam. The body's genitals were missing. It was clear that they'd been cut off. The first thing the Gunny had done, after we lay the body down, was to cut free the hands. Then we all stood around as the Gunny said a prayer.

The body lay at the water's edge while we waited for a chopper to pick it up. Since there was so much action all around Da Nang it took a long time to get a chopper. Finally, it was Captain X who agreed to come down to pick up the body.

Sergeant Chapelle informed me that Ani Bui knew the identity of the dead man. She had confided in Chapelle that this was a Special Forces soldier who had been captured in the mountains and brought to this area for interrogation. Ani remembered seeing him while he was still alive, and in the process of being transported through Dodge City, apparently to this place called the Warehouse . This information was invaluable in a number of ways. Given that the body was headed back to a very crowded morgue, identification of the remains would have been very difficult, if it happened at all. My guess was that this man was listed as missing. Captain X would be pleased that Ani Bui had been so forthcoming with these details. I would also make sure that Major Boden got this information back at the Special Forces camp at Marble Mountain.

While we were waiting for the chopper, thousands of white and yellow butterflies gathered along the water's edge. The butterflies began to land on the body, attracted by the ripe odor of decomposing flesh. Sergeant Chapelle, Hog, and I watched as hundreds of the butterflies descended to cover the body with a multicolored cloud of ivory and saffron. The vibrant butterflies became like a delicate, living shroud, landing everywhere on the body but the head. I noticed that the man's head was thrust backward, his neck muscles taut, his mouth gaping open in what must have been a final scream.

*   *   *

Day Seven, 1530 hours

We pulled our tracks out of the water at Cam Trung 2. The Korean Marines were waiting for us, having walked in from the east. I was surprised to see only a platoon. Captain X was also waiting at Cam Trung 2. He'd brought a grunt corporal who was called Propane. Propane had been sent over from Hoi An because he spoke enough Korean to get by. Propane called himself the gun master for the 106 recoilless rifle, which we graciously loaded on Track One-Nine. Captain X had picked Propane up in a chopper and hauled him out to Go Noi. It was that easy. I was beginning to have a greater and finer appreciation for Captain X. He'd also come through with a starlite scope that would help us see at night. It looked to me like he was making good with some of his big ideas.

"Lieutenant Kim, only a platoon. How about that?"

"I don't understand why Colonel Chai provides so few men," Kim replied.

"So few men also caught me by surprise. I was expecting more in the way of support. Colonel Chai must've had some other priority come up. I flew over at least a company of his Koreans further south, down at the foot of the Que Sons, near those My Son ruins," Captain X said.

"Strange. We have no operation going on that far south," Lieutenant Kim added.

"Shit happens. There's always competing priorities," I said.

I had an uneasy feeling as we finished loading and prepared to start back up the river. From this point our movement upriver would be slow because the river narrowed and the current grew stronger as a result. Looking through my binoculars, I thought I saw movement on the Dodge City side of the river. Along that side of the river the banks were steeper, and overhung with vegetation.

The narrow channel offered the VC a number of good ambush sites.

"Lieutenant, very bad along here. Number 10. Better watch out, easy for VC to shoot us," Ani Bui volunteered.

"I understand, Ani. You keep telling us what you can about hiding places, river crossings, weapons caches, any supply dumps. Captain X needs to know what you can remember."

"I help, and you take care of my brother?"

"Roger that, Ani. I'll make sure your brother is safe."

"Then I tell Captain X about big Warehouse in Dodge City. *Beaucoup* big supply dump."

"I bet you can show us."

"Too dangerous. Will show from chopper. Fly over."

"That will work. I'll tell Captain X. He'll be happy to hear that."

High thunderheads were building to the west. The occasional rumbles of thunder much like distant artillery. Maybe rain was on its way with the season's change. That would be some welcome relief from the heat.

"Monsoon coming. Better get to Warehouse before monsoon start.

"Roger that, Ani."

Oh yes, the monsoon, I thought. Our operations ground to a halt during the fall monsoon, a period usually preceded by the heavy buildup of cumulo-nimbus storm clouds over the mountain chain known as the Annamese Cordilleras. On Operation Oklahoma Hills we had gone into the mountains to deny the NVA their sanctuary. During that time several days of continuous rain had brought our activities to a halt. Socked in by the low cloud cover, I remember being stuck out on a firebase only a few kilometers from the Laotian border. At night it got so cold I had to wrap myself in two poncho liners to keep warm.

One morning I went out with a patrol to help a cherry lieutenant, a new guy with less than a week in country. Right off we entered a gigantic forest like no other I'd ever seen. This was triple canopy, where the trees soared, sometimes reaching a maximum diameter of four and five feet, with branches starting at fifty or sixty feet above us. The extraordinary height and spreading tops of the trees prevented the sun from penetrating to the ground. Under this shady canopy, vines thick as a man's thigh ran up the tree trunks to spread out their foliage in the sunlight above, adding to the darkness. There was little underbrush. Not enough sunlight reached the forest floor, where only a few, small, shade-loving plants grew. In places we were up to our waists in low clouds that had settled on the landscape and swirled around our legs as we walked through them.

We could move with ease among the massive trees, although we were soaking wet and chilled to the bone, winding in and out among the great trunks. Then we moved up a slope to find the terrain crisscrossed by game trails only a few inches wide, leaving just enough space for a wild animal, or a party of NVA to pass in single file. This gloomy forest was strangely silent, save for the distant call of an occasional bird.

The trail we were on continued upward until it reached the base of a steep cliff. For the better part of an hour, our patrol worked its way up the cliff face. Once we reached the top, we broke through the clouds, and the views were staggering. To the west, toward the Laotian border, the undulating green of the impenetrable forest stretched away as far as we could see. To the north, tight ravines tumbled down into rolling piedmont hills, thick with secondary forest. To the east, clouds of dense smoke rose, marking the spot where our Marines were in contact with the NVA. Beyond the rising smoke, I caught the sun glint off the tail of a plane heading northward. Whichever way I turned my eye, I was confronted by a vast landscape broken by deep solemn valleys and rugged rocky outcrops that rose above the green expanse, and my gaze became lost in the hazy, immeasurable distances that melted into the monsoon clouds gathering on the horizon.

Within this impenetrable sanctuary, the hidden base camps and supply dumps numbered in the hundreds. I couldn't help but be overwhelmed by the scale of the task before us. Clearly we didn't have enough resources to accomplish our mission. How could a few battalions corner the enemy in all that vastness? Our enemy simply fled before us, avoiding contact whenever possible. For a time we lingered, finally withdrawing just before the monsoon arrived, and the endless rains set in.

Now we were trying to deny the enemy sanctuary on a much smaller scale, Go Noi Island being some fourteen kilometers long, and from two to three kilometers wide at any given point. By comparison, what we were trying to do along the Laotian border with the resources we had at hand at the time, now seemed ludicrous.

At the close of Operation Oklahoma Hills I was asked to assist a Marine major on an air recon along the Laotian border. The area we covered ranged from the Ken Valley down to a place called Ngok Tavak, near the abandoned Kham Duc Special Forces Camp. The camp had originally been built for President Diem who enjoyed hunting in the area. The Dak Mi River flowed past the camp into a narrow grassy plain, with the long Ngok Peng Bum Ridge stretching to the west, and the towering Ngok Pe Xar Mountain looming to the east.

Based upon reports from our Recon Marines, the major was going to recommend a B-52 strike of the area.

Down in the wet, grassy plain I spotted something moving. At first I thought it was a water buffalo.

"Major, check out the water buffalo down in that little valley. Where there's a water buffalo, there's probably gooks," I said, motioning for our pilot to circle back. "That's no water buffalo, Lieutenant Gatlin. I'll be damned if it isn't a rhino, one of those rare forest species. I didn't realize they were so hairy," the major said. "It's got a calf with it," I pointed out.

We circled several times, watching the mother rhino and her calf cross the grassy plain and disappear into the wilderness, following a steep banked stream gushing down from Ngok Pe Xar Mountain. The major later decided against calling in the B-52 strike. His rationale was that if the mother rhino frequented that grassy plain, it was unlikely that NVA were in the area. Clearly he was a decent man, one who was also concerned about preserving the remnant of a rare species.

"Lieutenant, Ani Bui no VC! You take care of Ani and her brother! Ok? But you watch out. Maybe VC come to get Ani tonight."

"Holy shit," I whispered to myself, snapping out of my daze.

Of course, if VC hiding along the river had seen Ani Bui traveling with us, we were sure to have visitors. They would target Ani for elimination. Why didn't I think of that earlier?

Ani Bui's warning had me looking at the map. Just upriver I remembered passing the landmark we called the berm. The berm was all that was left of the railroad crossing that used to connect Da Nang with the south. Some twenty feet high and designed to protect the railroad from the Ky Lam's periodic flooding, the berm cut Go Noi Island in two. My plan was to use the berm as a defensive position for the night. From our high ground on the berm we could overlook two shallow river crossings. We would have excellent fields of fire and could utilize the recoilless rifle if necessary.

*   *   *

Day Seven, 1800 hours

Late afternoon found us digging at the berm. The Gunny had Propane mount the recoilless on top of the berm with the river at his back. We then placed two tracks west of the berm and three tracks east of the berm. The tracks were situated so that they had excellent fields of fire.

I sat in One-Eight pouring over the map, checking coordinates for prearranged artillery fire. Hair Trigger copied the coordinates down on a series of cards and had the cards passed out to Kim and the Gunny. In the process of checking out One-Eight's radios, Hair Trigger discovered Hog's spider. A tiny lizard had tangled itself in the spider's web. Soon we had the track full of Marines watching in fascination as the huge spider did a job on the tiny lizard. Ani Bui let out a howl at the sight of the spider. When Hog picked up the little lizard and offered it up to Ani, she slapped him, much to everyone's amusement. I had been prudent enough to take my trophy hand from behind the radio mount and hide it in a wooden ammo box. I couldn't tell you why the hand was still there.

*   *   *

Day Seven, 2000 hours

"So why do they call you Propane?" the Gunny asked.

"Because I'm a gas, Gunny," Propane replied, smiling.

"That right. Just be sure that you ain't one of these pot smokers. As long as you're burning beans and not marijuana we'll be fine. If you be a pot head, Propane, I'll be all over you like flies on shit," the Gunny said.

At that comment Propane looked shocked. He raised his eyebrows and looked at me. I shrugged my shoulders to say that there was nothing I could do. This was the Gunny. There it is, I thought.

Propane got up and went back to cleaning the recoilless rifle. The Gunny turned to me and just smiled. I walked down the berm to the edge of the river. The Gunny followed. Together we were plotting coordinates for protective artillery fire.

"Gunny, try to show some sympathy. Go easy on Propane," I said.

"Sympathy! The only place I know to find sympathy around these parts is back up on Hill 55, Lieutenant."

"What? Why do you say that?"

"Because that's where the nearest dictionary is, Lieutenant."

"You lost me, Gunny."

"The only place that you will find sympathy in Nam is in the First Sergeant's dictionary, Lieutenant."

"I see."

"And do you know where you will find it, Lieutenant?"

"No, Gunny. Tell me."

"Between shit and syphilis, Lieutenant," the Gunny said, spitting on the ground and walking away.

*   *   *

Day Seven, 2030 hours

I sat in One-Eight watching the oncoming darkness to the east. It was very still. Across the Ky Lam flowers were blooming and the fragrance passed over the water to our position. To the west, the sun had dropped behind the mountains, the afterglow reflecting off great cumulus clouds. Out on the Ky Lam, bank-swallows circled above the river, occasionally dipping down to skim the surface of the flow.

I got up and walked to the river. Lieutenant Kim was standing by the bank looking out at the water. Below, where the river current carried them close to the riverbank, hundreds of dead giant catfish were floating by, belly-up in the water. Others, near death, drifted by gulping for air, their movements at the mercy of the river current. I assumed these fish were part of the great swarm that we had encountered further upriver.

"Looks like the fish are all dying," I said.

"Ah, yes. I'm guessing that some chemical agents polluted this section of the river, or maybe residue from the heavy rain in the mountains, all of it washing down to the Go Noi. With all the Agent Orange sprayed in the mountains, something like this was inevitable," Kim replied.

"Yes, something like this was inevitable," I said.

*   *   *

Day Seven, 2100 hours

On the way back to One-Eight I picked up Half-Pint and put him on my shoulders. Ani Bui liked that. We discovered that the little guy had this thing for the beans and weenies from our C rations. He just kept putting them away. So he and I walked around the area talking to the men, scrounging all the cans of beans and weenies we could. Everyone thought it was real cool.

The action was hot and heavy over in the Arizona Territory to the west. The sky was lit up by the action as various elements of the Fifth Marines engaged the enemy.

"*Beaucoup* action over in Arizona," Ani Bui said.

"I wonder what it all means?" I said.

"We should cross to other side of the river, Lieutenant. This spot number 10, *beaucoup* bad," Ani said again.

"With all that's going down," Hair Trigger said, "it will be hard to get choppers tonight,"

"Roger that," Hog said, "I'm just glad we got Captain X. When the shit goes down we will need somebody who's not afraid to go into a hot LZ."

"Maybe Ani's right, Lieutenant," Hair Trigger said, "Maybe we should pull across the river into Dodge City. There's a place to ford the river a bit upstream."

"Never happen. The gooks would be watching that ford. Anyway, we got to keep our presence on the Go Noi side of the river. Major Hopkins is right when he says that being on this side of the river allows us to move around, more ability to maneuver," I said.

"Well, I don't know, Lieutenant. I'd be listening to Ani," Hog said.

"All we got to remember is to stand together back-to-back *when the shit goes down*, and it will go down," Hair Trigger said.

*   *   *

Day Seven, 2300 hours

I got up and walked to the top of the berm. Lieutenant Kim and the Gunny were scanning the area with the starlight scope, which allowed one to see in the dark as long as there was starlight. The starlight scope turned dark shadows into various images of eerie green light. It looked like a large telephoto lens, and worked by detecting faint reflections of starlight, magnifying them several times to produce an image. With a little training, one could pick out human forms moving up to two hundred meters away. From our vantage point on top of the berm it was an invaluable tool.

"So what keeps you going, Gunny?" I found myself saying, trying to make conversation.

"Going? Well, believe it or not, I like what I'm doing, Lieutenant. And I want to be remembered as a professional. Over twenty years in *the crotch,* and that's all I want and that's all I'm looking forward to. If I check out, I want to die knowing that I did my all to be remembered as a Marine's Marine. That's enough for me, and I don't give shit on what side of the river I die," the Gunny said with a smile.

"C'mon, Gunny. Sounds like you don't care if you live or if you die," I said.

"All my good friends have already bought the farm, Lieutenant... But I don't have no death wish. If I pull the wild card and die tonight, or tomorrow, I have no regrets. All I ask of myself is that I follow in the best traditions of the U. S. Marine Corps, taking as many gooks as I can with me. There it is. That's my philosophy. Hard core to the end," the Gunny said, spitting tobacco juice on the ground.

*   *   *

Day Eight, 0100 hours

Da Nang was being rocketed. Over twenty 122mm free-flight rockets were dropping throughout the Naval Support Activity area... Ani said it was the 68B NVA Rocket Artillery unit that was launching the rockets, and her volunteering that information was once more a good sign, another important indication of her willingness to cooperate with us. Hair Trigger had called in her information to Captain X to pass on to Major Hopkins.

Easily carried through the Dodge City area and assembled with little difficulty, both the 140mm and 122mm could be fired from either an earthen ramp, or a pair of forked sticks driven into the ground. The rockets were aimed by just pointing them in the direction of Da Nang. All that was necessary was elevating them to the correct angle for the desired range, and, naturally, salvos of these rockets often fell upon innocent civilians.

From our position on the berm we watched as Puff the Magic Dragon circled over the rocket launch site, sending down a steady stream of fire.

*   *   *

Day Eight, 0200 hours

Sergeant Chapelle and Ani Bui joined Lieutenant Kim and myself on the top of the berm… Chapelle had taken it upon himself to bird dog Ani, which freed me up from having to monitor her. Chapelle lit one of his strong cigarettes and offered it to Ani. She took it and smiled. Lieutenant Kim, who had not eaten, opened a can of Korean rations. It was what he called cuttlefish, another name for squid. He offered Ani a bite. She then ate the whole can. Cuttlefish tastes like a piece of baloney that had dried out in the refrigerator, but Kim claimed it was very good for you.

Ani spoke English well enough to make her needs and wishes known. She seemed very bright, having learned her English from a Combined Action Platoon that stayed for a time in her village.

"I like where Marines live in villages. That is *bea coup good*," she said, eating a bit of cuttlefish. "Must live in the villages to understand what must be done."

Lieutenant Kim opened another can of ROK rations. It was a can of that hot, pickled cabbage, *kim chi*. He offered some of the red, translucent strands to Chapelle and Ani.

Chapelle declined. Ani ate the whole can. Then she and Chapelle walked over to the river to wash out his mess kit.

"This Captain Chan called me on the radio. He say that this man, Seeker Six, wants him to bring in Ani Bui. Chan say you Marines need to be more flexible. Chan going to try to take Ani from you," Kim said, making sure that Ani was out of earshot.

"That right? Thank you for warning me."

"Yes. I was also told to be more flexible. So, you understand I will have to stay out of way."

"I understand. I'll get Captain X involved."

"Good idea. But Captain X vulnerable to this Seeker Six," Kim said.

"You don't think Captain X has any clout with this Chan?"

"I'm not sure about that. Chan take money from Seeker Six. I think Chan think money more important than Ani Bui and her little brother."

"I know Seeker Six, and he is no one to fuck with. But I'm not giving up Ani and Half Pint. There it is. You worried, Lieutenant Kim?"

"Yes. Chan very tough guy, and he say this Seeker Six is like the shadow of a cloud that moves across the land," Kim replied.

*   *   *

Day Eight, 0230 hours

The Gunny and the ROK platoon sergeant checked the perimeter. Sergeant Chapelle took Ani back to his track. He was acting as her protector, and I sensed a growing bond between them.

Tracks One-Eight and One-Nine were on the west side of the berm. Pineapple had One-Nine and Hog had One-Eight. The Gunny was to join Hog at the west side of our perimeter. Sergeant Chapelle would anchor the east side of the perimeter on One-Zero. Backing Chapelle were Weiner Dog on One-Seven and Cornflake on One-Six. Each of the track drivers had a track rat with them for backup. All of these backups were cherry privates who had little or no experience.

Counting Slammer I had eleven track rats. Add the Gunny, Hair Trigger, myself, and Propane, and the total of U.S. Marines came to sixteen. There were thirty-six in the ROK Marine platoon, including Lieutenant Kim who had assumed command.

I had decided to place myself on top of the berm with Lieutenant Kim, Hair Trigger and Propane. The Gunny and I had agreed that he would make the rounds till 0300 hours. After 0300, I would make the rounds, checking the tracks to ensure that one man was awake on each vehicle through the night.

Just after 0230 hours, the Gunny was making his rounds when he caught Ani Bui and Sergeant Chapelle making time in the bunker on top of One-Seven. The Gunny immediately started yelling at Chapelle, announcing to everyone the circumstances, much to the amusement of the men and the embarrassment of Ani Bui. At that moment, the Gunny gave Chapelle the nickname of *Gook Lover*, broadcasting a general order out into the darkness that from that time on everyone was to address Chapelle as Sergeant Gook Lover.

*   *   *

Day Eight, 0430 hours

Just before daybreak, the action started again over in the Arizona Territory to our west. It wasn't long before the sky was lit up by illumination, making the starlight scope difficult to use. Kim had been scanning the terrain prior to the illumination and he was sure that we had movement out in front of us. Kim and I monitored the action on one radio while Hair Trigger kept on the Mike Company frequency.

No sooner'd things died down in the Arizona when the NVA began to mortar Mike Company. Mike Company was dug in at Bao An Tay, overlooking that crossing site.

Bao An Tay was a good two kilometers away. I wished Wily luck. He would need it. From our vantage point we could see all the action as the enemy walked mortars through Mike Company. About that time our listening posts began calling in movement all around us. Kim called in the listening posts and alerted our perimeter.

The mortar fire raining down on Mike Company went on for about three minutes. I had a bad feeling that Wily's men were getting mauled. Then it was our turn. The Koreans covered up in their fighting holes as the first rounds came down. Track One-Seven took a direct mortar hit on top but luck was with Sergeant Chapelle and Ani Bui. Both of them had dropped down inside the track when the first mortars began to fall.

When the mortar fire let up I heard whistles. I'd heard such whistles before on my previous tour when a large group of NVA had charged my position. My left hand began to tremble. I pulled my bolo and stuck the knife in the ground beside me. I grabbed the handle of my bolo with my left hand and held on to the handle.

Hair Trigger was already on the radio calling in prearranged arty fire around us. Propane loaded a beehive round in the 106 recoilless rifle, ready to cut loose to our immediate front.

Within seconds the first battery of 105's had rounds on the way. The NVA must've sensed what was up because a barrage of RPGs came next, drilling One-Nine and One-Eight. Although hot slag from the RPGs spun around inside the vehicles, miraculously no track rats were hit. All the track rats were either hunkered down in bunkers on top of the tracks, or in holes dug along the inner sides.

The artillery fire slammed around us, churning up the earth, and creating a smoky haze. Through that haze some fifteen NVA charged our perimeter from the riverbank to our west. Using the cover of the riverbank, these NVA had crawled too close to us for our artillery to be effective against them. Hog immediately engaged them with M-60 machine gun fire, the ROK Marines surrounding his position holding their fire.

At the same time another twenty-some NVA rose up along the berm to our immediate front, and charged in a human wave, the heavy volume of their AK-47 fire forcing us to keep down in our fighting holes. The NVA closed rapidly. When Propane fired the 106 recoilless rifle with its beehive round containing thousands of tiny nails, the NVA couldn't have been more than fifty feet from our fighting holes. The beehive round stopped the oncoming rush of the NVA cold. The line of NVA simply disappeared.

Hog let out a rebel yell. When I turned to thank Propane, I found that he had been shot in the head. I jumped to my feet, loaded the 106, and fired again, catching a few dazed NVA who were straggling off into the darkness. I yelled for Slammer but there was no response. Propane never regained consciousness. I pulled him down into a fighting hole and continued on.

Hair Trigger continued to direct arty around us. Illumination soon burst overhead, and I could see that the west edge of our perimeter was in trouble. The NVA had penetrated the perimeter and overwhelmed One-Eight. Hog lay sprawled across the track's bunker. The Gunny was at the machine gun, clearing a jam. He had cleared the jam and was raising the weapon to fire when he was knocked backwards by a burst of AK-47 fire.

All around the base of the One-Eight ROK Marines had engaged the enemy at point blank range and bodies of both NVA and ROKs lay mingled together. Track One-Nine was starting to smoke, apparently from an RPG hit. One-Nine was known to have a leaky gas tank. If those leaky gas tanks exploded we would have a bonfire that folks on Hill 55 could see, some twelve kilometers away.

Pineapple, the big Samoan on Track One-Nine, jumped to the ground and ran to where the Gunny lay. I sprang to my feet and started to run down the berm. An RPG burst to my left, tossing me through the air like a leaf.

I flipped through the air and came down on top of a ROK machine gun. Both ROK machine gunners were dead from the RPG blast. I knew that I had seriously hurt my back but the adrenalin was flowing, and I grabbed the gun. I stumbled forward to Track One-Nine where Pineapple's cherry driver came to my aid. Together we positioned the machine gun in an empty fighting hole and Pineapple's cherry swept the riverbank, covering Pineapple's movement toward the Gunny.

Pineapple reached the Gunny who was stunned but otherwise conscious. The AK-47 rounds had impacted his flak jacket, sparing him. Pineapple began dragging the dazed Gunny back to our hole. A chicom grenade flew through the air toward them, flickering like a sparkler. Pineapple reached up, caught the chicom, and flipped it back toward the river. It exploded with a dull whump.

Then I saw Slammer run through the crossfire. Without hesitating he leaped aboard One-Eight and grabbed the unconscious Hog. Slammer dragged Hog across the top of the track, rounds zipping and pinging all around both of them. Another chicom arched through the air. It landed on the far side of One-Eight and exploded. Slammer and Hog fell over the side of the track and hit the ground. Out of nowhere an NVA rose up from the pile of bodies and stuck a bayonet into Slammer's chest. Slammer gasped. We cut the NVA in two with a sustained burst of the M-60.

At that point Pineapple reached our fighting hole with the Gunny. We pulled the Gunny into our fighting hole as green and red tracers zipped all around us, and I was amazed that Pineapple had made it through. If the Gunny had drawn a wild card that night it was surely a lucky one.

Pineapple got up and ran back to get Hog. Somehow I found myself noticing that the big Samoan, who didn't like to wear shoes because the Marine Corps had trouble finding double EEs for him to wear, was running barefooted. He picked up Hog like he was a baby and hauled him back to the cover of our fighting hole. Hog was unconscious.

An RPG flew over our heads toward the recoilless, and scored a direct hit. I saw Lieutenant Kim running down the berm to our position, dragging Hair Trigger behind them.

From the way Hair Trigger's head was hanging I feared he was history.

When Lieutenant Kim reached our position my fears were confirmed. Kim handed me the radio and I took over talking to Hill 55. Kim grabbed two ROK Marines and ran over to One-Eight to plug the hole. ROK and NVA bodies were scattered everywhere.

The tracks and men on the east side of the berm hadn't fired a shot. For some reason the enemy concentrated the attack along the top of the berm and from the west, along the riverbank. We'd stopped the rush from the west. Our only worry was the berm.

The ROK sergeant, Sergeant Hun, scrambled to the top of it with three ROK Marines. There was a brief exchange of fire from the top. Then everything went silent. In the distance, I could hear the action at Bao An Tay... Mike Company was still in contact. Sergeant Hun waved to me from the top of the berm. Just as abruptly as it started, our firefight was over.

There was a sudden bright flash as One-Nine's gas tanks exploded, and a great fireball lit up the night sky, rising at least fifty feet.

*   *   *

Day Eight, 0530 hours

My ears rang. A burning One-Nine lit up the dawn. The air was filled with a smoky haze from the artillery and our burning track. When I called Hill 55 to check artillery fire and to request an evacuation for our wounded, I was informed that chopper support was a problem, that the shit was again hitting the fan all around the greater Da Nang area. I bitched that I had both dead Marines and six seriously wounded. Hill 55 said that they would see what they could do. No sooner had I got off the radio than Captain X's chopper was overhead. He'd guided in on our burning track.

Captain X made three flights back and forth to Hill 55. All our wounded made it out, including the Gunny. I put Ani Bui and her brother on the last chopper. Major Hopkins sent word that he would bring a last chopper in for our KIAs.

"Captain X, Ani told me she can point out the location of this Warehouse from the air. I asked her to try and find it on my map but she kept pointing to an area south of Route 4."

"No way, Lieutenant Gatlin. Hopkins says the Warehouse is probably in the vicinity of Giang La. Yeah, the VC you captured told Seeker Six that the Warehouse was near La Huan and Giang La. That's north of Route 4," the captain said, shaking his head.

"Well, it doesn't hurt to check it out. But we got another problem. Kim tells me that Seeker Six is putting pressure on this Captain Chan to take Ani from us. Probably best to get Ani and Half Pint out of Go Noi."

"I don't like this continued interest in Ani. I'll take Ani with me but I'm reluctant to keep her back in Dien Ban District Headquarters. I've got a growing concern that my PRU Team, which is paid by that *certain agency* of yours, can no longer be trusted."

"No need to go any further with that. I fully understand. Let's take them up to Bo Boden at the Marble Mountain SOG camp for safekeeping. Bo will take them. He owes me a favor or two. Tell him I'll have them picked up once I get back to Hill 55."

"I'll try that. In the meantime watch out for this Chan."

"Roger that. Good luck finding this Warehouse ."

After the chopper left, I walked to the top of the berm and found my bolo where I had left it, stuck in the earth. For a moment I was afraid that I had lost the knife. But there it was. I slipped the knife back into its sheath. I noticed Lieutenant Kim was watching me. I turned and offered him a drink from my canteen. I couldn't think of anything to say.

*   *   *

CHAPTER TEN: THE KATU

Day Eight, 0600 hours

We got the word that Mike Company had taken nine dead and twenty-two wounded... The word came from Captain X who had flown to Mike Company's position just after the Kingfish. Captain X said that the Kingfish had relieved Lieutenant Wily on the spot. That angered all of us since it was the Kingfish who had insisted on keeping all of us on the Go Noi side of the river in the first place. The Kingfish didn't even give Wily time to pack his gear. He just ordered him on the first chopper back to Hill 55. Thus ended Lieutenant Wily's tour as a company commander, a real shame, for up to that point Wily was thinking about making the Marine Corps a career.

*   *   *

Day Eight, 0630 hours

True to his word Major Hopkins flew in to assess the damage and pick up our dead. One-Nine was a smoldering, burnt-out hull. Slammer and Propane were in body bags, ready for departure. The effect of their deaths had yet to sink in on the men. They went about their duties saying nothing, distracted. For the time being they seemed to have their heads on straight. They had survived.

Hog was evacuated with a concussion, as was Pineapple's cherry driver due to nasty shrapnel wounds. The ROKs had five KIA and twelve WIA. All told we had eleven Marines and seventeen ROKs left to cover the river crossing.

I sat back and reflected in the relative coolness of the track. There were four RPG holes through the port side of the track. When an RPG hits a track the point of the projectile melts through the steel, sending hot slag into the target. A lot of hot slag from the RPGs had whipped through the inside of One-Eight and it appeared that Hog's spider was history. The intricate web, woven between Hog's radios and communication equipment, was no more. The hand still floated in the pickle jar. The pickle jar, hidden behind the radio mount, somehow survived the storm of hot slag. Major Hopkins walked up to the track. I tried to muster a smile.

"Sorry that the Kingfish didn't come down himself. He got called up to Hill 55. The shit is still hitting the fan all over the Dai Loc map sheet."

"I understand, sir."

"I expect the Kingfish to be down sometime later in the morning. In the meantime you should prepare to swim back across the river to Dodge City."

"Major Hopkins, my tracks, especially One-Eight, can't swim because of the RGP holes."

"We could abandon it."

"Never happen, sir. One-Eight is full of all kinds of fancy communications equipment for tracking our sensors."

"Well Lieutenant, do you have a recommendation?"

I couldn't believe it. Hopkins was asking me for a recommendation, and he never once mentioned Ani Bui. Captain X must have made my position on Ani very clear to Major Hopkins.

"Major, the only thing we can do is to try to go overland."

"That will take you through the Lay Ban mine field," Hopkins said.

"I don't know of any other way we can go from here. We can't swim the tracks to go back the way we came, and I can't leave One-Eight behind."

"And you won't agree to destroy the track. Call in an air strike on it?"

"No deal, Major. If I have to, I'll call my company commander, Lieutenant Quick, to back me."

"Oh, yes, the infamous Lieutenant Quick. He's certain to scream loud enough for all the higher-ups in Division to hear him. Okay, Lieutenant Gatlin, we will do it your way."

Needless to say none of my men were high on the idea of driving out through the east end of Go Noi. Sergeant Chapelle just shook his head and looked off into the distance. At one point he turned and his eyes caught mine. I noticed that he was popping a couple of Slammer's little pills.

* * *

Day Eight, 0800 hours

The operation was over. Someone made a decision and just like that the word came down for us to get off Go Noi Island. Mike Company choppered out in a matter of an hour. Across the river from Mike Company's old position, the Kingfish ordered Lima Company in to cover the river crossing, only this time on the Dodge City side of the river. With eleven U.S. Marine track rats, and seventeen Korean Marines, we were going to cross the eastern length of Go Noi Island to the Korean Bridge before nightfall. Good luck, I thought to myself. Between us and the Korean Bridge lay ten kilometers of muddy ground, the Lay Ban mine field, and who knew what else.

* * *

Day Eight, 0830 hours

When Hopkins finally realized that I wasn't going to blow up One-Eight, and that there was a high probability that one of my tracks would hit a mine going through the eastern part of Go Noi Island, he had me call all the men together.

"You men did a hell of job! What you did last night at the berm, and what you have been doing the last few days serves as a positive example to all those in the First Marine Regiment," he said, like a true major of Marines. "When you get back up to Hill 55, I'm going to buy all the beer you men can drink! God bless you and I'll see you up on Hill 55!"

After that speech, my track rats were ready to go anywhere. Major Hopkins had a long history of being hard-nosed, and that made his praise of the track rats all the more meaningful to them. Here was Major Hopkins taking time to tell track rats that they had done good. It was a change for the better.

I noticed a tear in the corner of Sergeant Chapelle's eye as Major Hopkins finished his speech. I wondered if Chapelle could keep it together. It was a long way to the Korean Bridge.

"Well, what are you thinking, Val Jean?"

"A real waste, Lieutenant. It was all a real waste. Hog and Ani were right. We should have crossed to the other side of river."

* * *

Day Eight, 0900 hours

Before Hopkins left, to head back up to Hill 55, he pulled me aside.

"How do you feel about the support that you've been getting from Captain X?"

"Sir, I'm grateful that someone comes through with chopper support when we need it."

Hopkins said nothing in reply. He just looked off in the distance.

"Why, sir? Is there a problem?" I asked.

"I don't know, Lieutenant Gatlin. This guy is something else. He seems to get into everyone's business."

I didn't reply. I just smiled.

* * *

Day Eight, 0930 hours

I asked Sergeant Chapelle to drive One-Eight. He accepted, saying that he was the Neshoba Water Dog and he could drive anything. Chapelle promptly painted *Neshoba Water Dog Goin' Home* on the side of One-Eight.

If he had not accepted, I wouldn't have ordered him to drive the track. I would have driven it myself. For one had to be careful with track rats when a track's driver had been killed or wounded. Track rats were a superstitious lot, given to irrational attitudes concerning things like magic, the supernatural, and bad luck, and few track rats were willing to take a track once the driver had been hurt. While Sergeant Chapelle wasn't happy about taking One-Eight, I knew he did it to please me.

One-Eight would lead, followed by Wiener Dog driving One-Seven, and Cornflake still on One-Six. I asked Pineapple if he would bring up the rear with One-Zero, while I rode One-Eight with Chapelle. It was all set. Then, just as we were about to move out, a chopper appeared overhead. As soon as the chopper touched the ground Colonel Chai jumped from his chopper followed by two Korean Marine officers.

"*Colonel Chai!*" Lieutenant Kim said.

The colonel wanted to see for himself the great stand his ROK Marines had made at the berm. He was smiling and very upbeat. When he smiled his eyes twinkled and, with his snow-white hair, he reminded me of a burly Korean Santa Claus. Colonel Chai must have been pushing about fifty, but he looked very fit. Kim said his only vice was that he liked young women. Chai had a different one every night. Some nights he had more than one, most of them Chinese women flow up from Saigon by none other than Miss Swan.

Captain Chan, on the other hand, was not so happy. We had taken too many casualties, and he immediately inquired as to the whereabouts of Ani Bui. When Kim told him that Ani had left with Captain X, Chan walked off in a huff, laying down the law that there would be no more Korean casualties. Kim simply nodded, and replied that if we did sustain any ROK wounded, *they would not be evacuated* without Captain Chan's approval. Captain Chan spit on the ground and gave me a dirty look.

It seems the ROKs had certain limits for the number that could be wounded or killed in a given operation, limits set by the Korean Marine general. When the ROKs reached the limit, Kim said that they simply stopped operating. Under no circumstances did one allow the limits to be exceeded. Colonel Chai could do nothing to change these limits. I pointed out to Kim the obvious, that we were on Go Noi Island and such things were beyond his control. He just nodded and reaffirmed that the limits must not be exceeded.

*   *   *

Day Eight, 1000 hours

The chopper flew Colonel Chai and Captain Chan back to Hoi An. When Kim turned away from the departing chopper, he set two cases of cold Blue Ribbon on the ground. Sergeant Chapelle distributed the beer, and before I knew it, I had pounded down three cold beers.

"We did the right thing with Ani Bui and her brother," Kim said.

"Roger that."

"I wanted to have a word with you in private."

"About Ani?"

"No. Captain X told Colonel Chai that we have a big opportunity evolving in Dodge City. Captain Chan is very unhappy that Colonel Chai listens to Captain X. This has caught everyone on Captain Chan's staff by surprise."

"Tell me more."

"Captain X tells Colonel Chai that the NVA are playing by new rules. The NVA have left their sanctuaries and are striking back at us in a way that is very innovative," Kim continued.

"Innovative. Interesting word. Okay, I'm listening,"

"The NVA are moving along the boundaries of the Korean and U.S. tactical responsibility areas."

"Smart move on the part of the NVA."

"Yes. Captain X told Colonel Chai that if the NVA are exploiting the boundaries between the various areas of tactical responsibility, then we best communicate better among ourselves rather than depend upon the First Marine Division and the Korean Regimental hierarchy to give us direction. Chai calls Captain X a loose cannon."

"But it appears that we can depend upon Colonel Chai to support Captain X."

"Of that I am certain, and I agree with Captain X. It's obvious that your Major Hopkins is very frustrated. He sits up on Hill 55, the highest point in Dodge City, and overlooks the obvious," Kim said, shaking his head.

"And that is?" I asked.

"Simply, that the NVA are exploiting the boundaries, and the rules and procedures that limit how we operate among ourselves. But there is more. Based on the prisoner interrogations, Seeker Six tells Chan that the Viet Cong have stashed considerable supplies at a place code-named the Warehouse. Chan is very ambitious. He would like to find this Warehouse."

"I've already heard of the Warehouse. Captain X thinks that it is within the Giang La area."

"Lieutenant Gatlin, we have always had a buffer zone between the First Marine Regiment's area and the ROK Marine's area. That buffer zone existed so that we wouldn't kill each other with friendly fire. Now it seems the Warehouse is located somewhere within that buffer zone."

"Yes, I think that's true. The question for us is what to do about it. I believe our Colonel Humpski will provide some answers to that question."

"The one they call the Hump."

"That's him."

*   *   *

Day Eight, 1100 hours

We headed out, moving directly east. For two kilometers there was a sandy flat. The flat was easy going. After the flat we reached a creek that flowed northeast out of the heart of the Go Noi. We followed the creek to where it entered the Ky Lam River. There we paused to take a break.

At that point the Ky Lam River is about 500 meters wide. A long, fifty-meter wide sandbar runs for about two hundred meters parallel to the south bank of the Ky Lam. The distance from the south bank of the Ky Lam to the sandbar is about 50 meters. Thousands of dead catfish were floating belly-up in the channel between the sandbar and the south bank of the Ky Lam. Hundreds of sea gulls had gathered in a great flock, flying upriver from the South China Sea to scavenge upon the dead.

Since the sandbar was so flat, and due to the fact that we could sweep the area with machine gun fire at will, I didn't think that we were in jeopardy. With all the sea gulls around, things seemed safe. Then the crack of a sniper round proved me wrong.

The sniper round caught Weiner Dog in the shoulder. A few inches to the right and Weiner Dog would have had a sucking chest wound. Our machine guns opened up, sweeping the sand bar from one end to another. The hundred-some sea gulls rose into the air, obscuring our vision, startled into flight by our firing.

Within a minute I had a fire mission on the way from Hill 55. For another five minutes I walked 105's up and down the sand bar to make sure our sniper had bought the farm. When the smoke cleared, the sand bar was littered with dead gulls.

Once again we had trouble getting a chopper to evacuate Weiner Dog. Hell, it was the middle of the afternoon. Where were our Marine choppers? True to form, it was Captain X who flew in to pick up Weiner Dog.

During the firing, Captain Chan called Kim and demanded to know if there were any ROK Marine casualties. Kim replied that there were not and that things were under control.

*   *   *

Day Eight, 1300 hours

We struck east, crossing a narrow neck of ground where we had clear field of fire. By 1330 we had reached the old village site of Cam Lau Trung. There our tracks had to negotiate piles of rubble that had been left behind by the land-clearing operations of the previous weeks. This kind of mixed rubble was particularly hard on the suspension systems of amphibian tractors, so we had to pick our way through a maze of broken timbers and partially leveled walls. We were almost through when One-Six broke track.

Lieutenant Kim sent his ROKs out to secure a perimeter while my track rats began the dirty business of fixing the problem. Captain Chan was monitoring our radio traffic. When I reported our situation up to Hill 55, Chan got nervous and called Kim, ragging on him about keeping security tight.

It took us an hour to fix the track. When we were done, Cornflake tried to crank One-Six's engine only to find that the track's starter had burned out. This was serious. I didn't want to spend another night on Go Noi, especially in the exposed position that we now found ourselves in. Somehow I had to get a starter to Go Noi as soon as possible. Replacing a starter was about an hour's worth of work.

I called back up to Hill 55. Hill 55 had no starters, but called back to our home battalion, Third Tracks. Third Tracks had starters but there was no way to get one down to Go Noi. As usual chopper transportation was both the problem and the solution. Hill 55 tried to contact Captain X to see if he could accommodate us with his personal chopper. The word came back that Captain X was in Da Nang getting his chopper serviced. For the time being we would just have to wait.

While we were waiting, Sergeant Chapelle said that he wanted to take a nap inside One-Eight. I told him to go ahead, and that I would monitor the radio. Chapelle had been asleep for about an hour when he suddenly awoke with a shout. His eyes were wide with fear and he was sweating.

"What's the matter with you, Chapelle?" I asked.

"*It's Slammer, sir. Don't you hear him?*" Chapelle replied.

I felt a sudden chill go through me, as if there were a presence inside One-Eight. Out of the corner of my eye I caught a glimpse of something jumping down from a hiding place behind the radio. It was a large, golden-colored bamboo rat, the kind that infests certain areas of Dodge City. No ghost, just a bamboo rat, food for the small, marbled bamboo cats. Before I could react, the rat ran out the door of the track.

"All I heard was a bamboo rat scampering around," I said.

"He's stopped now. He told me not to give in."

"Could be a little heat stroke, or it could be those pills. Better lay off those pills for a while."

"He says that we're going to make it, Lieutenant."

"What?"

"Slammer. He told me that we're going to make it, that everything's going to be okay. *Don't give in.* That's what he said. And he said not to be afraid of the spook."

"The spook?"

"Yeah, the spook. What's he talking about Lieutenant? What spook?"

"I don't know, Val Jean."

I walked out the door of the track, feeling another cold shiver down my spine. Bad dreams, I thought to myself, just like the ones I had in Laos.

*　　*　　*

Day Eight, 1600 hours

By the time a chopper finally brought us the starter it was late in the afternoon. It took us only fifteen minutes to get it in, which was good, but when Sergeant Chapelle went to crank the engine nothing happened. The new starter was bad.

The problem was now serious to say the least. When I called Hill 55 to report the situation, they suggested that we prepare a perimeter for the night. My company commander, Lieutenant Quick, had another starter pulled off a track back at Third Tracks, but there was no telling when they could get it down to us.

About that time Chapelle got an idea. All of us had noticed the hull of an old mined track back about two hundreds meters. Chapelle suggested that we drive back to the old hull to see if we could pull off the starter. Even though the track had been mined, the hull hadn't burned. The starter could still be fine.

I gave the okay. The next thing I knew he'd cranked One-Eight and we were headed back to the old hull. We took four ROKs for security. I wrote down some map coordinates just in case I needed to call in some artillery support.

My only concern was if the old hull had been booby-trapped. Chapelle and Pineapple probed the dirt around the track, while I checked inside for trip wires. Everything seemed okay, but one never knew. Finally Chapelle took a deep breath and climbed down in behind the engine.

It took him a mere five minutes to pull off the starter. In less than a half hour we had driven back to One-Six and slammed in the starter. To my great joy and surprise, One-Six turned over and we were on our way. I turned to the Chapelle and slapped him on the back.

"Good job, Val Jean! It took a lot of guts to go inside that old hull."

"Yes, sir. But it was no sweat," he said, smiling.

"I think it took a lot of guts. And who would've thought the starter in that old hull would work," I said.

"It was the Slammer, Lieutenant."

"What?"

"It was the Slammer who told me about that starter. He whispered it in my ear, Lieutenant. I swear. I wouldn't tell anyone else but you. I swear it was Slammer. You know, sir, maybe its time for me to start reading the Bible again."

*   *   *

Day Eight, 1630 hours

Prior to our next departure, I sent Sergeant Hun and a fire team of Korean Marines up a dry streambed that ran west to east. Han knew the terrain well. With his men, Han was to recon the streambed, staying just ahead of us.

It was only two kilometers to the Korean Bridge, a piece of cake if it weren't for the Lay Ban minefield. To top it off, Captain Chan was getting nervous. He kept calling Kim on the radio to see how much progress we were making.

What Hopkins called the Lay Ban minefield stretched from the southern edge of Go Noi Island up to an abandoned village site we knew as Bac Dong Ban. Bac Dong Ban was about a half kilometer due west from the Korean Bridge. The mines were scattered throughout the area, but this was the only path that our tracked vehicles could take to get to the Korean Bridge. On either side of the minefield the terrain was too boggy for tracks.

There was no doubt where the minefield began because there were two amphibian tractor hulls and a burned out tank that served as landmarks. Two of those tracks had belonged to my company. On my last tour I had sat up on Hill 55 and watched them burn.

Earlier in the day, Captain Chan had called in an air strike on the minefield, attempting to clear a path for us. Kim, Chapelle, and I thought that the idea of trying to clear a minefield with an air strike might just work. Hill 55 agreed, but still had our Marine engineers at Hoi An come out to sweep the area where our air strike had cleared a path.

When we got to the edge of the minefield, our Marine engineers were only halfway through their task. Chan got impatient and ordered a ROK Tank to drive through the minefield where the air strike had cratered the minefield. The ROK tank drove through the cratered part of the minefield without any problem. Coming abreast of One-Eight, the ROK tank commander smiled and tossed me a cold Falstaff. I opened the beer, took a sip, and gave the rest to the ROK Marine next to me.

All our ROK Marines seemed to know this tank commander, and before I knew it, five Korean Marines had jumped off One-Eight and onto the ROK tank. The ROK tank then took off back the way it came, taking a slightly different angle through the cratered area. The ROK tank was halfway through the minefield when the air was split by the sound of a forty-pound box mine exploding under the right front track of the tank.

The Korean Marines, who had been riding on the front of the tank, flew through the air and landed scattered about like so many limp rag dolls, their clothes smoldering. I immediately went to the emergency frequency on the radio to call for an evacuation. No sooner had I finished the call than Captain Chan called Kim on another radio frequency and told him not to evacuate the wounded. Kim tried to say something about the seriousness of the wounded, but Captain Chan kept cutting him off. When I asked Kim what was going on, he said that Chan was coming out to assess the situation before he'd allow any of the wounded evacuated.

Pineapple, Chapelle, and Cornflake, had run out to the ROK tank, at great risk, and pulled the tankers out. With the help of the engineers, they then began bringing the scattered wounded back to One-Eight. About that time, Captain Chan's jeep appeared on the other side of the Korean Bridge. Chan was driving like a madman, careening down the road and throwing up a dust cloud.

The engineers parted to let Chan's jeep through. The sergeant in charge of the engineers tried to warn Chan but he ignored the warning. Chan paused only to downshift as he drove through the cratered area, confident of his safety.

When he reached the mined tank, Chan stopped, jumped out, and began to survey the damage. Chan was upset. In

his haste he had lost a tank and taken casualties, casualties
that would have to be evacuated sooner or later.

Chan started walking toward us… Suddenly he
stopped, as if he were pondering his next step. He was
only twenty meters in front of One-Eight. He tried to back
off but it was too late. In backing off Chan had taken his
last step, a booby-trapped 105 artillery round had detonated
under him.

The 105 round split him apart. His blood and flesh
peppered the front of One-Eight. By the time Kim and I
picked our way to him he was dead. Kim and I gathered up
the body and brought it back to One-Eight. When we
reached One-Eight, I was soaking wet with sweat and
Chan's blood. The evacuation chopper I had called for
earlier was just touching down.

*   *   *

Day Eight, 1700 hours

The radio was jammed with calls. The Operations
Center on Hill 55 wanted to know the details of everything.
The ROK headquarters in Hoi An radioed Kim that they
were sending out two officers to check out the incident.

About that time Sergeant Hun broke radio silence to
report that he had taken a prisoner… Since Hun was only a
short distance away, someone up on Hill 55 thought that
my tracks should go back, into Go Noi, and pick up Han
and his prisoner. The dry streambed Han had been
traveling angled southeast toward us. We could reach them
by crossing a small rise of ground.

The men couldn't believe it, but go back we did. When
we got to the dry streambed we found Hun and his fire
team hunkered down among a growth of elephant grass.
Squatting next to them was the tattooed one.

*   *   *

Day Eight, 1730 hours

According to Hun, the tattooed one was a Montagnard guide named Toc. Hun said that he was a member of the Katu tribe. I knew of the Katu, an elusive and secretive tribe who'd come under the influence of the NVA. They were a primitive people, barely out of the Stone Age; and if you studied Toc, he looked like something out of prehistory, with his scars and strange tattoos. His teeth had been filed to points.

Toc's left hand, I saw, had been severed at the wrist and, the moment Toc looked up at me, I knew that he knew. There was that tattoo of the dancer in the middle of his forehead. On my previous tour we had snatched a trail walker, out in Happy Valley, who was a Katu. That Katu hadn't been covered with so many tattoos. Someone'd once told me that such tattoos were an animist charm, meant to ward off evil. I noticed that Toc's eyes lingered on my bolo fastened to my flak jacket. Yes, I was sure that he knew I was the one who had sliced off his hand in the heat of combat.

Yet he talked freely. Like other Katu who'd been captured, he had no compunction about sharing information. Toc told us of the events of the last few days, and of his tribe. Originally, Toc was from the area around An Diem. He'd fled into the mountains when members of his family had been killed by South Vietnamese troops. The NVA had made him a guide and trail walker, the equivalent of a scout for the NVA. For the last two years he'd both scouted, and then guided, NVA troops. When necessary, he had scouted into the lowlands surrounding Da Nang. Toc was a good catch. Military intelligence would be excited. The few Katu who had been captured from time to time had proven to be a source of valuable information.

After the firefight with Mike Company, Toc fell back with the NVA to the edge of the Que Son Mountains where his wound had been cauterized with hot oil. Once his stub had been wrapped, and he had been given drugs, an NVA lieutenant ordered the tough Katu to take a message up to

Charlie Ridge. In order to get to Charlie Ridge, Toc had to cross Go Noi Island and travel back through Dodge City. He was traveling north, up the dry streambed when he ran into Hun and his fire team.

Looking at Toc, with his teeth filed to points, I found myself seeing a demon from the world of darkness. It was as if an inhabitant from an unseen and shadowy world had decided to appear to the living in bodily likeness. I recalled Chapelle's weird dream about Slammer, and the warning about encountering a spook. Toc was the bogeyman of all my bad dreams, a figure rising out of both my fear and imagination coming to haunt me like Slammer's ghost. This tough tribesman continued to stare at my bolo; and when he looked at me, Toc had a trace of a smile on his face.

*　　　*　　　*

CHAPTER ELEVEN: THE SAND CASTLE

Day Eight, 1830 hours

We crossed the Korean Bridge and headed towards Hoi An. The plan was to drop the tracks off at Highway One. Kim and I were then to proceed to Colonel Chai with our new prisoner. Chai'd got the word that we had a Katu. He wanted to see this trailwalker for himself.

When we reached Highway One, I gave Sergeant Chapelle the rundown. Kim and I were going to the Sand Castle, Colonel Chai's headquarters. I scrounged up a case of Falstaff from the Marine engineers and everyone kicked back. Chapelle was chain-smoking Camels. Although he looked better, he still had the shakes.

"You feeling better, Sergeant?"

"Yes, sir. I'm doin' good now that we're off Go Noi. Better go get me a Bible."

Chapelle took out a downer and washed it down with Falstaff.

"You know that when we get back to Hill 55, you're going to have to shitcan those," I said.

"I think I'll be okay, Lieutenant. Once I get me a Bible I'll be okay."

*　　　*　　　*

Day Eight, 1900 hours

The villa Colonel Chai called his Sand Castle sat on a piece of high ground within sight of the South China Sea. From a distance it looked like classic Greek architecture, white Ionic marble columns and white walls. Once owned by a Frenchman who was from the south of France, the villa was in fact constructed in more of an eclectic manner. This variety of building styles became more evident once one got closer to the villa.

In terms of color, however, everything was either white, or a shade of dark red, the thick plaster walls painted white, the roof red tile. Situated throughout the gardens which encircled the villa were large clay urns of the same dark red color as the tile.

A line of mature palms bordered the north and west sides of the Sand Castle. The east side opened onto a wide terrace of red tile surrounded by more white walls. Here and there a large succulent grew from a red clay urn, the former French owner being an aficionado of rare cacti, having served in North Africa.

The entrance of the Sand Castle faced southward, guarded by two large, stylized oriental lions carved from white marble. The grinning marble lions were more than eight feet tall and each weighed more than a ton. In the not too distant past a squad of sappers had assaulted the Sand Castle with satchel changes and an RPG. An RPG round had struck one of the lions in the neck, beheading the statue. The lion's head now sat in the middle of the broad stairs that ascended to the entrance of the Sand Castle; the expression on the lion's head was now more like a grimace than a grin.

It was starting to get dark by the time we reached the Sand Castle. A stiff breeze was blowing in off the South China Sea. One of Colonel Chai's aides met us at the door. He was wearing a white scarf, which trailed behind him as he brought us to the colonel.

We entered a large, well-lit room where Colonel Chai sat at the head of a long, white marble table. He sat composed and distinguished, his white hair quite striking. All around him, officers of various ranks ate and drink, laughing and conversing in loud voices. There was a party atmosphere, and there appeared to be little remorse for the death of their brother officer Captain Chan.

Chai appeared composed. But I sensed that he was an autocrat cut from the same cloth as the ancient Chinese warlords. Kim led the way and I followed. Toc brought up the rear. It was obvious from his smile that Colonel Chai was glad to see us.

With our exotic prisoner, we were the perfect after dinner entertainment.

A Korean officer we all knew as Scar, began to say something in a loud voice, pointing to the Katu. That officer's terrible scar began in the middle of his forehead, dipping down into his right eyebrow. With the Korean officer's comment, another heavy-set Korean officer with bulging eyes, who we knew as Mr. Toad, responded with a comment of his own, and the whole table, including Colonel Chai broke into roaring laughter.

Scar then sprung up from his chair, and stripped off the sarong-like garment Toc was wearing leaving the Katu stark naked. The crowd continued to laugh. Rice-wine and beer continued to flow.

"What the hell is going on?" I asked Lieutenant Kim.

"His tattoos. They want to see his tattoos," Kim said, pointing to the Katu's buttocks.

For the first time I realized that one of Toc's tattoos depicted a sexual act. I was amazed that this fact had escaped me. On Toc's left buttock was the tattooed outline of a man and a woman having sex. Toc stood there, in the bizarre atmosphere, not trying to cover his nakedness, head-down in humiliation. Mr. Toad shouted something to Scar, and the group laughed again as the Scar doused Toc down with a pitcher of ice water. The shock of the ice water brought Toc to his knees. From there he curled into a fetal position and began to moan as pitchers of ice water continued. Finally the colonel shouted for silence. The officers grew silent, rose from their chairs, and departed in an orderly fashion. Only Kim, Toc, the Colonel and I remained in the dinner hall.

The Colonel pulled the trembling Katu to his feet. He then brought up a chair and studied Toc's tattoos. At one point he asked Kim to inquire of Toc as to how the Katu lost his hand. Pointing to my bolo, Toc replied in a trembling voice, and sign language, that I had cut off his hand with the bolo during hand-to-hand combat.

The Colonel expressed great interest in the details surrounding the combat encounter between Toc and myself, asking Lieutenant Kim to translate endless questions. Satisfied, at last, with the accounts given by Toc and myself, he then asked to see my bolo. When I pulled the curved fourteen-inch high carbon steel blade from its sheath I could tell from the gleam in Colonel Chai's eyes that he loved the knife. Kim winked at me and I instinctively knew what I had to do.

Colonel Chai studied the knife in much the same way that he had studied the Katu's tattoos. When the Colonel handed the knife back to me, I instructed Lieutenant Kim to tell the Colonel that the bolo was my present to the Colonel. I then gave the bolo sheath to the speechless Colonel whereupon Lieutenant Kim told me that the gift of a knife or sword that had been bloodied in actual combat was a gift of great power and spiritual significance.

Colonel Chai jumped up from his chair and gave me a big hug. He called to his aide to take Toc off for further questioning. Chai also instructed the aide that the Katu was to be given medical care for his wound and was to be treated with dignity. Kim and I were led into another room, and there sat Miss Swan. Kim turned to me with a smile.

"The Colonel say that as a *collector of rarities* he will always treasure this special gift you have given him, this beautiful knife which you have bloodied in combat. Now you must honor him by staying the night as his guest, and accepting this gift as a small token of his regard for you."

"What gift?" I asked, still wondering what exactly a great *collector of rarities* was.

"Why, Miss Swan," Kim replied.

Miss Swan simply smiled and nodded, and it occurred to me that, although I loved that knife dearly, this time I definitely got the better half of the trade.

*   *   *

Day Eight, 1930 hours

Miss Swan suggested that we slip up to her room on the second story of the Sand Castle. We discreetly exited a side door to get to the stairs that took us to the second level.

At the foot of the stairwell I noticed a car-engine-sized brown sandstone Cham sculpture. It was a large stone head broken off at the neck from some greater statue. The floor around the stone head was littered with wire brushes and bottles of some kind of cleaning chemical. It appeared that the sculpture was being cleaned.

"A Cham sculpture," I said, surprised.

"Yes, a representation of Indra the rain god. It was recovered south of Go Noi Island, in the foothills of the Que son Mountains. Look closely and you will see that the god is weeping. Indra weeps to bring the monsoon rains. Colonel Chai intends to bring this find back to Saigon," Miss Swan said.

I nodded. Strange, I thought to myself.

We were midway up the stairs when a door opened at the top of the stairwell. Stunned, I found myself face-to-face with Fritz Lipske. But this encounter was not by design. He looked as surprised as I was by the chance meeting. He carried a new wire brush.

"Lieutenant Gatlin, *that's* the name as I recall. Lenny said he met some Jarhead lieutenant at the White Lotus. I guessed it was you. I've always been a good guesser," he said, a smart-ass grin on his face.

Lipske had been drinking. His eyes were bleary. He smiled and leaned on the stair railing with his left hand, gripping it tightly. His left knee was slightly bent, as if he were positioning himself for a kick at my face. He appeared unarmed. I was not. My ice pick was in the side pocket of my utility trousers, within easy reach. I backed off from Lipske, giving myself some distance from a potential kick, easing Miss Swan to my left so that she wasn't in my way. I was ready for any move he might make. But then something snapped in me, triggered by his smart-ass grin.

"You're blocking my fucking way."

"Be nice, Lieutenant. I was hoping that we would meet up. We need to talk. You know what I want. I'd like to visit with this Ani Bui, if you don't mind."

"I do fucking mind, and I have ten tracks and forty Marines in my platoon. That's a lot of firepower if I decide to drive up the beach and show up at your doorstep. I know where you live, Lipske. I understand this new interrogation center is right off the beach."

"Lieutenant, Lieutenant, we need to reach an understanding. I need your cooperation to interrogate this Viet Cong."

"She's not VC. She was kidnapped and forced into the service of the Viet Cong. Captain Graham and I consider her a Chou Hoi based on the information she has provided."

"Major Hopkins doesn't share your perspective."

"Fuck Hopkins and fuck you. I know what happened to the three wounded VC that Hopkins sent you."

"Bullshit. You know nothing."

"A Marine battalion commander told me all three were dead. I understand that one died by your own hand from a heart attack after you attached a field phone generator to his balls. Fuck with me or Ani Bui and I will blow the whistle up at division headquarters."

I could see the shock and fear in Lipske's eyes. He was, for the moment, speechless. No doubt Lipske was thinking hard about what I said, and he was dangerous. But here I was provoking him because I wanted to start something. I wanted to let it happen.

At six foot, four inches, the tall, thin Lipske was an inch taller than me, but I outweighed him by forty pounds of solid muscle. I could still bench press three hundred pounds and was no one to fuck with under any circumstances, drunk or sober. The street smart Lipske sensed that he was in trouble, and like most bullies, at heart he was a coward. I wasn't going to wait for him to make the first move.

With a quick sweep of my right hand I grabbed his bent right knee and pulled it out from under him. He fell hard on the stairs, hitting the back of his head. His long thin left arm immediately reached up to claw my face. I brushed away his skinny arm, and blasted his face with all my power, with three quick hard shots from my left hand.

The hours of punching the body bag at back at the Basic School in Quantico paid off. Lipske slumped back, spitting out teeth, his broken nose pouring blood. He kicked out at me, catching me in the groin. Without thinking, I pulled my ice pick, jamming into his thigh all the way to the hilt. Lipske gasped, holding his leg. I then grabbed him by the head with both hands and kneed him several times in the face, so hard I could feel his brain wobble inside his skull. It was all over in a matter of seconds.

Miss Swan cowered against the wall. Lieutenant Kim, Colonel Chai, and his aide stood speechless at the bottom of the stairs. I yanked my ice pick from Lipske's thigh. He sputtered, semi-conscious, flecks of white teeth on his bloody lips. Blood trickled down the white marble stairs.

"Lipske was drunk. I think he was jealous seeing me with Lieutenant Gatlin. He picked a fight with the Colonel's guest. The lieutenant was only defending himself," Miss Swan said quickly.

Lieutenant Kim translated for Colonel Chai who simply nodded. Chai said something to Lieutenant Kim, and went back the way he came, his aide following closely behind.

"What did Colonel Chai say?" I asked.

"He said that it looked like a good fight, and he was sorry he missed it. And, that I should clean up the mess," Kim said, as if in disbelief.

*   *   *

Day Eight, 2000 hours

Miss Swan and I sat in her bedroom next to a balcony that overlooked the South China Sea. The wind had picked up, and the temperature began to drop. The curtains billowed out and it started to rain, occasional heavy drops blowing in from the balcony. Then the downpour arrived in huge sheets.

"Indra the rain god is weeping," Miss Swan said.

"This may be the start of the monsoon," I replied.

She unfolded a red oriental screen to shield the room from the balcony. A blue dragon was painted on the screen. In front of the screen was a low table surrounded by several red cushions. In the middle of the table was a red enameled cloisonné bowl. The cloisonné bowl contained real Cuban cigars.

We sat down on a bed that was a simple frame covered with a red comforter and I pulled off my boots. I wasn't going to pursue the subject of Lipske, or how she had come to know him.

"Would you like a massage, Lieutenant?"

"Oh, yeah. First I would like to take a shower."

"Of course, you will feel more relaxed."

"Do you want me to bathe you?"

"Actually, I'd rather not. I just want to put my head under a hot shower for a few minutes," I said, wanting privacy in order to remove the sweat and filth of Go Noi Island from my body.

The shower stall was made of white marble and the water was very hot. The room filled with steam as I let the hot water run over my head and shoulders. Keeping both my ice pick and pistol handy, I toweled off and put on a red terry cloth robe that had a blue dragon on the back. When I returned to the bedroom Miss Swan had taken off the black dress and was naked but for a red kimono that fell open to reveal the surprising fullness of her breasts.

"How about a smoke?" Swan asked, offering a cigar.

"No, thank you. Not my thing."

"What is your thing?"

"Well, I like to drink beer. Sometimes liquor. Right now I just want that massage," I said, shrugging my shoulders and taking off my robe. As a precaution I chambered a round in my .45 and set it by the bed.

"That is not necessary, Lieutenant Gatlin."

"Yes, indeed it is Miss Swan. I always sleep with my .45, loaded."

"Such a big gun."

I liked Miss Swan's smile, and I liked the way she looked me over, her kimono falling open when she leaned forward. She moved toward me. This time the kimono slipped off her shoulders. She gave me a long hug, holding me very close. Then she let down her long black hair. It fell to her waist.

"I like your long hair."

"I like your big gun."

Miss Swan's hair smelled of sandalwood, and when I began to tremble, she took control. I was fascinated by the red and black Yin and Yang tattoo on the smooth, almond skin of her right shoulder.

"Yin and Yang," I said, pointing to the tattoo.

"Very good, Lieutenant Gatlin. The red is for Yang, the masculine, and the black is for Yin, the feminine. Yin and Yang are the symbols of the Tao. They are a dynamic force, constantly interacting with one another to create the Universe by their interaction."

"I see."

"Do you?

"Old Chinese wisdom."

"Very good. Now lay back. I promise to be very gentle."

I lay on my back while she slipped one hand beneath me. With her other hand she began a slow, delicious stroking. I knew then that there was a wild power within that allows us at times to touch the heavens.

*   *   *

CHAPTER TWELVE: LA HUAN AND GIANG LA

Day Nine, 0930 hours

The next morning I was up at daybreak. Miss Swan was still asleep when we left the Sand Castle, crossing over to Route 4. Once on Route 4, we cut across the northwestern corner of Dodge City. To our north, in the vicinity of the La Huan and the Giang La hamlet complex, a firefight was going on.

"Lieutenant Kim, do you have any idea what's going on?"

"Intelligence has reported elements of the Q-82d Battalion have linked up with a number of the local Viet Cong."

Kim's information greatly concerned me. The Giang La area was a patchwork of bamboo hedgerows, offering our enemy considerable cover and providing a perfect staging area for attacks throughout the Dien Ban District. It would be tough going getting that enemy out of the Giang La.

*   *   *

Day Nine, 1030 hours

The commanding officer of the First Marine Regiment sat at the head of the long table. He liked to be called Hump, and had a reputation for letting his people do their own thing. Hump had been at Guadalcanal during World War II, and had fought as a battalion commander in Korea. He was old for a full colonel, much older than the previous commanding officer. He appeared to be in his mid-fifties, but his records noted service prior to World War II as an enlisted man in China. That put him closer to sixty. He was an *old China Hand,* and part of what we called the Old Corps, Marines who had served in combat prior to Vietnam. His service in Vietnam had been confined to several staff jobs, and it was commonly understood that he was going to retire once he completed this tour. But for the assassination attempt on Colonel Fry, Hump would have never commanded a Marine Regiment.

Hump was thick and broad-shouldered, and a bit under six feet. Unlike the Kingfish he wasn't fat. Rather, he was barrel-chested, with hairy, club-like forearms covered with faded tattoos. His jaw was square, and he had his hair cut in a steel-colored flattop. But Hump's most distinctive feature was a great bushy eyebrow that ran in a continuous line across his low forehead. A smoker of White Owl cigars, at first glance one would guess that Hump was Old Corps through and through. However, Hump's reputation was quite the contrary. According to those who knew him well, Hump was highly literate, forward thinking, with a wide variety of interests. Hump even read poetry.

Today the Hump decided to have this briefing in the Hill 55 mess hall. It was the only place on the hill that was big enough. His various battalion commanders, including the Kingfish, were seated around him. Captain X and Colonel Chai were also at the table. Major Hopkins was completing his portion of the briefing as Quicksilver, Lieutenant Kim, Toc, and I entered. The discussion that followed was on the difficulty of getting helicopter support. It was very intense.

I noticed that Lieutenant Wily was seated in the back of the room, among the various company-grade officers in attendance. All told there must have been forty officers attending. Included in that group was Captain Sikes. His left arm was bandaged, and he looked pale. When I walked by him, I nodded. We were only a few feet apart. He winked back at me, taking a puff from a cigarette. I noticed that his fingers were trembling.

All heads turned toward Toc as our group entered the room. Colonel Chai nodded in my direction, smiling. I smiled and nodded back. There were murmurs from the crowd as Sergeant Chapelle came forward to escort Toc to another part of the building. I was surprised to hear that Captain X actually knew Toc from his previous tour in An Diem back in the early sixties. Also at the main table, sitting next to Colonel Chai, was Lipske. When our eyes met, Lipske looked away.

A colonel I recognized as being from the First Marine Air Wing continued to answer questions around the issue of chopper support. I knew him from the Basic School back at Quantico where he had been an instructor. Now he was a helicopter pilot from MAG-16, and he was sweating, seemingly frustrated by the questions the grunts had been asking him.

It was a difficult time for Marine air. The resources of the lst MAW were scattered throughout the I Corps Tactical Zone. The fixed wing aircraft were concentrated at two bases. At Da Nang, where the wing headquarters, support, and air control groups were located, was MAG-ll. MAG-ll included four jet squadrons. The other two fixed wing aircraft groups, MAG-l2 and MAG-13, operated out of Chu Lai, more than seventy-five kilometers to the south.

The primary task of the fixed wing attack and fighter squadrons was to provide close air support for ground combat units. Interdiction missions out on the Laotian border were supposed to be secondary. The attack squadrons flew A-4E Skyhawk bombers. The fighter attack squadrons flew F-4B Phantoms. The all-weather attack squadrons used Grumman A-6A Intruders, a plane that, in the opinion of many of the well informed, was underutilized.

Three aircraft groups also controlled the wing's helicopters. Those three groups were MAG-l6, MAG-36, and MAG-39. MAG-39 was way up in Quang Tri. MAG-36 was located a little farther south at Phu Bai. MAG-l6 choppers were located in Da Nang.

The helicopter's mission was both support and attack. Yet it appeared that troop redeployments were impacting helicopter resources in I Corps. There were not enough choppers to go around, and both support and attack missions were being impacted. The resulting problems were both tactical and political.

The attack mission involved both the Huey and the Cobra. The primary mission of the Huey was supposed to be observation, although an armed version of the aircraft was used most often as an escort until the introduction of the Cobra. While the Cobra helped meet the need for attack gunships, there were too few of them. But, the Cobra did have greater endurance and cruise speed than the armed Hueys. Armed with a mini-gun, a turret-mounted grenade launcher, and rockets, the Cobra, when available, offered significant firepower.

Again, with redeployment of Marines back stateside, the wing's lift and troop transport capability was also proving to be a problem. Ground units had been moved inland to set up firebases. To set up firebases required heavy artillery, ammunition, and ongoing resupply efforts from the air. These activities require the utilization of heavy lift choppers like the CH-53. The CH-46 Sea Knights lacked the heavy lift capability of the CH-53. All this was happening at a time when the word had come down to reduce flying time on the CH-53's.

It was a very complex situation. Each of the wing's helicopter pilots and gunships operated under the maximum number of monthly flight hours prescribed by the Navy Department. However, lst MAW constantly overflew the limits to meet the pressing needs of Marines on the ground. Wing helicopters routinely were flying at a rate of l50 percent of their authorized utilization, and during times of heavy commitment, such as the last few days, that utilization approached 200 percent. These usage rates created excessive pilot fatigue and a shortage of spare parts. Some internal rearrangement had to be made to accommodate the situation. As Captain X would say, we needed to start looking at things in new ways.

Quicksilver and I listened as the discussion took various turns. At one point, Hump rose from his seat and came to the defense of the chopper jock. He commented that the wing was operating with an inadequate number of helicopters, not only supporting two widely scattered Marine divisions, but Korean and South Vietnamese units as well. He added that there was a lack of understanding on the part of both air and ground commanders as to the capabilities and limitations of each.

Hump then called for a break. Everyone got up for a stretch and a smoke. Captain X shook his head and smiled. Captain X, Quicksilver, and I then walked down to the track park. Sergeant Chapelle joined us. A light rain was starting to fall.

"What a mess, Gatlin," Quick said.

"I don't have any solutions," I replied.

"Clearly," Captain X said, "the problems being discussed raise questions relative to basic Marine concepts of air-ground organization. Time for reinvention."

"Reinvention my ass! With all due respect Captain, I don't know what reinvention is. All I know is that people have to start doing their jobs, and that includes these hotshot flyboys. To win this fucking war every Marine has to do their job," Quick said with disgust.

"I think what the captain means by reinvention is for us to try to look at things in new ways, from different perspectives," I said, defending Captain X.

"Lieutenant Gatlin, all *you* got to do while *you're in my company* is make sure that your men do their jobs. We need to leave all this intellectual heavy lifting to the staff weenies," Quick said curtly.

"I can't understand why the Marines don't permanently attach their helicopters to their ground units," Captain X said.

"That's too easy," Quick replied.

"The Marine Corps doesn't have enough choppers to do that," I added.

"The problem goes beyond just helicopter support," Quick continued, lighting a Lucky Strike.

"What do you mean?" Captain X asked.

"What I mean is that if we ever intend to win this war we will have to go back into the mountains. To go back into the mountains means building more fire bases. Building more fire bases means we need to bring in more CH-53's rather than redeploy them. We need the heavy lift chopper, or we are history. But the heavy lift chopper is just a symptom," Quick said, blowing a smoke ring into the air.

"I'm all ears," Captain X said, leaning against one of our tracks.

"To me, the chopper problem is just one more indication that something is wrong at a higher level. Down at our level, we find ourselves trapped on the wrong side of the Ky Lam River because some politician wants to make a statement about who owns Go Noi Island. When it is over, we all have this empty feeling. On Hill 55 the grunts have a name for it. What is it they call it?" Quick asked, turning to me.

"The Dodge City Blues," I said.

*   *   *

Day Nine, 1300 hours

When the briefing reconvened, the group was smaller. Colonel Chai and Lieutenant Kim sat with Captain X on the right side of the table. Major Hopkins, Quicksilver, and I sat across from them. Hump sat at the end of the table. Lipske and the battalion commanders were absent.

"Captain Graham and I have been discussing this build up in the La Huan and Giang La hamlet complex. We got about four square kilometers to deal with, and from the earlier discussions that we've been having, it looks like we're going to have to do things in a new way," Hump said.

"Based on information provided by the Seeker Six, we have found what we believe is an extensive bunker complex, probably protection for an extensive weapons cache," Major Hopkins added.

"Now, my battalion commanders and Colonel Chai have been briefed. I'm going to turn this over to Major Hopkins so that he can respond to any questions you might have. I'm on my way up to Division to grease the skids. We may have some resistance. I know that I can count on all of you here at this table to keep quiet until you're given the word. Thank you for your support these last few days. It's been tough," Hump said, looking very old.

At that point the Hump got up and excused himself. Major Hopkins then explained how at this very moment Korean Marines were moving westward along Route 4 and elements of the First Marines were moving south and east off of Hill 55 to link up with the Koreans.

"Forget the choppers, we're marching in, but on a larger scale than ever before. We're trying a little different approach on this operation," Hopkins said.

This was all very surprising. I wondered what was driving this. Maybe I had missed something. There were many questions that had to be answered. As for assaulting the bunker complex, that would work as long as we softened it up with tanks and air support. Quicksilver was wondering the same things that I was. Before I could ask any questions, he did. Hopkins had anticipated our reaction and he had prepared a response.

"The plan is to cordon the four square kilometers that comprise the La Huan and Giang La hamlet complex and wait it out. Selected ambush patrols and snipers will work the area. At the appointed time, we launch a coordinated assault within our cordon," Hopkins said.

"Sounds no different than our previous operations. You need to make sure that your plan isn't compromised by spies within the South Vietnamese organization," Quick replied.

"Be patient, Lieutenant Quick. We are taking every precaution. We intend to make sure that there are no leaks. Yet, at this point in the planning, there seems to be some question if the South Vietnamese will support us? Certain South Vietnamese would be very concerned about damage to the ancient cemeteries in the La Huan and Giang La area. I've endured their protests on previous occasions."

"Major Hopkins, I've no crystal ball. I don't know how things are going to unfold. In the past both the ARVN and the politicians in Da Nang have said hands off Giang La and La Huan. La Huan is a productive rice area. Both areas are also very populous. Both areas have ancient pagodas that are of special religious significance," Quick said, rambling on.

"What we have here is an opportunity to expose our enemy, Lieutenant Quick. And I firmly believe the Giang La and La Huan provide sanctuary for this VC death squad that's been giving us so much trouble. To me, that is reason enough to mount this operation," Hopkins said, cutting off Lieutenant Quick.

Of course, I thought to myself, mounting out this operation and blowing away this VC death squad involved turning the Giang La and the La Huan hamlet complex, a most beautiful and historic area, into a wasteland.

*   *   *

Day Nine, 1430 hours

The truth of the whole matter came out later, when Quick and I were back in my hooch drinking a cold beer.

"Hopkins told me that Hump is most unhappy about how things went down on Go Noi Island," Quick said, lighting up a cigarette.

"Tell me more," I replied, opening a cold beer.

"The political aspects of the situation pissed him off. The truth of the matter is that he was forced to take a stand on the south bank of the Ky Lam River to keep in sync with some bullshit ARVN plan that never happened. As a result, the way things went down got some of our Marines killed."

"I think that's the case."

Someday official histories would be written, I thought to myself. Those histories would discuss strategy and tactical employment of men and equipment as well as body count. Events and language would be construed so that, given the circumstances, the course of action followed was appropriate. Proof of that course of action would be in the numbers of enemy dead, and in the leveling of the fourteen-kilometer long Go Noi Island. The fact of the matter was that most company commanders questioned our tactics, tactics that had been dictated to us from above. Through their spies, our enemy discovered ahead of time we were coming, and seeded Go Noi with thousands of booby traps and mines. As a result, many of our Marines were lost unnecessarily.

The preferred target had always been the northeastern corner of Dodge City. It wasn't that Go Noi Island wasn't a worthy objective; rather, it was just that much more would have been accomplished with less. Many thought the northeastern corner of Dodge City should have been the primary target. There were also those who, informally, were willing to express their doubts about the whole Go Noi effort, saying that it was orchestrated for political purposes so that it appeared that ARVN, U.S. Marine, and ROK Forces could work in concert. If the purpose of the combined operation on Go Noi Island had been to achieve maximum effect, couldn't we have accomplished the same task of leveling Go Noi Island with a series of B-52 Arc Lights? After all, Lieutenant Quick pointed out, that's what we did in the Sherwood Forest, and we didn't lose one track or U.S. Marine to a booby trap.

Outside, the rain was now coming down in heavy sheets. Distant thunder rumbled in the mountains to the west. Indra, the rain god, was on the move.

"Look at that rain. You know, Gatlin, I think the monsoon might hit us early this year. That certainly would slow things down. I think we may have a two-week window to pull off this operation. Then the rains will begin. Let's make sure that we have plenty of cable and bridge lumber with us when we head out."

"Roger that. You seem to be more involved in this operation," I said.

"Got to keep an eye on our assets. Making sure that grunts don't fuck with you."

"I see," I replied, still wondering about Quick's motives.

"Oh, and one more thing. Hopkins brought up this Ani Bui. He wants me to have you turn her over for interrogation to this new center in Da Nang," Quick said.

"The PIC?"

"That's the place. He claims she's withholding valuable information we could use."

"Hopkins doesn't know when to quit. Now he's sucking up to you. I don't know if she's withholding anything. I do know that she has rallied to our side. Captain X is treating her as a Chieu Hoi."

"Come on, Gatlin, who are you trying to shit? Ani Bui's no NVA soldier. She's VCI, if anything. She's Viet Cong infrastructure, and she's playing you for a sucker, big time."

"I don't think so."

"I'm going to order you to turn her over to Hopkins."

"Based on what authority?"

"Based on my fucking authority, Lieutenant Gatlin, or did you suddenly forget that I'm your company commander?"

"Never happen. Ani Bui is a citizen of Dien Ban District under the protection of Captain X, the District Advisor."

"Gatlin, this is very political. What are you, sweet on this gook pussy, or what?"

"No, I'm not sweet on Ani Bui, and this politics is bullshit as far as I'm concerned. It is very clear to me what authority is involved, and I intend to do the right thing with Ani. If you fuck with me on this one, I'll go to First Marine Division Headquarters and personally blow the whistle on all your questionable business dealings with the White Lotus, and that's just for starters. I know more about you and your corrupt Vietnamese business associates than you realize."

"Slow down, Lieutenant Gatlin. Before you start spouting off all this shit, I want you to know that Hopkins and I heard about a certain incident down at the Sand Castle. You stuck an ice pick in a civilian contractor's leg. You're very lucky that Hopkins wants to keep this under wraps; otherwise I'd have to bring you up on an Article Fifteen."

"His name is Fritz Lipske and he is responsible for torturing three wounded prisoners of war to death. Lipske made the mistake of threatening me down at the Sand Castle, and I wasted his ass. He's the same guy that wants Ani Bui, and Hopkins is playing his game. What game are you playing, Lieutenant Quick? Or maybe the question is, how much of the White Lotus do you actually own? Maybe we ought to let Division Legal find the answer to that question."

"What a minute you self-righteous asshole, you are no one to stand in judgment of me. I'm just doing what a lot of smart folks are doing, making some money off this war while I am able to do that. I'm making the most of my opportunities. That's what makes America great, and that's what I believe in fighting for."

"Smart people? What smart people? You mean crooks, don't you?"

"Gatlin, this war is going south; and when it's all over, you're going to look back and ask yourself why you didn't take more advantage of the opportunities."

"Not interested. I'm here to lead Marines. You know what I think? I think that you are close to losing your moral authority to lead this company."

"Moral what? Is this bullshit coming from the same guy who keeps a severed gook hand in a pickle jar? I'll tell you what, Lieutenant Gatlin. I'll back off on this Ani Bui business, but that don't mean that it's over, not as long as Hopkins and this Seeker Six are around."

"I understand."

"I hope so. Goddamn, I hate shit like this. Gatlin, try not to get yourself fucked up."

"Roger that."

Outside, the rain continued to pour. The wind picked up, slapping the canvas side tarps that covered the hooch screens. For a long time we sat in silence drinking our beers.

"Are we still friends? I'm not one to let some sweet little gook pussy get between me and my officers," Quick said, grinning and offering me a beer.

"Yeah, you corrupt asshole, we're still friends."

"I think you must be sweet on Ani Bui. You want a piece of that, I know it."

Captain X came rushing through the door, soaking wet, the rain blowing in behind him. The conversation on Ani Bui came to an abrupt end. Captain X flopped down in a chair and said that he had good news. He shared with us that he'd put together a small special task team of his district PRUs to check out the La Huan and the Giang La. At this very moment, under the cover of this rain, that PRU team was slipping into the northwest corner of Dodge City. The team's mission was to confirm or deny rumors that the La Huan and the Giang La were cache sites for the Viet Cong. The PRU team's leader was none other than the Gunny.

*　　　*　　　*

Day Nine, 1530 hours

Finally the rain let up. So I wandered back down to our track park to see how things were going. Sergeant Chapelle and the men had finished maintenance on the tracks and were looking at the old LIFE magazine that had the pictures of Woodstock. They were heavy into photos of the naked girls on Woodstock Pond.

"What do you think of all that, Lieutenant?" Chapelle asked.

"I think it's just one more thing that makes America great," I said.

"I ain't fightin for any hippies, Lieutenant," Pineapple said.

"Me neither, Pineapple. I'm fighting for the long-haired, naked girls," I replied.

Everyone got a laugh. But under the surface there was a great sadness. For Slammer was gone. Now that we were back on the hill the events of the past few days were beginning to have their effect.

I walked up the hill from the track park, my mind wandering back to Miss Swan. I wondered if I would ever see her again. How risky this business with women was. And maybe I had been too hard on Lieutenant Quick. He had always supported me without question, backing me up when I had issues with the grunts. In many ways I was very lucky that *Quicksilver* was my commanding officer.

"Hey, Sam!"

I turned to see Lieutenant Wily. He looked terrible, eyes sunken, face pale and gaunt.

"Wily, how's your bad self?"

"Not worth a damn. You heard what happened?"

"I heard that the Kingfish relieved you down on Go Noi," I said.

"You got that right."

"What are you going to do?"

"Sam, I don't know what to do. It looks like the Kingfish is going to make me a staff weenie. The word is that I'm supposed to go up to Division. As far as I'm concerned, that's the kiss of death. I don't know, any ideas that I had about making the Marine Corps a career are history."

"Wily, I know exactly how you feel. Let's go back up to my hooch and continue this conversation with a cold beer," I said, slapping him on the back.

*   *   *

Day Nine, 1630 hours

After opening a cold beer, Wily brought me up to date on the events of the last two days. I suggested that the best thing for Wily was to get off Hill 55.

Lieutenant Quick then entered the hooch, back from working with Captain X, Captain Sikes, and Major Hopkins. He flopped down in a chair and I handed him a cold beer. Hopkins had laid out an initial plan and was now on his way up to Division to find Hump. Quick was still pondering what direction this future operation would take. He shared the interesting details with us.

"While the battalion commanders have been involved in the basic planning, Major Hopkins is still concerned about the lack of coordination. Captain X also raised the same concerns, but is pushing a cordon and search operation with a unique emphasis on air power," Quick said.

"Air power takes time to plan, and I don't get it... Didn't we just hear from the Air Wing that they are strapped for resources?" I asked.

"Hopkins doesn't give a shit. He argues that we need to act now in order to take advantage of the element of surprise. The Koreans are already moving. Hopkins and Hump are to stop off at district headquarters on the way back from Division in order to bring Captain X up to date," Quick said.

While Quicksilver was frustrated, he hadn't lost his sense of the circumstances. As he related the situation, he emphasized how impressed he was with Captain X. There was actually a tone of optimism in his voice as he spoke of how they worked so well together.

"Well, I guess that puts a cramp on the little mission that you had for me," I said.

"Oh, no way. That little number hasn't changed. We are still going to support our friend Colonel Chai. We just have to be clever in how we handle it," Quicksilver said with a smile.

"But if there's going to be an operation in Dodge, I need to be here," I said.

"Stay loose, Lieutenant. I'll honco the tracks. Probably take two platoons of tracks anyway. You'll take headquarters platoon and move that hardware out of the club. In the meantime, we need to find us a few more lieutenants that have experience and training in tracked vehicles. There ain't many left in this division," Quicksilver said, sipping his beer.

"Would you take a grunt?" Wily asked.

"Say again?" Quicksilver said.

"They are trying to find a place for me up at Division. I'd just as soon be a track rat as sit back in Division packing paper," Wily said.

"Lieutenant Wily, you convinced me. Tell me who to talk to."

Quicksilver jumped to his feet and was out the door with Lieutenant Wily behind him. Quicksilver was never one to miss an opportunity. As they were leaving, Sergeant Chapelle knocked on the door of the hooch. He seemed lost in his thoughts.

"What's on your mind, Val Jean?" I asked.

"Hump looked really tired," Chapelle said.

"Yeah, real tired. I'm sure that he's feeling the burden of what happened down in Go Noi," I said.

"You know how it is, Lieutenant. Anytime Marines are lost, it weighs on the mind," Chapelle said

"I understand. You know, Val Jean, there's a lot happening right now. Things are getting real interesting. The Giang La and the La Huan have been off limits for any real action. The South Vietnamese wouldn't let us do our thing. In the past, all the district advisors had to play politics. Captain X is different. He's more action-oriented, and there are certain things that he won't compromise. This gook offensive has got everyone scared and he knows it. Something has to be done about the Giang La and the La Huan. Captain X will do something. He's the kind of leader that we need right now," I said, feeling the effects of too many beers.

"Roger that, Lieutenant. The men like Captain X. He's come through for us in a tight."

"Well, it's good that he inspires their confidence. I like him because he's a thinker, a thinker with the character to follow-through with his ideas. My take is that having him around has made the Hump look at things differently."

"There it is, Lieutenant. But old Hump doesn't want to think too much. If he's not careful, he'll get a dose of those Dodge City Blues," Chapelle said, sipping his beer.

*   *   *

Day Nine, 1730 hours

After I finished my beer, Chapelle started to doze off. I figured it was time to make my rounds again, first through the track platoon's quarters, then back down to the track park. I stumbled along, preoccupied with my thoughts, the loss of Slammer, and the events of the last few days. Once at the track park, I found Hog had returned from Medical. Hog had recovered from his concussion, and he and Mojo Man were hanging out, drinking a beer, which is what we all did in our free time.

"Hey Hog."

"Good to see you sir."

At the far end of the track park I could see Toc walking with Captain X and Ani Bui. We were too far away to hear their conversation, but Captain X looked quite animated, gesturing as he conversed with Ani and Toc.

Hog had heard from Captain X that Major Bo Boden at Command and Control North, SOG, was pleasantly surprised by Ani's willingness to cooperate. Her description of certain routes down from An Diem had been particularly valuable. Captain X asked Major Boden to keep Ani's little brother. Rather than bring Half Pint back to Hill 55, it made sense that he stay at the SOG camp in order to minimize the risk of a potential kidnapping.

Ani's effort to point out the location of the Warehouse to Captain X proved to be less fruitful. Captain X and Ani flew over much of Dodge City to no avail. She still insisted its location was south of Route 4, contrary to all other indications thus far. Ani also pointed out those villages that were VC supporters and those that were not. Her message was that Captain X had to evaluate each village in his district. Each village was different, she kept telling him.

"That Katu is a weird dude," Hog said.

"Captain X and Ani Bui are trying to talk Toc into coming over to our side. Toc knows all the paths through the Dodge City area, but Toc is uncertain," Mojo Man said.

Maybe it was all those beers I had, but I experienced a sudden inspiration, remembering things that I had heard about these mountain tribes. They were animists who believed in all sorts of spirits, and consulted their wizards to conjure up special magic. Maybe we could conjure up some magic of our own. As Captain X liked to say, it was thinking out of the box.

"Mojo Man, I got an idea. I think Hog and I can help out here. Tell the captain I need to talk to him."

*   *   *

Day Nine, 1745 hours

"So, you have this hand, right?" The captain asked.

"Affirmative, Captain," I replied, producing the jar.

"I'll tell Toc that we will give him a powerful talisman. We will give him back his own severed hand," Captain X said without hesitation.

"Holy shit, Lieutenant. With all due respect, how fucked is that?" Hog said, shaking his head.

*   *   *

Day Nine, 1800 hours

Captain X called to Ani Bui and Toc. When the Katu saw the hand, his eyes lit up. Toc then spoke rapidly, so rapidly that although I understood some Vietnamese, I couldn't follow him. When Toc spoke it seemed that the little tattooed dancer on his forehead became animated.

I presented the pickle jar to Toc. For a moment Toc said nothing, then he nodded his head and smiled. He said that getting back his severed hand was a great omen. He had regained part of himself that had been lost, and he would now bury his hand where no one would ever find it. It would be a powerful sign.

"This fucking country never ceases to amaze me," Hog said.

Captain X and Toc walked down the hill and dug a hole. Toc placed the pickle jar in the hole and covered it over with red, Hill 55 clay. Somehow, with the burial of Toc's hand, I felt some closure with our Go Noi Island experience and the events of the past few days.

*   *   *

Day Nine, 1930 hours

Quicksilver returned from the top of the hill in great spirits.

"Well, Sam, we are *indeed* on a roll. Lieutenant Wily has been transferred to our company effective today. Shit! I never saw anything so easy. You go ahead and take Wily with you on the run to the White Lotus. I'll worry about getting these tracks together for Dodge City. I tell you what! Do we have our shit together or not! We are *running right tonight*," Quicksilver said, obviously pleased with how easy the transfer had been made.

Quicksilver was like those darting fish that hunt on the top of the water. He moved in quickly to accomplish what he could, and was gone. He hated the messy details, and was reluctant to get down into the real depths of any subject. Always wary of those who asked probing questions, Lieutenant Quick either simply ignored the inquiry at hand, or promised to provide an answer at a later time, which almost never happened. It was impossible to catch this clever and elusive surface fish.

"We'll see," I said.

"Oh, what's the matter now?"

Lieutenant Quick's elation brought home to me how each man on Hill 55 had a different war. Each of us had our own unique story. Toc's burial of his severed hand had an impact beyond any explanation. No normal person would understand, nor would they believe how the strange circumstances arose to bring about such a burial. We all had much to learn. But now, as never before, I understood the complexity of this war, and the diverse nature of the men who were fighting it.

"Nothing. Nothing is the matter," I said.

*   *   *

CHAPTER THIRTEEN: STAYING LOOSE

Day Ten, 0830 hours

Quicksilver sat in the corner of the operations center, tapping a pencil on the table. Sikes and Lieutenant Kim were studying the wall map of Dodge City, using a grease pencil to draw what appeared to be a kind of corridor running north and south. The grunt battalion commanders were standing behind them, observing. Captain X was engaged in a conversation with the Gunny. Word had come down from Division that the operation into the Giang La and the La Huan was a go. The operation would now be a classic cordon and search. That is, a cordon and search with a subtle twist.

Wily and I walked over to Quicksilver and sat down.

Quicksilver offered me a cigarette. I lit up and inhaled the wonderful, relaxing smoke.

"Interesting situation," I said, trying to make conversation.

"Gatlin, I like this Hump. He's flexible. What we have here is a pulling together," Quicksilver said, watching the various people interact.

"What's the plan going to be for hauling the goods from the White Lotus?" I asked.

"You and Wily go into Da Nang and talk to Cowboy. He has the details," Quicksilver said, distracted by the action going on in the operations center.

"Why is everything so secretive?" I asked.

"Because it's the White Lotus," Quicksilver said with a sly smile.

"I see, because it's the White Lotus," I said, looking at all the action going on around me.

"That's a big affirmative. A lot of shit goes down in the White Lotus, the most political shit you can imagine. So, stay loose, Gatlin. This little assignment is right up your alley, just stay loose," Quicksilver said, leaning back in his chair.

* * *

Day Ten, 0930 hours

The plan to go into the Giang La area was blessed by Division, provided that we included the Korean Marines. According to Captain X, there were always political considerations concerning the ROKs. Part of the wheeling and dealing was to make our allies, the ROK Marines, look good. No lip service could be paid to the ROK Marines. The Koreans had to be involved, and Colonel Chai had to be kept happy. Based upon our Go Noi experience, Chai had a bad habit of sticking his nose into things at the most inopportune times. But the decision to keep the Korean Marines involved had been made at the Division level.

The plan was truly innovative. First and foremost, there was deception. What appeared to be a simple cordon and search, usually executed during daylight, turned into a subtle innovation involving night operations. It had taken both Captain Sikes and Captain X to convince Major Hopkins. But these men had been persuasive, pointing out that the concept had happened before, by accident, on a smaller scale down in the Go Noi. The subtle innovation was a feint, a mock blow into the Giang La in order to distract attention from the point on which the operation was really to focus, the La Huan corridor.

The La Huan corridor was a trail that ran east and west parallel to Route 4. The west end of the trail began in Giang La 1, on the banks of the A Nghia River and ran for two kilometers through the middle of the La Huan, to end at the railroad berm. The railroad berm ran north and south, providing the enemy with a means of crossing the wetlands that spread south of the La Huan on either side of the railroad berm. We had long known about movement up and down the La Haun corridor, but until now no one had come up with a way to utilize the information effectively.

It took the experience and know-how of both Captain Sikes and Captain X to refine the plan. As the Gunny once said, certain things in this war were a function of actual combat experience and knowledge from living in the villages. Captain Sikes and Captain X had sent the Gunny to recon the Giang La and the La Huan. In addition, as a CAP Marine, Mojo Man had once scouted these villages. Mojo Man's insights proved invaluable. I couldn't help but think of what Ani Bui had said about the effectiveness of the CAP Marines who lived down in the villages, close to the people. There was no substitute for having people on the ground, living among the folks in the villages.

The plan itself was elegant in its simplicity. There were three phases to the plan. The first phase was a cordon of the Giang La and the La Huan. The second phase involved a two-pronged assault.

During the second phase the Giang La bunker complex would be assaulted from the west by ground troops supported by tanks and tracked vehicles. This was the first prong. At the same time a second prong of tracked vehicles and ground troops would move north from Route 4 into the wetlands below La Huan until they reached the La Huan corridor. Once in the La Huan corridor, the second prong would insert teams who would plant seismic intrusion devices similar to those that were used on Go Noi Island. The second prong would then pull back while the first prong maintained its position. Both the first and second phase would occur during daylight.

The third phase would involve night action and fixed-wing aircraft in support and coordination with ground action. Since there had been persistent enemy movement through the corridor, the third phase would be an air-supported ambush. The well-traveled trail that ran through the corridor and the berm were flanked by wetlands on either side. Initial detection of the enemy movement would be at night by the seismic intrusion devices that Hog would monitor on seismic recorders in Track One-Eight. Using night observation devices, scout-snipers who knew the terrain would confirm the rate and direction of enemy movement. A-6's would then be vectored in for the kill using TPQ-l0 all weather radar.

*   *   *

Day Ten, 1130 hours

Wily was excited. He couldn't believe that Quicksilver managed to get him transferred into tracks. I told him that there was little that was beyond Quicksilver's imagination. Whether or not Quicksilver could accomplish all that he imagined, that was another question. But the mere transfer of personnel from one Marine unit to another wasn't even a challenge for someone with Quicksilver's ego and ingenuity. It would be interesting to see if some of Quicksilver's self-confidence rubbed off on Wily. Of course, there was that shady side to the illustrious Lieutenant Quick, and who knew what was really motivating his new interest in Hill 55 and the First Marine Regiment. I had a nagging suspicion that there were things going on behind the scenes, so-to-speak. Obviously these things were important enough to warrant Quicksilver's attention. I just couldn't put my finger on what they were.

"Sam, I keep seeing those blondes skinny-dipping in Woodstock Pond. I can't get them out of my mind."

"Wily, when we get into Da Nang I'm going to set you up at the White Lotus," I said, laughing.

"How are you going to pull that off with all the shit that's going down?" Wily asked.

"Wily, we got two days. Trust me. Sometime in the next two days we will get you some action. As Lieutenant Quick says, just stay loose, Wily. Just stay loose."

*   *   *

Day Ten, 1330 hours

Quicksilver pulled in a section of five tracks that we had placed over on Hill 37, near Dai Loc District Headquarters.

He then brought another section down from Hill l0 to our north. All together that gave him over twenty tracks to support the First Marines. Sergeant Chapelle seemed overwhelmed by all this action. Things were happening so fast. But I noticed that Chapelle's fingers had stopped trembling and that he had color in his cheeks.

"You look like you're doing good, Sergeant Chapelle."

"I am, Lieutenant. Don't need any more of those pills. I feel a lot better. Oh, once in a while I hear this voice whispering in my ear. But it ain't nothin that a few beers can't cure," Chapelle said.

"Good for you, Sergeant," I replied.

What I didn't tell Chapelle was that I had heard voices myself, from time to time. I wanted to tell him to stay loose but I couldn't get myself to say the words. Staying loose. Who was I trying to convince? Never fool yourself. Captain X once told me that he believed that at the center all things were one. What the hell did that mean? I didn't know. But I knew that he generated a power that influenced all of us through his example. In the future I would try to go with the flow, more of the Yin and Yang.

*　　*　　*

Day Ten, 1430 hours

I called a meeting of Sergeant Chapelle and Hog. I briefed both men on the details of the phased plan. It had been decided that Chapelle would organize the two teams that would plant the seismic intrusion devices. Hog would monitor the seismic recorders inside Track One-Eight.

Hog wasn't happy. He had heard that Wily and I were going into Da Nang. Hog wanted to drive the jeep. I told him that he needed to stay. As our key communications technician, he was a unique and vital part of the plan. I also told him that I was on a special assignment for Lieutenant Quick, and that I wouldn't be back for two days. Hog moaned, complaining that he'd missed out on a trip to the White Lotus.

"Lieutenant, when you're sitting there drinking a cool beer in the White Lotus, remember old Hog down in Dodge City. I'll be thinking of you."

"Hog, take it easy. Try not to get all worked up. This operation will roll out in phases, over a period of several days. Wily and I will be back to transport Marines and help monitor communications."

But Hog didn't buy it. He just nodded and went back to tinkering with his electronic gear. Out of the corner of my eye I noticed that Chapelle was watching me from the top of the track parked next to One-Eight. I looked up and smiled, trying to assume an air of nonchalance.

"Kicking back, Val Jean?"

"Yes, sir. And doing a little reading, Ephesians, Chapter Six."

"Oh?"

"*Put on all your armor that God gives you, so that you will be able to stand up against the Devil's evil tricks. For we are not fighting against human beings but against wicked spiritual forces in the heavenly world, the rulers, authorities, and the cosmic powers of this dark age,*" Chapelle said, reading from the text.

"It says that!"

"Yes, sir."

"Let me see that, please," I said.

Chapelle handed me his new Bible. I read the passage and thought how appropriate it seemed given the circumstances of the last few days. In the quiet of that moment, with the afternoon's long shadows beginning to creep across Dodge City's green checkerboard of bamboo hedgerows and rice paddies, somehow those words made more sense to me than all the other things I had heard and endured during the day's series of meetings and planning sessions.

I looked out over Dodge City. From my vantage point I had a good view of the muddy A Nghia River as it wound its way through Dodge. Here and there the red tile roof of a pagoda peeked through the green foliage. An unseen dog was barking down in the nearest ville. A rooster crowed.

Smoke from the cooking fires was rising straight up into the quiet rhythms of the afternoon. I realized that from my vantage point I could see the Giang La and the La Huan areas in the distance.

"Thank you, Val Jean."

"No problem, Lieutenant. As Lieutenant Quick likes to say, let's all stay loose."

*   *   *

CHAPTER FOURTEEN: PHASE ONE

Day Ten, 1800 hours

Wily jumped in the jeep and we were off, leaving by the south gate of Hill 55 and turning west on Route 4 toward Hill 37. Wily wanted to know why we were going to Hill 37. It was too late in the day to be traveling east along Route 4. Once we got to Hill 37, we would turn north on Liberty Road and that would take us safely back to Da Nang.

I told him that everything was cool. There were grunt patrols out along Liberty Road and it wouldn't take us more than fifteen minutes to cut over to Da Nang. On the way Wily took out his old issue of LIFE magazine and turned to the Woodstock article.

"It says here that they call themselves *flower children.* Look at this one, Sam. He's on a trip."

The picture was of some glazed-eyed, spaced-out dude who had departed on an acid trip. The guy reminded me of Lipske.

"You know, if I had been back in the States, I would have probably checked out Woodstock," I said.

"What are you talking about now?"

"Having fun."

"I can't believe that this Sam Gatlin is the same guy that I saw raging down on Go Noi."

"You'll see. I'm going to work harder on not blowing my stack."

I looked again at the picture of the spaced-out hippy on an acid trip. Better to think about more positive things, I said to myself.

*   *   *

Day Ten, 2000 hours

Top Chessman, our Alpha Company First Sergeant, met us when we got to Third Tracks. Top Chessman grabbed some Jack Daniels and poured us each a shot. We talked for a while about the offensive around Da Nang. Top mentioned that Sergeant Pabinouis was back to act as Wily's platoon sergeant. That gave me considerable comfort. I made up my mind to leave the White Lotus mission in the capable hands of Pabinoius. I didn't want to be associated in any way with Cowboy or any of Lieutenant Quick's questionable dealings. With that good news, I decided to have a couple more shots of Jack Daniels. Then we hit the sack.

For the first time in a long while, I slept through the night without waking. In my dreams I kept seeing the red and black Yin and Yang tattoo on Miss Swan's shoulder.

*　　*　　*

Day Eleven, 0400 hours

I was up before daylight. In the darkness of the early morning I walked across the sand dunes where the engines of our tracks were already rumbling. It seemed that the stars were extra bright in that time before the dawn. When I looked up into the clear and cold darkness I felt a primal rawness.

Third Platoon, Wily's platoon, was strung out in a line along the South China Sea. Since this was Third Platoon, the number three preceded all the track's numbers. I boarded Track Three-Zero. Sergeant Pabinouis was briefing his drivers.

There were eleven tracks behind us. Nine of the tracks were LVTP-5's, cargo and troop carriers, numbering from Three-Zero to Three-Nine. The eleventh track was a retriever, an R-l. I divided the tracks into two sections. Wily was disappointed with my last minute change of plans.

"Rather than you and I heading up the beach to the White Lotus, I'm going to send Sergeant Pabinouis to meet

Cowboy. Pabinouis will take one section of tracks as well as the R-1 to help load the ice machine. He will then pick up Lieutenant Quick's slot machines and haul them down to the Sand Castle. You and I will take the other section south to pick up our ROK Marines. Then we'll head back to Dodge City. Any questions?"

"Bummer. No massage for old Wily," Wily said.

"Wily, you will have to take a rain check on your massage."

Sergeant Pabinouis was clearly pleased that I put him in charge of the White Lotus mission. Once the White Lotus job was completed, he was to join the rest of us in Dodge City.

I threw my pack inside the eight by six foot bunker that was built on top of Three-Zero, sat down, and lit a cigarette. Wily was very quiet. I could tell he was disappointed about our not meeting Cowboy at the White Lotus. For some reason, one that I couldn't quite put my finger on, I was reluctant to send Wily up to meet Cowboy at the White Lotus.

Together we watched the sun come up over the South China Sea, monitoring the traffic over the radios.

*   *   *

Day Eleven, 0800 hours

The ride to Hoi An went without incident, and the ROK Marines we met on the beach began boarding Third Platoon's tracks. We then headed up Highway 1 and then cut over to Route 4. By 0900 hours we had reached the eastern edge of our operations area. Captain X and Major Hopkins were waiting for us on a slight rise of ground just north of Dien Ban. There I left Wily and choppered back to Hill 55 with Hopkins and Captain X. Wily was now on his own as platoon leader of Third Platoon, Alpha Company, Third Tracks.

Our mission was to clean out an area of Dodge City that up to now had been denied us for purely political reasons.

Sure, the area was the location of extensive, ancient cemeteries. But, in truth, the La Huan and Giang La village complex was an area where the black market of certain corrupt South Vietnamese officials was allowed to traffic with the Viet Cong.

As unbelievable as that sounds, it was true. Captain X had confirmed these facts using his special PRU team led by the Gunny. American medicine and equipment had found its way into the tunnels and bunkers of the Giang La and La Huan complex. Moreover, the NVA and Viet Cong who found refuge within the Giang La and the La Huan knew that certain corrupt South Vietnamese officials would do everything in their power to stall any operation into the area.

Captain X was now convinced of this. He also knew that his efforts to penetrate the area depended upon the fact that the Hump and Colonel Chai of the ROK Marines were individuals who were above politics. However, Captain X knew that his time was limited. That time limitation was not only due to the upcoming monsoon, certain to arrive in a matter of weeks, if not days, but our move into the Giang La and the La Huan was certain to generate big time political heat. In spite of the political threat, Captain X was setting things in motion, a lone, courageous aussie SAS advisor, who was the radical driving force behind the Hump. And for that, Captain X held my respect and admiration.

When I got to the track park I found Sergeant Chapelle standing off to one side, lost in his thoughts. Behind him, what was left of my old platoon, Second Platoon from Hill 37 and two tanks were waiting to move out.

"Val Jean, how are you doing?"

"Doing good, Lieutenant. Things have been busy here. Lieutenant Quick has our men jumping."

"Roger that. He's brought over additional tracks from Hill 37. The Dai Loc District folks must be up in arms over that."

"Yes, sir, they are. And Quick is about to drive me up the wall," Chapelle said, laughing.

I wasn't laughing.

"Maybe you will appreciate me more, Val Jean."

The tracks were moving up from the track park, sending up a great cloud of red dust. Lieutenant Quick led the column in Track One-Zero. Hog followed with Track One-Eight. Pineapple was driving One-Seven third in line and Cornflake was fourth with One-Six.

Second Platoon followed what was left of First Platoon. Since Second Platoon didn't have a platoon leader, Lieutenant Quick'd merged First and Second Platoons for the duration of this operation.

"Hey, Sam! Where have you been? I about gave you up for lost!" Quick yelled, jumping down from One-Zero.

"Doing your dirty work. Sergeant Pabinous is meeting with Cowboy as we speak."

Quick smiled and dusted himself off. India Company was forming next to us, preparing to board the tracks.

"I just heard over the radio that some gooks shot up that art exhibition across the street from the White Lotus. Took several of the sculptures. Word is they think it might have been this VC death squad. You hear anything about that?"

"No, I haven't heard anything about that. I am stunned, actually. Is nothing sacred to the VC? These collections of Cham art are a national treasure," I said.

"There it is. Hey, Sam, I need your help on something else. Next week, Top Chessman is due to rotate back to the land of the Big PX. We've been without an executive officer back at battalion headquarters. With the Top going, I need to appoint *you* the new executive officer of Alpha Company."

"Who's going to honcho these tracks?" I said in disbelief.

"I am. Since this operation is using all the available tracks that Alpha Company has, I feel that I need to be in the field with this one, as political as it is. Good chance for me to make some more contacts," Quick added.

"What am I supposed to do? Sit on my ass back at Third Tracks?"

"First of all, I want you to link up with Top Chessman. Get some transition plan in process before he leaves. I need you to facilitate some things. Yeah, that's a good word, 'facilitate.' You're my *facilitator*," Quick said curtly.

"I belong in the field. I'm not a paper pusher."

"I told you that the Top is due to rotate, and you belong where I say you belong!" Quick said, raising his voice.

That statement hit me like a load of bricks. It wasn't so much the content of the statement as the way Quick said it in front of Sergeant Chapelle and the rest of the track rats. The thought that I would be executive officer of Alpha Company had never occurred to me. I assumed that I would be going back out to the bush. Lieutenant Quick's decision to place himself back in the bush working with this reinforced platoon was highly irregular.

The grunts had finished loading and Hump walked up to the lead track. He gave the men a pep talk, explaining the importance of the operation. He then moved down the line, joking with the men. No doubt about it. Hump, the old China Hand, was a seasoned leader who could communicate at all levels. He inspired my confidence.

India Company's mission was to support the cordon and search of the Giang La and La Huan areas. Quick's tracks were to carry India Company into position. In order to accomplish this task, Quick divided his reinforced platoon into two sections. One section, under Lieutenant Quick, would push north from Route 4 to the villages of Giang La l and Giang La 2, a distance of two and a half kilometers.

Once in position at Giang La l the grunts of India Company would head east on line toward the La Huan and the great cemetery. The great cemetery was more than half a kilometer long and varied from two hundred to three hundred meters wide at any given point. The cemetery was enclosed with ancient walls and bamboo hedgerows, making any proposed assault difficult. According to Mojo Man and the Gunny, the ARVN patrols steered clear of the great cemetery. I found that fact most revealing.

While Quick's tracks were pushing north from Route 4, the other section, under Sergeant Chapelle, was to move further east along Route 4 until they had reached the railroad berm. The berm averaged about fifteen feet above the surrounding terrain and ran north to south. Sergeant Chapelle was to remain on the east side of the berm, traveling north and planting sensors until they reached the southern boundary of the great cemetery.

Upon reaching the great cemetery, Chapelle's tracks were to hold while the grunts of India Company swept the area. Having swept the area, the grunts were to pull back to a village called Thuy Bo 1 on the northern side of Route 4 and wait while the sensors did their work.

While Chapelle's tracks were moving, Lieutenant Wily and the ROK Marines would push north to the great cemetery in a parallel movement to Sergeant Chapelle's tracks, completing a cordon of the targeted area. However, once in place, Wily and the ROK Marines would remain, taking positions along the berm in case the enemy tried to break out.

The enemy, in this case, was the Q-82d Battalion, what we called main force VC as opposed to regional, paramilitary force guerillas. Main force VC proved to be highly trained military units, capable of attacking in formations. Elements of the R-20th were also supposed to be in the area, occupying a series of bunker and tunnel complexes south of La Huan 2. The Gunny, working his PRU team through the area, confirmed the existence of these bunkers. The tunnel complexes ran throughout the area, but there was one particularly extensive complex that was reported to run along the great cemetery.

The Hump'd finished talking to the men, and now walked over to our group. This tough old Marine was one of the last of the *Old Corps*. I sensed that he struggled with the powers-to-be up at Division Headquarters. Maybe no one wanted to take him seriously. He was Colonel Fry's temporary backup. But because of the Hump, we were going to make history. Because of the Hump, who didn't have anything to lose, we were going to go balls to the wall into Dodge City, at last. Certain South Vietnamese officials were going to be surprised.

"Good luck, Lieutenant Quick. I'm optimistic, very optimistic about this operation. I know that I can count on your track rats," Hump posting a big smile.

"Yes, sir! And sir, I'll have Lieutenant Gatlin available as a resource in case you need him," Quick replied.

With that, Lieutenant John Quick boarded One-Zero, gave the thumb's-up sign, and headed for Dodge City. Each track driver'd tied his state flag to the high antenna of his vehicle. At Quick's signal, each track driver released his antenna so that the flags rose in unison. The multi-colored state flags fluttered brightly in the mid-morning light as the tracks roared down into Dodge. Struggling with feelings of disappointment, I couldn't help but feel a great rush of emotion.

*   *   *

Day Eleven, 1400 hours

Cashed out of the game, so-to-speak, I followed the column through field glasses. Heading east on route 4, the sweep team immediately found a mine on the road. This they blew in place, while the column strung out along the road.

After blowing a second mine, the sweep team continued on. Somehow they missed another box mine fifty feet down the road. Box mines require various amounts of downward pressure, depending upon the nature of the firing device. The weight of a single Marine was not enough to detonate this last box mine. The sweep team and at least three grunts must have walked over the mine by the time our lead tank drove over it.

The explosion from this undiscovered mine blew the left track off the tank. Two Marines, walking to the immediate left rear of the tank, caught some flying gravel in the eyes. From our position on Hill 55 we could see the smoke from the mine's detonation. Bravo Tanks sent down another tank to replace the first, and a truck was sent down to evac the two wounded grunts. Within a half an hour the column was moving again, heading north from Route 4, into the thick bamboo hedgerows of Dodge City.

As soon as the tank hit the mine, Hump, Hopkins, Captain X, and several other staff officers gathered at the observation point that overlooked the area. The junior officers all shifted nervously, from foot to foot, as Hump studied the situation. I became self-conscious, suddenly aware that I was the only officer in the group with no shine to my boots. My boots were not only scuffed, the toes were worn to raw leather by the gravelly red clay of Hill 55. I found myself easing into the back of the group in order to remain inconspicuous.

Heat waves rose through the afternoon air, and far out, the deep green hedgerows of Dodge City seemed to shimmer. Hump didn't appear happy. Finding box mines along Route 4 was to be expected. But having these mines discovered so close was unusual. Upon further investigation, it turned out that an ARVN patrol had the responsibility for patrolling that particular section of Route 4 during the night. How had these mines been planted in the duration of a few hours? Once again the ARVN had demonstrated that they couldn't be depended upon.

The Hump had a scowl when he left the observation area. I walked over to Hopkins and Captain X to get their opinion of the situation. After all, I was now Lieutenant Quick's *facilitator*. I needed to know what was going on, however reluctantly I assumed that responsibility.

That I had more responsibility as Alpha Company executive officer was clear. Top Chessman called up on the radio and said that he was bringing out a bunch of paperwork for me to review and sign. I was not looking forward to my role as executive officer. I hated shuffling paper and the administrative procedures that went with everything in the Marine Corps. I preferred to leave that administrivia to people like Top Chessman who knew what they were doing.

Hopkins and Captain X were into an intense conversation. With a nod of their heads both men acknowledged my presence.

"So now comes the real test. You promised to get the 51st ARVN to do their thing. I want to see them jumping through their ass," Hopkins said.

"You know we can't be sure of anything at this point when it comes to the ARVN. My recommendation is that we stick to our plan. I trust that we can count on the Koreans. I have confidence in Colonel Chai," Captain X replied.

I stood there, saying nothing. A chopper passed low overhead, lifting off of Hill 55. Little swirls of red dust rose up around us, covering our faces and clothes with a red grit.

"Lieutenant Gatlin, Hump is going to have a meeting at 1600. You need to be there," Hopkins said.

"No problem," I replied, dusting myself off.

"I'm heading out. I told Hump that I would be linking up with the tracks going into the Giang La. I want to get a closer look at the terrain at a place called Cam Van 3. Is there anything that you want me to pass on to Quick?"

"No sir," I replied.

"Fine, I'll see you men later."

Hopkins walked down to the track park and boarded a jeep for his ride down into Dodge City and Cam Van 3. Red dust swirled after his jeep. A hot wind was rising, sending a spinning dust devil across the hot red clay of the track park.

Cam Van 3 was an abandoned village site that the grunts had decided to use as a staging area. Cam Van 3, in the northeast corner of Dodge City, was slightly higher than the rest of the terrain. North from Cam Van 3 the landscape sloped gradually downward to a stream bordered by tall hedgerows of bamboo. It was this unnamed stream that was the actual boundary between the Giang La and the La Huan.

The downward sloping terrain to the north and east of Cam Van 3 was thick, overgrown scrub, broken by mature clumps of towering bamboo. In recent years an area near the main road had been cleared for agriculture. However, with Cam Van 3 abandoned, the scrub vegetation had

quickly reclaimed what was once clear ground. The Gunny
had reported signs of the enemy movement along the trails
in this dark tangle.

So it was into this overgrown area that Lieutenant
Quick's reinforced track platoon had to carry the grunts.
Hopkins felt that this overgrown scrub area was too much
of an unknown. He was concerned about the Gunny's
observations. Accordingly, Hopkins was going down to
check out the area first hand.

*   *   *

Day Eleven, 1500 hours

"Well, Captain, Hump didn't look happy."

"Sam, don't mistake his gruffness. He's got too much on
his mind right now. But his officers are working better as a
professional team, much better than before. He's got more
involvement of key people in the planning."

"To look at the Hump you wouldn't think that he would
do business like that."

"Quite the contrary. Hump holds his battalion
commanders responsible for making the decisions. While
he will advise them, he won't make the decisions for
battalion commanders. Another thing, I gather that in the
past, weaknesses were covered up. The message everyone
got was not to rock the boat, if you found a weak stick,"
Captain X said, matter-of-factly.

"Very interesting."

"Now I see the issues being debated with wider
options."

"Options?"

"Hump is willing to use B-52's rather than go back into
the Go Noi and lose more Marines."

"No way, sir. The ARVN would never let that happen."

"We'll see, Lieutenant. At this point I would reserve
judgment. The ground rules have changed. Better
solutions are being proposed. I think that the effect of all
this will be greater flexibility to respond on our part. I see

the Marines doing more of the right things to take the fight into Dodge City."

"Roger that."

"We will be doing more of the right things at the right time, Lieutenant. That's what effectiveness is all about."

"Captain, how come these things that you are talking about didn't happen before?"

"Some of it had to do with the personalities involved. Also, I think that Hopkins kept changing his role. Beyond that, and I hate to say this, some of us weren't professional enough."

"Hump's predecessor seemed very professional. He projected a great image."

"Well, he may have projected a great image, but he didn't address the root causes for some of the problems that they were facing in Dodge City."

"Say again, sir."

"Keep in mind, Sam, in talking about Hump's predecessor, I realize that there were many things that were beyond his control. And there is a lot of history to this Dodge City."

"What are the root causes?"

"Well, all things considered, ask yourself two questions, Lieutenant. What things have kept the ARVN out of the northeast corner of Dodge City, specifically the La Huan and the Giang La? And what caused our military planners to go into the Go Noi first, rather than tackle the Dodge City problem, which was closer to home?"

"Politics," I replied.

"Politics is one root cause, the politics of a complex Vietnamese culture that, in their arrogance, certain generals simply ignore. We bullshit ourselves when we sit down and only look at data. On paper, looking at only the data, Go Noi, with all the enemy movement, appeared to be the priority. When in fact, what amounts to an enemy supply depot in the La Huan and the Giang La, is right under our noses! Absurd as it sounds, we allowed our enemy to move through Dodge City and create this supply depot in the La Huan and the Giang La! Sure, we curtailed movement for a time from Go Noi, but what the VC call the Warehouse still sits under the soft underbelly of Da Nang. And based upon my experience with the South Vietnamese Army, I believe that the ARVN know that the Warehouse is somewhere in the Giang La or the La Huan. They just don't want to pay the price to go get it!"

"I'm beginning to think Go Noi Island was a waste."

"Not entirely. We denied Go Noi to our enemy as a staging area, but we were playing a game of chess. We should've played the oriental game of Go rather than try to sweep the board clean. When we no longer occupy the area, our enemy simply returns. The game should have been one of contain and control."

"Ani Bui still says the Warehouse is south of Route 4."

"I doubt it, Sam."

"So, we should have contained and controlled Dodge City before we went into the Go Noi. As they say, hindsight is 20-20. I still believe that we could have leveled the Go Noi with B-52s. I'll never figure out why we didn't do that."

"I agree with you on that one. More politics."

"Does everything about this war boil down to politics?"

"No, everything in this war boils down to results. Another thing we learned from Go Noi is to think harder about what results we want. But, again, that's not a Marine problem, that's something that every professional officer in this country has to deal with."

"Captain, when it comes to results, things are no different in the Delta than they are here in I Corps. We count dead gooks. There it is. As Major Hopkins says, it's all about body count."

"Sam, we may have body counts all over Nam, but that may not always be the right measure for our effectiveness. We need to view our effectiveness in terms of the right measures. You Yanks try to do things on a scale that is impossible. I will say that some of the smaller operations are better than others, but generally speaking, most of your Yank operations take place on too large a scale. The objectives aren't always clear, and seldom does the right follow-up take place. We have generals who still don't understand that this is an insurgency we are fighting. As a result, we don't always have the resources we need."

"Like a heavy lift chopper."

"If we want to fight this war in the mountains, we will need heavy lift choppers. But that's just one symptom of the large problem."

"Sounds like a vicious cycle."

"Trying to operate on too large a scale, without the right planning or follow-up, leads to a meaningless waste of our resources. We go out to clear an area, only to find ourselves coming back later to do the same job all over again. That may be a second root cause."

"Like I said Captain, sounds like a vicious cycle. You think this operation is going to be any different in terms of results?"

"There are some good indications. First of all the operation is on the right scale. I think that we can do what we are trying to do in terms of the terrain with the resources we have available. That's very critical. Secondly, the objective is very specific and clear. That objective is to deny the enemy the use of the Giang La and the La Huan and the suspected Warehouse we believe to be located there. To deny use means to take away the tunnels, the bunker complexes, and to ambush and kill the enemy by way of cordon and search. If we blow up this Warehouse with its tunnels and bunkers, killing as many of the enemy as we can, those will be meaningful results, given our objective."

"But Captain, that's what we did in the Go Noi. We denied the gooks the area. We took out bunkers. We blew tunnels. We sprung ambushes and used our artillery and technology to take it to the enemy. To me we seem to be taking the same approach."

"Keep in mind what I said about scale. Go Noi Island is fourteen kilometers long, and anywhere from two to four kilometers wide, at any given point. The La Huan and the Giang La areas are much smaller. We are talking about saturating an area two kilometers by two kilometers. The scale of our objective on this operation, with the resources we have, is appropriate. By comparison, what we did on Go Noi was different. In this case we are going after something that we can deal with. I'm sure that you have heard of the term economy of force. Well, we also should have a term called economy of scale."

Captain X smiled and looked off into the shimmering green that spread below us. All around our high observation point the red dust continued to swirl. Out on the wide expanse of green that was Dodge City, I could see our line of tracks moving eastward.

* * *

Day Eleven, 1530 hours

Chapelle's tracks had reached Thuy Bo 1 and were moving north. As planned, Hog and Mojo Man were heading up teams that were in the process of planting sensors. These sensors were the same design as those that we used on Go Noi Island. Hog's guess had been that two teams could accomplish the task of planting the sensors in a matter of four hours, given the terrain. From the way things seemed to be going, phase one was way ahead of schedule.

At 1600 hours Hump addressed the First Marine Regimental staff. This time he was smiling, and his comments were brief and to the point.

"I am very pleased with both the progress that has been made, and with the kind of teamwork I've seen with the ARVN and the ROK Marines. I believe what we are doing in the La Huan and the Giang La is going to produce longer-term solutions to denying the enemy sanctuary. We have learned valuable lessons from our former Go Noi operation. Reliable intelligence has the NVA already building bunkers on the southern edge of Go Noi Island. On this operation we aren't going to repeat the mistakes of Go Noi. Those mistakes had to do with trying to do too much with our limited resources, given the terrain. That will not happen in Dodge City," Hump said, a White Owl cigar in his left hand.

What Hump didn't say was that he was taking a stand relative to the politics of the situation, and that the First Marines and the Second ROK Marines were going into the La Huan and the Giang La with or without the 51st ARVN. Hump was resolute. He was standing firm.

Hump's briefing was then interrupted. A corporal, out of breath, reported that one of the vehicles in Lieutenant Quick's column had hit a huge, command-detonated mine. The whole column was under heavy fire.

*   *   *

Day Eleven, 1630 hours

At the COC the most recent report had Major Hopkins seriously wounded and Lieutenant Quick KIA. Both men had been riding on top of a tank when the mine went off. The company commander of India Company was waiting for a dust-off to take out the casualties.

Captain X said that he was going to take his chopper in. I asked Hump if I could accompany Captain X. Hump pointed out that as executive officer of Alpha Company, Third Tracks, he expected me to assume command of the company. Hump's statement struck me cold. Company commander! Damn, I thought. I was now company commander of Alpha Company, and half my tracks were caught in a huge *u-shaped* ambush in the depths of Dodge City. I ran out the door to Captain X and the waiting chopper.

*   *   *

Day Eleven, 1700 hours

At 500 feet above Dodge City we could make out the irregular u-shaped ambush. At that low altitude we took a couple of hits from AK-47s. So we dropped down even further to a hundred feet, passing in low and fast before our enemy could hit us. Below me I could make out NVA uniforms. We were facing both main force VC and NVA regulars!

Pineapple's track was assaulting one side of the u-shape followed by two squads of grunts. His track was mounted with both a fifty caliber and an M-60 machine gun. Those guns were tearing up the scrub and laying down an intense volume of fire, too intense for the VC and NVA regulars with only AK-47s. Pineapple's rash assault had surprised the ambushers because the NVA line broke, falling back deeper within the scrub.

The chopper pilot dropped Captain X and me off at the rear of the track column, and the grunts brought us two wounded tankers and Major Hopkins. Captain X helped me load them.

"Hopkins' shit is weak. He's lost *beaucoup* blood," a grunt muttered to me.

In addition to injuries suffered when the mine had detonated, Hopkins had been shot through the side, the round exiting in a particularly ugly wound. He was shocky, and I was grateful that we were close to Hill 55. Captain X pulled Hopkins into the chopper and they were gone. The chopper was on the ground less than a minute.

Then two grunts carried over Lieutenant John Quick. He was wrapped in a poncho. I was afraid to pull the poncho back. When I looked at Hog, he shook his head.

"How bad?"

"Never knew what hit him, Lieutenant. He was sitting right on top of the mine when it went off."

Hog's eyes were glazed with fatigue. The noise around us was deafening. We all seemed to be moving in slow motion. We were settled in a kind of bowl, surrounded on three sides by tall bamboo and scrub. In that bowl, a smoky haze hung in the still air.

"Hog! Are you wounded?"

"No, sir. Shook up, but not wounded. Had an RPG explode pretty close to me."

Pineapple had turned his track around and was heading back toward our position. When the track turned, momentarily exposing its port side, an NVA rushed forward with an RPG and fired at a distance of less than twenty meters. A Marine grunt carrying an M-60 machine gun ran up and blew the NVA away. The RPG penetrated the track, slinging molten metal through the interior. Pineapple and his two track rats jumped clear. The track began to smoke.

"Lieutenant, they need help up at the tank. There's a tanker still inside the tank!" Hog yelled.

Pineapple ran up to me, keeping low to the ground. His driver had been wounded by hot slag. I directed Hog to take care of the driver, and grabbed my shotgun. It took me no more than a minute to get to the head of the column. I low-crawled most of the way.

The grunts were still in contact on the other side of the u-shaped ambush... There were several snipers to our immediate front, which was right at the bottom of the u-shaped ambush. Their accurate fire had pinned down the grunts on either side of the track column.

Pineapple and I reached a grunt lieutenant who was peering over a map, trying to figure out his position in the featureless terrain of the scrub. The grunt lieutenant was unfamiliar with the terrain and was waiting for guidance from his company commander before calling in artillery.

The mined tank lay to our direct front. The whole left front track was apart, and tangled in the road wheels. Since we were caught in a pocket of scrub that had no obvious terrain features, we had to gamble. Quickly I got a compass reading, sighting in Hill 55, the highest terrain feature. I calculated a back azimuth while the grunt lieutenant asked the 105 battery on Hill 55 to shoot a white phosphorus round at a point on the map where the railroad berm intersected the La Tho river...

Luck was with us. We were able to sight in on the smoke and took a back azimuth from that smoke, marking our position between Cam Van 3 and Thuy Bo 3. In the past we had found map errors up to one hundred meters on our map sheet, so it was with great concern that we called in our first artillery round.

The l05 battery dropped a round one hundred meters beyond the disabled tank. The grunt lieutenant told the battery to drop fifty, and fire for effect. The NVA, still firing on our right immediately broke contact as the arty rounds left the tubes on Hill 55. Once again, the 105mm Light Howitzer M01A1 saved our ass. Seven man crews on each of the guns in the six tube battery loaded their forty-two pound rounds into the breeches, and let loose a rain from hell, pulverizing the target with direct hits, three rounds per gun.

With no wind in this steamy pocket of scrub it must have been over one hundred degrees, with better than ninety per-cent humidity. The grunt lieutenant stood up to take off his flak jacket, and a bullet from a sniper's rifle caught him in the side. We all dropped to the ground, pulling the grunt lieutenant into the shelter of a nearby track. The sniper was very close to the tank, hidden in a spider hole along a slight rise covered with scrub.

Pineapple's track was still smoldering. Pallets of supplies inside the track were burning. It appeared that we might have a chance to put the fire out. Before I could say a word Pineapple and Hog took it upon themselves to grab fire extinguishers and rush across open ground to the smoldering track. Another sniper's bullet zipped inches over Pineapple's head. There was a shout, to my left, as Cornflake yelled that he'd seen the sniper's muzzle flash. Racing his engine, and spewing out a great cloud of exhaust, Cornflake's track churned away from the column toward the hidden spider hole. There was a second muzzle flash as the sniper continued to fire at Pineapple and Hog. The sniper must have known that his position had been revealed for he managed to crack off a third round in our direction just before Cornflake's track overwhelmed him.

The huge LVTP-5 amphibious tractor, traveling at twenty miles an hour, climbed the slight rise and engulfed the spider hole, catching the sniper as he attempted to crawl free at the last seconds. The sniper's scream was cut short as Cornflake executed a 360-degree turn, grinding the sniper into oblivion.

Pineapple and Hog extinguished the burning pallets. We called for a dust-off to evacuate the wounded lieutenant. A squad of grunts ran forward behind the cover of Cornflake's track and pulled the tank driver out. The tank driver was dead, apparently a victim of the sniper as he tried to crawl from the mined tank. The chopper arrived within minutes. We loaded the wounded lieutenant and the bodies of Lieutenant Quick and the tank driver. I turned away from the chopper to hear yet another sniper's bullet zip by, just inches over my head.

"Where the hell did that come from?" I yelled.

Pineapple was in the process of hooking a steel cable to his track. The big Samoan handled the fifty pound steel hooks as if he were handling a football. Another round cracked through the air, ricocheting off the track's hull and forcing Pineapple to the ground. There was a second sniper hidden in the scrub. This sniper was a shitty shot, but we were taking no chances. For this spider hole was close, very close.

The squad of grunts to my left opened up with all their weapons. I screamed at them for fire discipline. Fortunately the grunt platoon had a squared-away staff sergeant who took control of the situation, directing his grunts into defensive positions facing outward toward the direction of the fire...

The grunt staff sergeant then took out a claymore bag full of frag grenades. Keeping to the ground, his men low-crawled on line toward Pineapple's track, tossing frag grenades to clear the area ahead of them. The process took a good ten minutes but the grunt staff sergeant cleared the way to Pineapple's track. Then there was a burst of rifle fire and a shout of triumph from one grunt. The sniper had been found. A dying teen-age girl was pulled from the spider hole. It appeared that she was about the same age as Ani Bui.

*　　　*　　　*

Day Eleven, 1800 hours

Hump sent down word that he wanted the disabled tank brought back to Hill 55. The first step was to untangle the tank track that had been blown around the tank's road wheels. Pineapple went about the process of blowing off the tangled track with small blocks of C-4 explosive. This was tricky business. The block of C-4 had to be large enough to break the steel track, and small enough so that no one would get hurt. The track removal went smoothly.

Once the track was removed from the tank hull, we began pulling the tank back towards Route 4. The three tracks strained under the load but by 1900 hours we had reached Route 4. There we set up a perimeter for the night.

*   *   *

Day Eleven, 2000 hours

The evening sounds of the scrub-jungle began as the sun set. First the katydids snapped and clicked. Then came the quick and rhythmic peeping of the rice crickets. Occasionally, the high-pitched trill of a tree frog would break in. At 2130 the enemy fired a salvo of ten 122mm rockets at Da Nang. The rockets were fired from a position just north of Giang La. The offensive aimed at Da Nang's soft underbelly lived.

*   *   *

Day Eleven, 2300 hours

The singing night creatures abruptly ceased with the first dull thunk of an enemy mortar tube. We took mortar fire for about five minutes until we could direct our artillery to where the mortar tube was located. Because we had dug in, there were no casualties. Thus ended our phase one.

*　　*　　*

CHAPTER FIFTEEN: BUNKER COMPLEX

Day Twelve, 0600 hours

The ROK Marines advanced on line in the La Huan, moving east from the railroad berm into the area of the great cemetery. Wily's track platoon followed through a breach in the berm where a bridge had once spanned a small stream.

Hog and I were sitting along Route 4 eating breakfast when Captain X's chopper appeared overhead. Moments before, my battalion commander had contacted me on One-Eight's powerful radio to confirm that I was now company commander of Alpha Company. I could tell that my battalion commander was as shook up as I was over John Quick's death.

John Quick's death and my sudden appointment to company commander gave rise to a multitude of conflicting thoughts and feelings. I couldn't help but feel partially responsible for the fact that John Quick was dead. When he had made me executive officer and pulled me out of the field, I had been angry, very angry. Some of my freedom had been taken away. Behind that anger was the fear that if I had protested, Lieutenant Quick would have sent me to Division. Even though he was my friend, I didn't feel that I should confront him. And yet I hadn't trusted my own judgment. I felt guilty for not making more of an issue over his taking me out of the field.

I knew what I had to do to inspire the confidence of my men. I felt as if I were filled with a suppressed energy that was about to explode; but at the same time I was watching the events around me with a kind of detachment. These conflicting thoughts and feelings were dangerous not only for me, but for those that I was supposed to lead.

I made up my mind, then and there, that in the future I would hold myself to do a better job as an officer. Two weeks ago, I would have let Phase One grind itself into the ground before I would have taken it upon myself to try to rescue the operation.

"I was very sorry to hear about Quick," Captain X said.

"Yes, sir," I said, looking off in the distance.

"Hump sent me down to see if you wanted my chopper to take you over to Wily's position."

"Yes, sir," I said, picking up my shotgun.

Chapelle was sitting next to me eating a can of peaches. I noticed that his fingers were trembling again. I gave Chapelle a pat on the back. He nodded. It was obvious that Chapelle was as shook up by Quick's death as I was. I thought about what the Gunny once said about knowing when to leave your men alone. It seemed like this was one of those times. Captain X and I walked to his chopper.

"Things are jumping up on the hill," Captain X said.

"Yes, sir," I said, lost in my own thoughts.

"We have a low pressure system coming in. I expect that we'll get some rain before this operation is over."

"Sounds like the monsoon is coming early. That will cramp our style big time, sir."

"No. Not in this case. The weather factor was figured into the planning. Hopkins and I talked at length about it."

"They didn't talk to me about it. As my track rats say, *the monsoon will clean our ass and bog our tracks*."

"We'll get the tracks out before that happens."

"Sir, with all due respect, that remains to be seen. On my last tour, rain bogged my tracks down in the Go Noi and we were almost history."

"Keep the faith, Sam."

"It's easier to keep the faith on dry ground, Captain."

"Between you and me, Sam, there's some concern on the part of some of the officers on the hill that you got Wily running a platoon."

"Captain, sounds to me like a bunch of staff weenies. I know that Wily shoots his mouth off and has made some enemies. But I think Wily will be all right."

"It's more than a few staff weenies that are talking, Sam. Maybe you ought to think about calling your battalion commander for a more experienced track officer."

"Captain, a moment ago you were talking about faith. Well, I got my faith in Lieutenant Wily."

"We all know that Wily's your friend. It's easy to have a blind spot when it comes to a friend. Don't let your friendship get in the way of your better judgment."

"Say again, sir."

"Don't confuse your friendship with what the situation requires, or what objective analysis seems to suggest."

"Objective analysis! You got to be shitting, sir. What was so objective about the way Wily was relieved down on the Go Noi. The more experience that I get, the more that I think that there is very little about this war that involves objective analysis. Everything is subjective!"

"Right now it is enough for you to know that there are officers on the hill who will be watching Wily closely."

"Sir, I don't know all the circumstances as to why Wily was relieved down on Go Noi. Wily has never told me what happened. To me it doesn't matter if he ever does. Old Wily once came through for me in a tight, and I'll back him now no matter what."

"Wily made two mistakes down on the Go Noi," Captain X said, continuing.

"Sir, I don't need to hear it," I said, thinking about what the Gunny had once said about knowing when to stand firm.

"Sam, I think that you do need to hear this. Wily's first mistake was in expecting others to be self-motivated. It was a leadership mistake... He took the word of one of his men at face value that certain things were done when indeed those things were not done. That first mistake cost some lives. You need to know that was the first reason why he was relieved."

"There are a number of officers on Hill 55 who have made mistakes that cost lives."

"I understand. But Wily's second mistake was that he froze. He was unable to act, and some of his men had to act for him. That also was a leadership problem. One that couldn't be forgiven, and it was sufficient cause by itself to relieve Wily of command."

"Well, sir. I didn't know that. But I've got to hang tough with Wily. That's the way it is. But believe me, I heard what you said. What is it the track rats say? The first rule of combat is not to bullshit yourself."

"I thought that you needed to hear these things. If I were in your situation I would have wanted someone to tell me what was going on."

Captain X and I boarded the chopper. As the chopper rose, we could see more low, dark clouds coming in from the north and the east. We were in for a weather change. That was certain. I had this uncomfortable feeling that the monsoon season was beginning early.

*   *   *

Day Twelve, 0730 hours

By 0730 hours the ROK advance had reached a stream running north and south. Here things slowed up as advance elements had found a string of mutually supporting bunkers built into the opposite side of the streambed. That streambed was bordered by thick bamboo hedge. At that point Sergeant Pabinouis arrived with his section of tracks. The special supply run had gone without a hitch. Pabinouis heard about Quick over the radio. He was really shook-up over the news.

Wily, Pabinouis, Sergeant Hun, and myself waited with our tracks about 100 meters from the stream. The ROK company commander was none other than Scar. Scar, his platoon commanders, and Lieutenant Kim had gathered together to discuss the situation. The decision they reached was for us to pull back and call in an air strike.

Sergeant Hun said that Scar was a good officer who wouldn't waste either his men or resources. Hun added, however, that Colonel Chai had made it clear that he was out to support *his American allies* and that under no circumstances must the ROK Marines lose face. This situation had put tremendous pressure on Scar, because, despite his obnoxious manners, he was considered to be the best of the ROK company commanders.

"Sam, I don't see how this is any different than Go Noi. Do you?" Wily asked.

"Captain X tells me this operation is on a more manageable scale. He also thinks that the objectives are clearer than on Go Noi. Other than that, I don't know."

"You don't know! You're the company commander, Sam. You're supposed to know!"

*　　*　　*

Day Twelve, 0800 hours

The air strike came in two waves. An OV-10A Bronco carrying an airborne controller was on station to our west. Standing by to provide air support were two flights of three F-4B Phantoms, Marine high altitude interceptors adapted for ground attack. Circling over the bunker complex, the airborne controller gave the F-4B flights their target assignments.

Each of the Phantoms carried 16,000 pounds of ordnance, napalm canisters and snake-eye bombs. The first flight came in over us with a deafening roar, their napalm canisters scattering within the hedge and bursting into a cloud of all consuming fire. One of the canisters exploded within a hundred meters of us with a great whooshing sound. At that distance I could feel the heat on my face.

Then the second flight came in. Great sheets of liquid fire spread over the streambed followed by plumes of black smoke three stories high. The napalm run completed, two F-4's then dropped several snake-eye bombs. The earth shook under our feet. Bomb fragments whistled through the air over our heads. This was what Marines like to call *close air support.*

After the air strike, the artillery based on Hill 55 took over, responding to Lieutenant Kim's adjustments. I was sure that both the air strike and the artillery prep fire had reduced the enemy strong points so that we could now secure the opposite stream bed. I had seen air strikes soften enemy resistance before. The psychological value of our air support on Wily and my track rats was evident. My track rats cheered as the F-4 Phantoms flew over.

"There you go, Wily. That shit will soften them up."

"We will need something, Sam. Hun tells me those bunkers are some of the best that he's seen."

"We'll see. I like Hun. He was with me on Go Noi."

"Hun's okay. But I worry about this Scar. He runs around like a man obsessed."

"Stay loose, Wily, and listen to Pabinouis. He'll keep you out of trouble."

"I heard Pabinouis is real shook-up over Quick."

"Yeah, but he's proven himself, Wily. He's proven himself under fire, which is what you got to do!" I blurted out.

"What do you mean by that?"

"Just what I said, Wily. Hey, I don't know what happened down on Go Noi Island. And you don't have to tell me. But don't bullshit me and don't bullshit yourself. If you listen to Pabinouis, he'll give you some good advice."

"Is this the same man who I saw scream at Sergeant Chapelle, down on the Go Noi?"

"Don't stand in judgment of me, Wily," I said, my voice loud enough to attract the attention of several track rats.

"You're right, Sam. And I'll stay loose… Look, I never told you what happened on Go Noi. Basically, I fucked up."

"On the hill they are saying that you froze up. That you lost your nerve."

"That's true," Wily said, looking at the ground.

The smell of napalm drifted through the air and the thick bamboo hedgerow was no more. There was roar overhead as the jets made another pass. Somewhere out in the bush I heard Marines cheering.

*   *   *

Day Twelve, 1000 hours

We reached Hill 55 to find the COC busy. I got on the radio and talked to my battalion commander in order to status him on the operation. He only asked a few questions, and, as a former tanker, he seemed to have a lot of assumptions about how tracks should be deployed. This was his first battalion command and he had been on the job a month. The past weeks'd made him extremely cautious, and he seemed restrained even in his communication to me. His restraint made me wonder how I fit into his universe as a company commander. When I finished talking to him, I felt very tentative. Hump walked up and slapped me on the shoulder.

"How's Lieutenant Gatlin doing?"

"Just right, sir. Although I understand that some of the officers on the hill are concerned about one of my platoon leaders."

Hump smiled knowingly.

"You're talking about this Lieutenant Wily."

"Yes, sir."

"I hoped that Lieutenant Wily learned from his experience."

"Yes, sir. I wonder about that myself."

"Lieutenant Gatlin, I've asked around about you. I talked to that Gunnery Sergeant who was down on Go Noi with you, the one now running a PRU team over at Dien Ban District. He said good things. And I watched you. You impress me. But let me give you some advice. Forget about the past. You're strong. Strong people always have weaknesses. You will do fine as a company commander. Just remember what you stand for. Do what you think is right, and the men will follow your lead."

Hump then looked at me for a moment, saying nothing. It was as if he were looking right through me, and that he could read my mind. Hump had some strange kind of insight. I wondered what he would say if he saw the beautiful Miss Swan, or my green bottle of absinth. Perhaps he had heard of my trembling episodes, or maybe of Toc's tattooed hand floating in the green juice of the pickle jar. This grizzled old relic from the Old Corps smiled again, still saying nothing, and then walked away.

*　　*　　*

Day Twelve, 1130 hours

I walked to my hooch in a drizzle that was turning into a steady rain. The pervasive dust of Hill 55 had already turned to slick red clay. I opened a cold Sapporo.

"*Here's to John Quick,*" I said to myself.

I sat down and drank in silence. Quick would have appreciated that. Quick was gone, and I was struggling. What had he died for? He had died for the Marine Corps. No other explanation was needed.

At that moment, I felt a profound despair. I could now see that Quick had been endowed with at least some quality of genius. His *Yin,* an imagination gifted with an insight into the circumstances surrounding us, and his *Yang,* moving forward with confidence, acting upon what he believed in, grounded in his own unique and comprehensive vision of the world. His Yin and Yang.

I bummed a poncho and walked down to the chopper pad. The rain had picked up, and it appeared that the cloud cover would hinder our air support. On the way I met Captain X.

"Welcome to the monsoon, Captain. This weather will kill us," I said, disgusted.

"Negative. I've told you this before. The weather was a factor that we considered for our great ambush."

"Great ambush, my ass. I'll believe it when I see it."

"Technology, Lieutenant Gatlin. This is about technology and patience. *Patience is the hunter.*"

"And I've heard that before. Patience is the hunter. I'll be sure to tell that to my men as they are digging out their bogged down tracks."

*　　*　　*

Day Twelve, 1430 hours

Rain beat on our chopper as we headed back down into
Dodge City. To the north and east the sky was black with
more high thunderclouds, and a twenty-knot wind was
blowing them in our direction. The ROK Marines had
mopped up the area of that morning's air strike using
explosives to blow up the bunkers. At l530 I reached
Wily's tracks, hiking in over the blown bunkers. As of yet,
there was no sign of the Warehouse we were seeking, nor
had any weapons cache been uncovered.

What we moved into was a burned-out wasteland.
Where the tall bamboo hedgerows had been, there were
now only a few leafless, blackened shafts. Our tracks
crossed this gray wasteland to a wide savanna surrounded
on three sides by more scrub. In the middle of the grassy
savannah, on a slight rise, the ROK Marines had camped
among the remains of an ancient pagoda.

Scar made the decision to make the pagoda ruins his
headquarters for the night. The drizzle had increased to a
steady rain, and Scar said that, because of the tracks, it
would be best to keep to the higher ground. That decision
gave me some comfort. Scar was tuned in to our needs.

Wily directed the tracks to circle the pagoda. With ten
tracks around him, Scar was protected. He then ordered his
men to dig in for the night. I jumped down from the track
and walked around the perimeter with Wily to discuss the
best positions for our machine guns.

Although the walls of the pagoda had holes blown in
them, the structure supporting the roof seemed intact. Wily
and I sat under that roof and out of the rain. I looked up to
see the Gunny and his PRU team coming out of the high
grass. Mojo Man and Blitz were with the team.

Mojo Man sat down and broke open a case of Korean
combat rations. I noticed that he now had three different
little Buddhas hanging on chains from his neck.

"Think that you have enough of Buddha's luck with
you?" I asked.

"Never can have enough luck, Lieutenant," Mojo Man said.

"Roger that," I replied.

"I like Jack Daniel's myself," the Gunny said.

Mojo Man took one of the Buddhas from around his neck and offered it to me. I took the Buddha and put it around my neck. The Gunny made a face.

"Thanks, Mojo Man. Thanks a lot," I said, pleased with the gift.

"How come you wear those fucking things? Are you going gook on me?" the Gunny asked.

"Well, Gunny. When I left the World to come back to the Nam for my second tour, I kept wondering why. Then I met this little lady in a ville called Nui Kim Son, just south of the Special Forces Camp next to Marble Mountain. She gave me my first Buddha, said it would help me, that it would bring me luck."

I was opening a can of *kim chi* and listening to Mojo Man. I stopped what I was doing and looked up. Clearly the little lady Mojo Man had met in Nui Kim Son had helped him.

"Tell me more about the little lady," Wily said, now curious.

"Yes, sir, the little lady is my number one," Mojo Man said.

"Sounds cool, very cool," Wily said.

"Cool my ass. Mojo Man, don't go messin up Lieutenant Wily's brain housing group," the Gunny said gruffly.

Everyone laughed except the Gunny. Mojo Man appeared to have a sweetheart down in the ville. I respected Mojo Man for that, and I trusted that his sweetheart would help him hold firm to doing his job as best he could. I was proud to keep his Buddha around my neck.

Lieutenant Kim and Sergeant Hun had caught the tail end of the conversation. They sat down and opened a couple cans of seaweed and little fishes. The rain was coming down hard, straight down. I sensed that each wanted to say something but was holding back.

I had come to the Nam an iconoclast. Before Nam, I had been turned off of religious images and, in general, was opposed to their veneration in any form. For I saw myself as a totally rational person who had a handle on what reality was. Now, after my experience in Laos and my second tour in I Corps, I could see myself changing. Maybe I was getting religion. Mojo Man and Pabinouis each carried on their person a powerful symbol that they believed in, a thing that gave them comfort, and that they held close.

No such comfort for me, I thought. I knew in my heart and mind that there were things that were fundamentally, perhaps even chemically different, about the psyche of each of these men who sat with me under the roof of the ruined pagoda. That difference caused each of them to perceive reality in a different way. Yet each of us was bound to the other by way of the Marine Corps. It occurred to me that those bonds were no longer rational, and the more combat I saw, the more it seemed that I had become a mystic who had surrendered to an enigma called Vietnam. The *Nam* was a mystery that defied individual interpretation. Perhaps understanding the *Nam* was something that could only be attained through the experience of living it.

*   *   *

Day Twelve, 1700 hours

I walked into Wily's track and found an entrenching tool. I started clearing an area inside the pagoda, my plan being to dig myself a hole. For a few minutes I worked hard, clearing away the rubble and debris. Then I sat down to have a smoke. Before I knew it a bluish-green creature with a hundred or so orange legs ran out from under the rubble and up my leg.

I screamed, jumped up, and pulled off my trousers. The creature was a centipede over a foot long. The centipede tried to hide in my cast off trousers, but I went frantic, hacking the creature to pieces with my entrenching tool. The centipede's sharp claws had left tiny red marks at every point where the claws had touched my skin. The little red marks formed a trail up the outside of my leg.

"You skated that one, Lieutenant. Doesn't look like you got bit," Mojo Man said, examining my leg.

"I guess so," I said, out of breath.

"Your Buddha brought you some luck," Mojo Man said.

"There it is," Wily said, his eyes wide at the sight of the centipede.

*   *   *

Day Twelve, 1800 hours

My face was flushed and my leg was swollen. I put some rubbing alcohol on the red marks that had turned into welts. It seemed to help. The welts burned and itched. I put on a pair of shorts, elevated my leg, and sat back to watch the rain.

It began to rain harder. At 1830 Scar had sent out several squad-sized ambush patrols to catch any of the enemy that might try to move in on us. Scar left the perimeter about 1845 to check each of those patrols, concerned about poor communication. He was also upset about the fact that the so-called assault on the bunker complex had turned up nothing. The Warehouse had yet to be uncovered. Scar was feeling the pressure to do something. His men felt that pressure and everyone was very up-tight.

It was 1900 when we heard a burst of rifle fire. Scar had been zapped by his own ambush. The chopper that took Scar and his wounded radioman out also took me back to Hill 55. Halfway to hill 55 Scar died, victim of friendly fire. Thus the assault of the bunker complex ended with the great Warehouse still undiscovered.

*   *   *

CHAPTER SIXTEEN: PHASE TWO

Day Thirteen, 0300 hours

I was sent up to medical for observation. At one point in the middle of the night I walked out to get some fresh air. The rain had let up for a time. Through a break in the rain clouds, the moon even shone, and the NVA choose that moment to launch six 140mm rockets at Da Nang. Hill 55 responded with artillery. After our artillery pounded the launch site for five minutes, Puff the Magic Dragon came on station with its steady, orange stream of fire. For the next ten minutes I watched while Puff tore up the earth. Then more clouds rolled in and the rain returned. Puff disappeared in the clouds.

* * *

Day Twelve, 0830 hours

The welts on my legs continued to rise and the rain continued to pour. The doctor gave me a couple pills and said the swelling would stop. The itching didn't stop, however, and I still had a bit of a temperature when I left medical about 0900 to head back down to the chopper pad.

Captain X was waiting there with Toc. Together we watched as the Gunny choppered in with Mojo Man. The news was bad. At 0630 that morning Colonel Chai's chopper had got into trouble while on the ground in an area southeast of Hill 55. What they were doing on the ground in that area was a mystery. Stranger still, Lipske was with Colonel Chai for some unexplained reason.

Colonel Chai's hiding place in the scrub south of Route 4 was also the site of an old minefield. The Viet Cong had enhanced the minefield with numerous booby traps. I simply could not understand why Chai's U.S. Army pilot had set the chopper down at the edge of the minefield.

Shortly after setting the chopper down, they had taken fire and were forced to make a run for it. During that time Lipske had been separated from the rest of the group. Colonel Chai and the two Army pilots were now hiding in a tree line. It was a replay of the incident where Captain X had been shot down over the Xuan Diem Cemetery.

A squad of Marine grunts had already been put on the ground. The grunts had moved to within 400 meters of Chai's position when they took 50-Caliber machine gun fire from a tree line. Two Army choppers were in the area, prepared to give support as best they could, but the heavy machine gun fire complicated matters.

*   *   *

Day Twelve, 1000 hours

Toc agreed to guide the Gunny and Mojo Man through the minefield. Captain X was to drop the group in. Captain X immediately used his authority to designate the group a special task team. That team was made up of Mojo Man, the Gunny, Toc, and myself. The Gunny decided not to bring his PRU Team. It appeared that he no longer fully trusted them.

This time there was good cause for the special task team. Captain X was responding quickly to a real need. As the team was preparing to board the chopper, I noticed that my hand began to tremble slightly. Was I trembling with anticipation, or was this the returning result of my head trauma? Maybe both, I thought to myself.

"You run the team, Sam," Captain X said.

I grabbed my shotgun and an M-79 grenade launcher. Captain X looked at me strangely. My decision to go with the team was crazy. No one had forced me. It was a decision that grew out of the situation at hand. I felt that they needed me. *It was the right thing to do.*

Through both long study and experience, I was the one most familiar with this area of Dodge City along the border between the Dien Ban and Dai Lac Districts. Now, that study and experience seemed to integrate itself into a unified whole. I was no longer separate from the Dodge City that appeared on the map. I was part of the bamboo hedgerow. I was keen as a bamboo cat.

Perhaps it was unconscious. But the moment that the minefield had been mentioned, it was as if I had made a great leap forward, and I had found new energy. Since then, I have never again had that feeling. It was a feeling of power that came from within. I was centered and at one with everything around me. I knew that what I was doing was right. Even though I had my role as company commander for Alpha Company, Third Tracks, I knew that I would be saving lives by going with this team.

By the time our chopper was in the air, the heavy rain had changed to a drizzle. We circled the minefield, coming in from the east, just over the treetops in order to avoid fire from the 50-Caliber. I could see Colonel Chai's chopper in a clump of scrub. I marked its position on my map. Then our chopper touched down and an instant later we were hunkered low in knee-high grass.

The grunts were 100 meters to our immediate left under the cover of a rice dike. I checked my map and determined Colonel Chai's chopper to be about 200 meters directly west. The firefight had stopped, and the grunts were consolidating their position, a position that was too exposed. An NVA mortar attack would do a job on the grunts.

These grunts had been put on the ground without much guidance. The corporal in charge didn't know where he was on the map, but he knew the old minefield was to their front. Beyond the minefield, which was some 50 meters wide, was a tree line of scrub. I guessed that the 50-Caliber was 300 to 400 meters further west into that scrub. While it was firing at any chopper that passed overhead, no one had been able to get a fix on the gun's position.

Due to the heavy machine gun fire, any chopper that wanted to land had to come in very low from the east. Normally, we would have called in an air strike. The problem was that Chai and his American pilots were now hidden in the same scrub that concealed the 50-Caliber.

Mojo Man and I quickly devised a plan. The Gunny was to take charge of the grunt squad and hold the position. When it came time to get out, the choppers that came in to pick us up would have to again come in low from the east. The Gunny was to move the grunts to the most advantageous position. Mojo Man, Toc and I would head south for about 100 meters. At that point Toc felt that he could get us across the minefield. As a trail guide for the NVA, he had crossed this minefield on a number of occasions.

We were in radio contact with the Army chopper pilot. The pilot said that they had movement all around them. He had no clue what had happened to Lipske. I directed him not to move unless it was to avoid immediate capture. He also said that the 50-Caliber was very close. That fact I found confusing. My understanding was that the 50-Caliber should have been farther west.

Mojo Man carried our radio. I carried a bag of M-79 ammo along with my shotgun and an M-79. Toc didn't carry a weapon. With Toc leading the way, we low-crawled south to find an opening across the minefield.

The light rain favored our movement. Moreover, the minefield had grown up into waist-high grass crossed by narrow animal trails. Small animals could run over these old French-type mines without incident. It took the weight of a man to detonate this type of mine.

Toc studied the ground and the little trails through the grass. It all looked the same to me. Finally, Toc found a path that he knew. We crawled into the grass on all fours, completely hidden from any eyes.

Through this tunnel in the vegetation, we made it across the minefield. Soaked to the skin, I was tempted to shed some of what I was carrying in order to move more freely. The rain began to come down harder.

Once through the minefield, we made radio contact with Chai's pilot. My compass reading had them 75 meters directly to our north. The pilot said that he still had *beaucoup* movement all around. I took point as we crept carefully through the scrub.

I guessed that we were halfway to Chai's position when we heard voices to our west. Through a hole in the vegetation I could see a small clearing that was the result of a bomb crater. At the other end of the clearing was Chai's chopper. Four NVA were moving toward the chopper. Each one was carrying either a different part of a 50-Caliber machine gun or an ammo box. The NVA had broken the gun down and were moving to a better position.

I was surprised at the boldness of the NVA. They must be very confident, I thought. Mojo Man tapped me on the shoulder and pointed east.

There, some fifteen meters to our left, was Fritz Lipske. He had been stripped, disemboweled, and impaled through the rectum upon a large bamboo stake. I could see that one of his eyes had been gouged out. The other eye hung down, partially pulled out, dangling. His entrails spilled out onto the ground, still steaming in the drizzling rain, a tangled, ropy gray and blue mass.

Mojo Man tapped me on the shoulder again. Six more Vietnamese were moving toward us down a narrow animal trail in the waist-high grass. Where had they come from? These Vietnamese weren't wearing NVA uniforms. They were wearing the black pajamas of the VC. The Vietnamese leading the group was none other than Cowboy, the bartender from The White Lotus.

Mojo Man must have read my mind for he pointed to the ground and pointed to a trap door. I nodded. No wonder the machine gun team was confident. We were sitting on top of an extensive tunnel system. The placing of this tunnel system, within easy walking distance to Hill 55, was both bold and ingenious. These NVA had exploited the boundary between the Dai Lac and Dien Ban Districts as well as our Marine battle plan for the Hill 55 area of responsibility.

The six VC, including Cowboy, were carrying AK-47s. They joined the NVA gun team and began talking excitedly, pointing in the direction of Lipske. Then, as a group, they started in our direction. I was certain that they would see us so I radioed the Gunny to fire a burst into the air in order to get the NVA's attention. The Gunny fired, and the distraction worked. Cowboy and his group stopped in their tracks, allowing us to move back, out of sight of both the narrow animal trail and the trap door entrance...

A long minute passed. The six VC were still talking with the NVA machine gun team. I knew what I had to do. I shifted my position and I suddenly found myself with a shot through the scrub. Without a moment's hesitation I dropped an M-79 round into the group. I followed with another round. Mojo Man tossed two frag grenades in rapid succession. Then all was silent in the light rain.

Chai's pilot called on the radio. He was shook. He wanted to know what the hell was going on. I told him to stay loose and asked him where he was in relation to the M-79 explosions. He replied that he was to the northeast. I was sure that we were only some 50 meters away from them.

Mojo Man then ran to Lipske. He stopped ten meters from Lipske and studied the ground. He pointed to what I guessed was a booby trap. It was clear that the NVA were using Lipske as bait. At that moment Lipske raised his head. My God, I thought, *he's still alive.*

For several seconds I just stared. But Mojo Man knew what he had to do. He put a single M-16 round through Lipske's forehead. Then quickly, we moved forward through dense vegetation and drizzling rain, crossing the animal trail the six NVA had used. At the other end of that animal trail I guessed there must be another trap door entrance. I committed the spot to my memory.

Colonel Chai and the two Army pilots poked their faces through the scrub. Chai looked bad. The Army pilots were shaken up but able to tell us their story. They told us that Cowboy had flown out with them, directing them to land at the site. Once on the ground they had been caught in an ambush. They would have all been wasted but for the fact that Lipske took it upon himself to assualt into the enemy, allowing Chai and the pilots to escape.

Apparently Cowboy had been an informant to Colonel Chai, feeding bits of information and promising to reveal a weapons cache. It was clear now that the whole thing had been planned from the beginning. Colonel Chai, Lipske, and the two Army pilots had been lured into a trap. The dead VC had all the hallmarks of an assassination squad. Mojo Man recognized their leader. He said this was the same VC assassination squad that had taken out the last Dien Ban District Advisor, predecessor to Captain X.

Talking in whispers with Mojo Man, I decided that we would gamble and head directly east as quickly as possible. We moved east until we came to the edge of the scrub and the minefield. We were further north than I expected, but Toc said that he could get us across. Again we proceeded on all fours, alerting the Gunny on the radio that we were coming through.

Once we were through, Mojo Man tapped me on the shoulder again. He handed me my Buddha that had apparently fallen off its chain. The rain was coming down even harder. Mojo Man made a gesture. He was pointing back the way that we had come. Mojo Man was going back to secure Lipske's body.

*   *   *

Day Twelve, 1300 hours

I watched while Marines from India Company loaded Lipske's body bag onto chopper. A corpsman from India Company was treating the welts on my leg. They had festered into little pus-filled sores. The corpsman had broken them open to drain the fluid and then cleaned them with alcohol. Once again I was running a low-grade fever.

Captain Sikes had deployed his company with no further resistance. They also found a huge weapons' cache that Ani Bui confirmed to be the Warehouse. Ani turned out to be right. The Warehouse was south of Route 4, an extensive tunnel complex revealing sacks of rice as well as weapons. It would require *beaucoup* manpower to bring all that rice in. More importantly, Sikes men found a large cache of 122mm rockets. The sixteen 122mm rockets were blown in place. Our finding and destroying the now legendary Warehouse would be a profound setback to the enemy.

Captain X choppered down to see the Warehouse for himself. In addition, upon the advice of the Gunny, Hump decided to move the section of tracks that I had at Giang La south to link up with India Company. It was 1400 by the time I boarded Captain X's chopper for the flight back to Hill 55. It was still pouring rain.

Back on Hill 55 I called down to Wily on the radio. He was nervous. The ROKs' hadn't back-filled Scar's position. A lieutenant was acting company commander. As a result of the vacuum caused by Scar's death, the ROKs hadn't patrolled the area to Wily's satisfaction. Wily felt that their position was vulnerable. To make matters worse, due to the heavy rain, the stream east of Wily's position had risen from its banks, marooning Wily's tracks. I calmed Wily as best I could and called my battalion commander.

My battalion commander was livid that I had gone off with the special task team. He was so angry that his voice quivered over the radio. If he would have had someone to replace me, I'm sure he would have relieved me of my command. When I finally got off the radio it was 1930 and I was drained. At 2000, phase two was to end and phase three to begin.

*   *   *

CHAPTER SEVENTEEN: PHASE THREE

Day Twelve, 2100 hours

I pulled off my wet clothes and opened a cold Sapporo. My temperature was normal and I felt good. I sat with my beer, rubbing alcohol on the sores on my leg. The sergeant of the guard was making his rounds. He gave me a couple of ham sandwiches from the midnight guard rations that I quickly ate. Then I heard that Major Hopkins was going to make it. He was on his way out of country to hospital in Japan.

Captain X knocked on the door of my hooch. I invited him in for a beer. Together we turned on two PRC-25 radios and monitored the ROK frequency on the first radio. On the second radio we monitored the Hill 55 command center where Hump and his staff were preparing the great ambush.

During the day, while I was getting Colonel Chai out, the First Marines had tightened their cordon, advancing eastward through the Giang La and on toward the La Huan. NVA and Viet Cong units had stayed ahead of the Marines, avoiding a fight and using both the rain and the dense vegetation of Dodge City to their advantage.

But at 1500, Hump had ordered his Marines to halt their advance. The miscellaneous NVA and Viet Cong units, trapped between Hump's First Marines and the blocking force of the ROK Marines, must have breathed a sigh of relief, thinking that once again our Marines had stopped short of their objective. Nothing could have been further from the truth. Hump and his staff now had the enemy trapped.

The various NVA and Viet Cong units that found themselves between the U.S. Marines and the ROK Marines had only one way out. ROK Marines blocked escape to the east. U.S. Marines were pushing on the enemy from the west. Movement to the north was blocked by water. The only way out was to the south, and for all practical purposes, the way even appeared clear to the Viet Cong scouts who knew the area well…

Meanwhile, as evening set in, Sergeant Chapelle's tracks had made it back to Route 4 and hard ground. Once on Route 4, Chapelle'd split his tracks, sending half to Captain Sikes. The enemy, familiar with the limitations of the amphibian tractor, had assumed that Chapelle's pull out was due to wet terrain. It was a safe assumption, but it wasn't an accurate one.

*　　　*　　　*

Day Twelve, 2300 hours

I was pleased with Chapelle's performance. He was doing very well, and since tracks were to play a crucial role in the great ambush, I was proud for Chapelle and his track rats.

Track One-Eight, with its special monitoring equipment, was positioned on the hard ground of Route 4. Sitting in One-Eight was our special communications team. Hog and the communication jocks began to pick up movement at 2330 along the string of sensors being employed on this effort.

Of the two types of sensors being employed, the most effective was the seismic intrusion sensor device, called the SID. The SID responded to ground vibrations such as footsteps. The second type was an acoustic sensor that picked up audible sounds. Both these sensors were now transmitting information to Track One-Eight, an innovative, mobile monitoring station.

The sensors had been planted in strings, positioned along the southward route out of the La Huan corridor. Hog was already picking up the direction of enemy movement through the corridor.

All signals had been prearranged by Hump's staff, and were in code. I listened to the great ambush beginning to take shape, drinking a cold Sapporo and eating the last of a cold ham sandwich. Outside the rain still fell, and the heavy raindrops hitting the metal roof created a din.

A forward air controller, sitting in the track with Hog, initiated radio contact with a flight of A-6A Intruders circling over Hoi An. Standing by to provide radar-controlled bombing guidance was an air support radar team on Hill 55.

An estimated enemy column of some one hundred men was moving into the La Huan corridor. Captain X's great ambush was about to take place as the enemy column moved into a kill zone some 200 meters long. Water on both sides of the enemy column made the kill zone narrow. The enemy would need to be walking the high La Huan dike to pass through the corridor. But the enemy had never encountered sensors in this area, and they were probably confident that rainy weather would mask any movement southward.

With the column of one hundred men stretched out along the high La Huan dike, the radar team, using TPQ-10 all weather radar, began vectoring the first A-6A Intruder on target. More than twenty 500-pound bombs were dropped on the column during the next two hours. The flight of the Intruders was followed by artillery from Hill 55, responding to the continued sensor information coming in as the enemy tried to drag away their dead.

Thus was Phase Three, a highly successful combined operation. All that remained was for the ROK Marines to mop up in the morning.

*   *   *

CHAPTER EIGHTEEN: WILY

Day Thirteen, 0100 hours

It was 0100 and I insisted that Captain X have one more beer with me in celebration of his great ambush. Hump and his staff were still down at the command center. The Gunny was with them, having been elevated in status by virtue of recent events. Captain X said that the Gunny was on his best behavior. Jokingly, the Gunny'd said that he didn't know how to behave after being out in the bush so long. I didn't take that as a joke. For the Gunny it was only a matter of time. He was a bomb waiting to detonate. Once the Gunny got back to his old friend, Jack Daniels, anything could trigger that detonation.

Our artillery continued to fire sporadically.

"Well, here's to success," Captain X said.

"And here's to Lieutenant Quick," I added.

"By the way, we got word from Major Boden back at SOG that they made a positive identification of that body you and the Gunny recovered from the Ky Lam. The major was very grateful."

"If Ani Bui hadn't shared that information, that soldier might still be listed as missing, his family living without closure."

"The major is interested in talking further with Ani. Do you trust him with Ani?"

"Yes, sir, I absolutely trust him. Major Boden kept Ani's brother for us. That worked out. You know, Ani tells me that she has a sister in Saigon. With all his contacts, maybe Major Boden can get her situated down in Saigon. We need to get her out of Dodge, so-to-speak."

"I agree. Let me handle those details. I've found Major Boden easy to work with, and I have a couple of ideas that I want to ask him about. Those ideas involve Toc, and going back into the mountains. Major Boden may see some mutual benefit in what I propose. Transporting Ani back to the Special Forces camp at Marble Mountain will give me an opportunity to talk to him."

"Thanks Captain, anything we can do to get Ani down to Saigon would be outstanding."

"Yin and Yang," the captain replied.

"Roger that," I said, draining my beer.

*　　*　　*

Day Thirteen, 0130 hours

Suddenly I was very dizzy. I figured that I'd better go back to medical. A Navy corpsman that looked at me said that I was in a world of hurt. My temperature had risen to 100 degrees, and a pink rash was breaking out all over my ass. The corpsman called the doctor, a new guy who had come down from Division only a few days before. The doctor asked me if I had been in an area during the last two weeks where there had been lots of mosquitoes. I thought he was joking. I laughed and told him that I had been down to Go Noi Island.

The doctor raised his eyebrows and said that he was keeping me under observation until morning. Several grunts had come down with something called dengue fever. Since my joints hurt, and I had this rash over the lower part of my body, the doctor said he was worried. I related my encounter with the centipede, but again, the doctor said that he wasn't taking any chances. At that point the fingers on my left hand started trembling.

"How long has that been going on?" He asked nonchalantly.

"Hard to say, maybe a few weeks, maybe a month," I said.

"You've had a serious head trauma in the recent past, which may cause such symptoms. Over time that may disappear."

"My corpsman gave me some pills. They helped control the trembling. But I don't have any left," I said.

"Well, Lieutenant Gatlin, I'll fix you right up."

True to his word, the doctor loaded me up with various pills. I then called up my battalion commander on the radio and told him that I was in Medical. My battalion commander said that in the morning he was sending out a newly arrived captain to take command of Alpha Company. I was to pack my gear and report back to our battalion as soon as Medical released me.

Thus ended my command of a company in Vietnam.

*   *   *

Day Thirteen, 0300 hours

I lay in Medical, unable to sleep. I was in deep reflection, and what occurred to me, as I stared up at the ceiling, was that I had *reconciled myself with death, but now I needed to keep death at a distance.*

The many sticky-toed little lizards in the hooch ran across the screens under the light of a single bare bulb. The bulb hung from a single cord, and a lizard would run down the cord until it reached the edge of the bulb. There the lizard would bask in the heat of the light until another lizard came and a struggle for position would ensue.

For the lizards in the hooch it was as if on a cold, rainy night the light and heat of that bulb was the dominant power in the universal scheme of things, and they adjusted themselves accordingly. But that adjustment was the function of the cold and the rain that drew them to the light.

It was no different for me. The chill of death was drawing me into deep introspection. But there was no metaphorical light bulb providing illumination. Looking up at the ceiling, I reflected on the men with whom I had shared both hardship and good times. Captain X, a.k.a Captain Graham, was an inspiration, even though I found his ideas difficult. He was a man of character, as was the Gunny, who in his own way had held me to a high standard. Then there was the Mojo Man with his Buddha and his unyielding optimism. From each of these men I could take many lessons that I could read into my own life.

What was important was how that reading would give me
the will to move forward. That was what I needed to think
about.

*   *   *

Day Thirteen, 0600 hours

Hump came in to wake me from a drowse. He sat down
next to me while I shook myself awake. My mind had been
wandering, my fever coming and going. One minute I'd
be dreaming of Miss Swan. Because of her, my past
disappointments in Australia now seemed unimportant.
But then faces would appear, the faces of those we had lost,
Slammer and the others, even Lipske, silent faces
suspended in a dark thicket of tall bamboo. Where did
these faces come from? And those that we had lost, where
were they now? Then, as quickly as they appeared, they
would be gone, and I would break a sweat. Maybe it was
the new pills I was taking.

"Sam, I wanted to come by and personally thank you for
your support. Your tracks were an important factor in this
operation, and your taking the initiative saved Colonel
Chai," Hump said.

"Thank you, sir. Coming from you that's the highest of
compliments."

"And we didn't lose any of your tracks."

I nodded, swinging my feet off the side of the cot.

"Sir, do you believe in a God?" I asked.

"Do I need to go get a chaplain?"

"No sir, I was wondering if you believed."

"Since you ask, Lieutenant Gatlin, I believe in
Spinoza's god who reveals himself in the lawful harmony
of all that exists, but not in a god who concerns himself
with fate and the doings of mankind. Let's leave it at that."

"Spinoza. That sounds Italian."

"Actually, he was a Jew."

"So you see your god in the craziness and chaos that
surrounds us?"

"I do. What surrounds us is reality, a reality governed by certain immutable laws."

"Immutable?"

"Unchanging."

Well, Sam Gatlin, I thought to myself, what we have here, in all this craziness, is an opportunity to find god! I chuckled.

"You find my beliefs that amusing?"

"No sir, what struck me is how we all find our god in different ways."

"Well, I didn't come to see you in order to act as a chaplain. I came to thank you for your efforts."

"Sir, I understand that, and I am grateful."

"We were lucky. Take it from this old China Hand, operations never go as planned. This time we had the right combination of experience and planning, and we had enough resources. Things came together for us."

"Quite a difference from our efforts on Go Noi Island."

"On Go Noi we tried to do too much with too little. And we were impatient."

"Captain X would agree with you. His perspectives make a lot of sense."

"I know, Lieutenant Gatlin. I've heard his point of view. He and Hopkins had me suffer through their lectures. That took quite a few cold beers. What I told them, I'm telling you, and that is all things are revealed over time. The real driving factors at work behind the scenes are seldom clearly understood. I'm sure you have heard the old saying that hindsight is 20-20."

Well, I thought to myself. Sure, hindsight is 20-20. But I wondered if all things are indeed revealed over time. That might be the cure for the Dodge City Blues. I had a sudden, unreasoning desire for a cold Foster's Lager. I needed to find Captain X. He would have a cold Foster's stashed away. Captain X had his shit wired.

"Sir, I give Captain X a lot of credit. Look how he was able to influence Colonel Chai.

"I give our Marines a lot of credit, especially those who are no longer with us. Speaking of Colonel Chai,

Lieutenant Kim brought this for you. Kim said it's from Colonel Chai. Lieutenant Kim said that Colonel Chai feels a great debt to you and your team. Kim added that the colonel would like see you before you return to the States, if that is possible."

"I don't see why not. I'll find a way to get over there," I said.

The fever had sapped my energy. My body's equilibrium was upset. But my mind was clear. Slowly I opened the package. It was my bolo. Colonel Chai was returning the knife that I had given him. And there was a card. The card was written in Miss Swan's fine hand. It said that she hoped to see me again before I left Vietnam.

Hump excused himself. I sat up and lit a cigarette. There are some sparks in the darkness, I thought. It was as if the fever had brought me across a threshold. For a long time I sat, smoking a cigarette, and gazing out into the darkness.

*   *   *

Day Thirteen, 0900 hours

Lieutenant Wily's position was being mortared. I pulled on my boots and listened to the radio while the command center tried to help Wily. The operations officer told Wily to get a listening fix on the mortar tubes. The enemy mortars had already wounded Wily and several ROK Marines, but Wily sounded calm. He climbed to the top of one of the tracks, exposing himself, in an effort to get a visual fix on the tubes.

The enemy continued to walk their mortars through Wily's position. Wily radioed back that he had been wounded, but he stayed on the radio to verify his fix on the mortar tubes. He gave us an azimuth that put the tubes in the middle of the great cemetery. Hump didn't hesitate, immediately ordering artillery to cover the huge cemetery with airbursts. The batteries on Hill 55 responded quickly for the coordinates had been prearranged as part of our planning. A chopper then evacuated Wily up to Hill 55.

I ran down to the chopper pad and met the evac as it came in. Wily was bleeding from what seemed to be a multitude of small wounds. His helmet and flak jacket had saved him. The mortar bursts had caught his legs and arms, but his vitals had been spared.

"How'd I do, Sam?"

I looked at his glazed eyes. He was in shock. We had to get him to NSA as soon as possible.

"You did good, Wily. You did good," I said, afraid for my friend.

"I didn't cheese dick out, Sam."

"No, Wily. You didn't cheese dick out."

I radioed Pabinouis that he was in charge, and that a new Alpha Company CO would be arriving on Hill 55 within the next twenty-four hours.

*　　*　　*

Day Thirteen, 1100 hours

Hump was taking big political heat from Division over two things. The first thing was that the ARVN claimed the great ambush killed a number of innocent civilians. The second thing was that Hump's artillery had fired upon the great cemetery. Division told Hump to hold up any operations involving the First Marines until further notice. Thus phase three officially ended at 1000 hours.

Word came down that Wily had stabilized. He was already on his way out of country to a medical facility in Japan. Captain X was relieved to hear that news. He offered to fly me up to Third Tracks. I accepted his offer, and during the trip we flew over the La Huan corridor.

I saw Wily's tracks, now under the direction of Pabinouis, heading south to Route 4 over firm ground. The plan was for Pabinouis to haul the Koreans back to Hoi An. I had confidence in Pabinouis that he would be able to get the job done without any problems.

Down along Route 4, Sergeant Chapelle was also doing his part. Chapelle's tracks were in the process of hauling the First Marines back up to Hill 55. Chapelle seemed to have things under control. I was still running a low fever, but the welts on my legs and the pink rash had disappeared.

The chopper pilot circled over the La Huan corridor. Below, the earth looked as if a giant had taken a spade and dug a series of gaping holes in the vivid green. The rain had stopped and the sun was breaking through the cloud cover. At 500 feet, I could see the bodies floating in the water of the rice paddies. The bodies lay jumbled together in groups of four and five, arms and legs askew at odd angles. Other parts of limbs and headless torsos were strewn over 200 meters. I noticed that many of the dead were not soldiers, but older men and many women, probably pressed into service like Ani Bui. The terrible effectiveness of the great ambush was evident.

Looking down at the carnage, the villagers mixed with the NVA, I couldn't help but think of the setback these dead civilians would bring to the pacification efforts in the La Huan. The dual nature of this war had always been confusing to me. To speak of pacification seemed contradictory to the cold facts below me. What was it that Hump had said? Operations never go as planned. Nothing is ever truly complete.

*   *   *

Day Fourteen, 1900 hours

I figured that down in Hoi An, the night was young. So I hitched a ride out of battalion with two tracks heading south, running the hard-packed sand. As night came on, the stars seemed to rise out of the South China Sea, and because of the moonless night, one could plainly see phosphorescence in the waves breaking on the sand. The long curve of the shoreline swung in a ten-mile arc that ended in the lights of Hoi An. A strong wind was blowing in off the South China Sea.

*   *   *

Day Fourteen, 2100 hours

The Sand Castle was bustling with activity. The game
room, with its new slot machines, was particularly
crowded. I wandered around, looking for Miss Swan.
Then I caught a glimpse of her on the level above me. I
waved and she waved back, descending the staircase.
When she reached the bottom of the stairs, she gave my
cheek a peck.

"Hello, Miss Swan," I said.

"Hello, Lieutenant. Did you get my card," she replied,
smiling.

"Yes. I did."

"Good. Colonel Chai was called to Saigon in
preparation for his new assignment. He will be
disappointed that he missed you."

"Please give him my regards."

"I will indeed. Saigon is much more to his liking than
Hoi An. You would like Saigon, Lieutenant. I am gratified
to say that he will be moving back there."

So, I thought to myself, Colonel Chai was going back to
Saigon. Maybe getting shot down over Dodge City had
shaken him up.

"It seems that Colonel Chai's command time was cut
short. I felt he was just getting started with Captain X."

"On the contrary, with My Son his purposes here were
accomplished."

"My Son?"

"Protecting My Son was Colonel Chai's primary
concern when he came up from Saigon."

"This is the first that I have heard of his interest in My
Son."

"When his interest arose, the Colonel wanted simply to
visit the ruins as a lover of antiquities. But then he saw the
damage done by your Marine aircraft during one of the Go
Noi Island operations. Colonel Chai took this command to

ensure My Son was preserved from further destruction; and thanks to our Captain X, a true visionary, that objective was achieved. Extraordinary, I'd say."

"What you are talking about are those ruins down around Hill 119, in the valley at the foot of the Que Son Mountains."

"That's correct, Lieutenant Gatlin."

It all came back to me. We were kicking off our big operation on Go Noi Island; and Hill 119, down at the edge of the Que Son Mountains, offered a clear view of all the action. As we flew in to Hill 119, I remembered looking down to see the ancient ruins of My Son far below, stretching across a narrow valley, many towers and crumbling walls, like Wat Phou, only much older. A religious site belonging to the Chams, rulers of Champa someone had said.

"Of course, the Colonel brought back that exquisite stone head of Indra, the rain god, to Saigon," Miss Swan added, fiddling with her hair.

"A *collector of rarities*."

"Exactly, you seem to understand. That is indeed what he is. The colonel has an interest in all things ancient, both artistic and primitive. Thus, his fascination for that disgusting montagnard you captured. Or perhaps, even yourself, with your big knife."

"You mean Toc, the Katu."

"Frightening."

"Toc helped us save Colonel Chai."

"Oh, I must share that with Colonel Chai when I see him. He would find that of great interest."

"I think he already knows that, Miss Swan."

It now seemed that much of Colonel Chai's cooperation and willingness to work with us was driven by his personal interest in My Son. I wondered how many Korean Marines had died for the cause of preserving My Son. And of course, from Colonel Chai's perspective, using B-52's to blanket-bomb Go Noi Island and the Que Son foothills would have been put My Son at risk.

"Miss Swan, do you believe that all things are revealed over time?"

"Why, yes, I do. That's a bit of old old Taoist wisdom. Lieutenant Gatlin, I continue to be most impressed by you. How did you come by this?"

"Well, let's say that it came to me by way of China."

Then Miss Swan smiled and whispered in my ear.

"Give me fifteen minutes to freshen up and then come up to my room," she said.

I waited about ten minutes before ascending the stairs to the upper level. During that time, it occurred to me that, in the midst of all the craziness, Colonel Chai had retained a kind of moral authority with regard to My Son, and in preserving the religious site of the ancient Chams. Call it his decision of conscience. He had done the right thing at the right time.

While I was walking down the long hallway to what I thought was Miss Swan's room, my arm began to tremble. I knocked on Miss Swan's door. There was no answer. Opening the door slightly I peeked in to see that I had chosen the wrong room. This was not Miss Swan's room, but as I was closing the door, something caught my eye. On a table by the window was a Cham statue. It was Dr. de Fillio's Cham sculpture, the Devi. What was the Devi doing down here in Hoi An?

Picking up the statue, I examined it closely. It was apparent that the base of the Devi was slightly damaged, as if it had been torn from the sandstone pedestal on which it had been mounted.

"Lieutenant Gatlin, I see that you appreciate the gift Colonel Chai left for me," Miss Swan said.

I looked up to see Miss Swan wearing a dark see-through slip.

"A gift, the Devi?" I said, breathlessly.

"You are trembling."

"Yes. I can't help it," I replied.

She kissed me on the cheek.

"Do you want me to let down my hair? As I recall, you are fond of long hair," Miss Swan said, letting down her hair.

That thick, dark abundance of perfumed hair fell across Miss Swan's almond shoulders. She sighed, guiding me towards the bed, her wide eyes glowing, and at that moment I could only acknowledge a sense of wonder at my present circumstances. I was still holding the Devi. Then I understood what had happened.

"It was a set-up. Wasn't it? Quick's supply run for Colonel Chai wasn't about hauling slots or an ice machine. It was about transporting priceless Cham art treasures, sculpture stolen from the Musee' de Cham."

Miss Swan sat back, saying nothing. *I had been such a fool*, I thought to myself. This wasn't about saving the religious site of the ancient Chams. Colonel Chai was no more than a sophisticated art thief. I remembered what Hump had said about the real driving factors at work behind the scenes, how they are seldom ever really clear. *Now I needed to do the right thing*, and at a time and a place where everything was being measured against death, I got up and walked out the door, taking the Devi with me.

"Where are you going?" Miss Swan called after me.

"I'm returning the Devi to Dr. de Fillio. Call it a decision of conscience," I replied, chambering a round in my pistol, just in case someone tried to stop me.

"Oh, Lieutenant Gatlin, watch that big gun."

*　　　*　　　*

EPILOGUE

Day Fifteen: 0700 hours

At first, light, heavy rain blew in from the high
Annamese Cordillera to the west. As Miss Swan once said,
Indra the rain god was weeping. This was indeed the start
of the monsoon.

Earlier I'd set the Devi on the stairs in front of the
Musee' de Cham, near the spot where Miss Swan's hair had
appeared lustrous black in the late afternoon sunlight, the
cobalt-blue sheath she was wearing that day revealing her
shapely thighs as she ascended the stairs, seemingly cool
and relaxed, her red and black Yin and Yang tattoo so
distinct on her bare right shoulder.

Dr. Jean de Fillio, old enough to be my grandfather and
a relic from French colonial days, stood at the top of the
stairs of the Musee' de Cham, poking at the Devi with a
long thin stick of bamboo. He looked out into the rain, his
eyes magnified by thick, Coke-bottle-like glasses. I was
observing him through field glasses from the balcony
outside my room on the third floor of the White Lotus. Dr.
de Fillio must have assumed that someone was watching
him, for he waved at the empty street. Then, quickly
picking up the Devi, he disappeared back into the depths of
the Musee' de Cham.

The big caramel-colored pieces of Cham statuary that
represented the various gods and goddesses worshipped by
the Chams were gone, now hidden away. But in my mind
the images of these ancient Southeast Asian sculptures
lingered, providing me not only with a sense of Cham
history, but also with an insight into the complexities of my
own confused experiences.

I had followed behind Miss Swan quite willingly,
watching her beautiful ass sway back and forth, seduced as
she took me on a tour of the Cham divinities, first showing
me Brahma, the Creator, with his four faces; and then dark
Shiva, the Destroyer, with his third eye. How could I
forget when she laughed, giving me a wink when we found

Kama, the god of love, in the act of mounting the celestial dancer Apsara?

My flight was due to leave in four hours. But I had plenty of time to get to the airport. Lost in my thoughts, I would wait for the rain to let up. It occurred to me that in the last few days I had found something that had been beyond my previous understanding. What I found could only have been revealed to me when I was ready and willing to accept it. Soon a plane would take me across that wine-dark South China Sea, and knowing Ani Bui was now on her way to Saigon, I felt a new lightness of being. I had a similar feeling when I heard that Toc had buried his lost hand in the red clay of Hill 55.

Cham Sculpture: replica of Devi, Quang Nam, Vietnam 1968

Photo by Dave Scott

Glossary

A-4: Douglas Skyhawk, a single-seat, light jet attack aircraft.

A-6A: Grumman Intruder, a two-seat, twin-jet, all-weather attack aircraft.

ACTUAL: A Unit Commander

AK-47: Russian-designed Kalishnikov gas-operated 7.62mm automatic rifle, effective range about 400 meters.

AMTRAC: An amphibious tractor, LVTP5, mounted with a .30 Caliber machine gun and used to transport Marines and supplies.

AN HOA: Key town in the An Hoa Basin. An Hoa served as the Regimental Headquarters for the Fifth Marines from 1968 through 1970.

ARC LIGHT: Code name for B-52 bombing missions in South Vietnam.

ARIZONA TERRITORY: Contested area south and west of the Thu Bon River that was the tactical responsibility of the Fifth Marine Regiment from 1968 through 1970.

ARVN: Army of the Republic of Vietnam.
B-52: Boeing Stratofortress, a US Air Force eight-engine, heavy jet bomber.

BLUE LINE: Military map jargon for a river.

BOO-COO or *BEAUCOUP*: Many.

C-4: Plastic explosive.

C-130: Lockheed Hercules, heavy transport aircraft.

CAP: Combined Action Program. Combining a Marine rifle squad with a South Vietnamese Popular forces squad for village security.

CH-46: Boeing Vertol Sea Knight, a twin-turbine, tandem-rotor medium transport helicopter.

CH-53: Sikorsky Sea Stallion, a single-rotor, heavy transport helicopter powered by two shaft-turbine engines.

CHAMPA: Champa was a kingdom that evolved beginning in the 2nd century along the central coast of Vietnam, growing over the centuries from maritime trade and becoming increasingly influenced by Hinduism. During the 4th century Hinduism was adopted and Sanskrit used as a sacred language. From the 4th to the 9th centuries Quang Nam Province was the heartland of the Cham Kingdom, My Son being the spiritual center. In 1999, My Son was designated a World Heritage Site.

CHAM SCULPTURE: Classic period, 6th and the 14th centuries, when the Chams flourished, producing an art and architecture reflecting the influence of Hinduism in Vietnam. The Cham Museum (i.e., Musee' de Cham) in Da Nang houses the largest single collection of Cham sculpture in the world.

CHARLIE RIDGE: Spur of the Annamese Cordillera to the northwest of Hill 55 that juts into the An Hoa Basin.

CHIEU HOI: Open Arms, a program where enemy soldiers could surrender without penalty.

CHINA HAND: Marines and Sailors who served in China prior to 1939, and from the period of 1945 to 1949.

CHOPPER: Slang for helicopter

CIDG: Civilian Irregular Defense Group. A South Vietnamese paramilitary force made up of Montagnards, mountain tribesmen advised by US Special Forces. In I Corps, members of the Bru tribe were utilized by Command & Control North, US Special Forces, Da Nang. On at least one occasion, the Special Forces attempted to recruit the Katu at An Diem for CIDG activities, but those efforts were unsuccessful due to the influence of the NVA. The NVA were to make use of the Katu as scouts and trailwalkers.

CP: Command post. They were established to coordinate unit activities.

C-RATS: Combat rations. These standard meals came in a box to be eaten while in the field. K-Rats were the Korean Marine Corps version of combat rations.

CTZ: Corps Tactical Zone. These were the principal military and political sub-divisions of the Republic of South Vietnam (i.e., I Corps, II Corps, etc.).

DAI LOC DISTRICT: The district to the immediate west of Hill 55. The area known as Dodge City included the eastern boundary of Dai Loc District. Each province in South Vietnam, led by a Province Chief, was broken down into districts. Each district had a chief who had two lines of authority, one political and one military.

DA NANG: Second largest city in South Vietnam during the Vietnam War. Da Nang served as the Headquarters for both the First Marine Division and the Third Marine Amphibian Force (MAF) from 1965 through 1971.

DEVI: The Great Goddess. Known also in India as Devi, she is all-important in Hinduism through one of her many aspects. For some she is considered a primary deity while for others she is part of a greater pantheon. As Jaganmata, or Mother of the universe, she destroys evil and addresses herself to the creation and dissolution of the world. In some forms she is gentle, while in other forms she is ferocious. The preserved outside wall of My Son's E 1 Tower, now in the Cham Museum in Da Nang, contains a half-length statue of Devi.

DODGE CITY: Contested area south of Hill 55, bounded on the north by the La Tho River and on the south by the Thu Bon and Ky Lam Rivers. Dodge City was the tactical responsibility of the First Marine Regiment from 1969 through 1970.

DIEN BAN DISTRICT: The district to the immediate east of Hill 55. The area known as Dodge City included the western boundary of Dien Ban District.

E-TOOL: An entrenching tool, a small shovel.

F-4B: McDonnell Phantom II, a twin-engine, two-seat, long-range jet interceptor and attack bomber.

FRAG: Noun: a grenade. Verb: to frag someone was to harm them using a grenade.

GET SOME: A common Marine exhortation to kill the enemy.

GO NOI ISLAND: Contested area south of Hill 55, bounded on the north by the Thu Bon River and northern branch of the Ky Lam River, and on the south by the southern branch of the Ky Lam River. Go Noi Island, fourteen kilometers long and from two to three kilometers wide at any given point, was the site of numerous Marine Corps battalion and regimental-sized operations. Go Noi Island was the tactical responsibility of the First Marine Regiment from 1969 through 1970.

GOOK: Originally Korean slang for "person," this term was passed down by Marine veterans of the Korean War and used to describe all Asians.

HE: High explosive artillery, tank, or mortar shells.

HIEU DUC DISTRICT: A district south of Da Nang and to the immediate north and east of Hill 55. From Dodge City the NVA would slip into Hieu Duc District to terrorize villagers and launch rockets at Da Nang.

HIGHWAY ONE: Main north-south highway running the length of I Corps.

HILL 55: Tactically dominant hill, approximately one and one-half miles in length and three-quarters of a mile wide, 55 meters above sea level and seven miles south of Da Nang. Hill 55 was utilized as a combat base and a logistical support area.

HOI AN: City near the South China Sea on the north bank of the Ky Lam River to the east of Go Noi Island. During the Vietnam War Hoi An served as Headquarters for the Blue Dragon Division of the Republic of Korea Marines (ROK).

HOOCH: A dwelling, either Marine-made or a typical home in a village.

HUEY: Bell Huey, a single-engine light helicopter used for a variety of missions ranging from observation to operational troop insertion and evacuations.

I CORPS: The military and political sub-division of Vietnam that included the five northern provinces of South Vietnam.

ILLUM: Parachute flare or illumination artillery round.

KATU: One of the Montagnard tribes. The Katu tribe lived in the remote mountains west of Da Nang in an area stretching to the Laotian border and beyond.

KIA: Killed-in-Action.

KOREAN BRIDGE: Key bridge across the Ky Lam River in eastern Go Noi Island.

LP: Listening post

LZ: Landing Zone

M-16: The standard rifle carried by Marines.

MAF: Marine Amphibious Force.

MAG: Marine Aircraft Group.

MAIN FORCE: Regionally organized Viet Cong units of battalion and regimental size as opposed to local VC guerrilla cadre and terror squads.

MEDEVAC: To medically evacuate a wounded person.

MIA: Missing-in-action.

MOST RICKY TICK: Marine jargon meaning immediately, if not sooner.

MONTAGNARD: General term used for the many different mountain tribes such as the Katu, Bru, Rhade, Sedang, Jurai, Phuong, and Pacoh.

MY SON: My Son, located in Southern Vietnam, was a religious center for the Champa Kingdom. The current My Son Sanctuary is a large complex of religious monuments, originally comprised of more than 70 structures. Twenty-five of these structures remain today. While the monuments on the site, remains of a series of impressive tower-temples, are in ruins, it is still possible to grasp the importance of this beautiful UNESCO World Heritage Site. The builders of My Son were the nobility of the Champa Kingdom, and the site represents the longest continuous occupation for religious purposes, not only of the Cham Kingdom, but also of Southeast Asia as a whole. The site was inhabited from the 4th until the 15th century AD, far longer than the more famous sites of Angkor Wat in Cambodia, or Ayutthaya in Thailand.

NUMBER ONE: Marine jargon for the very best.

NUMBER TEN: Marine jargon for the very worst.

NVA: North Vietnamese Army.

OLD CORPS: Marine jargon referring to veterans of wars prior to Vietnam.

OPEN SHEAF: Rounds of artillery fire spread along an axis rather than focused at one point.
PF: Popular forces, South Vietnamese village militia.

PHOENIX PROGRAM: Counter terror program funded by the CIA.

PUFF: Puff the Magic Dragon, also called Spooky by the Marines, was a C-47 cargo plane mounted with Gatling guns.

PRU: Provincial Recon Units created to support the Phoenix Program.

R & R: Rest & Relaxation leave, often in an exotic place.

REACT: Noun: a reserve unit designated to aid other units in need.

RED LINE: Military map jargon for a road.

RF: Regional Forces, South Vietnamese Provincial Militia.

ROKs: Republic of Korea Marines.

ROUTE 4: Major east-west road in southern Dodge City connecting the towns of Dien Ban and Hoi An on the east, with the town of Dai Lac to the west.
RPG: Rocket-propelled-grenade, fired from a shoulder-held launcher, and used for both antitank and antipersonnel targets.

STROBE: A bright, neon-like light used to mark landing zones at night.

SAS: Special Air Service, an elite Australian unit.

T.O.T.: Time on target, a prearranged mortar or artillery barrage scheduled to occur at a specific time.

VC, or VIET CONG: A contraction of the Vietnamese phrase meaning "Vietnamese Communist." It is important to distinguish two types of VC, cadre and main force. The first type were small cadres living in the villages. The second type were larger, main force guerilla units, capable of conducting full-scale military operations.

VILLE: Marine jargon for a Vietnamese village.

WAT PHOU: Wat Phou (Vat Phu) is a ruined Khmer temple complex in southern Laos, located at the base of mount Phu Kao, some 6 km from the Mekong river in Champassak province. While there was a temple on the site as early as the 5th century, the surviving structures date from the 11th to the 13th centuries. Over time Wat Phou was converted to Theravada Buddhist use. This continued after the area came under control of the Lao, and a festival is held on the site each February. Wat Phou was designated a World Heritage Site in 2001.

WIA: Wounded-in-action.

WILLIE PETER: Marine jargon for a white phosphorus artillery or mortar round, often used for marking targets or creating incendiary effects.

THE WORLD: Marine slang for the United States.

About the Author

Dan Guenther was a captain in the U.S. Marine Corps. His first novel, *China Wind*, (Ivy, 1990), (Redburn, 2007), was based on his combat tour in Vietnam. He has also published poetry in several small magazines and anthologies, most recently in *Open Range: Poetry of the Reimagined West*, (Ghost Road Press, 2007). Dan has a BA in English from Coe College and a Masters of Fine Arts in English from the University of Iowa where he attended the Iowa Writers' Workshop.
www.danguenther.com

About Redburn Press

This is the newest Redburn Press title. Redburn Press gets its name from the early Melville novel. In it, the autobiographical narrator goes to sea for the first time, excitedly. The ship is full of fascinating types, eccentric human nature in its motley richness. Wellingborough Redburn then encounters more "life and life only".

I want Redburn Press to be that ship in a bottle, so to speak. I will publish – and republish --- eclectic, various, good books full of life. Dan Guenther's *Dodge City Blues* is such a book. This novel is the second in Guenther's Lost Vietnam trilogy. *Townsend's Solitaire*, the third in the series, will follow.

China Wind, the first book of the trilogy, is still available from Redburn Press online or through your local bookstore.

Mark Kohut
Publisher
December, 2007

Marine Amphibian Tractor, LVTP-5, along the shore of the
South China Sea, 1969

Photo by Author

Author, on right, with a wild boar shot west of the
Sherwood Forest, Hill 10 area, 1969. The shooter, who I
remember only as being from Texas, is on the left

Photo by the Author (Note: Amphibian Tractor, LVTP-5,
in background, and bolo style knife on poncho in the
foreground. Taken on Hill 10, May 1969.)